SPECIAL MESSAGE TO READERS

Juliet Nicolson has two daughters and lives with her husband in Sussex.

ABDICATION

England, 1936. After the recent death of George V, the nation has a new king, Edward VIII. While another war threatens world peace, and unemployment is rampant in England, the nation has yet another secret to keep from its people: the new King's affair with a married American woman. In the midst of all this, a young woman, May, is starting a new life away from home. Working as a chauffeur for a kind and very busy government official, May is learning about life, secrets, and love. There's also Evangeline Nettlefold, a friend of the family May works for, and Wallis Simpson's old classmate and occasional confidante. But Evangeline's building resentment towards Mrs. Simpson may prove to be destructive for her.

JULIET NICOLSON

ABDICATION

Complete and Unabridged

CHARNWOOD
Leicester

First published in Great Britain in 2012 by
Bloomsbury Publishing Plc
London

First Charnwood Edition
published 2013
by arrangement with
Bloomsbury Publishing Plc
London

British Library CIP Data

Nicolson, Juliet.
  Abdication.
  1. Windsor, Edward, Duke of, *1894 – 1972*- -Fiction.
  2. Great Britain- -History- -Edward VIII, *1936*- -
  Fiction. 3. Biographical fiction. 4. Large type books.
  I. Title
  823.9′2–dc23

  ISBN 978–1–4448–1481–1

Published by
F. A. Thorpe (Publishing)
Anstey, Leicestershire

Set by Words & Graphics Ltd.
Anstey, Leicestershire
Printed and bound in Great Britain by
T. J. International Ltd., Padstow, Cornwall

This book is printed on acid-free paper

For Clemmie and Flora and Charlie
with all my love,
and more.

Winter

Arrival

1

On a gloomy February afternoon in 1936 a young woman, nineteen years old, brought a dark blue Rolls-Royce slowly to a halt. Managing the mahogany steering wheel with surprising ease for someone so slight, May Thomas parked the car outside the country home of a middle-aged man and his married mistress.

The journey from London to Sunningdale had taken about an hour and shortly before reaching the town May edged the car along the boundary of Windsor Great Park before turning off the road into an unmarked opening. She was enjoying the unaccustomed feeling of stylish authority given to her by the new chauffeur's uniform of blue trousers, jacket and matching navy-blue cap with its shiny patent leather peak. Driving through a pair of wide open and crisply painted white gates, she took the car slowly up a rising avenue of plump-trunked oak trees and thick rhododendron bushes. There were signs that substantial clearances had been made within the undergrowth but in some places, where the tangle of branches at the top formed a thick canopy, the snow had failed to make its way down into this melancholy landscape.

As the sand-coloured house — although no one could actually call it that — appeared round a bend, lit up by an ingenious series of concealed electric floodlights, May was relieved that she was only dropping off her passenger and would not be required to stay the night. The series of battlements surrounding the central tower that protruded from a mass of crenelated buildings were very un-house like; and yet its diminutive size made it ineligible for the status of castle. May was reminded of a picture she had seen in one of her brother Sam's old cowboy books, a turreted fort out of which an invading Red Indian leapt, complete with bow and arrow.

A woman in a slim fitting and tightly belted black dress with long sleeves and a white collar was standing at the front door. She looked a bit like a nurse or a school matron. As May eased the car slowly alongside her, the woman stepped forward and opened the car door.

'Evangeline, my dear!' said the woman in a hard-edged accent that sounded like coins rubbing up against each other in a pocket. 'You have no idea how pleased I am to see you!'

May's passenger was struggling to get out of the car. In fact, Miss Evangeline Nettlefold was wedged between the back seat and the back of the front passenger seat and the harder she struggled to get free the more stuck she became. A little dog, a Pekinese that had been sitting on his owner's lap throughout the journey, appeared to be having an asthma attack and when May ran round to the other side of the car to release her passenger she saw that the dog had drooled onto a patch of Miss Nettlefold's grey wool skirt, leaving a black stain on the front panel.

After an awkward tussle between May, Miss Nettlefold and a now frothing dog, the large

4

woman found herself suddenly catapulted into the open air.

'Oh, Wallis, you know me! Too many delicious English cookies for my own good!' she apologised, in a surprisingly unflustered and rather beautiful voice. Her chubby cheeks resembled pink gobstoppers. 'But how *divine* it is to be here at last.'

And with a wave to May, she turned towards the front door, her fur coat flapping open in the wind. The two women immediately fell into conversation, glancing briefly backwards in May's direction before vanishing inside. Miss Nettlefold's arm had been tucked tightly into that of her hostess, a woman with an unnaturally wide smile, a doll-like body, high shoulders and an enormous head. She reminded May of someone, although May could not quite identify the memory. After several deep breaths of cold winter air May returned to the car, removed her cap and shook her hair free. She was about to resume her place at the wheel when she noticed the flat package on the front seat. The brown paper parcel was imprinted with a store logo, a sharp edged four-leaf clover separating the letters H and K.

'I brought this all the way from Baltimore,' Miss Nettlefold had told May when they set off from St John's Wood that afternoon. 'Can you put it somewhere safely for me? Knowing my luck, if I find a space for it here in the back with me and Wiggle, I will probably sit on it, and records have a funny way of snapping when sat on, don't you find?'

5

With the parcel safely under one arm May returned to the front door and pulled the bell. A black-suited butler answered the ring. He was as compact and elegant as a Russian Sobranie.

'Sorry to trouble you, Sir, but Miss Nettlefold has left something in the car.'

'I will make sure she gets it immediately,' he replied with unequivocal authority. But May felt uneasy. From early on in her life she had discovered that trust must be earned.

'If you don't mind,' she said, raising her voice to a level beyond the tremble that threatened to unseat her resolve, 'Miss Nettlefold left the package in my care and I would like to make sure she gets it myself.'

'I assure you, Miss, that if you give the package to me it will be delivered safely to Miss Nettlefold.'

But May kept her composure, holding onto the parcel tightly and wishing she had remembered to put her cap back on her head. A short silence elapsed between them.

'Oh well, you better follow me,' the cigarette-slim butler snapped, before moistening his lips with a thin tongue.

Walking a pace behind the stiff back ahead of her, May followed the butler into a short passageway which billowed out into a high-ceilinged hall painted white, the starkness relieved by eight bright yellow leather chairs positioned in each of the octagonal corners. May's hard-soled driving shoes clicked in echoing reply to those of the butler as they crossed the black-and-white marble floor. A pretty maid in a pink uniform, a lace-edged hat perched on her blond hair, put her head round a corner.

'Excuse me, Mr Osborne,' she said, 'Miss Spry is on the telephone and wants to know whether it would be convenient to come over later and do the flowers for the weekend?'

'Tell her to check with Mrs Mason if that will suit. We don't want the housekeeper upset. You know what she's like,' Mr Osborne replied abruptly and crossed the hall ahead of May.

A cloying sweetness came from the vases of lilies that sat on plinths at every few feet. A faint sound of barking could be heard from behind a closed door far away. May felt unnaturally hot. There was no warning, no time to ask for a mirror to check her newly bobbed hair, no time to think before she found herself at an open doorway and saw two faces turned towards her in surprise.

'Why May? Whatever are you doing here, my dear? Is something wrong?'

But the butler spoke before May could answer.

'Forgive us the interruption, Madam. Your driver *insisted* on bringing this parcel to you herself.'

'Please bring her in, Osborne,' Miss Nettlefold's friend instructed. 'And by the way, have you ordered a car to meet the hairdresser from the train?'

The butler's previously impassive expression reflected irritation. 'I have of course,' he retorted, adding 'Madam' in afterthought.

Bending over a tray laid with china cups as

thin as eggshells, he poured out the pale tea before offering Miss Nettlefold a plate of miniature salmon sandwiches.

May wondered what sort of impression she was giving in her dark suit, her fringe still clamped damply onto her forehead. While reminding herself in future to remove her cap when driving, she struggled to place the familiar face of Miss Nettlefold's friend. Had she seen her in a famous painting, maybe? Miss Nettlefold took a step or two nearer.

'Waaaah-llis,' Miss Nettlefold began in her long-vowelled, slanted voice, 'I would like to present my driver, Miss May Thomas, a most unusual young woman who I dearly wanted you to meet. You know? Remember I just told you how, like me, she has recently crossed over the sea to England?' Turning to May with a reassuring smile she said, 'May, I would like you to meet Mrs Simpson.'

'Most delighted to meet you,' said Miss Nettlefold's friend with her mesmerising symmetrical eyebrows. But she did not sound delighted at all, and shook May's hand with an aggressive grip. 'You are very young,' she remarked, in a tone of accusation, her face close enough for May to smell the strangely pleasant combination of musky perfume and eucalyptus that scented Mrs Simpson's breath.

'I am nineteen, Madam.'

'Nineteen,' Mrs Simpson repeated, rolling the word around her mouth like a boiled sweet. 'Nineteen. I was married at the age of nineteen. First time round, mind you. I was far older and

8

more prepared for the second attempt!' Laughing at her own youthful absurdity, she turned her attention to the package in May's hand. 'Is this really meant for me?' she asked, looking at Miss Nettlefold.

'I think you might be able to guess what it is!' Miss Nettlefold replied with a little excited clap of her hands, 'I hope your dancing shoes are in need of a little exercise!'

'Oh David, do come over here and have a look.' Mrs Simpson glanced over in the direction of the window across which yellow velvet curtains had been drawn.

A man was sitting on a sofa next to a grand piano, a couple of sleeping terriers lying at his feet, their heads resting on his shoes. His own head was bent over a tapestry canvas that he was poking at rhythmically with a needle threaded with green wool, but at the sound of his name he looked up.

'Come on, Cora, move off. And you too, Jaggs,' he said, shifting the dogs off his feet and onto the floor. Putting the embroidery down on the sofa he reached for the silver monogrammed box on the table beside him and, lighting a cigarette, came to join the others. May had seen photographs of him, of course. In fact there was one hanging in a gold frame in the schoolroom at home, a cigarette in his mouth. But, for the second time in a month, it was a shock to see that black-and-white picture not only in colour but moving and breathing. He looked thinner than he had in the photograph and even smaller than the mournful figure he had presented to the crowds at the recent funeral of his father. His face was the colour of a plum and his left eye drooped a little as if halfway towards a wink. He was wearing a grey-and-red kilt with black checks and a thick blue jersey. A couple of small burn marks on one of the sleeves were just visible beneath a dusting of cigarette ash. He was clearly as unprepared for introductions as May was.

'So, Miss . . . ?'

'Thom-Thomas' she supplied, stumbling a little over her own name before adding, 'Sir, I mean Your Royal. King. Sorry, Your Majesty, I mean.' She tapered off.

But he appeared troubled neither by her confusion, nor by her wobbly attempt at a curtsey and turned to watch Mrs Simpson open the brown paper parcel.

'What *have* we here, my dear Evangeline?' Mrs Simpson exclaimed in her jangly voice as she removed the flat slipcase from the wrapping paper. 'Oh my! I do declare it *is* something to get the foot tapping!' And then, 'But Evangeline, darling! How clever you are! A foxtrot from Handy's Memphis Blues Band,' she exclaimed, reading the words of the record sleeve. 'Oh my! David, do you see?'

Mrs Simpson held the bright yellow disc out to show him. Printed along the bottom of the record were the words 'Manufactured for Hochschild, Kohn and Co.'

'Oh, Evangeline! Hochschild's! Our favourite store, the lipstick store, the place of refuge from our mothers! Were we all of sixteen, even fifteen years old I wonder?'

Her eyes shone at the recollection. But Miss Nettlefold was not quite finished with her surprise.

'And Wallis, there is a rather divine coincidence that I think will surprise you.' Miss Nettlefold pointed to one word denoting the record label that was imprinted on the top of the disc. Belvedere. Just the same as Fort Belvedere, the house in which they all stood.

'*Well!* I do declare this is quite the best gift I ever did see! What about it, David? Do you see what a clever, imaginative, generous friend I have brought to stay with us? We will quite forget all our worries when we start dancing to Handy's Band. It will be quite like the good old times before you became . . . '

But she stopped herself mid-sentence and ran over to the gramophone, the record in her hand.

'Come here, Evangeline darling! Let's listen to it at once. And let's have a martini! Whoever said it was too early for a martini? It's never too early for a cocktail, is it, Vangey?' Her hands were as expressive as her smile, opening up and outwards as she spoke.

The King appeared startled by this girlish gush of reminiscence and, spotting May dawdling uncertainly in the corner near the door, went over to speak to her. May had been trying to edge out of the room, with its soft lamplight and its glossy furniture, without anyone noticing.

'I believe Miss Nettlefold mentioned that you learned to drive in the West Indies?' the King began. 'A most glorious place! I know it myself: travelled all through that area by ship just after the war! Such friendly people aren't they? Which one exactly is *your* island?'

'Barbados, Sir,' she murmured, but his attention had returned to the figure of Mrs Simpson, who was gliding round the room to the sound of the music. As she passed by the King's hand brushed her cashmere elbow. He was unable to take his eyes off her.

'Just imagine, darling. May is from Barbados. One day, *soon*, darling,' he said, raising his voice to compete with the bluesy crooning coming from the gramophone, 'I promise *WE* will go and find some sunshine.'

On hearing the emphasis the King put on the personal pronoun, Mrs Simpson put her purple-polished finger to her lips in a sign to him to say no more. Her face was abnormally pale, and apart from the mole on one cheek her skin was as smooth as the inside of a seashell. Whirling away from the King's touch, Mrs Simpson turned her back on them and May could see her wide jawbone jutting out from either side of her head like the back view of a cobra. The King pulled a cigarette from a leather case that was tucked into the silver sporran hanging from his waist and lit the end from the burning ember of the one he was about to extinguish. The intimacy of the little procedure unnerved May further and she was wondering how much more of this unexpected encounter she could manage.

'I am most impressed to hear of your skill

behind the wheel,' he continued in his semi-transatlantic accent. May could feel herself breathing hard. 'I love cars myself,' said the King. 'Matter of fact I'm thinking of ordering one of those new American station wagons. My own driver Ladbroke is a little sceptical. Perhaps you would care to have a turn in the machine when you next bring Miss Nettlefold to see us? You might be able to persuade Ladbroke that one must keep up with the times?'

But May found herself unable to supply anything more than a blush in return to this friendly line of enquiry. And suddenly it was all over. Mr Osborne had returned and was lingering by the door. With a barely discernible inclination of his head, he indicated to May that it was time to leave.

Past the yellow chairs, across the marble floor, and there at last was the February wind restoring some coolness to May's flushed cheeks. It was as if she had been released from a conservatory where rare plants were lovingly tended, unable to survive without careful nurturing. Outside felt like the real world. Inside resembled a hothouse of make-believe. She reached the car, inhaling the familiar leather smell of the seats. This strange house, about which she had already been warned in advance not to ask questions, had well and truly shaken her.

'Fancy that,' May murmured out loud settling herself back in her seat. It occurred to her that Mrs Simpson must be a very good friend indeed of the King to be so in charge in the King's own house.

'Well, *I* must get back to my *proper* place where I belong, darling,' she continued out loud.

'Darling' mattered to May. Her father never uttered the word when speaking to her and she was glad of that. The term of endearment was reserved for rare usage by her mother alone, and its power to soothe always took her by happy surprise. May could not imagine ever using the word herself. It did not seem to fit anyone she knew. For a moment she wished desperately that her mother could be there with her now.

Pulling the door shut, and adjusting a small cushion that Mr Hooch the Cuckmere Park odd job man had suggested would give May extra height, she put the engine carefully into reverse. She was still feeling jumpy after the recent scene in the drawing room and as the car began to crunch over the gravel, her shoe became caught in a small tear in the fitted carpet on the floor below the steering wheel. As May tried to release her foot, she inadvertently pressed down hard on the accelerator pedal. The car jolted backwards hitting an object that May was certain had not been in the driveway earlier.

A prickling on her arms was coming from underneath her skin. The sensation, May's infuriating response to anything that made her nervous, travelled up towards her shoulders, then her neck and right into her cheeks as she fought the instinct to look round. *Take it slowly*, May told herself. *There is no need to panic*. Had Miss Nettlefold been carrying her handbag with her as she entered the house? May felt certain she had. And then a dreadful thought occurred to her. Still facing forward and sitting up very straight May was able to see the reflection of the back seat in the driving mirror. It was empty.

Just then Miss Nettlefold appeared at the front door of the house. For a second or two she stood quite still, a large and in some ways absurd figure in her black fur hat, and her voluminous coat and her shoulders rounded and hunched forward, as if she was trying to reduce her height. Miss Nettlefold was smiling as, shielding her eyes with her hand against the surprisingly strong glare of a setting wintry sun, she searched the driveway.

'Wiggle!' May heard her call in a deep American voice, and then again, a little louder with an extended emphasis on the first syllable. 'Weeeg-le!'

Miss Nettlefold turned in the direction of the parked car, a woman happy in her ownership of a temporarily missing dog, as she scanned the gravel for the wag of a tail. But her glance fell quickly on a small, still shape just visible beneath a back wheel of the Rolls-Royce.

In an instant the Fort driveway filled up with several black-suited servants, alerted by Miss Nettlefold's agonised cry. Towered over by the straight-backed Mr Osborne, they hovered crow-like over the large figure that lay on the gravel, unsure how to lift the comatose Miss Nettlefold inside. In her thick-haired fur coat Miss Nettlefold resembled a bear that had lumbered out of the evergreen rhododendron bushes surrounding the driveway and collapsed in confusion.

Mr Osborne approached May and suggested that it might be best if she leave now, adding, after a theatrical clearing of his throat, 'And remove the instrument of death before Miss Nettlefold regains consciousness.'

A yard or two away, his outline just identifiable beneath a plaid rug, lay the motionless body of Wiggle.

2

The following morning, May stood cap in hand in Sir Philip Blunt's study at Cuckmere Park in Sussex as he faced her, employer to employee, from behind his large mahogany desk. She had returned to the house late the previous evening, and had gone straight to her bedroom without speaking to anyone. She feared the worst. She had tried to prepare herself for the inevitable consequences of her carelessness, and had been unable to stop herself reliving the minutes following the second of impact. She could not absorb the shocking knowledge that she was responsible for the death of a living thing.

Sir Philip put a match to his cigar, igniting it with big billowy puffs. May watched one end of the brown cylinder darken with saliva while the other end glowed with menace. For a moment a large puff of smoke obscured his face.

'I am happy to come straight to the point and tell you that Miss Nettlefold has concluded that yesterday's incident was not your fault.'

May tried to swallow but her throat felt blocked.

'In fact, it is to you whom Miss Nettlefold now wishes to apologise,' he explained, looking a little bemused. He had received a telephone call from Miss Nettlefold at Sunningdale just an hour ago. She had begun speaking in a state of understandable anguish, even anger, declaring that Wiggle had been 'the love of her life', and the only living soul she could trust. But she had calmed down and in the end registered *her* distress at the distress that must have been suffered by Miss Thomas. The dog had been unwell for a few days — an allergy to offal, apparently — and that weakness must have prevented Wiggle from dodging the approaching wheels of the car.

At that moment May wished she still had enough hair to cover her face which she was sure betrayed a vestige of the guilt she felt. Sir Philip had not finished.

'There is one other small matter that I wish to raise. I understand you met certain people when you delivered Miss Nettlefold to the address at Sunningdale yesterday?'

May nodded.

'Well, far be it for me to question the wisdom of introducing you to those particular individuals. What is important is that I already know you well enough, May, to say that I feel you to be a dependable person. And an intelligent one too.'

She was not quite sure where this was all leading.

'So I want your confirmation that you will never discuss with anyone that meeting yesterday. And when I say 'anyone' that includes not only the staff in the house here but your own family when you return home. Have I made myself clear?'

May nodded vigorously.

Sir Philip smiled. 'Good. I knew you would understand.'

May left Sir Philip's study, relieved on two levels. First, she was happy to escape a smell that reminded her of smouldering socks, the result of the accumulated decades, if not centuries, of cigar smoke that had impregnated the ancient stone walls of the Sussex manor house. But mostly she was astonished to have held on to her job and to have been exonerated so completely from the consequences of yesterday's accident. Considering how things might have turned out, May felt herself to be most fortunate, although she hated to think how much she must have upset Miss Nettlefold. She was startled by the forgiving nature of the woman who, the previous afternoon, had settled herself into the back of the car. As for the caution that she should be discreet about yesterday's encounter in the yellow drawing room of Fort Belvedere, she felt no anxiety. Keeping secrets had been a way of life for May for as long as she could remember.

★ ★ ★

Up until the moment when Miss Nettlefold had slid the glass partition aside May had maintained the respectful silence that was expected of a chauffeur. As a courtesy, she had formally introduced herself to her passenger at the beginning of the journey but Miss Nettlefold had been so preoccupied with her bags and parcels and small snuffly dog that she had paid little attention to the driver. However, in her driving mirror May could see the surreptitious stares Miss Nettlefold began to give her from the back seat and had expected to hear the whoosh of the screen that separated the passengers from the driver being pushed back even sooner. The little window had not closed properly from the first day May had begun driving the car and although she had considered getting it fixed she had changed her mind. The almost imperceptible gap through which private conversations reached her was too much of an unexpected bonus to relinquish.

'I do declare you are a girl!' Miss Nettlefold had finally concluded aloud, in a rich and lilting accent that was unequivocally American. 'Tell me I'm right,' she said, already chuckling deeply at the accuracy of her deduction. 'My, oh my, you certainly have some pluck in choosing this profession at such a young age! And what with you being so pretty in such a male line of work!' she continued. 'Tell me, how did this all come about?'

After a little hesitation, May described briefly how she and her older brother Sam had left their home at the sugar plantation in Barbados and had sailed to Liverpool on the sugar consignment boat two months ago. She told her passenger how, with the encouragement of her mother's London cousins, she had looked in the newspaper and applied for this chauffeuring job.

Miss Nettlefold professed herself to be 'quite fascinated' by everything May told her and had kept up her chatter for the last twenty miles of the journey. Both women were amazed to discover they had disembarked from their respective ships at the Liverpool dockyards on exactly the same day. Miss Nettlefold felt certain that the coincidence was a fortuitous sign of a future amicable relationship between them. Indeed, her passenger appeared so effusive that May began to feel a little uncomfortable. But she listened politely as Miss Nettlefold explained how she was on her way to meet an old school friend from Baltimore, Maryland, whom she had not seen for years. If she was honest, she was apprehensive at seeing her again after such a long interval.

'Of course, we stayed in touch by letter, you understand, May? Oh forgive me? Do you mind if I call you May, Miss Thomas? I wanted to ask, rather than presume, especially as we Americans can sometimes run away with our manners over here in England. I guess we can be too informal for some folks.'

'I don't mind being 'May' in the least,' May replied. 'In fact Sir Philip asked to call me by my first name only last week, so you are in good English company.'

'Oh, you have no idea how pleased I am to hear that,' Miss Nettlefold sighed. 'It's so good to meet up with someone who understands what it is like to be a bit on the outside of the insiders, if you get my meaning? My word,' she continued, 'there are so many things one is not allowed to talk about over here, and it takes a Yank a bit of time to figure it all out.'

May sensed a further confidence teetering on the edge of Miss Nettlefold's fashionably red-painted lips.

'I expect you've heard whispers about . . . well

21

. . . you know . . . the goings on at the top?' Miss Nettlefold went on. Her remark was more a statement than an enquiry.

May gave what she hoped was a non-committal movement of her head.

'Most people think it will all blow over just as it did with his earlier married girlfriends, but they don't know Wallis like I do. Death of a King, crowning of a King, whatever happens, when Wallis wants something, boy, does she hang around until she gets it and blow the consequences!'

May's silent concentration on the road quieted Miss Nettlefold but only for a moment.

'Oh, there I go, opening my big mouth again! Forgive me, May.'

But May had pulled the car over and was examining the written directions that lay on the front seat beside her and a few moments later the car was making its way across the gravel and Miss Nettlefold was wishing out loud that the journey had not been over so soon. Chauffeur and passenger assured one another that after this agreeable beginning, they would look forward to meeting again before long.

*   *   *

The day after the accident, May had left Sir Philip's study and gone to her room in Mrs Cage's house, eager to clarify her thoughts by writing in the blue cotton-bound diary given to her by her mother, Edith, just before May had stepped on board the ship. Sir Philip had not mentioned a diary in his list of forbidden confidantes.

'Don't forget to write everything down, darling,' her mother had said. 'Nothing has really happened until you write it down.'

May did not write every day. Sometimes there was not much to say. Sometimes she was nervous that if she put down the truth someone might read it. There was also another drawback to confiding everything to paper. The shortest of entries could trigger the memory of experiences best forgotten. Her mother was right. Once something was committed to writing it became a reality, whereas if she failed to record an incident, or sometimes skipped a whole day, she could pretend it had never happened at all. But with her brother Sam already away at the beginning of his training in the voluntary naval service, and in the absence of anyone else she was allowed to or trusted enough to talk to, she took the diary down from the shelf beside her bed, hoping that the exercise would simplify her confused state of mind.

'I am keeping this diary for you, Mamma,' she began, 'although it feels good to be able to write it for me too, without feeling I have to be careful what I confide. Did you know that Dad has been reading my diary for years? I never mentioned it in case he took it out on me. Although the last few weeks have been unpredictable nothing has happened to make me regret boarding the ship to England, except of course for missing you.'

May's mother Edith had been born and brought up in considerable hardship in the

23

Hebrides in the north of Scotland and when she reached her twenties, she had gone south to Liverpool with her elder sister, Gladys. Both girls hoped to find their freedom and their fortune and, with those aspirations in mind, they found employment in the kitchens of a transatlantic cruise ship. Two months later they had reached the port of Bridgetown in Barbados in 1911 and Edith had been enchanted by the fertile abundance of the island, a landscape in arresting contrast to the bleak beauty of the Scottish moors. Not long after Edith's arrival she had met Duncan Thomas, a fellow Scotsman. Duncan's great-grandfather had made little money from trading in peat and wool and hating the cold and the damp of Scotland had emigrated to the West Indies in the 1850s. There Mr Thomas established a life of relative affluence, and incomparable warmth, as the proprietor of a small sugar plantation.

Two more generations of Thomases followed the first Mr Thomas into the sugar business but by the time the third owner, Duncan's father, had succumbed to a fatal dose of malaria, the world sugar markets were suffering and the Thomas plantation was no longer so prosperous. Duncan was in his early twenties when he inherited the family business and met the lovely young woman who had recently arrived from the Scottish highlands. The charm of the palm-covered island, the lure of its balmy water and the prospect of financial security convinced Edith to accept a proposal of marriage from a man she barely knew. Gladys, her feisty elder sister, the fight for women's suffrage powering the blood through her veins, decided that life on an island in perpetual sunshine was not for her. She returned to England, saddened by the parting from her much-loved sister and burdened with the task of telling her parents that they would probably never see their younger daughter again.

Back in England, Gladys married Bob Castor, an ex-miner and a Scottish trade unionist. Their only son Nathanial was born in London shortly before Edith gave birth in Barbados to her own son Sam. Three years later Edith became the mother of a daughter, May. At the outbreak of the war Duncan had joined the British navy and, apart from one brief spell on leave in 1915, did not return to the island until 1917, when the seriousness of his wartime injuries ensured his future permanent exclusion from national service. A year after the war ended Gladys had died in prison, where she had been detained for her militant role in the suffragette cause, leaving her sister Edith shattered by the news. Shortly afterwards Bob also became fatally ill with tuberculosis, a casualty of years of inhaling the noxious air of the mines, and within eighteen months Nathanial Castor had become an orphan.

Seventeen years later, May and Sam set off on their sea passage to Liverpool on one of the plantation's regular sugar cargo ships. The decision had not been without its challenges, especially as May was leaving the island of her birth for the first time. If it had not been for

Sam's repeated assurances to their mother that he would look after May on the ship, and deliver her safely to Bethnal Green and the front door of cousin Nathanial, their only remaining family member in England, May would not have found the courage to leave and her mother would not have found the strength to let her go.

Both children had longed to come to England for as long as they could remember. Sam had been working on the plantation since he left school at the age of sixteen. He had grown up around ships and had accompanied his father several times on board the consignment boats to England. His ambition was to join the British Royal Navy, just as his father had before him.

But while Sam was motivated to follow the profession of his father, May thought of little other than how she could escape Duncan. On the face of it, Duncan appeared to be a doting father. He encouraged Sam with his studies and insisted on reading bedtime stories to May every night. As a very young girl May had lain in her bed, too hot to tolerate a nightdress, as her father had pulled up a chair beside her. Only May had known that those bedtime stories were accompanied by a 'little nip', the term of endearment, or so Duncan made it sound, that he reserved for those sneaky tots, upended in one swift movement into his mouth from the silver flask he kept in the pocket of his cream tea planter's jacket.

'Just one little nip to oil the wheels before we get going,' Duncan would whisper through the gap in his teeth, half speaking to himself, his small bloodshot eyes looking down at May's body in her bed, as soon as he heard Edith's shoes receding down the stairs.

'Our little secret,' he would say, as May tried to conceal her instinct to draw back at the moment when he began to trail his fingers through her hair, his dirty and broken nails snagging as they made their way down through her ponytail, towards her back, flicking the familiar switch of alarm. But May's mother had suspected nothing and May had been too frightened to tell anyone, feeling that Duncan's behaviour must somehow be her fault.

When May grew too old for the bedtime stories, Duncan left her alone, staying away from the plantation for nights at a time and reappearing with no explanation for his absence. A few years later he had seemed genuinely pleased by May's interest in learning to drive the plantation car and by her cautious acceptance of his offer to teach her. Her skill behind the wheel led to her employment as the official plantation driver. But during the driving lessons Duncan would stroke the back of her head as May, powerless to stop him, gripped the wheel in revulsion. He would put his hand on her knee as she worked the pedals at her feet. He would appear through the high stalks of sugar cane when she was out talking to the women in the fields and offer to walk her home, or he would think of a reason to accompany her on her weekly trips to the bank and the post office in nearby Speightstown. May became practised at avoiding him but she knew that however much she tried to protect herself, one day he would succeed in crossing the final boundary. In the end it had been Sam's persistent pursuit of his naval ambitions that had opened up the opportunity for escape and freedom.

★ ★ ★

In the very early days of January 1936, May and Sam Thomas stepped off the ship, up onto the high Liverpool quayside at Albert Dock. May shivered beneath the inadequacy of her thin cotton coat. The pale-blue summer-flimsy material had been perfectly suited to the warm climate back home, wrapped around her narrow shoulders by her mother before she had pulled her daughter close to her and kissed her goodbye. But May had been quite unprepared for this feeling of real English coldness. Not only was her skin cold to the touch, but she felt as if her blood had stopped pumping round her body altogether.

From the warmth of her bed in Mrs Cage's house, May thought back over the past few weeks. At home the brightness of the overhead sun could dazzle with a light that filtered scarlet through closed eyelids. But on that first day in Liverpool, the greyness of the early morning had given her the illusion that night-time was already falling. The sky hung so low that it appeared to be collapsing onto the Pier Head.

Sam knew his way around the dock from his previous trips to Liverpool. He had tucked his sister's right hand into that of his own glove and joined together in that manner they walked the length of the quayside. The grey water, until so recently their exclusive landscape, had vanished behind the frosty sea mist that rose above the harbour walls. The walkway was thick with people, almost all men, all travelling in different directions. The level of noise was nearly as hard to tolerate as the freezing air. Men pushed carts so precariously laden with vegetables and fruit that the weight caused the carts to weave uncontrollably from side to side. Warehouse workers rode bicycles with huge trailers packed with cardboard boxes hooked behind them, and the occasional private car nudged its way through the crush, granted special permission to draw up at the water's edge only because of the importance of the human cargo it had come to collect. May pulled at Sam's sleeve to stop. A beautifully kept dark blue Rolls-Royce was parked up against the harbour wall. The plantation car that she loved for the freedom and independence it gave her had been one of the hardest things to leave behind.

Glad to be on land for a few days before the return journey, Sam's sailor friends were full of good humour, telling the sort of jokes generally too risky to tell in the presence of a woman. They had accepted May as one of them, warming to her on the voyage partly for her brave-spiritedness in the rough seas but also for her unusual and delicate beauty. The ration of rum distributed on arrival in port had induced a friendly boisterousness towards her that bore no resemblance to the threatening, drunken silences

29

that accompanied Duncan's lingering looks.

A couple of the crew offered to help carry their few pieces of luggage and the little group made their way along the bustling fog-draped pier, to the nearby Pier Head bus station. The timetable for the Crosville Motor Services to London was pinned onto the waiting-room wall and a gas fire was sputtering in one corner, doing its best to warm the cramped space. The room began to fill up with people blowing air into their hands. When the squat green-and-cream bus drew up outside, just visible through the smeary condensation of the only window in the waiting room, the passengers gathered up their bags and cases. The driver, his mood avuncular, stood at the foot of the coach steps.

'Come along, Ladies and Gents,' he said, taking May by the crook of her elbow and helping her up onto the bottom step of the coach. 'Mind how you go, my dear.'

Some of the male passengers saluted as they boarded and the driver returned the gesture of mock-deference, touching his cap, the smartest part of his otherwise shabby uniform. Several of the women around May clutched thermoses, their curlers visible beneath their headscarves. They spread woollen rugs over their knees and soon the driver was swinging the bus out of the station, the large steering wheel sliding easily through his fingers like a seal slipping through a circus hoop.

May settled back into the velvety moquette seat, tucking her gloveless hands beneath her thighs to warm them up. As a child she had often hidden her hands, not for warmth but in embarrassment, longing for them to turn as pale as those of her brother and mother. Only recently had she accepted the inexplicable, that just like the rest of her body, they would always be a slightly deeper colour than the rest of her family.

The journey to London took up much of the day as flasks of tea were passed up and down between the aisle, and jam sandwiches in greaseproof packets were offered to those who had come unprepared. May had not eaten since leaving the ship and was grateful when an elderly man gestured to her and Sam to help themselves to his own supply. Each time the coach hit an uneven patch of road the man put his hand to his mouth.

'It's my teeth,' he explained. 'These new ones cost me an arm and a leg and I don't want them shooting out onto the floor. Might never find them again.'

Eventually the soothing sway of the coach encouraged sleep. Every so often the coach stopped in a city bus station to pick up and drop off more passengers and twice the coach drew into the forecourt of a public house where a chatty queue formed outside the door to the ladies' facilities, while the men vanished behind the back of the building, whistling. Each time the coach paused, first at Birkenhead, then Chester, and then Whitchurch, the interruption to the motion woke May from her doze. She watched the tiny breath clouds that hung for a moment in the outside air as more London-bound travellers came huffing into the bus, visibly disappointed to find that the presence of a group of human bodies had made little effect on the cold inside.

At Oxford, the last stop before the end of the two hundred-mile journey to London, May and Sam left the coach for some fresh air. A barely lit cigarette stub was clinging to the corner of the driver's bottom lip and the front crease down the length of his trousers had disappeared. He looked crumpled and tired, the bonhomie of the early part of the journey squeezed out of him. Sam offered him a Player's from his own packet and, with an embarrassed shrug of the shoulders, the driver apologised for his dishevelled appearance. He confided that he still preferred his winter uniform to the summer variety. The white linen jacket, compulsory throughout July and August, was never free from oil and smuts and he dreaded the ignominy of being confused for an ice-cream salesman.

An insipid watercolour sun was setting as the men stood and smoked outside the bus as in the half ghostly light. May stared at the skyline ahead of them.

'Matthew Arnold says 'the dreaming spires of Oxford need not June for beauty's heightening'.' Sam recited. 'I learned the poem at school but I never thought I would see the place for myself.'

May was mesmerised by the dramatic outline of the city and the silhouetted buildings with their towers and spires which glinted with a romantic beauty. She was barely awake when she felt Sam putting his hand inside her own glove before leading her across the bus terminal at

Victoria. The National Omnibus Company let them off at Bethnal Green Road. Night had fallen and struggling through the darkness with their heavy cases they left the busy main road and soon arrived at a short terrace of small brick houses abutting a park. Children swung off ropes tied to the waists of the gas lamps and May had to step into the street to avoid trampling the chalked-in numbers of a recently abandoned game of hopscotch. All along Cyprus Street, wooden shutters painted black opened out flat against the wall on either side of the ground floor windows. A brightly coloured display of flags decorated part of a wall opposite the Duke of Wellington pub and a memorial stone had been set well into the brick. Despite her tiredness, May tugged at Sam's arm to stop for a moment so she could read the words.

R.I.P. In loving memory of the men of
Cyprus Street who made the
Great Sacrifice 1914–1918.
Erected by the Duke of Wellington's
discharged and demobilized
soldiers and sailors benevolent club.

Spelled out clearly beneath the plaque were more than two dozen names.

Turning the corner into Oak Street they saw a broad-chested man, his curly hair breaking on his shoulders, standing at the open door of number 52.

'At last,' he said, beaming at May and Sam. 'I am Nat. And you are really here at last.'

Nathanial Castor, the son of their mother's adored elder sister Gladys, had been expecting his cousins for an hour or more and even though this was their first meeting, he enfolded May in his arms before embracing Sam with equal warmth.

May looked back in the direction of the Cyprus Street war memorial.

'We call it the Shrine,' Nat told her. 'It commemorates the highest number of men from any one London street to have died in the War, and reminds us all how they did their duty to their country.'

'It's beautiful,' May said.

'Yes, isn't it?' Nat agreed. And then he said, 'Come in, come in, Sarah is longing to meet you.'

3

As Miss Evangeline Nettlefold reached across the dining-room table for a second piece of toast, she felt the seam at the side of her woollen dress give way.

Despite her size, Evangeline often surprised her friends with her stylishness, particularly when everyone knew she was all but penniless. Her often admired hats, the straw boaters, berets and feather-decorated combs, changed as frequently as those pictured on the pages of fashionable magazines, were thought by some to be a little *jeune-fille* for a woman who had just entered her fifth decade. Beneath the hats were a variety of wigs that cunningly concealed the ravages of alopecia and gave Evangeline a little of the confidence she craved. However, the current trend for close-fitting clothes was not making her life easy. She wished she had been born in an earlier era of flamboyant, floaty gowns, which must have conveniently masked the evidence of too many rich desserts. She had registered with a wince that the American fashion pages had pronounced the 1936 waists to be 'in', and had been debating silently whether the discomfort would be worth the effort.

She reflected with some regret on how she had indulged herself royally in the ship's first-class dining room on the way across the Atlantic. And now that she was here in England, those pounds continued to amass in the most disconcerting manner. She comforted herself that what might look like a small lapse of self-discipline was often beyond her power to change. How was she expected to refuse the exquisitely rolled balls of butter that the British invited their guests to unfurl onto a piece of bread? What control did she have over the volume of cream-filled pitchers they stirred into their puddings? She remembered with nostalgia how in the summer they served a particularly delicious cream-and-fruit-based dessert that resembled melted ice cream. Fool, they called it, but there was no fooling Evangeline with the amount of calories it must have contained. Calories interested her. Back home she had been following reports of some scientific experiments with rats whose lifetimes had been significantly extended when their calorie intake was reduced. Something to bear in mind for another day, perhaps, Evangeline thought as she buttered her toast. She had recently become aware of her zipper catching the small but disturbing pinch of flesh beneath her armpit and had prayed that the already weakened stitching would hold up — at least until after breakfast.

She had an inkling of what it might feel like to be slim. She had once been left alone in a fitting room when the dressmaker had gone to fetch a measuring tape. Seizing her chance she had run her hands along the sides of a small-sized tailor's dummy, beginning just below the bust and travelling all the way down past the neat indent at the waist and further on to the pleasing gentle swell at the hips, closing her eyes as she did so. Her hands encountered no lumps or rolls, simply smooth straight lines. *That,* she thought to herself with envy, *is what it must be like.* The evidence of her ill-fitting clothes was becoming impossible to ignore, even though the height that she had been lucky enough to inherit from her father helped to spread some of the extra weight across a larger area. Such a bonus would not have been hers if she had been born with her mother's diminutive stature. Even so, there was no avoiding the truth: several of the dresses she had brought with her from Baltimore would soon have to be altered. Altered? Dear God! What was she thinking? If she was being truthful what she meant was they would have to be let out. Evangeline felt sure that Wallis would be able to give her the name of a good English dressmaker.

Evangeline shifted uncomfortably in her seat, wondering whether to help herself to another sausage from the silver dish sitting on the hot plate. She felt a familiar shiver of self-loathing. She knew that her public excuse for eating too much was that the curves were part of her character: rounded; jolly; up for a laugh; not in the least bit sensitive about the odd tease. But the secret truth was that Evangeline had no expectations that her status as a forty-year-old 'virgo intacta' would ever change. So what difference was the odd fleshy roll here or there going to make to her solitary progress through life?

Sometimes she felt like a caricature of a

middle-aged spinster. She wondered for the hundredth time when real life — by which she meant *happy* real life — was going to begin. As she scooped out a dollop of marmalade from the pot whose label confirmed it came from Oxford and must therefore be the best of its kind, she reminded herself that at least for now during her time here in England she had a purpose. Ever loyal to friends that needed her and indefatigably romantically optimistic, she felt sure her luck would change soon.

She could hardly believe that it had only been a matter of days since Wiggle had been squirming in discomfort beside her on the floor. After an initial flash of fury at the stupidity of the sweet young chauffeur, she had forgiven May. After all, Pekineses, like their mistresses, were often choosy about their food, and the chopped up kidney in thick gravy that the London cook had prepared for Wiggle had been causing havoc with his digestion. There had never been any question of leaving Wiggle back at home in Baltimore. Besides, who else would have shared the lonely nights with Evangeline? The ever-present warm body at her feet had been the only nocturnal companionship she had ever known. Admittedly she had taken a gamble with the quarantine laws and had been careful not to produce Wiggle too often in public places. Before leaving Baltimore, she had persuaded herself that at least his dear little bark would not betray an American accent. And when the customs officers had waved her through at the dock she had been relieved that the capaciousness of her coat ensured there was ample room to hide a small dog within its folds.

Evangeline debated for a moment whether to have a third and definitively final slice of toast to go with the sausage. Joan had already left the table and there was as yet no sign of that tiresome Rupert in his absurd lacy cravat or of his captivating young friend Julian. She was alone. No one was here to count.

She had been delighted, if surprised, to receive the first letter from England. Only six weeks earlier (although it felt like much longer ago. My, oh my, didn't time play tricks?), she had been at home, helping her sister-in-law with preparations for the family Christmas. Her mother's death and the consequent terms of the will had left Evangeline without a home or any independent means and she had come to live with her brother Frank and his family at their invitation. Evangeline's father, an affluent businessman, had died so soon after his daughter's birth that Evangeline had no memory of him. A large man, fond of his food and drink, he had suffered a heart attack after breakfast when his wife was out shopping. Mrs Nettlefold had returned to the house to find the barely warm figure of her husband spread out on the dining-room floor, a buttered roll lying, as if tossed away in overdue disgust, a yard or so from his rounded face.

During the subsequent years Evangeline had served as companion to her cantankerous widowed mother, putting up with an endless succession of Mrs Nettlefold's 'suitors', the covetous glint of her inherited wealth in their eyes. Evangeline's filial devotion had gone quite unrewarded. Mrs Nettlefold rarely failed to draw a visitor's attention to Evangeline's size and had long made it clear that she considered her big-toothed, accident-prone, spinster daughter to be a disappointment. Since the age of twelve, her pubescent breasts evidence of approaching adulthood, Evangeline had dreamt of the day she would be set free from her mother's critical presence.

'How many times have I told you to sit up straight? No man wants to marry a humpback,' Mrs Nettlefold would say, producing a pencil from nowhere as if it were a magician's wand, and prodding it deeply and painfully into the small of Evangeline's back.

Once when Evangeline had already embarked on the hairpin bends of puberty, she overheard her mother on the telephone to a friend. 'Evangeline reminds me of a tombstone. She is huge, grey and lifeless. She might as well be in the ground beneath that stone right now for all the trouble she causes me.'

A few days later Evangeline had woken to find her pillow covered in hair. Putting her hand to her head a whole section of pale brown fluff came away as if she were scooping up a field of dandelion clocks.

'Has your daughter had a recent shock?' the doctor asked Mrs Nettlefold.

'Nothing that I know of, doctor,' Mrs Nettlefold replied. 'She leads the care-free life of a cosseted child.'

But Evangeline *had* experienced a shock. If

pressed, the doctor might have confirmed that a declaration of lovelessness delivers a severe shock from which it is difficult to recover. But the doctor was not consulted again and the hair on Evangeline's head had never grown back. For several months her mother's friends, ignorant of the real reason why Evangeline always insisted on wearing a hat, even at mealtimes, had talked among themselves of how such an attractive mother did not deserve such a plain child. Hats became a passion for Evangeline. And ever since the shock she had paid extra attention to any outfit on the street that was topped off with a cloche or a bonnet.

No one was more aware than Evangeline herself that Mrs Nettlefold felt cheated. Where was the vivacious elegance that would have ensured Evangeline's inclusion in the society magazines? The Great War had obliterated so many of America's eligible bachelors that Mrs Nettlefold had joined a band of socially ambitious and avaricious mothers who escorted their unmarried daughters across the Atlantic to England. There they hoped to take advantage of a country that had proved until recently to be a reliable source of rich and titled young men. But the British upper classes had suffered still worse wartime casualties, and while second sons had become an acceptable second best in the bazaar for upper-class husbands, in desperate cases third-borns had come to suffice. However, despite some of the very best introductions effected by her well-connected English god-mother Joan, no one had so much as invited

Evangeline for a cup of tea, let alone lavished upon her dinner, candlelight, romance and a seat as the châteleine of a decent Georgian rectory. Well before Evangeline's twenty-fifth birthday Mrs Nettlefold gave up all hope of her daughter ever marrying, concluding that the root of the problem was not a scarcity of candidates but a matter of size. Evangeline was just too fat.

In her twenties Evangeline had read Michael Arlen's best-selling, romantic novel *The Green Hat*. A passage about discomfiture, nothing in fact to do with hats, struck a note of empathy. Searching for something to fill the void created by a dissatisfaction with life, Iris Storm, the heroine, rejects cigarettes, cocaine, sex and even chocolate.

'Yes,' Evangeline said aloud in recognition of herself. That is how she spent her time: searching for the elusive *something* to banish the feeling of emptiness. On countless occasions she had thought chocolate might be the answer, but the relief the sugar brought her was evanescent and the emptiness invariably returned. Every day of her life Evangeline Nettlefold battled to suppress the bitterness that threatened to consume her. Jealousy and resentment remained her most pernicious enemies. She was jealous of people's looks, of their popularity, of their self-confidence, of the loyalty they received from others and above all of their apparent ease at attracting love. All her life Evangeline had felt unregarded, unimportant and unloved. And all her silent resentment was directed at the woman who had caused this state of affairs.

Evangeline's brother Frank had long been distressed by his mother's victimisation of Evangeline but like everyone else was too wrapped up in his own life to do anything about it. However, he was grateful to Evangeline for accepting almost single-handedly the nursing of their mother, who rarely spent a week without discovering she was suffering from some new ailment. She was plagued by aches and pains in every part of her body and Frank and Evangeline joked behind her back about their mother's tedious 'organ recital'. Eminent specialists had been unable to make a diagnosis. They could find no explanation for the intermittent fainting fits, shortness of breath and trembling limbs that could confine Mrs Nettlefold alternately to the sitting-room sofa or, more extremely, to a demanding existence tucked for several days into her bed, waited on by her daughter. Evangeline felt persecuted, throttled and trapped and there had been occasions when she prayed her mother would not recover from her latest affliction.

In the end, for the first time in Evangeline's life, a wish came true and a weakened heart was given as the medical consensus of the cause of Mrs Nettlefold's eventual death. Seeing his sister homeless and, valuing the uniqueness of a sibling bond, Frank and his wife had offered Evangeline board and lodging. Because of her generally cheerful and phlegmatic presence, and despite her occasional clumsiness, her dependency never felt like an imposition.

* * *

43

Six weeks ago, when the Baltimore morning post had been placed on the hall table, Evangeline had turned to the small pile of envelopes and the new Christmas issue of *Good Housekeeping* magazine, the publication that was her single modest flash of self-indulgence. Most of the envelopes contained Christmas cards and shop catalogues filled with pictures of tempting seasonal highlights. She had saved the best for the last. The sight of the stamp with its crowned head in profile always brought her a little lift of pleasure, for she knew who had placed that stamp on the envelope.

Cuckmere Park, Near Eastbourne, Sussex.
10 December, 1935

My dear Evangeline

We have not seen you for so long. Our plans to come over to the United States keep on getting interrupted by Philip's demanding parliamentary schedule. But recently I was at a dinner party and found myself talking to an old schoolfriend of yours. I believe you knew her as Wallis Warfield, although you may not have heard that since leaving school she has been married (twice in fact!). Miss Warfield became Mrs Spencer and then not long after her divorce (most painful I believe, as he drank) she married an Ernest Simpson who is half American and has an English mother. So now your friend is Mrs Simpson.
Although Wallis and Ernest settled here a

few years ago, I do not know them well. During our chat the other night, I got the impression that Wallis, although devoted to her husband, was a little lonely, and would, I am certain, be much comforted by the presence of one of her countrymen here in England. In fact when I mentioned your name as a long-standing friend of our own family she lit up!

I wondered, dear child, if you might make two lots of people happy by agreeing to come over for a lovely long visit? Of course I do know how tight money is. Perhaps that final illness took its toll on your mother's mind? I do hope you can manage to join me in blaming ill health for her otherwise inexplicable failure to remember you in the will?

Anyway, my dear, I am enclosing a small cheque that might help persuade you to book a passage on the first ship to England to sail after Christmas. That way you could be here with us at the beginning of the New Year. I can already hear your protests, but you must know that it is actually an act of pure selfishness on my part as the pleasure of having you here will be mainly mine. And if you stay with us long enough you will be in time to travel home on the new Cunard liner in the summer. I hear that the Queen Mary is even to have a dog walking deck so perhaps (if we are careful to avoid any nasty quarantine rules: a convenient blanket could be readily to hand!) you could bring Wiggle with you too? And, if I dare suggest that you might discover *you are enjoying yourself, you might even extend your stay beyond the summer season. There are always so many jolly parties to go to and you would be welcome to join in everything as an honorary member of the Blunt family.*

I know you will keep it to yourself when I tell you that I have been suffering one of my worst glooms recently. Philip says that another war is a distinct possibility and I do not think I could manage to go through it all again, especially with Rupert leaving Oxford this coming summer and being the right age for being called up. I am praying it will not happen. But if you write and say yes to coming to see us, you will be giving Philip and me the very best of belated Christmas presents.

This comes, as always, with a kiss from us both
Your loving godmother
Joan

Joan's family and the Nettlefolds had known each other for as long as Evangeline could remember. Her mother and Joan had met in England one summer while Queen Victoria was still on the British throne, two reigns ago. Mrs Nettlefold had been visiting London on a sightseeing visit to Europe, or what she later referred to as 'an eye opener' (named after her favourite cocktail). In the summer of 1894 she had met the eighteen-year-old debutante Lady Joan Bradley (as one of three daughters of an

46

earl, the title had been hers from birth). They had been seated on adjacent gold chairs at a fashion show at the Maison Lucile in Mayfair, a new salon to which society flocked in the wake of the patronage of the elegantly bustled Lillie Langtry, the Prince of Wales's favourite. That day when they had each bought a daringly diaphanous tea gown, and had marvelled at Lucile's crêpe de Chine and rose silk underwear, a friendship had begun to develop between the young society woman and the socially ambitious American tourist. A year or two later, after Evangeline's mother had found herself a rich suitor willing to play the several roles of banker, husband and father, she gave birth to Frank and then to Evangeline. The two godmothers selected to take care of Evangeline's spiritual well-being were Madame Lucile, who gave Evangeline her love of fashion, and Joan, who instilled in her a hesitant affection for England. Charming as the country was, Evangeline always felt the weather and an occasional propensity for unfriendliness let the place down.

The Blunt and Nettlefold families had remained in touch by letter and through occasional visits across the Atlantic, although the fortunes of the two godmothers had not prospered during the war. Madame Lucile, the one-time queen of the fashion world, found herself reduced to bankruptcy, her wafty Edwardian tea gowns no longer fashionable, and she died alone and poverty stricken in a bedsit in south London. Misfortune had struck Evangeline's other god-mother far earlier. At the beginning of the War at the late age of thirty-eight, Joan married a successful politician, and soon afterwards became the mother of first a son, Rupert, in 1915 and then a daughter, Bettina, the following year.

But only a month before the Armistice was signed in 1918, a monstrous stray shell had torn with annihilating force into the body of Joan's beloved younger sister Grace, a nurse stationed right up at the front line at Ypres, and despite a desperate search by her medical colleagues, no remains were found. This loss had permanently fractured Joan's emotional equilibrium. Nearly twenty years later, and now sixty years old, Joan continued to suffer bouts of deep depression. Sometimes her husband Sir Philip Blunt was at his wits' end trying to bring his wife back to the state of capable sunniness that had first prompted him to fall in love with her.

Evangeline also knew what it was to question the point of getting out of bed in the morning, and whether it would be worth the bother of dressing, washing, brushing her hair or speaking to a living soul. But through the dulling agents of food and shopping Evangeline taught herself to force the immediacy of the pain to recede and to diffuse her propensity to despair by making it a habit to think of the welfare of others. Pursuing responsibilities made Evangeline feel needed and worthwhile.

But should she go to Joan? England in the winter was hardly an enticing prospect. Her last trip had been five years ago during one of her mother's visits to Royal Ascot and had proved most unenjoyable, what with the lack of male company and the incessant drizzle. Despite Joan's generous invitation, Evangeline was doubtful if there really was anything worth going to England for.

4

A day or two later, slipped within the final late post of the Christmas season, another letter bearing an English stamp arrived for Evangeline. Helping herself to a handful of the sugar-covered almonds from the glass bowl on the hall table, she examined the envelope carefully before inserting into one corner the silver, flower-engraved knife that she used for opening letters. The flourishing loop that finished off the first letter of each word took her back to those Baltimore boarding schooldays at Oldfields where the teachers often quoted the school motto to them: 'Gentleness and Courtesy are expected of girls at all times.'

As ever, the circled, underlined and hyphenated code word was reliably in place in the top left-hand corner of the envelope, the word she and Wallis had used in all correspondence with each other since their teenage years. At school, the custom had been for best friends to merge part of their own first names into one, and the middle part of Evangeline and the last part of Wallis had formed Gel-Lis. The two of them had always laughed when saying the made-up word out loud because although it sounded like 'jealous', that particular emotion played no part in their friendship. The other girls thought they made an incongruous pair as the stooped, cumbersome figure of Evangeline towered over

50

her shorter, skinnier friend. Wallis had another soulmate, the pretty Mary Kirk, with whom she was almost as close, and Evangeline, while grateful for her primary position in Wallis's life, wondered if Wallis chose the company of herself over Mary solely for the shiny glamour bestowed on her by Evangeline's contrasting dowdiness.

In the holidays, Wallis and Evangeline would go shopping in downtown Baltimore. The girls were just turning sixteen and the new department store, Hochschild Kohn, was a favourite place to meet. Evangeline would arrive early and spend stolen time in the store's tempting hat department, swaddling her poor bald head in the latest velvet and silk models, her appearance in the mirror briefly confusable with a sophisticated young woman of fashion like Mary Kirk instead of the plain-faced egg-head that usually stared back at her. It was in the coffee shop at Hochschild's that Wallis confided to Evangeline that she had 'done it'. The boy in question was the son of a friend of her parents, although much more beyond that Wallis was not prepared to divulge. It was clear from Wallis's satisfied expression that Evangeline had reacted to her shared confidence with awe. In fact, Evangeline had found the information almost impossible to comprehend. When had it happened? How had it begun? How long did it go on for? Were they wearing clothes all the way through? Who unhooked the hooks? Was there any sound involved? Words? Shrieks? Many other mysteries demanded answers but Evangeline had not the courage to ask them. Evangeline was further perplexed when, having settled their bill with the waitress and returned to the street, she noticed that Wallis had no trouble at all swinging herself onto her bicycle and pedalling off at speed. A hard bicycle seat that tapered to a point? Surely after such an 'interference' it must now *hurt*? Nonetheless, Evangeline left the department store that day feeling as if life had lurched forward a notch or two. If Evangeline herself remained innocent of the interlocking physical jigsaw that two human bodies were evidently capable of, she could at least glow in the reflected smugness of her newly worldly friend.

★ ★ ★

Two decades ago Wallis had returned to Baltimore from China where she had been living for two years with her first husband, Earl Winfield Spencer, a naval pilot known by everyone as Win. Evangeline had been looking forward to their reunion in Wallis's old family home but had spoken little during the meeting as Wallis described the drama of the Orient and the horror of dealing with her husband's alcoholic temper. After more than two hours of chat Wallis gave Evangeline a silver Chinese paperknife, engraved with flowers and sheathed in its own silver holder.

'I bought it in a bazaar in Peking,' Wallis told her. 'I thought you might like it.'

Evangeline was moved by such thoughtfulness. Friendship was everything she thought content-edly, as she put the knife in her bag and Wallis announced she had an even more special present to show her in the bedroom.

'What do you think of this?' Wallis asked, her usual macaw-like voice suddenly unnaturally soft. In her hand was a flesh-coloured metal cylinder about four inches long and a generous inch in diameter. 'We could have some fun with this, Vangey. I learned how in China. I could show you if you like.'

Evangeline could smell Wallis's spice-scented breath as her provocative expression was accompanied by the slow unbuttoning of Wallis's beautiful silk blouse. Before Evangeline could move out of the way, Wallis had reached for the pussycat bow at the neck of Evangeline's dress and loosened it with one short tug.

'What in the world do you think you're doing?' Evangeline cried, sending Wallis stumbling backwards with a forceful shove, the stifling intimacy of the bedroom suddenly intolerable as she made a rush for the front door.

That horrible misunderstanding had reverberated in Evangeline's thoughts during all the intervening years, and at first Evangeline had vowed privately to have nothing more to do with her old schoolfriend. She had learned through the Baltimore grapevine that Wallis and Win had been divorced and that Wallis had gone on to marry an English shipping executive named Ernest Simpson. Evangeline and Wallis had not met since the unfortunate incident in Wallis's bedroom and no reference had ever been made to the occasion in their infrequent letters.

Maybe that was all about to change,

Evangeline wondered as she removed several folded pages from the envelope. The letter-head was unknown to her. Had Wallis and her new husband made friends with some sort of military family? What sort of people lived in a fort? There was no accounting for the English and their old-fashioned ways. Despite the incident in the bedroom Evangeline could not help looking forward to Wallis's letters. They were always so amusing. Wallis had made Evangeline laugh at her aversion to Britain's lumpy pillows and her unease with the complex etiquette at table. Why for example did the British fall upon their food as soon as it was placed in front of them, as if they had not eaten for months, instead of an hour or so earlier?

'Do start, oh DO,' a hostess would apparently call down the table even though the butler had not yet completed his rounds and half the guests still had nothing to start *on*.

Wallis had also written of her relief at finding a new husband, half English to boot, with whom she got on so well. Their relocation to Ernest's mother's home country and the fun they had been having over choosing antique furniture for their small flat had confirmed for Evangeline that this second marriage had been a good decision.

Wallis had also described the filth of the capital city and how the sulphurous-smelling pea soupers, the greenish fog that Londoners called the 'London Particular', restricted the visibility in the city streets making it impossible to tell the house numbers without peering right up against the door. She told of how the smoggy dirt from coal fires that belched night and day from the city's chimneys was intensified by the diesel fumes from the increasing number of cars on the road. What is more, Wallis could not abide the dust and grime that found its way *inside* the houses.

Dirt and chaos did not suit Wallis. The photographs of herself that she sometimes enclosed always confirmed that everything about Wallis was clean and tidy; she was as assured as a flamingo on one leg. The attractive waviness of her youthful hairstyle had long since disappeared. Instead she had become streamlined in every detail from the fine symmetry of the parting of her hair right down the middle, to the precise manner in which she posed for the camera in her chic and cinched dresses. Even the pencilled-in shape of the upended smile of her eyebrows that brought some relief to the otherwise empty expanse of her broad forehead had apparently been subjected to the same strict dietary regime. Some of the girls at school had nicknamed her 'Skellis'. Evangeline tried not to dwell on the name they might have called *her* when she was out of the room, but skeletal she was certainly not.

Evangeline settled herself further into the faded blue velvet chair next to the fire, the silver paper knife as always on the table beside her. Realising from the startled yelp beneath her that she had sat on top of the new kitten, she extracted the tiny animal from underneath the cushion, relieved when it shook itself out and headed unruffled for the door. Smoothing out the folded pages of blue stationery, she began to read. Wallis wished to ask Evangeline a favour. Mentioning the dinner party at which she had chatted with the 'charming Lady Joan Blunt', Wallis expressed her sadness in discovering so late in the day that Mrs Nettlefold had passed away. Wallis had heard that Lady Joan was encouraging her god-daughter to take a trip across the ocean and expressed the hope that a word from Wallis, her 'oldest friend', might help to convince Vangey to come.

'I would love to show you how life is so different over here,' Wallis had cajoled. 'It might amuse you to know that this democrat has been taking dancing and curtseying lessons, though my curtsey is more of a mop than a floor sweeper!'

Given that her aunt Bessie was now too elderly to cross the Atlantic more than once a year, Wallis was missing the company of someone to talk to about the way they did things back home. She was not sure if Evangeline was acquainted with a fellow compatriot, Thelma Furness, with whom Wallis had previously spent a good deal of time. Sadly Wallis saw little of her these days, and if Evangeline could keep this one confidence to herself for now, the truth was that Wallis was beginning to feel a little overwhelmed by the British. Sometimes she did not know which nationality she belonged to. She loved the British dignity and their wide outlook but she preferred the American sense of humour and its peculiar brand of 'pep'. Sometimes, despite the social swirl around her, Wallis felt a little out of things. Even the friendship of one or two special individuals (other than that of her dear husband, of course) did not wholly eradicate her sense of homesickness. She wanted to discuss all this and much more with Evangeline in person.

'Do come! Oh *do!*' she had written, underlining the words three times for emphasis. 'We might even find you that elusive beau over here! He is bound to be waiting for you somewhere.'

A longing for her schooldays engulfed Evangeline. That long-gone sense of innocence and trust reminded her of the feeling she now had when about to put on a new dress, or when given a box of chocolates sealed up in its wrapper. Everything was lovely in the anticipation; there must have been a time, she thought wistfully, when disappointment was an undiscovered emotion. The warmth and wit of her old school friend suddenly seemed deliciously tempting. The misunderstanding in the Baltimore bedroom with the 'Chinese Wand' was behind them and need never again be mentioned. Putting the letter back in the envelope, Evangeline made her mind up to go to England at once.

★ ★ ★

As the SS *Thalassa* switch-backed its way through the Atlantic waves in one of the worst crossings in memory, most of the passengers clutched their queasy stomachs in the privacy of their staterooms. The outside temperatures dipped so low that the bottom of the empty swimming pool had cracked in the freezing weather. Evangeline counted her blessings that she was making this journey during the winter months so that one of her secret shames would remain undiscovered. Evangeline had a profound fear of water and had never learned to swim. Deck tennis and table tennis were also impossible activities in the heaving ship, but movies and bridge filled the hours between meals most satisfactorily. Evangeline found herself unaffected by the rocking motion of the waves, as long as she kept away from the terrifying sight of the rolling, cresting seascape. As a result she was often one of just a handful of diners in the restaurant and, lavished with the constant attention of dozens of under-occupied waiters, she felt the glee of a hippopotamus that had just landed on a thick and oozy mud bank.

With Wiggle in canine paradise, devouring as many sausages and biscuits as his small jaws could manage, Evangeline wished the voyage would take double the time. There had been cocktails and cigars, caviar and canapés, and she had enjoyed herself, the many invitations to dance with the perspiring assistant captain notwithstanding. Evangeline was not a gifted dancer despite the hours of lessons that she had undertaken at her mother's insistence on the premise that you never knew when they might come in useful for 'Important Society Gatherings'. On the final evening on board Evangeline and her naval suitor stumbled their way through the Viennese waltz, his clammy hand suctioned to a small area of Evangeline's exposed flesh. The cutaway lozenge on the back panel of her evening gown provided the impetus for a whisky-drenched suggestion that the assistant captain might introduce her to his widowed mother who lived in Liverpool and who would so enjoy hearing tales of the New World in Evangeline's charming accent.

In more ways than one, Evangeline was looking forward to reaching Liverpool but above all she was excited about the reunion with her schoolfriend. She was particularly pleased to have found the perfect gift for Wallis, a belated Christmas present as well as something that would remind them both of the years of affection and of memories that still bound them together. A week before she sailed for Britain Evangeline paid a visit to Hochschild's. The shop's familiar yellow-and-black delivery vans still darted through the Baltimore streets, bringing a flash of colour to the grey streets. After much thought, nostalgia encircling her as she browsed through the departments she and Wallis had once known so well, Evangeline had stopped in the music department and come across a box of jazz records marked 'old stock'. There, near the top of the pile, was a recording of WC Handy's 'Memphis Blues', the band's top hit in 1909 and re-released in the 1920s under Hochschild's own record label 'The Belvedere'. The name was clearly imprinted on the yellow vinyl record. What a perfect present to take to Wallis at her new address at Fort Belvedere! The coincidence could not fail to delight her friend. How the gift would confirm to Wallis how much she had missed her teenage companion! She had made a couple of other purchases, too. For Joan there was a stylish umbrella with the Hochschild logo stamped on the black-and-yellow waterproof. And for Philip there was a pair of the latest casual shoes, a 'loafer', all the rage amongst fashionable men, who had adopted the American variation on the Norwegian moccasin with gusto.

Even as she made her way down the gangplank at the crowded Liverpool docks, with Wiggle hidden underneath her coat, Evangeline was still trying to shake off the persistent assistant captain's attentions. She was relieved to spot her name written in uneven script on the large piece of card held up high by a bulldog of a man in uniform. His cap was sitting slightly askew on his head as he waited for her beside a glistening blue Rolls-Royce on the quayside.

Philip's chauffeur, Cropper, was to bring her straight to London and Evangeline's luggage had been strapped to the back of the car by the taciturn driver, who was evidently reluctant to open his mouth even in cursory greeting. Not until she had settled herself and Wiggle on the leather seat beneath a thick plaid rug did Evangeline detect a whiff of whisky in the air.

Deciding that the least confrontational and therefore most pleasurable way to spend the long journey was to remain silent, she gazed out of the window, relieved when they left the grim-looking streets of Liverpool behind them. As the car gathered speed along the monotonously grey roads of the north of England, Evangeline fell asleep. She only came to during brief stops at the side of the road when Cropper muttered that he needed to check that the luggage was still securely tied to the back of the car, but she soon dozed off again until they eventually arrived in London.

5

When May and Sam squeezed their way into the tiny front room in Bethnal Green they found three people waiting for them. A tall girl with wide-open grey eyes, rose from her chair beside the coal fire to greet the new arrivals. An older, balding man, his shirt buttons perilously close to detaching themselves from the straining fabric of his shirt, tucked his arm into the crook of Sarah's elbow and smiled at May and Sam. His facial resemblance to Sarah was unmistakable.

The third member of the greeting party, a woman wearing a floral apron tied tightly over her cardigan, faced the visitors from her position in front of the fire. She had hitched up the back of her skirt almost to her waist and was warming herself on the coals. Releasing her skirt she bustled over to May and peered at her over the top of her glasses. May could smell something faintly farinaceous.

'Well now! Here you are. Nat's cousins! And let me say we are very happy to have you here in Oak Street, aren't we, Sarah? Aren't we, Simon? Simon, are you paying attention to me?'

'This is Mrs Rachel Greenfeld, my mother-in-law, Simon my father-in-law, and my wife Sarah,' Nat began.

'Was it rough on the boat?' Nat's mother-in-law interrupted, her grey bun pinned in a graceful coil at the back of her head. 'And was the coach on time? I hope your mother packed you both off with a lot of warm clothes and a nice flask for a hot drink. I expect you could all do with a nice cup of tea. Simon, put the kettle on at once, Simon. Did you hear me, Simon? These children are half dead with thirst, I shouldn't wonder. Now then, did your mother warn you that it's very cold here in England? Did you tell your aunt to warn them, Nat?'

Rachel tapped her neatly laced shoe on the floor as she spoke, as if keeping time with the rhythm of her own speech. Her questions came like bubbles popping from a child's blowpipe, with one bursting into the air only to be replaced at once by another.

'Well, tell me, May, what was the food like on the ship, Sam? Not enough of it by the look of you both! Well you won't have to worry about quantity in *this* house!'

Sarah sat quietly, occasionally rolling her eyes at her father and husband as she watched two strangers encountering her mother's inquisitive but affectionate volubility for the first time.

'You look peaky, Sam. Simon, doesn't Sam look peaky? Come over here by the fire and warm yourself, my boy. You don't look so bad, May. Got a bit of colour on you, I'm glad to say. Still, come over here near the heat. Now, is that kettle on, Simon?'

As Rachel continued to interrogate them, May noticed Sarah smoothing down the neat waistline of her dress. For as long as she could remember, May had watched the young women in the plantation fields, their pregnancies advancing gradually to a size that made it uncomfortable for them to bend their distended bodies over the sugar cane without splaying their legs. The absence of even the hint of a swell convinced May that Sarah was still dreaming of the day when she might have a child of her own.

The Greenfeld and Castor's house was the showcase of the street. Number 52 had been one of the first to be connected to electricity, and the chrome plate warmer was displayed on the sideboard with as much fanfare as a cup awarded to the comeliest cow at a country show. The house was fit to burst with possessions accumulated over many years but it was neat, aromatic and well ordered, like a baker's tray of buns. The front door opened directly onto the front room where an ironwork basket on the hearth of a blue-and-white-tiled fireplace was filled with a hillock of coal, shining black-red with heat. Rachel had returned to her position on the hearth and May could see the lace edge of her petticoat peeping out from beneath her skirt. Arranged around the fireplace was a mottled leather three-piece suite and on either side were a couple of lumpy armchairs covered in a brown matte material speckled with pink flowers. A large chestnut wood wireless sat prominently on a low table between the chairs and on the wall hung two shelves full of books.

'Come and see the rest of the house while we wait for the kettle to boil,' Nat said, leading May and Sam next door.

A schoolroom table, covered with a dark-green velvet cloth with thick fringed edges, was laid for tea at one end while neatly arranged at the other were the tools of Sarah's trade. Several pairs of polished scissors, a collection of pink hedgehog-spiked rollers, a variety of different-sized hairbrushes, a silvery tin marked 'bleach' in handwritten letters and a couple of razors were all laid out in precise lines. Along the back of one shelf was a display of beautifully coiffured wigs, waiting for their owners to come and reclaim them from their wooden stands. A small mirror fixed at eye level to the wall opposite a comfortable-looking chair with armrests completed Sarah's salon. The whole effect smacked of efficiency. The source of Rachel's elegant hairstyle was obvious.

Nat took May and Sam through the tiny passageway to the back of the house where an unplumbed bath sitting on decorated metal feet had been squeezed into one corner. A cake of pink Lifebuoy soap in a saucer was balanced on the edge. Outside they were shown a tiny yard with a meat safe, the shed that housed the privy and an earth-filled wooden box in which some bedraggled sprouts clung to life. Ducking under the line of washing May could just make out a door leading into the back alley.

There were two bedrooms upstairs, one for Nat and Sarah, light and sunny and dominated by a pretty bed piled with cushions and brightly coloured shawls from beneath which something lacy and feminine peeped. Nat paused at the second door.

'This is Rachel's boudoir,' he said laughing at his use of the fancy word for the only room in which clutter had got the better of orderliness. A large dresser took up most of the opposite wall, its shelves crammed with Russian icons and gilt candlesticks, the wax of the half-melted candles arrested mid-drip. Beside the dresser was a full-length mirror with faded photographs and postcards stuck all around the frame. A small bookcase hung just inside the door supporting, instead of books, a row of flower and coronet embellished mugs, each one bearing the portrait of a British King or Queen. There was Edward VII and his Queen Alexandra on their Coronation Day, his son George V and Queen Mary on theirs, and the same regal couple again on the occasion of their Silver Jubilee only last year.

'Only one more room to show you,' Nat said as he moved a ladder into position and began to climb.

Stacked along one side of the attic from ceiling to floor were dozens of bolts of material, the overflow from Simon's workshop, Nat explained. But on the other side was a child's brass bed with gleaming copper knobs at each corner. A coal fire was already lit in the corner grate but May's attention went at once to the skylight. By standing on the bed and craning her neck a little she had a terrific view right up the adjoining Cyprus Street towards the war memorial.

'Auntie Edith always said you were trim,' Nat said, clearly delighted by May's pleasure at the room. 'So we hoped you would be able to squeeze in here. At least you will have it to yourself. I am afraid that Sam will have to stretch out on the sofa downstairs.'

A room of her own, whatever size, with a ladder leading nowhere except to a door of her own was something May had always longed for. At home in Barbados, despite the comfortable size of the house, she had always slept in her old childhood room, which led through a connecting door to her parents' bedroom on one side and down to the stairway on the other. She had never liked the sense of being within earshot of her parents and their ineffectively muffled arguments, but out of habit, she had never thought of asking to move.

The house in Barbados had once been a splendid dwelling with its elegant Jacobean proportions, curved staircase, British-designed cornices and beautifully carved wooden doors. But the West Indian sugar export business was no longer thriving as it had done in her grandparents' day. Financial strain following the Great Depression in Britain and competition from other sugar-growing countries had eroded the demand and May had been conscious of the necessary economies her parents had been forced to make. In the past few years the number of household staff had dwindled from a dozen servants down to a couple of maids who came in to clean and dust and to help Bertha, the rotund and cheerful cook. Bertha prepared all the meals for the family as well as lunch for the plantation workers. Her pillow of a shoulder was famously available for any member of the community to lean on or weep on whenever they wished. Bertha's husband Tom completed the complement of staff, a man whose strength lay in his head for figures as he organised the weekly accounts with impressive precision. The ancient plantation chauffeur had died two years ago and it had been Duncan's idea to replace him with his own, unpaid daughter. Even the Rolls-Royce, for so long the pride and joy of May's grandfather and father, had begun to show irreversible signs of age, no matter how much time May gave to the polishing of its green paintwork.

May followed Nat back down the creaking Oak Street ladder thinking how happy her mother and Bertha would be to know of the extent of Nat's welcome and of the excellent character of Gladys's only boy. May had heard all Edith's stories about her adored sister, a passionate campaigner for the vote for women who had been locked up in Holloway Prison before the War for hurling bricks through government office windows. After Gladys's and Bob's deaths Edith had stayed in touch by letter with their son Nathanial, and when the news of Nat's marriage to a beautiful Jewish girl reached Edith she felt happier than she had for years.

To her knowledge, May had never met a Jewish person and she and Sam had been fascinated by the written accounts of Sarah and his new family that Nat sent out to Edith in Barbados. His great-grandparents-in-law had moved from Russia to live and work in London's East End in the middle of the last century where they raised half a dozen children. Rachel's grandfather had been a tailor and his five sons, including Rachel's father, had all joined the

68

same trade. A talent for needle and thread had evidently been ingested with their mother's milk. The only daughter of the family, Rachel, had fallen in love with Simon Greenfeld, the son of her father's partner, and that marriage had produced one child. Rachel had suffered horrible complications at Sarah's birth making her incapable of conceiving again and while there had been some hand-wringing over cups of consoling tea at the news that there would never be a son, the disappointment was soon forgotten in Rachel and Simon's devotion to their daughter.

Beneath her nagging outer shell, Rachel was committed to the care not only of her daughter but of her husband too; she fussed over Simon night and day. She was anxious to prevent him from developing an excessively fatty heart like their neighbour Mrs Cohen's husband. Mr Cohen had reached such a size that his coffin would not fit through the front door. He had been carried out of the house, stiff as a poker, with the whole neighbourhood watching. It was an undignified scene, especially as Mrs Cohen, in her distress, had failed to dress her husband in his best suit and Mr Cohen attracted some comments as he left Oak Street for the last time wearing a pair of striped woollen pyjamas.

Food, whether too much or too little, was not Rachel's only preoccupation. Rachel fussed and worried about everything. When her daughter began walking out with Nat Castor, a gentile apprentice in Simon's workshop, both her parents were cautious. Marrying outside the faith was not to be encouraged. But the vigorous and charismatic young man won them over and by the time the young couple announced their engagement Simon showed as much pride in Nat as he would have done in a son of his own. Nat had written a funny letter to his aunt Edith describing the conversational convolutions that had led to his marriage.

'Of course there will have to be a conversion, Nat, *and* all the trimmings, if you will forgive me putting it that way,' Rachel had declared. 'I am afraid it might be a bit painful, but God wants you to know in no uncertain terms, Nat, that you are promising to trust in Him. Isn't that right, Simon?'

In the Jewish tradition Simon invariably gave way to his wife's running of all matters relating to the house and the family. If the truth were known, he enjoyed spending time in his own company at the workshop, or with his friends down in the Bethnal Green Road bookies where he could find some respite from Rachel's incessant chatter. It was therefore a shock to Rachel when her deferential husband announced that the surgical knife would not be necessary prior to Sarah and Nat's marriage and that no religious conversion would be taking place either. There would be none of the customary sitting Shiva, the week-long period of mourning observed when a Jewish girl marries a gentile. So long as any children, God willing, were brought up in the Jewish faith, Nat could hang on to his God-given genitals intact. Nat had proved himself to be a good Jewish boy in all but name and that was good enough for Simon.

Privately delighted by Simon's rare display of assertiveness Rachel came out fighting, demolishing every bit of street gossip on the matter.

'Look here, Mrs Cohen,' she said, her arms folded in defence across her flowery bosom, 'Nat's not Jewish but at least he's a tailor and that's a good profession. My daughter has a good husband who can provide for her. That's all that matters.'

★ ★ ★

Within minutes of May and Sam's arrival at Oak Street, and even though it was a little late for tea, a cake still in its shop-bought box was brought to the velvet-covered table, an extravagance usually reserved for the birth of a new baby or the Coronation of a new king. Covered in pale creamy brown icing, with a few flicked-up sugar peaks skipping across its otherwise smooth surface, the cake boasted a single halved walnut smooth side down in the middle.

'You can always tell a Fuller's coffee cake,' Nat whispered, shushing his chattering mother-in-law as he cut into the soft icing. A tiny sound, and the barest of visible agitations of the surface as the sharp knife made contact with the glazed sugar, caused those sitting around the table to moisten their lips in anticipation.

'Not a noise you get from any other cake,' promised Nat, as he pushed the knife on down until it made contact with the china beneath.

'What about a lemon bun?' Rachel said,

handing a plate round.

'Have a drink, May. Help yourself, Sam,' Nat added, indicating six miniature, flower-patterned glasses, brimming with liquid.

May closed her hand around the delicate stem with care. The honey-coloured wine was sweet, but not sickly.

'*L'Chaim!*' Nat, Sarah and Rachel and Simon cried in unison as they raised their thimble glasses in welcome to the new arrivals.

★   ★   ★

The next day May and Sam's cousins took them to The Trocadero at Piccadilly Circus, the most famous of all the white-and-gold-painted Lyons Corner House teashops. A Jewish tobacconist had founded the company nearly forty years earlier, Nat explained, and some, the proud Greenfelds among them, considered the restaurants to be the height of luxury.

May watched, impressed, as one of the Lyons' 'Nippies', the black-and-white-uniformed waitresses popularly named for their agility, nipped between the packed tables, balancing trays of teacups, teapots and plates of curranty scones and jam. Across the other side of the huge dining room was a 'Trippy' threading her way cautiously through the closely packed chairs, clumsily clearing away the dirty crockery onto her trolley, looking forward to the day when she stopped tripping up and became eligible for Nippy status.

Rachel was already ordering a second round of

chips, belching gently but unapologetically as she instructed the Nippy to be sure the next serving was extra hot and generously salted. May traced the rim of her plate with a tepid chip but she could not bring herself to actually eat it. She had smelled the same smell on her journey from Liverpool, mingled with the stench of cigarette smoke inside the coach, and it had made her nauseous. Even so, May longed to have the money to pay for the tea. May had arrived in London with twenty pounds that her mother had given her. 'I wish I could afford to give you more, my darling,' her mother had said. The sum had seemed to May like a lot at the time, but the cost of everything in London meant that the twenty pounds was fast running out.

Hanging on the walls of the restaurant were a series of framed posters from Lyons' long-running advertising campaign featuring a fictional character called George. The gag was that George was never where he was expected to be. George was never at home, never in the office, never appeared on the railway platform to join his wife waiting to catch a train, never turned up to watch the Punch and Judy show with his children, and consistently failed to arrive on the golf course, his golfing plus-fours pictured hanging limply over the frame of a scarecrow instead.

'The trouble with George,' Nat explained, 'is that he has *always* 'gone to *Lyonch*'.'

★ ★ ★

Three days after May's arrival in England she was sitting in one of the brown armchairs in the front room, looking through the small collection of books on the shelves and wondering what had happened to Sarah. Simon and Nat were in the tailor's shop, and Sam had gone down to the Royal Naval headquarters to investigate how he might join its Voluntary Service. In a corner was a tailor's dummy dressed in the half-finished wedding suit Nat was making as a favour for a best friend. After the excitement of arrival, May was at something of a loss to know what to do with herself. Everything, the cold weather, the food, the traffic, the clothes, all proclaimed how different life was back home. She felt as if she had been turned upside down. She had considered going up to her attic bed but as she had passed the ever-open door to Rachel and Simon's room she had caught sight of Simon standing in front of the mirror, his back to the door. He was juggling his huge stomach from one hand to the other while chanting to himself loudly enough for May to hear 'wobble, wibble, wibble wobble'. He was stark naked. May did not want to attract his attention by climbing the squeaky ladder and instead silently retraced her steps downstairs.

She had hoped to find Sarah there, but then remembered how her cousin had packed up her rollers and hairbrushes before setting off to give a shampoo and set to one of her richer clients, one of several, bored, indulged wives who were only too happy to fill the vacant hours by having their hair curled and styled. May had learned quickly that hard work was the habit of the Oak Street household. Simon and Nat's buoyant tailoring business brought relative affluence to number 52, and between them the family tried their best to ease a little of the poverty that surrounded them. The neighbourhood was a poor one, with unemployment and the resulting deprivation often leading to desperate behaviour. Petty thieving was rife, even within Oak Street itself. Only the other day, after a pair of prized racing pigeons disappeared from the backyard at number 73, a delicious smell had come seeping from under the Smiths' front door at number 54. There were ten children in the Smith family and the elder ones wore shoes with a hole punched into the side, a warning sign to pawnbrokers that these shoes were the property of the local school and only out on loan. The children tried to hide the hole from their friends by stuffing an extra sock in the side but no one was fooled. Simon and Nat would pass on cast-off coats and waistcoats that came their way, Rachel was forever popping next door and into other houses in the street to see if they could do with a bit of left-over pie and Sarah cut the neighbours' children's hair and helped them with their letters and numbers, in exchange for the occasional bantam's egg supplied from the backyard coops.

Apart from Simon wobbling away in his bedroom, the house was empty.

Glad for the chance to be alone, May went into the parlour where a two-day-old newspaper was lying on the leather sofa. Nat was fascinated by politics and had heard long ago that *The*

Times was the paper of the educated classes. His neighbours, if they were interested at all in reading the news, got their daily information from the *Daily Worker*. But Nat had become friendly with a butler, a customer from a big house in the West End, for whom Nat had made a smart black working jacket and matching pair of trousers. Each morning, the butler would collect the previous day's copy of *The Times* from his employer's smoking room, have a quick look at the sports pages and then pass the paper on to Nat. They would meet at the bus stop on Bethnal Green Road when the butler was on his way to work or at Goides, the Whitechapel café where Jewish intellectuals went to discuss politics and literature over small cups of thick Turkish coffee and glasses of lemon tea.

May turned the pages of Nat's second-hand paper, looking for the names of the latest winners of the Littlewood's Football Pools. Sam had suggested the Pools might make their fortune.

'Every day someone wakes up to a morning of good news,' he argued, 'and to a means of escape from a hard life. Maybe one day it will be me. Then I will buy a yacht,' he promised, 'and we can sail round the world like kings and queens.'

But May could find no reference in the dog-eared newspaper to anyone celebrating a windfall. The first few pages were covered with columns of boxed-in advertisements. The front page carried notices from financial advisors, personal advertisements from spiritualists promising to 'restore confidence' for those living in uncertainty, and details of a sumptuous antique Persian tapestry for sale at a bargain price of two hundred pounds. The second page was devoted almost exclusively to educational positions in boys' schools but on the third she came across the columns reserved for domestic situations. Most required skill in the kitchen and May's culinary expertise was based on little more than watching Bertha preparing huge mounds of rice and peas for the plantation workers' lunch back home.

May tucked the paper under her arm and went upstairs, passing Simon's now-closed door and climbing the complaining ladder to look through her skylight from where she gazed yet again at the memorial stone with its poignant message of sacrificing life for duty. She began to wonder what sort of occupations would have awaited those young men had they not lost their lives before life had barely begun. A man's world had been on offer for those boys, but it had been replaced by one top-heavy with women.

A man's world . . . snippets of a conversation with Nat the day before began to re-form in her mind. Nat was proving quick to notice anything that interested her. On the morning after their arrival the Greenfelds and the Thomases had gone for a brisk walk in nearby Victoria Park and as they crossed the road May had been conscious of Nat studying her face.

'Tell me, May,' he had asked, 'am I mistaken or do you have a secret passion for these smelly machines?'

May blushed at his observation but nodded,

admitting to being mesmerised by the sight of so many beautiful cars.

'Why not look for a job as a chauffeur?' Nat said. 'Loads of women drove cars professionally in the Great War. Women wore the trousers in those days. And many still do,' he said, darting a look in Rachel's direction. 'Even though there is talk down at the workshop of another war,' Nat continued, his eyes meeting Sarah's, who was nodding in agreement, 'none of us think it will come. Even Mosley and his fascist thugs are losing power in this country and anyway, Baldwin will do everything in his power to prevent it.'

Nat did not sound optimistic.

'But whatever happens there is no reason for women drivers to wait for another war to give them a professional role. Especially if they have a real skill for it.'

'What sort of car would I drive?' May asked. 'And who would be inside it?'

'Well, they say the test to drive a London taxi is a hard one. You have to know all the streets of London backwards as well as forwards. They call it the Knowledge and it is said to be more difficult to pass than the exam to get into Oxford or Cambridge!'

'She's a quick learner,' Sam interrupted with brotherly pride.

'I am sure she is,' replied Nat, 'but it might be an idea to see if any private work is advertised in the paper.' Perhaps a *Times* reader was looking for her in the same way that she was seeking them? he suggested.

May sat on her bed and opened the newspaper once more, beginning again with the third page. She ran her finger down the situations vacant columns. With the cutting back of numbers of servants since the Depression, even the grandest houses were looking to double up on staff roles. That day the advertisements for 'cook-generals' outnumbered all the others, a euphemism that according to Nat disguised something closer to general slave labour.

'You would never have found such a job advertised before the war,' he had said.

Even so, a parlour maid was required for a family in South Kensington and a head house-maid was needed to head a team of four other servants near Southampton, the advertisement assuring all applicants that the employers were a 'titled family'. Neither position sounded at all what she was looking for. Further down the page, however, May drew in her breath a little. Her finger hovered for a moment and then putting her hands in her lap, she read the five compact lines slowly.

'Discretion is an essential qualification for the successful candidate who applies to work as *chauffeuse*, with additional general secretarial duties for a busy Member of Parliament, based both in London and in Sussex. Flexibility, a willingness to work hard, a head for bookkeeping, a smart appearance and an impeccable driving record are all requirements.'

May circled the advertisement with a pencil, went downstairs and waited for Sam and Nat to come home. She planned to seek their advice even though her mind was already made up. Later that evening, she had rung the number printed in the newspaper from Nat's workshop telephone, and an arrangement had been made for May to take the train from Victoria down to Polegate station where she would be met and driven to Cuckmere Park. She had been told by the housekeeper, who in deep voice introduced herself as Mrs Cage, that Sir Philip Blunt would be at the house and would be pleased to interview her himself.

'He needs to be certain of getting the right one this time,' Mrs Cage had said. 'And he's not the only one here at Cuckmere who doesn't want any more balls-ups, pardon my French,' she continued. 'Spent too much time abroad with men and their bad ways with language, I have. Mind you, a woman might cause a bit of attention behind the wheel. I hope you scrub up nice and smart,' a note of warning in her voice as she replaced the receiver.

Nat had made Sarah a warm coat for the winter in thick tweed. Sarah insisted that the coat was ideally suited to May's neat figure and would be perfect for impressing Sir Philip. She also lent May a pair of cotton stockings. May, who had never worn such things before, pulled the stockings up and clipped them to the suspenders just as Sarah showed her. She did not know that legs could experience claustrophobia, even though Sarah assured her the stockings would soon expand and wrinkle at the knees and ankles. At the last moment Nat had produced a striped, battered box from which he lifted a small, black, velvet hat with a jaunty feather on one side.

'Mum would be honoured to think of the daughter of her favourite sister wearing her best hat on such an important day. This is the only piece of clothing the prison returned to us after Mum died. All her other clothes had been burned because she was too thin to wear them.' Nat's voice faltered. 'But Mum didn't mind. 'Anything for the suffragette cause', she always used to say. I always wish she had lived on just a bit longer to see women given the vote and Lady Astor taking her seat in Parliament. Then she would have known the fight was worthwhile.'

'Well, I want to try and do Aunt Gladys *and* her hat proud,' May said, reaching up to give Nat a kiss on his cheek. 'So here comes a woman aiming for a man's job.'

Placing the hat on May's head, Sarah pronounced it a perfect fit.

★　★　★

As May sat on the train in her third-class carriage she passed innumerable back gardens and yards. The scene passing her eyes was as strange as anything she had seen at the pictures. Some of these tiny patches of horticulture were pristine in their winter tidiness, the flowerbeds turned and forked with the care given to the potato topping of a meat pie, paths swept of leaves and the still stark trees forming a skeletal silhouette against the sky. Other gardens were overrun with weeds, and sometimes the train passed an abandoned swing settee, just visible in the thick mist, its seat rotting in the damp, a reminder of summers past. Most of these small plots were devoid of life, although as the train slowed down for a station, May spotted a sleepy cat curling itself around the back fence of a house and a bent-over figure emerging from his potting shed, probably escaping the demands of domesticity in the house. And yet this unlikely jigsaw of semi-tended earth, despite the apparent mismatch of the pieces, slotted together to form the overall effect of a satisfying collage.

As the London suburbs gave way to the muddy greenish-brown of the Sussex winter countryside, a thin white frosting covered the fields. May had never seen snow before. The pictures illustrating Hans Christian Andersen's icy queen in her white fur coat were the closest she had come to such a sight. There was no one in the empty railway carriage with whom she could share her excitement. Sam had wanted to come with her but that day he had an appointment on board HMS *President,* the huge ship permanently moored at King's Reach near the Law Courts at the Embankment. She wondered how he was getting on. His hope that the Royal Naval Volunteer Reserve would take him on as a rating was a long shot but even so Sam was confident that he would soon be wearing a jacket with the volunteers' herring-bone-shaped stripe at the cuff.

Nat had also offered to come with May on the journey, but she assured him she would manage fine on her own. Just at that moment she felt deliriously independent. The train made its way through the frozen landscape, the bosomy undulation of the South Downs rising into view as if the backdrop of a theatre had just been changed for a new scene. May tried to count the number of flint churches with pencil spires that pointed upwards towards the grey skies and felt the return of an old tumble of words from a poem that her mother used to read to her when May was very small, the rhythm of it dependably sleep-inducing even if the words did not then mean much.

'Faster than fairies, faster than witches,
Bridges and houses, hedges and ditches;
And charging along like troops in a battle,
All through the meadows the horses and cattle
All of the sights of the hill and the plain
Fly as thick as driving rain.'

As the painted stations of the Sussex Downs whistled past her window, May only just had time to read the letters on the wooden signs announcing the successive towns of Plumpton and Lewes, Glynde and Berwick, until at last the train began to slow down and a ripple of nerves overtook her. Sarah had suggested she might suit a bob cut, and had offered to give her a shining blonde Jean Harlow-style, with a little help from her infallible tin of bleach. May had resisted the offer but wondered whether she had been right to do so. Now she could only hope that her hairpins would hold their place.

A man in overalls was standing at the far end of the platform, holding a tweed cap. He raised a hand to May in greeting. She waved back. A sharp gust of wind lifted off her black velvet hat and, bending to retrieve it, the pins that she had carefully tucked into her hair two hours earlier slithered out onto the ground. *They will never take me seriously now*, she thought, as she stood up, juggling hair, hat, and pins and made her way towards the man who was standing beside a beautiful car.

6

May was waiting for Sir Philip in the library, attempting to calm herself by laying her open handkerchief out flat on the table in front of her and folding down each corner, one on top of the other so the handkerchief became an ever-decreasing square. This schoolgirl trick, if done correctly with paper, resulted in a fortune-teller's cup. But the corners of the cotton handkerchief were too bulky to stay in place and no sooner had May flattened the edges than they bounced back up again. She felt horribly unprepared for the interview ahead of her. She was still getting over her arrival at the station.

Reaching the end of the platform, she had put her hand out in greeting towards the man waiting for her, only to notice his misshapen chin and a nose resembling a squashed fig that was nowhere near the centre of his face.

'Hooch,' he said. 'Mr Hooch,' by way of introduction.

'I'm May Thomas,' she replied. 'Nice to meet you.'

She had avoided looking at the disfigurement that was plainly visible in the driver's mirror during the ten-minute drive from the station and had instead allowed herself the unaccustomed treat of being a passenger in such a lovely car. The familiar smell of the Rolls-Royce's red polished leather seats was comforting while the comfort of the upholstery felt fit for a king.

When the car reached the end of the single-track road lined with huge elm trees, in the grand French manner, she saw Cuckmere Park rise out of a dip, its Sussex flint stones the colour of the rain-clouds above, each window in perfect proportion to the next. The front door was wide open and a woman wearing a black dress reaching almost to the ground was standing just inside. Her white hair was caught in a ponytail, an old-fashioned style for a woman who must only be in her early forties, about the same age as May's mother.

'Good afternoon, Miss Thomas, welcome to Cuckmere Park. I hope Mr Hooch looked after you? Brought you in the Rolls, I expect, just so you could feel the movement?' she asked in the rolling accent that May had heard on the telephone the day before.

May followed the housekeeper into a stone-flagged hall where two deer-sized dogs were lying asleep in the centre of the floor. The flags must have been laid centuries ago, May thought, wishing that Sam were here to show off his knowledge of history; he would love this old house. May stumbled slightly on the uneven stone as she hurried to keep up with Mrs Cage.

'Isn't January blooming awful?' Mrs Cage said, her voice echoing around the high grey walls. 'Mind you, Sussex in winter can be beautiful, and I've known some lovely ones over the past nine years,' she continued, the words flying up to the ceiling and returning in shadow form. 'But I cannot help thinking about how nice

86

it will be to be warm again.'

'I miss the warmth too,' May said, agreeing with her enthusiastically.

'Do you like swimming?' Mrs Cage asked, turning to look at May.

'Yes, I love it. Is there a beach near here?'

'Yes, there is, in matter of fact, down at Cuckmere Haven. Florence and I sometimes go there even though it is a bit of a walk.'

'Florence?'

'Oh sorry! Florence is my daughter. She is nine, well, nearly ten, as she is constantly reminding me! She lives for the chance to swim in the sea!'

Mrs Cage pushed open the panelled door at the end of the long corridor.

'Sir Philip has a telephone call or two to make so if you wait in here I am sure he will come and find you shortly. Shall I send you in a cup of coffee?'

May declined the offer and was left alone. She sat down in a chair in the far corner. A powerful smell, a combination of freshness and spiciness, puzzled her until she spotted a neat line of hedgehog-like balls placed along the windowsill. She recognised them from the linen cupboard at home. Every Christmas she and Sam had punctured the pitted skins of oranges with little clove heads and tied a ribbon around the fruit from which the perfumed ball would hang and scent the sheets.

Books were piled on every surface, their multicoloured spines displayed in the shelves stretching from ceiling to floor on three sides, while on the remaining wall of the room the brick red wallpaper was obscured by two fraying tapestries of ancient wooded hunting scenes. Curtains made of rich dulled gold silk had the fullness of Cinderella's gown. May tried to work out how long it would take to read every book in the room. A week, maybe a month for each volume? A year for each shelf? She gave up, giddy with the calculation. Abandoning the improvised fortune-telling cup, she shoved the handkerchief back in her pocket, closed her eyes and wished she felt less nervous.

The sound of the door opening startled her. A tall young man in spectacles burst into the room and flung himself onto the hessian-covered armchair opposite her, spread-eagling his legs. Evidently he thought he was on his own. He opened a yellow-jacketed book on which the words 'Left Book Club' were stamped on the cover. In case he unexpectedly caught sight of her and suspected she had been deliberately hiding, May felt she should say something.

'Hallo.'

The young man looked up at her from his book. His hair was almost white, the colour of thick honey. Putting his finger to his lips he motioned to her to be quiet.

'I am escaping from the dreaded sister,' he hissed. For a moment he studied her closely. 'I must say, you look awfully smart sitting inside with your hat on.'

'Oh,' May said, suddenly unsure. 'Do you think I should take it off?'

'Well, it depends what you are planning to do

next. If you were staying for lunch, I would definitely take it off. But if you have a head cold and are here to study branch formation of Elizabethan oak trees in the garden, then I suggest you leave the hat where it is.'

'I'm waiting for Sir Philip,' she explained defensively. 'I am hoping he will ask me to be his driver.'

'Oh I *see*,' said the young man, examining her a bit more closely. 'What fun! You are nothing like Cropper, although I hope there isn't a small flask of whisky hidden under that hat.'

May looked puzzled.

'Oh dear. Sorry. I *must* learn to be a bit more discreet. Joan has a phrase for it. PD, she always says to me. *Pas devant*, meaning 'not in front of'. It's the Blunts' private alert for discretion in front of the servants. Awful outmoded way of talking, isn't it? I can't bear it. And anyway I think there's far too much secrecy in this world. Always tell the truth is what I say, no matter whom it is you are talking to. Did Hooch collect you from the station?'

May nodded. 'Poor man,' she said. 'Poor face, I mean.'

'Yes, I know,' the young man agreed, his earlier expression of curiosity suddenly replaced by one of deep seriousness. 'We all think it's amazing that Hooch still wants to get behind a wheel. He got those injuries when a fragment of shell hit him as he was driving a tank somewhere in the Somme. That's twenty years ago now but he'll have the scars for the rest of his life. He's an inspiration, really.'

At that moment the door opened again.

'Ah, Julian, I see you have already met Miss Thomas.' An older man holding a box of matches was standing at the door. 'I'm afraid you will have to continue your conversation another time. Miss Thomas is coming with me.'

And before May could say goodbye she was beckoned into the adjoining study. Just before the door closed behind her, a stage whisper floated through the open gap.

'I really hope you get the job'.

The older man turned round and smiled. He had heard the whisper too.

'How do you do,' he said to May, addressing her directly for the first time. 'I'm Philip Blunt. Have you been offered some coffee? Good. Well, come in. And *do* take that hat off, you must be so hot under there!'

Sir Philip shook the box of matches in his hand but it was empty. Picking up a cigar that was lying half smoked but extinguished in an ashtray on the desk, he tried unsuccessfully to blow it into life, pulled the anglepoise lamp closer and ran a hand through surprisingly dense and unfashionably long hair that was the colour of a well-worn penny.

'Well, shall I kick off then?'

'Yes please,' May replied, trying not to squash Aunt Gladys's hat as it lay in her lap.

Sir Philip outlined the responsibilities involved in the job with efficient economy. He explained that he was one of a handful of Deputy Chief Whips in Stanley Baldwin's Conservative government. He had formerly been a lawyer and still occasionally gave advice in that capacity.

'It certainly makes for varied and interesting work, but I need to keep my wits about me, and that is why I could do with a first-class secretary and chauffeur.'

He needed someone to drive him from appointment to appointment during the week-days in London and to take him up and down from town to the country. When he was tied up in day-long parliamentary sessions, he liked the car to be available for his wife, Lady Joan, and occasionally for their two adult children. The job advertised came with free board and lodging with Mrs Cage in the housekeeper's house in the village. For the occasional overnight stay, especially during late-night sittings in the House, a small room next to the butler's pantry in St John's Wood was on offer.

'And now it's your turn,' Sir Philip said, puffing ineffectively at his lifeless cigar.

May described how she had come to live in England with her cousins after leaving behind her working life in Barbados. She explained how she was not only the daughter of the plantation owner but also had been his employee. At the age of seventeen, her father had taught her to drive the plantation car and she had discovered an unrivalled pleasure when the driver's door was closed, the engine was cranked and the motor responded to her touch. She had spent long hours alone in the car, collecting the weekly account books from the office before driving to Speightstown to post letters at the post office, cash the workers' wages cheque at the bank as

91

well as being responsible for the maintenance of the old Rolls-Royce.

From the authority as well as the passion with which she spoke, Sir Philip could tell she knew more about automobiles than a male mechanic twice her age. He needed no more convincing that the right person for the job was sitting in front of him, twiddling her hair unselfconsciously as she told him how she had heard that the older models of the Rolls were so much more reliable than the later versions. He had heard of a special two-day practical course for advanced drivers that perhaps she might be interested in joining 'if things work out'. May nodded enthusiastically at the prospect.

The second part of the position involved some secretarial work within the house.

'I have helped my father with the book keeping at the plantation since I was twelve,' she told him confidently. 'We could not afford a proper secretary but I can type sixty words a minute, and before I left home I was getting even faster.'

Sir Philip looked impressed.

'There are four main qualities I require in my staff. The first three are flexibility, willingness, and sobriety,' he said

May nodded at each of the conditions.

'And the fourth,' Sir Philip continued, 'is probably the most important of the lot, and that is discretion. In my job I am entrusted with a lot of confidences, some of which I am compelled to share with my secretary, and some of which will by default become apparent to my chauffeur.

Since you are applying to fill both of these roles I think you will understand why I labour the point a little?' He smiled at her. 'And you are single, I hope? Not that I don't approve of romance, you understand, but it tends to interfere with the working schedule.'

This time May shook her head, and then, in order to dispel the idea that she might have been disagreeing with him, she changed the shake to another nod. Despite her age, Sir Philip found something beguiling about the eagerness of this young woman with her flopping hair. She had no references for him to follow up and he had only her word. But his instincts led him to a quick decision. Stubbing out his unlit cigar Sir Philip's voice became persuasive.

'Well, Miss Thomas, it has been a pleasure to speak to you. I know it is rather short notice but do you think you could start the job at once? We have had a bit of trouble with the previous incumbent in the job, and he had to be asked to leave rather smartish,' he explained, 'which is why we are in a bit of a pickle. We've even run out of matches, as you see! Anyway, perhaps you would like to telephone to your family. Do they have a telephone?'

Telephones are part of the British way of life, May thought to herself, realising how readily they and so many other things that she had not been used to at home were becoming part of her new existence. She hoped that Nat would still be in the workshop and that she might catch him if she hurried. Sir Philip had already mentioned making arrangements for her uniform. His tailor could make her something in a twinkling of an eye. Trousers or skirt? Any preference? Yes, yes, Sir Philip had agreed, trousers: far more practical. He certainly thought of everything.

The high-pitched pips of the switchboard, announcing that her time was up, sounded in the earpiece before May could fully explain to Nat what had happened during the preceding hour but Nat had heard enough to shout to Sarah who was in the workshop that day.

'May's landed the job! They didn't even ask for references!' and May heard a distant but exultant 'Hurrah for May!' before the operator told her that her time allowance had expired and she must replace the receiver.

* * *

Very early the following morning, before it was even light, May woke up in the tiny bedroom in Sussex that she was now entitled to call hers. She shook smooth the dark-red-and-green paisley eiderdown, and pulled it up over her. The eiderdown had slithered off her bed during the night, and landed in a heap on the floor leaving behind just a thin sheet for covering and a blanket that was more holes than darning. The seams of the eiderdown were weak with age and curled up feathers had floated out all over the carpet. May could see from her raised position in bed that a few of them had attached themselves to the dark velvet of Aunt Gladys's hat that was lying on top of the chest of drawers.

The room appeared not to have been used for

94

a while as a musty smell floated up from the dark carpet. May wished sometimes that her nose were not so sensitive. The clove-studded oranges in Sir Philip's study had been delicious, the cigar smoke in Sir Philip's study headache-inducing, but dampness smelt depressing. The floor-length, soap-scented cotton nightdress, lent to her last night by Mrs Cage, was covered in tiny pink roses and must have shrunk in the wash judging by the way it clung to her hips. May longed for a cup of tea but did not dare go downstairs until it was light enough for her to see to get dressed in her day clothes. Mrs Cage had promised her that the new trousers and jacket of her uniform would be ready in a day or two but meanwhile she would have to make do with the interview suit and a pair of stockings borrowed from Mrs Cage. May had reluctantly accepted Mrs Cage's offer of a pair of old step-ins but the elastic had given way on the housekeeper's intimate second-hand garments and were far too loose to stay in place round May's slim waist. May hoped that her own underwear would have dried on the fender where she had laid it after a thorough rinsing the night before.

A thousand things were running through her mind and she wanted to get them all down in the blue diary as soon as it was light and before recent events crowded out the earlier ones from her mind. Pushing her long dark hair back from her forehead, she wondered if Bertha was missing her. She wondered if she would ever be warm. Was anyone looking after the car? And then she was unable to prevent the bigger questions from tumbling right into the forefront of her mind. Was her mother lonely? Had May made a terrible mistake by leaving her? For a moment a sense of panic overwhelmed her. Sitting bolt upright, by now painfully awake, she wondered if, in all the excitement of this new life, she was forgetting what it felt like to be a daughter?

She shifted back down in the bed and checked the catch of the bracelet of silver forget-me-nots that encircled her wrist to make sure it was secure. Another puffball of feathery curls escaped from the gap in the lining and floated into the air. She closed her eyes and tried to go back to sleep but at once she found herself thinking about Julian Richardson. She had been taken aback by the speed and the familiar ease with which he had teased her about her hat. Had he been flirting with her? She wondered what it would be like to kiss him. How did that sort of kiss work? Would he remove his glasses or would she have to duck beneath them to reach his mouth? Her lips puckered at the thought and she felt a flutter of curiosity. That experience, mouth-to-mouth kissing, that she had read about so often in books, seen so often in movies, and watched so often when courting sugar cane workers were unaware they were being observed, remained for May frustratingly mysterious.

A year ago her mother had spoken to her about the nature of happiness. One evening Edith had suggested that they sit on the terrace together and have what she called 'a coming of age talk'. The conversation had assumed an air of finality about it as if Edith was making the most of a last chance to tell her daughter everything she held to be wise and precious.

'The first thing I want to say, my darling,' Edith began, taking her daughter's delicate hands in hers, as she had done ever since May could remember, 'is that there is no man on this earth who can fulfil all the requirements of a wife. A sense of humour and a passion for books are strong bonuses, I would suggest. There will always be a few tolerable minuses: snoring, or a lack of interest in flowers, for example.'

May smiled. She had lost count of the times she had heard her mother complain to her unresponsive husband about the rose-intolerant earth of the West Indies. The whole family had grown used to Edith's yearning for the sweet-smelling bushes that she had coaxed into growth against the odds in the small garden of her Scottish childhood home.

'But if one is lucky,' her mother had continued, 'one will find enveloping love, even if it is only for a short time. And if one is luckier still, one will find someone to cherish and be cherished by for a lifetime. Oh yes, and it is important to marry someone who listens, and of course you must listen too, not just hear. There is a big difference between the two. I want you to learn to listen so that you make choices about the way you lead your life rather than falling for any opportunity that presents itself.'

A knock at the door interrupted May's thoughts. A child of about ten years old was standing in front of her using both unsteady hands to balance a cup and saucer from which steam was rising. A good part of the liquid had already slopped over the edge.

'Mum heard the floorboards creak and said you might like a cup of tea,' the freckled-nosed girl said, and continued without giving May a second to say anything. 'So I said I would like to take it to the new lady driver. I am Florence and I wanted to have a look at you. Do you mind?'

'Of course I don't mind,' May said reaching out to take the wobbling liquid. 'And a cup of tea is what I would like more than anything else in the world.'

Florence looked pleased.

'Have you been in the sun?'

'Yes, I certainly have,' replied May, a little surprised.

'I thought so,' said Florence. 'You look browner than everyone else. I'm not allowed to go in the sun. Well, actually, there isn't any at the moment but if there were I wouldn't be allowed in it. I have to wear a hat even though I am nearly ten. My mother says my freckles are bad enough already and the sun would make me have even more.'

May was intrigued.

'Perhaps you could tell my mother the sun won't hurt me? I'm always being made to do things I don't want to do *and*,' and here Florence allowed her voice become very low and quiet and ominous sounding, 'keep secrets that I'm not meant to tell.'

May tried to conceal her smile.

'I think your freckles are lovely.'

'No one else thinks so, except Mr Hooch. Do you like Mr Hooch? He comes to our school sometimes to tell us about the tigers and elephants he used to see when he was growing up in India. And he reads us stories by Mr Kipling.'

Florence flipped her reddish gold plaits behind her so they hung down her back, stretching well below her shoulders. Two green ribbons, half untied, trailed off the bottom of each plait.

'That sounds wonderful,' May replied, beginning to enjoy herself. 'Mr Kipling is one of my favourite storytellers too,' she said.

'I like Mr Hooch much more than Vera.'

'Who is Vera?'

'Vera's the gardener. She is called Vera Borchby and she wears dungarees all the time, never skirts or dresses, and she never lets me eat the raspberries from the cage in the summer. It's really unfair because I really like raspberries. She says they have to be saved for the Big House.'

For a moment Florence looked downcast as her forehead wrinkled and her top row of teeth bit firmly onto her bottom lip for a moment before the round little face brightened as if a curtain had been suddenly drawn back and let in the daylight.

'Would you like to meet Mrs Jenkins who runs the post office?' she asked. 'I could introduce you. She sometimes smells of cheese. I don't know why. Sometimes she tells the truth by accident. She doesn't know she's doing it. Mum says it's a sort of illness. Anyway, I like her

99

because not everyone tells the truth. And sometimes she swears by mistake too.'

'Yes, please. I would certainly like to meet Mrs Jenkins,' May said. 'Perhaps we could go and see her on a bike ride together?'

May was keen to get a bicycle as soon as possible. Back home, when she wasn't driving the car, she had bicycled everywhere.

Florence was looking worried again.

'Haven't you got a bike?' May asked her.

'No I haven't because, well, because I don't know how to ride one. Mum says she would love to teach me but she hasn't got the time at the moment. You won't tell anyone from school, will you? I have to keep it a secret or my friends will tease me.'

'I will teach you if you like? Perhaps Mr Hooch has a couple of old rusties in his shed and we could find a time to practise?'

Florence's eyes shone as she jumped on the bed, kissed May on the cheek and was out of the room before May had time to say another word.

7

May had been working for the Blunts for two weeks when news of the King's illness prompted the cancellation of their weekend guests and May was given the next few days off. It seemed very strange to May that after only two weeks in a new job, and barely a month in a new country, a decision about her own working hours had depended on the health of the King. As she left Polegate and once again watched the country stations pass by her window, she reflected for a moment on how well the train served her as the connection between her two contrasting lives. And then she remembered how much she was looking forward to taking up Sarah's offer of a haircut.

All along the length of Oak Street the customary preparations for the weekend were underway as women in floral aprons crouched on their knees, a pail of soapy water beside them as they scrubbed a half moon of cleanliness into the pavement outside their front doors. Despite the King's illness nothing was going to interrupt number 52 Oak Street's weekly observance of the Sabbath, when for twenty-four hours, from sundown to sundown, the family would gather together to say prayers, eat well and remove themselves from all the small anxieties of life.

Before the Sabbath feast, May and Sarah joined the crowds taking their weekly walk before sundown along the Whitechapel Road. Children were out in the streets, swinging from lamp posts and eating hot chestnuts from twists of newspapers bought from the temporary braziers on every street corner. Butchers had laid out their displays of kosher meat in the front of their shops, and no one seemed to mind that flies crawled all over the jointed chicken and slabs full of tripe. The atmosphere in Petticoat Lane resembled a carnival. Contortionists wriggled their way out of strait-jackets, china salesmen threw entire dinner services into the air, catching them just before they smashed on the ground, women stood with their arms folded behind stalls packed with beigels, kippers, salted herring and salt beef. An Indian man with a turquoise turbaned headdress and a barrowful of tiger nuts and liquorice root was attracting a healthy custom. A blacksmith was clamping red-hot shoes onto the sole of a horse. A boy balancing on one leg leant on a battered crutch muttering, 'Thanks, Ma'am' every time a well-dressed woman put a coin in the small cap that lay at his feet. After five minutes May saw the child reach behind himself as if fiddling with a knot. As his second leg dropped to the ground the boy carefully picked up his cap so as not to spill the morning's takings and ran off into the crowd.

Rachel prepared the Sabbath dinner each Friday afternoon, and May knew from her mother that for gentiles such as herself and Sam it was an honour to be included. The Greenfelds did not follow the strict orthodox rules of some Jewish families that forbad all modern intrusions, not even so much as a light bulb was turned on, let alone a wireless. But for the Greenfelds the Sabbath nonetheless remained a sacred day.

May watched the elaborate preparations wide-eyed. Sarah's hairdressing tools had been temporarily removed and the long table had been covered in a delicately embroidered cloth. The best plates had been taken out of the glass-fronted cabinet in the front room and been dusted off, the double candlestick had been lit and a new loaf of challah, the sweet eggy bread, lay under a piece of linen as white as an old rabbi's newly washed beard. Plates of pickled herring, chopped liver and thinly sliced smoked salmon were brought to the table by Sarah as soon as the prayers were over. The buttery smell of a chicken cooking had been filling the whole house for the past hour or two and Simon's hand was making little circular motions of hunger round and round his large stomach. Simon was rarely hungry. His wife made sure of that. But on the Sabbath the cooking smells got the better of him.

'Have you made any matzo balls for our guests?' Simon asked as he moved round the table, filling the glasses. 'Better watch out for Rachel's matzo balls, Sam,' he cautioned. 'They're what you'd call a dumpling. Stop you up for a week they will!'

May watched the wax drip and pool in a small hardening mass at the base of the candlestick as at the conclusion of the meal, Sarah brought the noodle-based lokshen pudding to the table. The sweet vanilla taste was pronounced by Simon to be more splendid even than Rachel's splendid orange-flavoured lokshen of the week before and a sense of pleasure received by a group of people comfortable in each other's company filled the room. Rachel dominated the proceedings, ever busy with the ceaseless open-handed gesticulations that illustrated her speech.

'Be careful when you go out in the street, won't you, May? You need to hang on to your purse, May, and keep that driver's cap firmly on your head. Gives you an air of knowing what you are about. Otherwise some fool will have the whites of your eyes if you aren't careful.'

The following evening Nat and Sarah took May and Sam out to the Queen's Arms near Petticoat Lane. They wanted to know how her job was going but May was careful not to say too much beyond the beauty of the car, mindful of Sir Philip's caution that discretion was a paramount rule for those in his employ. Daniel, the publican, or Danny Boy as everyone called him, was popular with all his regulars. He was a handsome fellow, Jewish, and originally from Liverpool but with an Irish accent picked up in the various pubs in which he had worked all his adult life. With his sealskin-black hair, smoothed and centrally parted, a sharp-edged moustache and a physique to make other men wilt in envy, he had the kindest heart in the business. The pub was often the warmest place to go on a wintry afternoon for someone who had no job. Survival on bread and dripping, and without a penny to spare to activate the gas fire led the poor, lonely and despairing to the welcoming embrace of the

Queen's Arms. No predicament was overlooked by Danny, or his gentle wife Ruth, and as a result the pub was always full of misfits and people down on their luck, confident of a kind word or a slice of pie. Most Saturdays the pub was packed and on May and Sam's first visit they had to push their way through rows of flat-capped drinkers. Sitting on the long oak bar, and swinging the bruised and scratched knees endemic to one of his generation, was a young boy of about eight years old.

'Hallo, Howard,' said Nat. 'Had a good week at school? Been schmoozing those lady teachers, I bet?'

Danny and Ruth's young son blushed.

'Go on, Hoppy Teddy, move over a bit,' Nat said to a man with a peg leg who was chewing on a cooked chop.

Behind the bar were three framed pictures. The first was of Queen Mary wearing the familiar five-stranded pearl necklace that habitually hung just above her impressive embonpoint. The second was of George V, taken on the day of his Coronation in 1911, his shoulders weighted down with gold braiding, his dark full beard in contrast to the thin and pointy grey version in the third picture that showed the King and Queen together, taken during last year's Silver Jubilee. Danny had been in the crowds when the Royal Couple had come to the East End and the crush had been so great that people had fainted before getting the chance to glimpse them. Beneath the earlier picture of the King were two lines from Lord Tennyson.

One with Britain, heart and soul!
One life, one flag, one fleet, One Throne!

Danny caught Nat's eye as he looked away from the photographs.

'Yes, I know. If the news I heard on the wireless is correct, we may need to put a new model on display if the poor old King snuffs it. Ruth wants to wait until Edward chooses himself a wife, but I told her we might be waiting till the cows come home.'

'Even so,' Nat said, 'we better keep an ear out later on for the evening news.'

May was listening to this conversation, watching the smoke that Danny had inhaled from his cigarette a good five minutes earlier make its slow, thin reappearance through the corners of his mouth. During the two weeks May had been working for Sir Philip she had heard him speaking earnestly on the telephone on several occasions while discussing the intricacies of the constitution. Twice Sir Philip had asked May to put a call through to the Prime Minister's office before asking her, with the utmost politeness, if she would mind leaving the room for a few minutes. There was clearly considerable anxiety around something that concerned the Prince of Wales's personal life although May had not yet discovered the truth of the problem. However, she had heard enough to realise that people like Sir Philip, with their status of privileged authority, knew a lot more about the prospects of a Princess of Wales taking up her position than anyone in the Queen's

Arms or, for that matter, anyone else in the entire Bethnal Green community.

★ ★ ★

The Castors and their cousins were making a weekend of it. On Sunday at noon the shrimp and winkle man had called by on his weekly rounds, his horse pulling a cart laden with shrimp and winkles, cockles, whelks and mussels. Bunches of watercress and sticks of flowery green-tipped celery were laid out next to the molluscs on a white cloth providing the better-off residents of Oak Street with a feast for Sunday tea.

'Rachel's got an eye for a nudge and a winkle,' Nat said grinning at May before pushing a pin into the shell of a particularly tenacious whelk. Rachel loved these flirty exchanges with her son-in-law. Nat was always having a laugh but while his easy male attractiveness was impossible to ignore, he reserved his most loving looks for Sarah.

That evening, Sunday 19 January, the family went into the front room and gathered round the wireless, listening to the tunes played by Radio Luxembourg, tapping their feet and sometimes standing up to dance, cheek to cheek, to the accompaniment of Fred Astaire's romantic song from the new movie *Top Hat*. They hummed along to the heart-tugging notes of 'These Foolish Things' that floated into the room from Leslie Hutchinson's creamy voice. The West Indian singer known as Hutch was a glamorous figure whose voice, according to the popular press, had attracted the admiration of the Prince of Wales himself. As Hutch sang of the scent of gardenia perfume and the taste of wild strawberries, May's thoughts drifted away from the reality of cold winter days to dreams of a life of romance. She could not help noticing Nat's eyes resting on the figure of his sleepy wife in the chair opposite.

As the song came to an end Nat lent over to the brown wooden set and twirled the dial, watching the small line flickering hesitantly along the concentric coloured circles visible through the glass window at the front. Passing by Florence, Fécamp, Paris and Stuttgart, the little needle arrived at the point marked Home Service. The leading BBC broadcaster Stuart Hibberd was speaking. George V's life was moving peacefully towards its close. They were barely able to believe their ears. No one had realised the full seriousness of the King's illness. Last year's Silver Jubilee celebrations and George V's recent Christmas broadcast had lulled people into the belief that national life was entering a settled phase and that the long years of the Depression were a thing of the past.

Big Ben tolled with the passing of every quarter of an hour, and with each set of chimes a further bulletin on the King's health was made. Rachel made everyone a cup of tea but the plate of homemade cinnamon buns sat untouched beside the wireless. Sarah put some more coal on the cinders of the fire before going to lie down for a while. The others remained close by the wireless set, chatting and reading a little, and all the while listening out for the next bulletin from Buckingham Palace. At the sound of the sombre voice they would all stare fixedly at the set, as if the disembodied speech was coming from a visible person and not from an inanimate brown box. A further two and a half hours elapsed before another even deeper voice came across the airwaves; beginning with the words, 'It is with great sorrow . . .'

They all knew what Sir John Reith the Director-General of the BBC was going to say next.

So much death was in the air. Only three days earlier May had read of the grand funeral plans for Rudyard Kipling. Florence would be sad to know that her favourite storyteller had died. Perhaps May could follow Mr Hooch's practice of reading aloud some of those magical stories to Florence. The idea of a bedtime story being a time to develop friendship and affection appealed greatly to May, and perhaps the experience would help to excise the memories of Duncan's bedtime nips.

* * *

Ten days after the King's death May was once again given a couple of days off. The Blunt family and the Cuckmere staff had been equally shaken by the news. But when Mrs Cage had remarked to Sir Philip how at least the Prince of Wales was a first-rate successor to good old King George, Sir Philip had replied rather ominously that he hoped she was right. Oak Street had been equally curious about the character of the new King.

'He really cares, Edward does,' said Rachel with conviction. 'He's got the welfare of us all in his heart, he has. And I think we cannot be alone in wishing that a nice girl will come his way soon. The whole world, especially his mother, must be hoping that a foreign princess will melt his heart and give him that son and heir.'

The voices around her acknowledged their mutual sympathy for poor Queen Mary.

'Mind you, it's a good thing we haven't got that brother instead. Half-baked, he is, if you ask me. Can't even string two sentences together without losing his way. I heard him on the wireless the other day. Stumbling all over himself, he was.'

Rachel always had a great to deal to say about the Royal Family. They were one of her pet fancies. That Bertie, he needed feeding up a bit, she thought, although the Duchess of York, now she was all right. Maybe she would be in the procession tomorrow. Rachel would love to see her in the flesh. No. She would not be dissuaded by Simon from going up to watch the funeral tomorrow, even if he tried. Nothing, not even her painful bunions, was going to prevent her from going into the West End for a Royal funeral. She might even pick up a mourning mug to add to her Royal china collection.

The Greenfelds made preparations for the following day as chicken sandwiches were made into portable greaseproof parcels and black armbands were retrieved from drawers where they had been put away on Armistice Day in 1918. On the wireless the gay patter of music hall comedians and the sound of dance bands had been replaced by the mournful tune of 'Oh God our Help in Ages Past', the long thump of lament broken by official statements concerning arrangements for the state funeral.

On Tuesday 28 January 1936 Rachel, Simon, Sarah, Nat, May and Sam took the underground train, 'up West' to St James's Park, emerging to find themselves surrounded by flags flying at half-mast and black bunting hung between the gas lamps. The cheerfully decorated streets of the Silver Jubilee six months earlier were no more than a cherished memory. Menacing-looking crows touched down briefly onto the boot-worn grass only to be airborne again within moments. In some places the pavements were ten deep with people. All cinemas and theatres had been closed for the week but there was promise of enough of a real-life spectacle to make up for the temporary lack of entertainment on stage and screen. May had never seen so many flowers as she gazed at the mass of bunches lying dozens deep, along the pavements on the approach of Westminster Abbey. A policeman informed the party from Oak Street that the queue to get into Westminster Hall for the lying in state stretched for two and a half miles. Instead Nat led his family back into the underground.

At Paddington Station they waited for what seemed like an age for the royal coffin to arrive to pay their respects to George V before his final

111

journey on board the royal train to Windsor. May's eye fell on two exhausted-looking women half-kneeling on the pavement beside her. One wore a battered mauve felt hat that looked as if it had been put through a mangle while her friend was equally down at heel in a brown coat of limp and ragged fur.

'Funny how things can change in a jiffy, isn't it? Seems like only the other day we were cheering George for sticking around for twenty-five years,' the mauve-hatted woman murmured. 'God bless his soul.'

'Mind you, it'll be a nice change to have a young one on that throne,' her friend replied.

'Young?' spluttered the mauve hat as people around her stared and uttered a reprimanding shush. 'You must be having a laugh!' she continued, dropping her voice to a more respectful pitch. 'Edward's going on more than forty if I'm a day. Should be married by now. It's not natural at his age, if you ask me. A King needs a wife, just as I need a husband.'

'You volunteering then, Dot?' asked the woman in the fur coat.

'If only,' was the wistful reply from the battered mauve hat.

Slowly the mood of the jostling crowd began to change from anticipation to irritation. Impatient mutterings grew louder as the procession for the dead King continued to fail to appear. With a sort of inevitability it was not long before someone bellowed 'Where's George?' from somewhere deep within the crowd. The words broke into the solemn shuffling and neck craning and

112

prompted a wave of laughter. Someone else shouted that George himself, such a stickler for punctuality, was not the sort of man to be be late for his own funeral.

'He must be shuddering with horror in his coffin,' they tittered, the previously restless mood restored to good humour.

Despite the sadness of the funeral, May could not help thinking it was a bit of luck to be present at such an occasion so soon after her arrival in England. Never in all her wildest dreams had she expected to find herself so close to royalty. Judging by the sound of weeping all around her, she realised the old King must have been much loved. But instead of feeling tearful, May was exhilarated by it all.

Eventually the gun carriage arrived at the station, the coffin resplendent with its glinting crown, giant sword of state and large cross fashioned from white flowers all laid on the top. May found herself thrilling to the spectacle. The procession formed by sailors, so smart in their uniform, who had been chosen to escort George V on his final journey, was equally impressive, although May's first glimpse of the new fair-haired King himself, so alone, his slight figure weighed down by a floor-length woollen overcoat, was definitely a letdown. He was so *small*. But the carriage bearing Queen Mary had an altogether different effect on her.

May watched the Dowager Queen, her peaked coif just visible through the window of her carriage. Her black clothes, elaborate, lacy, stifling, looked as if they should be on exhibit in a costume museum. They were the sort of clothes pictured in the piles of yellowing British magazines, their pages curling at the edges in the damp heat of the doctor's surgery back home. Queen Mary's face was almost entirely hidden from public view behind a thick crêpe veil but as the carriage passed by her May caught a sudden glimpse of the woman's eyes. They were brimming with tears. May wondered if she herself would ever love a man enough to feel as sad as Queen Mary looked in that moment.

That night after a day of such excitement May found it difficult to sleep. She did not think she would ever get used to the passing traders who called by at all hours. There was the man who sold caustic stinking carbolic, the thick white liquid used for keeping everything in the bathroom and kitchen clean, and the old gent who pushed around a grubby supply of sticky tape in an old tin pram. Her favourite callers were Loafy, who brought the bread still warm from his oven at midnight, and the lavender lady, a clear, summery smell floating up from the purple-headed stalks in her wicker basket. Standing on her bed to peer through the skylight into the darkness, May could just make out the street's human alarm clock, an elderly woman who earned her living by shooting dried peas at windows behind which men slumbered too deeply, anxious not to oversleep and miss the working day.

May rammed the window shut against the sound of pinging pulses. She was looking forward to catching the train to Cuckmere early the following morning, conscious of the contrast between her two lives. Nothing was ever hidden in Oak Street; people spoke their minds, wore their hearts on their sleeves. The Blunts' way of doing things, however, was secretive. The glass dividing screen in the Rolls was perpetually sliding backwards and forwards; information was classified into categories for those either permitted or prevented from hearing it; open doors were closed with confusing regularity. And yet May had begun to feel herself part of the Cuckmere community, enjoying the friendships she was making not only with Florence but also with Mr Hooch, Cooky, the chatty cook, and the somewhat inscrutable Mrs Cage. Even Vera Borchby, the gardener who kept herself to herself for much of the time, had responded with enthusiasm when May had asked if she may see the rose garden.

'My mother loves roses,' May had ventured one day when Vera came into the garage to ask Mr Hooch for some poison for the pesky rabbits. 'And in the summer I would love to be able to watch them come alive so I can tell my mother about them.'

'It would be a pleasure to show you, May,' the deep-voiced gardener had replied, as Mr Hooch gave May a little wink of approval behind Vera's back.

'Vera's very choosy about who she shows her roses to,' he had told May later. 'You should be honoured that she's taken a liking to you.'

Sir Philip and Lady Joan had also treated May with the utmost consideration, and she was starting to derive equal enjoyment from her seat at the wheel of the Rolls-Royce as she did from her desk in Sir Philip's study.

Above all, May was looking forward to seeing Mr Richardson again. As a friend of the Blunts' son, Mr Julian had been staying at Cuckmere for much of the university holidays and he had taken to popping in and out of Sir Philip's office on a very regular basis. He was always asking questions. He was the most curious man she had ever met. On reflection, she liked almost everything about him. Perhaps it was his unusual honey-coloured hair that attracted her? Or maybe it was his long low laugh as he talked to Lady Joan at the breakfast table when May brought in the post in the mornings? Or was it simply that May was curious to see what he looked like without glasses?

When Mr Hooch met May at the station he let slip that both the young men had already returned to Oxford for the new term. She tried not to betray her disappointment at this news, while Mr Hooch passed on Sir Philip's instructions for the following day. She was to pick up Miss Nettlefold in London and continue on to an address in Sunningdale. May could see the inkling of a conspiratorial smile form at the edges of Hooch's twisted mouth and uncertain of its implication, she smiled straight back at him. She had grown accustomed to looking at his face and no longer flinched at the sight.

116

8

Evangeline had been temporarily resident in Joan's comfortable St John's Wood townhouse for over ten days and had almost forgotten her previous urgency to see her school friend. She was enjoying herself walking Wiggle round the leafless but still elegant Georgian streets, despite the time when Wiggle had squirmed his way under the fence at the nearby Lord's cricket ground and felled a terrified rabbit right there on the famous pitch. In his excitement Wiggle had become caught in the netting. The daily newspaper which was spread open to cover the guard's face had slipped to the floor as Evangeline's sharp 'cooee' woke him in his hut on the periphery of the grounds. His weary eyes reflected his alarm at seeing a double chin framed in fur peering at him through the window, mouthing some words he obviously could not identify.

'We gals stark?' he queried from behind the window.

'Wiggle . . . my little dog . . . he's stuck. And I can't unravel him!' Evangeline yelled back at him.

The guard had eventually untangled the trapped animal with the help of an old golf club he kept in the hut for such emergencies, and appeared mightily pleased to be allowed to get back to his midday nap.

There had been another mishap a few days later. Evangeline and Joan had been out to tea at The Grosvenor Hotel in Park Lane when Evangeline became caught in the revolving door at the entrance. A queue of expensively dressed and impatient-looking women had formed on the other side of the glass and for a few minutes, despite the strenuous tugging of the doorman, and a hastily summoned back-up team of waiters, there was no budging the obstinate door. The claustrophobia was intense and Evangeline, in a flash of temper born of exasperation, felt like smashing the glass if only she could. She reminded herself of Alice in Lewis Carroll's story but without a magic biscuit to start the shrinking process. Only when a bowler-hatted gentleman went down on his knees, inserted his umbrella handle into the lower hinge, agitating it back and forth, did the glass door finally come loose. With no warning at all, Evangeline found herself whooshed round in a circle at an unseemly pace, while the previously stern-faced women laughed at her from behind their hands.

★　★　★

On the whole, however, Evangeline had settled down into a most agreeable way of life with the Blunts. They had taken her out to dine at Rules and at Wheelers, two of their favourite restaurants, and Evangeline was enjoying time spent with these two older people, their affectionate ease with one another evident as they lobbed and returned well-rehearsed teases nurtured during many years of contented marriage.

'I cannot think what Winston thinks of the length your hair has now reached, my darling. Does he imagine the government has appointed a rather dishevelled elk hound for a chief whip, I wonder?'

But Philip had long resisted his wife's attempts to get him to cut his long and infrequently brushed hair. It was part of his identity.

The Blunts had embarked on the New Year with considerable energy for a couple in their sixties. They had begun by treating Evangeline to a performance of Noël Coward's new play at the Phoenix Theatre, *Tonight at 8.30*, a sequence of one-act dramas Coward had written for himself and his favourite leading lady, Gertrude Lawrence. After the show the Blunt party met the playwright for a drink in the Café Royal. Evangeline could not help staring at the man whose work filled theatres on both sides of the Atlantic and who had helped make Gertie Lawrence such a star. In Evangeline's opinion, Coward's looks just missed qualification for heart-throb status but he was so funny and warm, referring to Gertie as 'Gert' whom, he told them, he had loved ever since she was an unknown fourteen-year-old. Evangeline remembered her mother mentioning a scandal involving Coward and the Duke of Kent, the Prince of Wales's younger brother, although the precise nature of that friendship had never been explained. To Mrs Nettlefold's frustration, British newspapers always maintained absolute discretion as far as stories about the Royal family were concerned.

First nights at London theatres, especially a Noël Coward first night, were glamorous occasions, providing an opportunity for the stars of London society to dress up, turn out and show off to one another. But Evangeline preferred the evening parties at Hamilton Terrace. The Blunts' guests tended to be older than herself and demonstrated a gratifying interest in life in America. They were curious about the racial tension that dominated so many cities, in the tallness of the new buildings, in the new museum that had opened just before Christmas at the New York home of art collector Mr Henry Clay Frick, in the goings-on among the film stars in Hollywood and most particularly in Baltimore itself. Evangeline was enjoying the novel experience of being 'interesting' and a little giddy with the notion that she was bringing 'insights' into how American and British ways of life differed. Privately she felt a little deflated when the conversation turned to the two other insatiable topics of the early spring.

Speculation about the Prince of Wales and his relationship with Mrs Simpson was rarely off the agenda. The British newspapers were silent on the subject and the couple in question moved easily and without inhibition within the upper circles of London Society. They would regularly be seen in each other's company at the theatre, at nightclubs, and at dinner parties in the private houses of the rich and well connected. Mrs Simpson's husband was usually included in such expeditions and hostesses marvelled privately not only at Ernest's tolerance of the Prince of Wales's devotion to Mrs Simpson but also at how Wallis herself seemed to manage the threesome with such dexterity. She seemed to feel genuine affection for both men. Nevertheless, London drawing rooms were fizzing with talk about how long this arrangement could last and also how long the story could remain out of the newspapers.

War was the other subject that monopolised conversation. Despite Philip Blunt's insistence that some sort of martial conflict with Germany was inevitable, he often found himself to be a lone voice in the matter. There was indeed little evidence to convince anyone of the imminence of war. The Olympic Games this coming summer were to be held in Berlin and opened by the German Chancellor himself, Adolf Hitler. '*Le Tout Monde*', according to the Blunts' daughter Bettina, by which she meant a large delegation from the upper ranks of British Society, was planning to be in Germany in August for the many Olympic parties and balls in Berlin and Rupert Blunt was intending to go straight out there to celebrate the end of his final exams at Oxford. He and Bettina had accepted a stylish invitation to attend the Games from the American bon-viveur Chips Channon, a Member of Parliament and friend of their father.

Scattered throughout the gaiety of Evangeline's days there had been moments alone with her godmother that reminded her of the hidden challenges of life. Although nearly two decades had elapsed since the death of Joan's sister, her grief was rarely far below the surface, evident when her eyes would suddenly lose their natural shine, as if shrouded by a layer of dust. One of Joan's closest friends, Lady Cynthia Asquith, had spoken to Evangeline at dinner only the other night, expressing her pleasure at Evangeline's extended visit.

'You have brought a new purpose and an interest into her life,' Lady Cynthia told Evangeline. 'We all worry about her so much as she still seems incapable of recovering fully from Grace's dreadful sudden death. Grace was her favourite sister, you know.'

Evangeline nodded in sympathy.

'Every anniversary seems to be as bad as the one before,' Lady Cynthia continued. 'We had all hoped that time would ease the pain, but it does not seem to be doing the trick. Men seem able to handle their grief better. They go to their clubs and talk about it there among themselves, if indeed they talk about it at all.'

'I heard there was another sister?' Evangeline asked.

'Oh yes, but Myrtle has never been a big part of Joan's life. She is a good five years older and they are such different people. In fact, I cannot remember the last time I heard Joan even mention her.'

'Where is Myrtle now?'

'She lives on her own, I think, somewhere near Settle in Yorkshire,' Lady Cynthia replied. 'A good safe distance from London and Cuckmere. So Joan relies on her friends mostly.' Lady

122

Cynthia sighed and for a moment the two women were silent.

'The trouble is barely anyone escaped losing someone they loved in the war. And yet many of us who will never get over our own grief also know that unless we find a way of accommodating it we will go under.' Lady Cynthia's expression of despair confirmed her own private feelings as she continued and not without a hint of bitterness. 'I am afraid Bettina and Rupert are too absorbed in their own young lives to think of sparing a moment to look after their mother, although of course Philip does all he can, but he is so busy with his parliamentary work. Rupert's Oxford friend, Julian Richardson, has been lovely to her though. Have you met him?'

Evangeline nodded. 'Oh yes. He's rather a dish isn't he?' she replied enthusiastically.

Lady Cynthia raised her eyebrows.

'Oh no, don't get me wrong, Lady Cynthia! Of course he's *far* too young for me to be paying him any attention! I was just remarking; in an objective way, you understand?'

Lady Cynthia continued, although a little chill had entered her voice.

'Well, you obviously know what I mean about him. And anyway, now you are here to help cheer Joan up as well. Forgive me saying so, but we all think it is an added bonus that you don't have a demanding husband to take care of.'

Evangeline blushed, but this time said nothing. Lady Cynthia seemed to take her blush as a sign of pleasure at the compliment.

'What's more,' the older woman continued, 'I

do believe that even those deep lines in Joan's face, like swallows' wings I always used to think, appear to be fading a little.'

For the time being Evangeline managed to dampen the prickles of resentment that the mention of her single status had ignited. Evangeline had been the recipient of her godmother's full confession. No one else, not even Philip, knew that Joan sometimes felt trapped in a dark cave hung about with colourless cobwebs, great skeins of grief that waited to trip her up. Evangeline's concern for Joan was empty of the hollow, bored pity with which the bereaved are so familiar and as a result Joan felt able to confide her feelings and to weep, even to laugh and especially to remember with an unprecedented freedom.

Joan acknowledged that there were so many things to be grateful for. She had a life that, when viewed from the outside, appeared blessed. But the emotional tug that pulled her down when she was least expecting it was something that no husband, son, or daughter could truly understand, let alone eradicate. She had developed a habit of not talking about the events of nearly two decades ago. She was frightened of making a scene and yet this tendency to withdraw was beginning to affect her relationship with Philip.

Sometimes she would leave their bed in the middle of the night and creep into an empty guest room where she would muffle her sobs deep within a pillow, clutching at the hems of the sheets as if they were the tiller on a ship that might steady her. During the daytime she kept herself busy. But roaming the open-ended corridors of night-time thoughts, she could find herself stuck in the dusty, neglected attics of childhood memories. Reliving those experiences, even the happy ones, was more painful than any physical experience, childbirth included, that she knew of. At least with childbirth there was a purpose to the suffering. The futile open-endedness of grief was sometimes impossible to accept. Sleep was elusive. Once, she confided to her god-daughter, she had woken from hard-won unconsciousness to see her husband holding a feather beneath her nose.

'I just came in to see you were all right, my darling,' he said, his over-long hair falling over his eyes as he reddened a little, clearly ashamed at being caught checking up on her.

★　★　★

Nearly a month had gone by since the docking of the *Thalassa*, and Evangeline had still neither seen nor heard from Wallis, even though Evangeline had given her the Blunts' address and the date of her arrival. Just when Evangeline was steeling herself to lift the receiver to the school friend that she had not seen for so long, and who was the subject of so much discussion, George V had died. And then *everything* changed.

There had been little warning; the King had been out riding his horse only five days earlier. Philip told Evangeline about the exuberant

Jubilee street celebrations of the summer before, still talked of in pubs and clubs. On that day men had worn hats fashioned from Union flags, children had eaten chocolates wrapped in Union flag imprinted foil, women had flashed finger-nails painted with miniature crowns, and red white and blue bunting had looped itself in gay abundance through the city streets. Philip was clearly much saddened by the death of the old King, describing for his American visitor the level of affection most Britons felt for a King and a Queen who had steadied the country through the Great War and out of the troubling times that followed it. With King George and Queen Mary at the helm it had almost been possible on that one Jubilee day of pageantry and joy to forget the truth: that Britain was still a country struggling with poverty, unemployment and a persistent fear of the return of international conflict.

★ ★ ★

The invitation for Evangeline to visit Fort Belvedere came by telephone two weeks after the old King's death. Wallis apologised for the long delay in getting in touch. Life had been so busy. But she would almost certainly be alone for the next day or two. Ernest was delaying his return from a business trip to America, having met up with their old school chum, Mary Kirk. Although Mary had been married nearly twenty years ago to a Mr Jacques Raffray, a French insurance broker, her husband rarely appeared in public

126

with her, and Mary had obviously been delighted to run into Ernest and for a chance to catch up on news of Wallis. And anyway, wouldn't it be fun for Wallis and Evangeline to spend time together without anyone much getting in the way of their long-awaited reunion?

'Oh, and just one last thing, before I hang up!' Wallis had concluded the call with an after-thought. 'If you had been worrying about it, there is no question of you packing any mourning clothes. The Prince, I mean the King, has expressly forbidden them to be worn at the Fort. He does not like us all going round looking like blackbirds! And I must say, Vangey, I am delighted at the rule as I haven't worn black stockings since I gave up the Can-Can!'

Evangeline had been nervous on the drive to Fort Belvedere. Wiggle had been experiencing one of his dietary upsets and had looked so pathetic in the hallway at 44 Hamilton Terrace that at the last moment Evangeline had scooped up his lead and whisked him into the car. She had been glad of his small comforting little body on her lap. Recently there had been more talk than ever around the St John's Wood dining table about Mrs Simpson and the complications her relationship with the new King would inevitably cause. Queen Mary's grief at the death of her husband was fully understood among those in the Blunts' circle. Her dearest friend Lady Airlie had let it be known that the Queen operated under 'a façade of self-control' but that the romantic intentions of her eldest son were causing her dreadful anxiety. According to Joan's own sources of information, George V had shared his wife's concerns. His refusal of the Prince of Wales's request that Mr and Mrs Simpson be invited to a state dinner last year had resulted in a family row and the heir to the throne had been seen banging his head against the lemon silk walls of his mother's private sitting room.

Evangeline was aware of the constant reminders not to discuss any of this in front of the servants. 'PD,' Joan would mutter, with a finger to her lips as Mrs Cage carried the evening cocktail tray into the Cuckmere drawing room. There were other subjects that fell into the '*Pas Devant*' category. Sex was one. Money another. As both of these topics were of utmost concern to many of Joan's friends there were frequent pauses in conversation as the time came for curtains to be drawn, plates to be cleared, or wood to be added to an already blazing fire. Sometimes guests, including Evangeline herself, would forget themselves and run on indiscriminately, in which case a servant would find themselves summoned to the study and told to forget everything they had heard.

★ ★ ★

As the Rolls-Royce travelled along the country roads towards Sunningdale, Evangeline tried to imagine how the woman at the heart of all this talk would be feeling and whether at their first meeting she would even raise the topic. Evangeline promised herself she would not

128

touch it unless Wallis herself did first.

Although Joan had explained that Cropper's affection for the whisky bottle had prompted Philip to replace him with a more level-headed driver, Evangeline had uncharacteristically paid little attention to the new incumbent behind the steering wheel of the Blunts' navy-blue Rolls-Royce. Evangeline was always curious to meet someone new whether they were a king, a famous playwright or someone employed to make the wheels of life roll more smoothly. While motoring with Joan one day to fulfil her long-held ambition to visit the famous food halls in Harrods department store, she had learned a good deal from Joan about the sleek car in which they were travelling. Philip, a fan of the motor-car since before the war, would have far preferred the more racy Bentley but there was so little room in the back seat to spread out his work papers that they had opted several years ago for the more conventional Rolls.

But Joan's explanation had somehow never proceeded beyond the vehicle itself to the person who sat at the controls. During the couple of theatre visits and shopping expeditions that Evangeline and Joan had made together in the car, and on the one occasion when they had been driven to lunch with Philip in the fashionable Ivy restaurant, they had sat together in the back, too full of their own conversation to have time to chat to the new driver. He appeared to be even more silent than Cropper, but his steady gloved hands had conducted them through the London traffic without a hitch.

Therefore, on the way to Sunningdale, it came as a surprise to Evangeline, deprived of Joan's diverting chat, to find herself looking at the chauffeur's hands resting un-gloved on the steering wheel, the delicacy of his olive-coloured fingers unexpected in such a profession. Examining the straight-backed figure in front of her a little more closely, and observing the slightness of the shoulders, Evangeline tried to catch the reflection of his face in the driving mirror. The leafless Berkshire lanes had offered little scenic beauty to comment on but Evangeline, always one for having a go at establishing intimacies, moved the dozing Wiggle from her lap onto the seat beside her and pushed back the glass dividing screen.

9

A week after Evangeline's visit to the Fort, Wallis made one of her now daily telephone calls. She wanted to discuss the dinner party that she and Ernest were giving in honour of the Blunt family. It was to take place in their first-floor flat in Mayfair and, Wallis assured her, was to be a most informal event.

'I have had Mary Raffray on the horn this morning,' Wallis explained. 'She cannot move without telephoning me it seems! Anyhow, I must say I am quite relieved to know that our old school friend is otherwise engaged for that night.'

Evangeline too felt some relief. The competitive spirit between the two scrawny Oldlands girls was not something she had ever enjoyed witnessing.

'Honestly, Vangey, I seem to have been entertaining that girl for days on end since her arrival in England. She is never out of the flat! I barely get a chance to have an appointment at Antoine's and as a result my hair is a perfect fright! And my old digestive problems have been playing up again. Life is never quite simple, is it?'

What is more, Wallis explained, she was not going to invite any of those London hostesses who came so regularly to dine at Bryanston Court. This was not an occasion for Sybil, Emerald or Margot or even Diana, entertaining as all those society lionesses could be. They were all coming with Chips next week anyway. No, this was to be more of a family party, even though they would be a little cramped around the dining-room table.

'I usually limit my dinners to six people as that is what my most regular guests like best, but tomorrow a table of twelve will make a happy exception.' And would they have some fun, she promised! Wallis was looking forward to meeting Lady Joan and her husband once again and was delighted to include not only their daughter Bettina and son Rupert in the invitation, but also his friend Julian from university and Julian's girlfriend Charlotte.

'Don't you just love the younger generation?' Wallis had twinkled at her old school friend. 'Especially the male part of it!'

Evangeline had agreed with her wholeheartedly.

Despite the insistence on the casualness of the evening ahead, Evangeline had taken particular trouble with her choice of clothes. Wallis had just returned from a shopping trip to Paris where she had ordered a complete spring wardrobe from Mainbocher, the most fashionable of all Parisian dressmakers.

'The King insists on indulging me with so many lovely new clothes!' she had said with a smug look at Evangeline, who privately vowed to herself she would not be outdone in the fashion stakes, particularly when that charming young man Julian was going to be present. Of course there were a few years in age between herself and the young undergraduate, she was the first to acknowledge, but people cared so much less about that sort of thing these days, didn't they? And after all, people often remarked on the youthful quality of Evangeline's complexion.

The Blunts had assembled in the Hamilton Terrace drawing room and drank a glass of champagne while waiting for May to bring the Rolls to the front door.

Charlotte was sitting on the leather arm of the semi-circled fire fender, crossing and uncrossing her legs, and occasionally reaching down to smooth her silk stockings from ankle to knee in a gesture that Evangeline felt to be inappropriately provocative. Bettina was wearing a floor-length silver sheath dress and was telling her parents about the ball she had been to last night. Evangeline, ever up to the minute with the fashion pages, noticed that dangling from Bettina's arm was the very latest thing in chic: a velvet evening bag with a working watch for a clasp. Goodness knows which eligible young man had been persuaded to make this silly girl such an extravagant gift. The young woman's habit of using French words and phrases within perfectly good English sentences seemed to Evangeline both affected and irritating. She knew from the roll of Philip's eyes that he shared her opinion.

'Oh honestly, Mummy, every joke told by the spotty specimen I got stuck with was *such* old *chapeau*. But then things looked up when Le Grand Fromage himself arrived hot foot from Nombre Ten! *Quelle* excitement!'

The silver sheath shimmered as Bettina darted around the room, swinging her velvet bag and doing little pirouettes as she spoke. But no one was really listening.

Evangeline sat in the corner, hoping that the experimental and girlish 'natural curl' that she had agreed to wear, finished off with a large, dressy feather, would be an improvement on the habitually static appearance of her wig.

She tried to adjust the shoulder straps of her cut-away black silk evening gown without Philip, Rupert, Joan, Bettina or Charlotte noticing. The notion that she would be dressed in something beyond the limitations that her body could tolerate had been worrying her since breakfast. Even before she had removed the dressmaker's cotton sleeve that protected the gown from attracting dust, she suspected her choice had been a mistake. And she had been correct. Despite the efforts of Wallis's own seamstress the straps were struggling to hold up the bodice and already cutting into her exposed shoulders, forming ugly raised welts. She remembered all over again why she was usually so careful not to expose too much flesh and became resigned to wearing the matching and concealing shawl, even though Wallis had assured her that her apartment would be warmly heated.

In the middle of this undignified hitching and tugging the door opened and Julian stood there looking straight at her. He was wearing a red velvet tie and winked at her from behind his glasses before announcing that he had seen May waiting for them in the hall and were they all ready to leave? Immediately Evangeline began to feel more confident of the enjoyment the evening surely now promised, crossing her fingers tightly, as she always did when she wanted a bit of luck to come her way.

Julian spent a great deal of time with the Blunt family, even though Evangeline had been unable to identify the basis for Rupert and Julian's friendship. The two undergraduates were so different; one all loud bluster and back-slapping, the other quieter, cerebral, and yet unhesitatingly flirtatious. Julian's charm rarely landed on Rupert's obnoxious, loud-mouthed sister; however, the quiet conversations that Evangeline had observed between Julian and Joan made her wonder whether it was his need for a warm-hearted mother that brought Julian back again and again both to Cuckmere and to St John's Wood. Encouraged by the sight of that fleeting wink, she failed to repress a bubbly thought that maybe there was another, a recent addition to the household, whose presence persuaded him to return so often.

★   ★   ★

Bryanston Court was a large purpose-built apartment building just round the corner from Marble Arch. Wallis's guests walked through the imposing entrance lobby, lit by a magnificent central chandelier, past a polished Georgian table on which two huge Chinese vases sat resplendent, and across the shining marble floor, pulling the concertinaed lift gate shut behind

135

them, assured of further elegance ahead. Conscious of Wallis's pledge to find her friend a beau, Evangeline was hoping that Wallis would seat her next to Julian. She was also looking forward to the dinner itself. Mr and Mrs Simpson prided themselves on serving delicious food.

'You know, Vangey, how we folks from the south love to provide our guests with a good table, and Ernest has always been something of a gourmet, you know,' she had said with unexpected pride on the telephone earlier that afternoon, leading Evangeline to question momentarily whether Wallis's feelings for the King yet came anywhere near replacing those she still had for her husband.

Whatever the truth, Ernest and Wallis were jointly proud to have 'brought on' Mrs Ralph in her culinary skills. Initially a kitchen maid to Lady Curzon's French chef, Mrs Ralph had been trained at the hands of a master. By the time she came to Bryanston Court she had developed a flair in the pastry and sauce departments that few could rival. Her preference for vegetables steamed al dente instead of the British boiled-to-slush method had been much remarked on by Wallis's guests.

If Ernest encouraged a concern for the menus, Wallis's own particular taste was evident in the furnishings. An unusual yellow-and-black Italian painted table and a William and Mary walnut chest both looked perfect in the pale-green-painted drawing room with its heavy cream curtains. Glass vases of Madonna lilies were placed on every surface, filling the air with a sweet, decaying smell that was intensified by the over-heated apartment. Fragile, pink-edged orchids rose from cane baskets in the corners of the drawing room. A pair of gold leaf and ebony blackamoors doing handstands at each end of a side table were balancing small trays on the soles of their feet on which matching arrangements of white-washed leaves with white roses had been placed, proof that Mrs Spry had been working her magic here earlier in the day. A letter rack on the small desk in the corner was visibly stashed with thick white cards printed with the two words 'At Home' in copperplate across the centre.

After a cocktail or two had been prepared with some expertise at a low table by Wallis herself, and after Evangeline had re-acquainted herself with Slipper, the dear little Cairn terrier that had been a gift to Wallis from the King, the guests were invited to gather in the pretty dining room. The walls were covered in a bucolic blue-and-white French paper depicting cows and milkmaids, and the table laid for twelve glowed with the visual warmth of a dozen lit candles. Small bowls of miniature pink rosebuds had been positioned at each guest's place and an elevated silver stand at the very centre held a generous cascade of out-of-season Muscat grapes. The place settings were magnificent with the gold cutlery that Wallis had confided to Evangeline was on loan from the King.

'He loves to make sure I have everything just so!'

Eleven people assembled in the charming

room and stood leaning over the backs of the white leather chairs, allocated their place in turn by Wallis as she consulted a handwritten seating plan of the table.

'Now you are here, Vangey, though, don't forget your wrap. Those poor shoulders look as if they could do with a little protection.'

Comforting herself that she could catch up on news with Julian at another time, Evangeline took the chair that Wallis indicated, between Ernest Simpson and George Hunter.

'Of course, you know Ernest already I think? And we have been friends with Kitty and George since our earliest days in London,' Wallis explained as she moved away to seat her other guests. Evangeline had indeed met Ernest on a couple of occasions, finding him the most congenial of companions. She greeted him with a kiss before extending a hand to George Hunter.

'I have not yet had the pleasure, Mr Hunter. Are you in the shipping line of business with Ernest?'

'Oh no, Miss Nettlefold, I confess I have never been bothered by the nuisance of having to go to an office.'

As the guests spoke among themselves, Wallis slipped out of the dining room, returning moments later with a small fair-haired man, evidently so familiar with the Simpson apartment that he straightaway took his place next to Wallis at the top of the table with Lady Joan on his right. For as much as half a minute the new guest's arrival was so unobtrusive that it went almost unnoticed among the energetically chattering guests. But gradually a feeling grew that the quality of oxygen in the room had been enhanced, and deference and respect settled on the assembled company as attention was concentrated on the twelfth amongst them. The women dropped a middling low curtsey just where they stood at their chairs and the men bowed in the manner appropriate for a private party, using the dignified nod of a neck bow as opposed to the dramatic bend from the waist they had been trained as schoolboys to reserve for state occasions.

'So sorry I am late,' the King said, all cheery informality and smiling at each guest in turn as, exercising his prerogative, he was the first to sit down, indicating with a hand, that they should all join him.

General conversation resumed. The King leant across the table to speak to Sir Philip, his voice audible to all, with its hard-to-place accent that combined a touch of American with an unlikely dash of London's East End. As the individual spinach soufflés were placed in front of each guest, the deep green of the aerated surface contrasting deliciously with the lighter colour of the accompanying watercress sauce, Wallis encouraged them all with a firm 'Do start!', directing a meaningful look towards Evangeline.

Soon the conversation turned from talk of the tiresome length of the dark winter months to the political news of the week. The empty soufflé dishes were cleared and the King lit a cigarette. Wallis put her hand so briefly on his that Evangeline only just caught the gesture. The

King immediately stubbed out the lighted end, a film of ash floating onto the black waistcoat he wore beneath his dinner jacket. Hitler's soldiers had reoccupied the Rhineland in violation of the rules laid down by the Treaty of Versailles six months after the end of the Great War. Some people felt that Hitler was only re-entering his 'own back garden'. But others took it to be a worrying indication of things to come. Had not the Italians allied themselves with Germany against the rest of Europe after their invasion of Abyssinia the preceding October? And this latest development in the Rhineland came on top of the recent reintroduction of conscription in Germany.

The King was the first to reassure the assembled company. War is a dreadful thing of course, as he could himself testify, having spent many months in the army, often equipped with little more than his dependable bicycle during a spell right up there with the finest of men at the front line.

'But may I remind you,' he said firmly, 'that not only was the Rhineland formerly part of legitimate German territory, but Adolf Hitler himself has seen a war at first hand. He too suffered the appalling effects of gas, lost friends and family.'

The King stressed that he was certain the Führer would not want his experience to be repeated in his lifetime. Julian could see Rupert smiling in agreement. He knew that smile. It was the one that appeared on Rupert's face every time the fascists were given some sort of conversational endorsement. Bettina was nodding vigorously and indiscriminately at every syllable the King uttered. At one moment she joined in with her own observation.

'Oh yes, Sir! I *do* agree. I hate it when people are *très* unkind about the Germans. I think they are the giddy limit. Rupert and I are going off to the Olympics in Berlin in August with Pommes Frites Channon and I bet it will be *parfâitment* fun over there!'

The conversation began to feel a little dangerous. Evangeline, Joan and Philip were all looking down at the plate of escalope de veau en crème that the butler had just placed in front of them. Evangeline tried to keep her mind on the talk rather than the food. Droplets of sweat had broken out beneath Julian's hair. He had originally contemplated abandoning the black tie dress code for dinner after a couple of his socialist-minded friends at Balliol told him that they sometimes flouted the long-established and constricting rule and came to formal dinners in an ordinary day suit. At the last minute Julian had conformed out of respect to Joan, more than anyone else. The centrally heated air was getting to him as he dabbed at his face with his napkin. He could no longer remain silent.

'Forgive me, Sir, but I hope you will forgive me for mentioning your brother-in-law's views on all this?'

'Of course. Please do remind me. Mr?'

'Oh I am so sorry. Of course. I am Julian Richardson.'

'We share digs at Oxford, Sir,' Rupert added.

141

'Ah yes, Oxford. What a wonderful place! Spent some of the happiest days of my life there. Of course, Mr Richardson, please do go on.'

'Thank you, Sir. Yes, well I was going to mention that the Earl of Harewood was highlighting the dangers of Germany's wider territorial intentions as early as last summer. You have only to look at the far-reaching and catastrophic influence Hitler already commands. I mean, Sir, it's not just fascism per se, but how could one not be worried about the increasing anti-Semitism that is infecting huge parts of Europe? Look at Italy. And if I may say so, Sir, look at England. Mosley may not yet have had the success he craves for his blacker than black shirts, but he is having a damn good stab at corrupting the gullible in this country!'

As Julian felt the wave of anger break over him he wondered if he had gone too far. But the upper classes, and royalty in particular, so it seemed, had an entrenched antipathy to telling the truth.

What on earth am I doing here among all these people? he wondered silently to himself. He took a large gulp of wine and the butler was instantly at his elbow refilling the glass.

He was debating whether to continue, when, through the flickering candles, he saw Charlotte scoop up the wedge of lemon floating in her glass of water and begin to suck it very slowly and deliberately while not moving her eyes from his face. The age-old trick of forcing an involuntary response at the sight of a mouthful of lemon juice had its instantaneous effect on Julian. The inside of his cheeks began to pucker and he found himself unable to utter another word.

The King, a man whose informality and approachability had been a hallmark of his popularity as the Prince of Wales, stared across at Julian with a look that combined incomprehension with pity. Easing out an American Chesterfield from the small silver drum on the table in front of him, the King turned his immaculate manners to his right. Julian could see his diamond cufflinks glinting at the edge of the dark sleeve of his dinner jacket.

Nostalgia and a vestige of pride had seemed to sweep over the King at his own earlier mention of his part in the Great War. When the King turned to Joan asking what sort of a war she had been through, Evangeline saw her godmother flush.

'Not so good, I am afraid, Sir,' Joan began.

The King inhaled long and deeply on his cigarette. 'Oh?' he said encouragingly, his left eye half-closed but the right one in full focus as he waited for her to continue.

Philip stiffened in his white leather chair.

'You see, Sir, my sister was a nurse, stationed up at the front and she saw sights that no human should ever see. She was the kindest woman on this earth.' Joan's voice had dropped to a whisper and the guests were now leaning forward to try and catch her words. 'She saw men who had lost their hands, arms, feet, legs, chins, noses,' Joan listed the missing parts as if she were reeling off a shopping list at the Harrods cheese counter.

The King extinguished his cigarette. Philip stood up but a look from the King prompted him to sit down again as Joan, finding some sudden volume, finished her litany at something approaching a shout.

'And penises, Sir,' she announced definitively and audibly enough for all to hear. 'Is there any man here who could describe what it feels like to be missing a penis? Anyone know any penis-free bodies? Anyone ever actually *seen* a penis blown off?'

With each taboo-laden repetition, the assembled company winced, until Joan appeared to run out of breath and, closing her eyes, lay back, her face as white as her chair. The butler, well trained in unforeseen situations, lifted the claret jug and embarked on another round. For several minutes the only sound in the pale-blue dining room was the splash of wine filling the empty glasses. Even Wallis had lost her social savoir, and remained sitting in her chair, a look of horror on her face.

'Tell Miss Thomas to bring the car round immediately. Explain that Lady Joan and I are leaving at once,' Philip whispered into the butler's ear as the crystal decanter reached him. With his wife lying half slumped opposite him, he drained his full glass in one. Everyone began to move from the table. Evangeline saw Wallis jump to her feet and, taking the King's arm, guide him into the passage, away from the shocked silence that had filled the space left by Joan's outburst, and out through the heavy, bronze front door towards the waiting lift. The other guests were ushered discreetly into the drawing room by Ernest where they remained

144

talking in whispers among themselves, the ladies helping themselves from a tray laid with tiny glasses of a substance resembling toothwash, the men accepting Ernest's offer of balloon-shaped glasses of brandy. None of them saw Joan's bundled-up figure being helped out of Wallis's flat, Philip holding one of her arms, and May the other.

While Wallis was showing the King out into the night, into the care of his waiting detective, Evangeline appeared more distressed than anyone else. She looked around for Wallis's dog to derive some physical reassurance from stroking its warm wiry body but could not see the animal anywhere. All at once she realised she and Julian had been left quite alone together in the dining room. It was too good to be true. Torn for just a moment between retaining her dignity for her godmother's sake on the one hand, and her own romantic interests on the other, she chose the latter and with a delayed, though long-planned answering wink, whispered, 'What a shame poor Joan chose that moment for her little outburst. I had heard there was to be a splendid Grand Marnier bombe glacée for dessert and now we will have to miss it.'

Realising her misjudgement instantly, Evangeline lifted her hand to her head, inadvertently dislodging her carefully positioned wig. Screaming inwardly at herself for her clumsiness, she stood helpless as, with a look of disgust on his handsome face, Julian quietly took the coat and hat being held out to him by the butler, and walked out of the front door without a backward glance.

Spring

Discovery

10

One early spring evening, just as dusk was beginning to fall, an unfamiliar car came slowly down the Cuckmere drive and parked in front of the house. A tall figure in a dark suit emerged from the backseat, was greeted by Lady Joan, and marched into the stone hall as if he was leading a platoon of soldiers behind him.

May was on her way to the study to catch up on the large pile of correspondence. She had been so busy recently with the chauffeuring side of her work and was worrying about the backlog of papers that were piling up on her desk. She stood to one side as the visitor followed Lady Joan through the hall. May noticed his snappy, black moustache and his neatly slicked back hair, and then the man turned his head and looked directly at her. For a second his eyes connected so deeply with her own that she felt an intense physical jolt before he looked away and was hurried upstairs by Lady Joan. Sir Philip followed the pair climbing the stone stairs two at a time and closed the door behind him while May went into the study, disturbed by the unexpected encounter.

Back in January at May's interview, Sir Philip had made clear that her job depended on keeping certain things to herself and not sharing confidences with the other staff, either in London or at Cuckmere. In theory, the rule

149

applied to all Sir Philip's employees, but May was aware of its flouting by the others on a daily basis. In the Cuckmere kitchen fierce differences of opinion were voiced about employers, weekend guests and other members of staff. 'Pantry football' was how Lady Joan referred to the clatter of pans and raised voices that sometimes broke through the barrier of the baize door. It was clear that from the clandestine manner in which the dark-haired man had been brought into the house, Sir Philip and Lady Joan were going to some trouble to stop his presence being discussed below stairs.

A cold dinner for three had been left in the dining room, rendering redundant the need for any serving staff. The following morning May was standing in the hall, her hand absent-mindedly stroking the glossy head of one of the golden Labradors when the door to the kitchen opened and Mrs Cage emerged carrying a tray laid for breakfast with a tiny glass vase of miniature narcissi sitting on one corner of the white cloth. The housekeeper, dressed in her usual long black woollen costume, her hair tied back in her neat grey ponytail, was concentrating so hard on balancing the tray that she did not notice May watching her. The job of carrying breakfast upstairs to a guest was always reserved for one of the daily ladies and it was surprising to see Mrs Cage taking on such a lowly duty. May might have thought no more of it if she had not looked at her watch half an hour later and realised she had forgotten to ask Mr Hooch to fill the car with petrol in readiness for Sir Philip's journey to London the next day. She nearly collided with Mrs Cage who had just reached the bottom of the stairs and was breaking into a sort of run, a red flush filling her cheeks. But Mrs Cage was in no mood to pause to chat and hurried out of sight through the door to the kitchen.

May went straight to the garage where she found Mr Hooch smoking a Woodbine, an angry expression on his face.

'Don't know what they're doing inviting a man like that to this house,' he muttered when he saw May. 'I know Sir Philip says Sir Oswald Mosley is helping him with important constitutional matters, but I don't care if he's come about the bleeding Saviour himself, pardon my directness.'

May had never seen Mr Hooch either so animated or so agitated.

'Who is Sir Oswald Mosley?' May asked.

'Who is Oswald Mosley?' spluttered Mr Hooch. 'Oswald Mosley is the man in charge of the British fascists, that's who. And a Jew-hater to boot. If we left things up to him, we'd have Hitler himself over here running the country. And then where would we be? If it wasn't for Sir Philip and his reputation, I would have been tempted to put some of my supply of rat poison in the tank when his driver came to the pump for a fill-up. I mean, I ask you, what did we all go through for four and half bloody years, if now we're entertaining one of 'them' to tea as if he were my aunt Molly.'

May did not press Mr Hooch any further. She stopped herself from making any remarks about the dangerous attractiveness of the recent house

151

guest. Nor did she say anything about the housekeeper's furtive behaviour. She trusted Sir Philip implicitly and was sure he would not invite someone with those sorts of views into the house unless he had a good reason. But she was puzzled by Mrs Cage. What could she have been doing upstairs for so long alone with the head of the British fascists? Much as she liked Mrs Cage (who had never asked May to use her first name) at times she could not fathom her. May was trying to put her finger on this troubling feeling as she left Mr Hooch and went to her room in Mrs Cage's house to pick up a sweater before resuming the afternoon's work.

Just inside the small hallway, and almost hidden under the stairwell, was a small open door. May had never noticed it before and was about to look inside when Florence appeared, sliding down the banister shouting dramatically, 'Save me, save me,' as throwing her arms wide, she flung her arms round May's neck.

Releasing herself from the embrace, Florence slammed the open cupboard door shut with one hand while grabbing May's with the other.

'Shall we go down to the lake?' she asked, pulling May towards the front door.

'I wish I could, Florence, but I must get back to work,' she said.

Neither of them mentioned the cupboard.

★   ★   ★

The following Saturday afternoon May was alone in the study at Cuckmere catching up on the filing. She had no time to answer a knock on the door before Mr Julian came straight in. He appeared unusually nervous, clearing his throat, as he came straight over to her desk. He was standing so close to May that she could smell the smoke from a recently extinguished cigarette clinging to his blue suit jacket.

With her anglepoise lamp tilted to shine directly onto her papers, she looked up, seeing bright spots dancing in front of her, the light momentarily dazzling her. Mr Julian had a favour to ask. He began with a confession: he had not yet learned to drive although he had promised himself that after his final exams he would take lessons.

'The thing is, you see, I want to travel around a few of the towns up in the north of the country. I keep reading about these places where so many people are out of work, especially in the mining areas, and I want to see those towns for myself, stop where I want to, look about a bit, not be dependent on taxis or train times, you know?'

May moved the lamp to one side.

Mr Julian continued. 'Quite a few of my friends at Oxford have already been up there to take a look. Not Rupert's crowd, obviously, but some of the others in my politics year. What I am trying to say is that I am beginning to feel like such a hypocrite. I mean, I keep talking about how awful it must be up there but actually I don't really know what I am talking about.' The favour was turning into a ramble. 'It might sound odd but I am frightened that when I leave

153

Oxford this term, my time won't be mine any more. I can see just as many obligations as opportunities; exciting but limiting. Maybe Philip, if he did not need you one day . . . ?'

Mr Julian paused.

May said nothing. He was leaning on his right hand on the desk. His second and third fingers were stained slightly yellow by tobacco. May stared at them.

'The thing is, perhaps I could see if Charlotte could come too? You could both chaperone me if . . . ?' He trailed off.

'Shall I see if Sir Philip can spare me during the Easter recess, Mr Julian?' May interrupted.

'Oh would you? Would you really?' he replied, pulling a packet of Woodbines out of his pocket and spilling the contents on the floor. 'Oh and please don't use the Mr bit. I'm Julian. Just Julian.'

Without waiting to hear her answer he bent down, gathered up the cigarettes, stuffed them in his pocket and walked out of the room. May could just hear his tuneless humming as he reached the garden door at the end of the corridor.

Hard as she tried, May found herself incapable of returning to work after her spontaneous suggestion to Julian. What had she been thinking of? Her concentration was all over the place. The beautiful spring weather shone through the window and, getting up from her desk, she went to find Florence. They had taken to spending time together whenever May was not working and Florence was home from school. On the first

154

of these expeditions May had agreed to be introduced to the legendary Mrs Jenkins, despite Mrs Cage's warning about the unpredictability of such a meeting. Florence had dragged a reluctant May through the post-office door and up to the counter.

'This is my friend May. Don't you think she's beautiful, Mrs Jenkins? My mother says all the men are cracky about her.'

'And I am not surprised to hear it,' Mrs Jenkins replied, a harmless-looking middle-aged woman, her hair caught back in a net. She was giving May a thorough once over from behind her position at the counter.

'She's gorgeous, Florence darling. Mind you, she's as dark as a cup of over-stewed tea. And that awful chopped-off hairstyle. She isn't one of those frightful lesbians is she?'

A gleaming bicycle had appeared on Florence's tenth birthday, a present from Lady Joan, accompanied by a very serviceable second-hand version for May. After twenty minutes of wobbles, with May running behind, her hand on the seat to steady the machine, and Florence's occasional violent kick of frustration at the spinning spokes as the machine fell to the ground beneath her, Florence had found her natural balance. As May left the study to go and find Florence, the sun falling in pools on the stone floor of the great hall, she knew that if there had ever been a day for bicycling this was the one.

The fields around Cuckmere Park were bisected at many points by the meanders of a

155

small river that led out to the open sea at Cuckmere Haven. One morning May and Florence had biked up onto the small rise above the house to see the winding river from above, finding themselves eyeball to eyeball with the thrice-life-size figure of a white horse sketched into the chalky hillside. Florence's new proficiency on wheels had coincided with the transformation of the rolling fields into a giant nursery. On this sunny spring day May and Florence went up onto the Downs to see the new lambs, the wool of their lithe week-old bodies like peaks of whipped egg white. Their drowsy mothers with their grey matted coats, the colour of the chalky flints that dotted the landscape around them, chewed rhythmically as beside them their lambs leapt into the air on all four legs. Florence imitated the young animals, jumping up and down on the spot like an escaped spring from a mattress. Sometimes they would tire of bouncing off the earthy mole-made hillocks and come to nuzzle at the ever ready source of milk, their catkin tails waggling as they drank. Occasionally they would lie down on the warm earth, exhausted by their own energy, kneeling first, before tucking their forelegs neatly beneath their chests. The new mothers would stand shielding the whip of the wind from the young bodies, and every so often would gently touch their mouths to their offspring in a grassy kiss. On the periphery of the fields, at the foot of the newly green hedgerows, lurked a kindergarten of young rabbits. Sentimentality was rationed and discouraged up here as May and

Florence both knew that these young innocents would eventually end up in the large copper cooking pots of the Cuckmere kitchen. But May found a beauty and a peace in this place that excelled even the memories of the sandy, wave-lapped expanses on which she had walked as a child.

★   ★   ★

A few days later May was once again working in the study. She had changed her mind entirely about agreeing to drive Julian up north. Even though she had originally gone along with his proposal, she now felt the idea to have been quite mad, partly because of the alarming prospect of spending time alone with someone so clever and so, well, so different. She had a further reservation. She belonged to a different class of society and her experience of life in England had already taught her that different classes, like different nationalities, did not mix. If she was to keep her job, she should also know her place.

May pulled the typewriter nearer. There was an urgent letter to Sir Oswald Mosley to complete, suggesting a second overnight visit. The trust between May and her boss grew daily and confidential papers passed through her typewriter daily and often without explanation.

'I was happy to discover during our enjoyable conversation recently here at Cuckmere that political differences can be laid aside most willingly when matters affecting the constitutional roots of our Nation are concerned,' Sir Philip had dictated.

Next there was a pressing call to be made to the editor of the *Daily Telegraph,* offering him a choice of dates to discuss what Sir Philip referred to as 'the American problem'. May lifted the unwieldy mouthpiece, and was about to ask the exchange operator to put her through when the instrument rang.

'Is that May?' a familiar voice asked. 'Oh, May. It *is* you. Can I come down and see you? Straight away? I have been given leave for the afternoon.'

Her brother Sam spoke with practical urgency. A mist of unreality descended as May was about to ask him why he wanted to come and yet realised she did not want to know. Not yet.

'I will take the train from Portsmouth and be with you in two hours.' And then, just before she replaced the earpiece back on its cradle, she heard his half whisper, 'I love you.'

May sat at her small desk in the corner of Sir Philip's study uncertain what to do next. She examined her hands. As usual, her fingers were covered in the inky film that rubbed off from the carbon paper. She had to use a scrubbing brush to get them properly clean. Today the sight of the smudgy ink stains did not trouble her. They felt like part of a normal working day. But still she sat, unable to get on with her work. The telephone call to the editor and the letter to Mosley would have to wait. The pile of correspondence that she had been about to reply to on Sir Philip's behalf was in front of her, skewered through the middle on the dangerous-looking letter spike on

158

the desk. The letters were a humdrum collection, typical of the Cuckmere post during the Easter parliamentary recess: early requests to attend two summer fetes in nearby villages, the weekly cigar bill. But there were also two envelopes marked 'Strictly Private', which she should put on Sir Philip's desk but she could not bring herself to move.

At least two weeks had elapsed since May had received the letter from her mother in which she expressed her contentment at the news that May and Sam had both settled into their new life.

'I have always felt sure that Nat would look after you with the loving care that my sister would have given you both,' Edith had written, sounding reassured about the welfare of her children.

May began thinking about the last time she had looked closely at her mother's face. She had been surprised to see a network of tiny lines running around her mouth and chin which, when Edith concentrated or smiled, puckered into a criss-crossed pattern like a honeycomb. How could May not have noticed that her mother was growing older? On the day of her departure from Barbados, another existence away as the Caribbean sun shone down on the Bridgetown quayside, May and her mother had tried to ignore the distant shouts.

'Anyone sailing better hurry now.'

But Sam had come dashing and panting over the gangplank and onto the jetty beside them.

'We really must get on board,' he said, looking pleadingly at May. He was wearing the uniform of the cargo ship's management, even though the Thomas sugar consignment formed only a small percentage of the total number of crates packed into the vessel. Business was tough and the plantation managers had taken to sharing cargo ships between them.

It was time to leave. May's hands were enclosed within those of her mother.

'All I want is for you to know true, enveloping happiness,' she said.

Edith's tears were on the brink of falling. Her huge grey eyes had a recently washed but not quite dried haze about them, suggesting the weeping she might have done recently and alone.

'Stay safe,' her mother whispered, pressing a tiny black velvet pouch into May's hand. 'Whenever I think of you wearing this, I will know that you are thinking of me. Stay safe, my darling girl. And look after Sam. You and Sam are more precious to me than anything.'

In the study the anglepoise lamp flickered for a moment before returning to its full strength. May stroked the silver flowers of her forget-me-not bracelet. She willed Sam to arrive. Twice she thought the moment had come. Girlish shrieks could be heard a long time before Bettina actually burst into the study. She was, she said, 'looking over *tout la terre*' for her father. May told her he had bicycled over to Beddingham to see his friend Eric Ravilious. The artist had wanted to show Sir Philip his designs for souvenir mugs, commissioned for next year's Coronation.

Bettina left May alone. No wonder her voice

drove Julian mad. He was always confiding things to May that they both knew he shouldn't. The second time the door opened it was Mrs Cage. Without actually entering the room, Mrs Cage peered round from the cover of the door and wanted to know if there was anything she could fetch May. The unusual gentleness of her tone increased May's sense of apprehension. Did Mrs Cage know something? Had she spoken first to Sam on the kitchen telephone extension?

When Sam eventually walked into Sir Philip's study, still wearing his naval volunteer's uniform with its smart white collar, May momentarily forgot her anxiety. He came straight behind the desk and held his sister close. She was the first to speak. Somehow she already knew what he had come about, even before he produced the telegram from his pocket.

'It's Mamma,' she said. He did not contradict her.

No one disturbed the brother and sister as they spent the afternoon alone together, trying to make sense of their tragedy. The telegram gave only the very basic details.

Regret to inform Sam and May Thomas. Edith Thomas drowned 21 March 1936, while swimming off Bathsheba Beach, Barbados, West Indies. R.I.P. Duncan Thomas

Over and over it all again and again they went, as if by imagining the exact circumstances and the exact manner and cause of their mother's death the fact of it would seem real. May and

Sam both knew the seductive beauty of Bathsheba beach. It had been part of the landscape of their lives. They knew the easy temptation of racing out towards the water along its sandy expanse, always deserted (and for good reason). At one end of the beach there was a dramatic rock formation, a huge stone mass, the under-part whittled away by the remorseless pounding of the sea to form a sharply defined jaw. May and Sam had often risked leaving their towels on the rock just where the scrubby trees petered out, before running towards the spray that was thrown up high into the air when the colossal waves hit the shore. But the rule had always been never to go into the water itself. The rip tides were deceptively powerful, carrying with them an undertow that was notoriously difficult to battle against. Years ago the locals had put up a huge red-and-white-painted notice to warn strangers. But the sign had become part of the landscape of the beach and the urgency of the message had faded along with the paint of the letters. No one really noticed it any more. In the absence of a witness, or any explanation from their father, they could only conclude that Edith Thomas must have been swept away in the strong current on the east coast of the island. Could their mother, who knew the power of those unpredictable waters so well, really have been so careless? Perhaps they would never know.

The talk turned briefly towards their father. What must he be feeling? His telegram, except for the one word of 'regret' had revealed nothing of his own state of mind. Would he now wish both children to return to the plantation? They would have to wait for a letter from him if they were to know more. For once May was relieved that there was no telephone at the plantation. The prohibitive expense of the installation had meant that urgent messages had instead been delivered on horseback or by May herself in the car.

Both of Edith's children had their reasons for wanting to stay in England, but neither was quite prepared to share them with the other. Sam's motives were more transparent. He was relishing a career in the Navy that was already on the ascendant. In February, the government had approved a report calling for the expansion of the Navy and Sam, until then a mere volunteer, had impressed the 'high-ups' enough to have been selected as a permanent employee of the Fleet. He was blowed if he was going to be sent back to the confines of the sugary fields of Barbados.

Sam had never discussed with May or his mother the other reason he was enjoying his new life in England. It had to do with Duncan. There was something about his father that made him recoil. On countless occasions Sam had caught him staring at May in a way that unsettled him. And then there was the time when he had burst into his parents' bedroom to see Duncan's hand raised over his mother's head, only for him to lower it as soon as Sam appeared. Although there were four members of the Thomas family Sam always felt there were only three. For some reason Duncan seemed like an outsider. He did not even look like Sam, who had inherited Edith's blonde hair. More curiously, May, with her olive skin, did not look like either of their parents but her temperament confirmed conclusively enough for Sam that she was related by blood to himself and their mother. Nothing of Duncan's abrasive nature was ever evident in his sister.

May knew she would never return to Barbados. The presence there of her father had been one deterrent. Now the absence left by her mother's death and the opportunities offered by her new life in England gave her two more. As well as the deep affection she felt for her cousins and the endless challenges and excitements of her job, there was her growing interest in one particular individual who occupied her thoughts more every day.

Eventually Sam said he wanted to walk to the river that May had told him about so often. The prospect of being by water always calmed him, and he set off, oblivious to the irony that it was water which had taken his mother from him so recently. Exhausted by trying to restrain her tears May went to lie down on her bed in Mrs Cage's house where she stroked each of the little forget-me-nots in turn as they hung on the silver chain round her wrist. At last she allowed herself to weep wildly and loudly and without control, before burying her face in the paisley quilt, soaking the edges of the silky material. Picking up her diary she pressed the blue cloth covers against her face, and knowing how her mother had held the small lined book in her own hands, she willed her mother's touch to be somehow preserved within the binding.

The storm of crying was over with the suddenness with which it had begun, and May became still, the blue book still held to her cheek. New images began to jostle for space in her thoughts and the previously sharply focused picture of her mother became suddenly elusive as memories of her father returned with a rush. Hard as she tried to will Edith to fill her thoughts, the cold touch of Duncan's ever-damp hands continued to fill her mind. She remembered how he would interrupt conversations when she was alone with her mother. He had been jealous, she now realised.

'What's going on here?' he would ask angrily, a pool of sweat gathering across the top of his forehead from which two tributaries would run down onto his nose. His long tongue would flick out through the gap in his teeth and catch the drip, his lips glistening with the moisture. 'Got all the time in the world to waste, have we? All right for some.' His ill-matched front teeth enhanced the muffling of his words.

'Secrets.' May now said the word aloud, slowly. The sound, with its snakelike consonant at beginning and end, contributed a sinister meaning to the word. Her life was littered with secrets, but the story-time nip had been the first.

Opening the blue book she turned to the pages at the back and for the hundredth time, she tried to cheer herself up by reading through a list of notes she was making for herself headed 'Qualities necessary for true love'.

1. Must not rule out short-sight, snorers or strange tastes in food.
2. Cherish and be cherished.
3. Listen as well as hear.

These initial points had been inspired by her mother, of course, but May decided that now was the time for some of her own additions. First, there were to be no secrets between her and the man she chose to marry. And secondly, she would have to find him infinitely desirable. The concept made her feel nauseous. One man's body had evoked feelings of revulsion for so long. How could the hairiness of a male body and the sensation of her skin crawling and pricking as if infected by some termite as he stroked her ever be a source of pleasure? How could she trust her own nakedness in the hands of someone so much bigger than herself? How could she be sure she would not be hurt? Her curiosity about Julian and her fascination with the beauty of his mouth was invariably eclipsed by the nightmares of those 'little nip' moments in her childhood bedroom.

Suddenly she remembered Sam and, standing up, she brushed her hair, and washed her smudged face, before going over to the house. Sam was sitting in the hallway pretending to read a newspaper, waiting for her, trying to smile a lopsided smile. She drove him to the station and clung to him on the platform before promising they would be together in Oak Street soon.

Florence was sitting in front of an empty bowl at the kitchen table when May returned, holding a spoon with the remains of Cooky's sponge-cake mixture smeared around her lips. Both plaits were in their familiar state of disarray, the coppery strands of hair escaping as ever from their loosened ribbons. Florence put her arms around May's waist and then stood on her chair so she was on the same level as May. As Florence kissed her quickly on the lips, May could taste the uncooked sponge mixture on her own mouth. The sudden, intimate, reassuring contact made her feel she could not bear to be alone any longer, so instead of returning to her room she went upstairs to see if Sir Philip had arrived home. She had made a decision about something that had been troubling her for a week. She wanted to ask Sir Philip if she might have permission to drive Julian up north.

11

During the night, Julian's bed in the Wigan boarding house had come to life beneath him. He had been warned about bedbugs and other species of vermin that sprang into action in darkness. Last night in the pub Julian had heard a story about a rat that had recently fallen through a small hole in a tenement ceiling a few streets away, landed on top of a young boy and removed a substantial chunk of flesh from his arm. The child had developed septicaemia and died shortly afterwards. Julian's eyes scanned the flaking plasterboard above him for rat-sized gaps. Meanwhile, he doubted whether the mattress beneath him, or indeed any of the other mattresses in the boarding house, had ever been cleaned and tried not to think about how many transitory bodies they had supported over the years. The stench from the canal that ran along the side of the street seeped through the barely open window. Julian tried to stop up the smell by burying his nose in his arm but the power of damp and dirt had already impregnated his skin.

As he lay on the flea-infested mixture of horsehair and foam rubber, he opened John Gunther's new book on Europe.

'Adolf Hitler, irrational, contradictory, complex, is an unpredictable character; therein lies his power and his menace,' it began.

But Julian's concentration was disturbed by

the intestinal emissions coming from the snoring occupants of the two other beds. Although his glasses lay on the floor beside him, he did not reach for them. He preferred for now to leave the detail of his surroundings in soft focus. What would the new King make of the sights of Wigan? Julian wondered. As Prince of Wales, Edward had been so unexpectedly concerned with the underdog and had been applauded for his genuine empathy with the British people. Lady Alexandra Metcalfe, a frequent dinner-party guest at Hamilton Terrace, who with her husband Fruity knew the King well, had spoken of how the King had on more than one occasion shared a beer with out-of-work men in the makeshift bar of an abandoned church crypt. Had this pleasure-loving American woman stoppered up the King's concern for suffering? The confrontation at that dreadful dinner party had left Julian sceptical of the worthiness of the man who for such a short time had occupied the throne. Julian liked to think he would never understand someone who put personal feelings in front of moral principle. Of course, the best thing would be if the two sides of the argument could merge but Julian was uncertain in what circumstances that might occur. He wondered for a moment whether he dared risk discussing all this with May before remembering how, not long ago, Philip had emphasised to him and Rupert how important it was not to speak about that dinner to anyone, including the servants. Delicate negotiations with the national news-paper editors had so far ensured that Mrs

Simpson's name had been kept out of the British papers. The government had agreed to do all they could to keep it that way.

'Best to keep one's trap shut until things die down or, if we are lucky, fizzle out,' Philip had said with a little knowing tap of his forefinger on the side of his nose.

'What with all the other problems facing the government both at home with Mosley's fascists as well as abroad with Germany and now the potential for revolution deepening in Spain, the Prime Minister does not want any . . . ah . . . um . . . *complicated* personal relationship sending jitters through a public that is just settling down to the idea of a new, modern and popular monarch on the throne.' Looking over the top of his glasses he asked if he had made himself clear.

'Perfectly, Sir,' the two friends had replied in unison.

★　★　★

That morning Julian's main worry however was not politics, bed bugs nor the love life of the King but the welfare of May. She was only a flight of stairs away in the cramped room usually occupied by the landlady's three daughters but he felt as if an entire terrace of houses might be between them. Julian tried to imagine May wrapped up in his spare, grey-flannel shirt, probably the cleanest garment in the whole place. He smiled at the thought of the sleeves of his shirt enfolding her naked body. Julian shifted

170

his weight in the bed, pushing the sleeping figure that lay beside him clean off the mattress and onto the floor where it just missed toppling a nearly full chamber pot. Without a word the still-drowsy man climbed back into bed and resumed his sleep.

As he had explained to May when he asked her to drive him to Wigan, Julian had hoped that a few days in the North would show him something of the poverty in which, so he had read, a third of Britain's city dwellers lived. But he was beginning to think it was perhaps not as simple as that.

May's scepticism had been quite obvious in the car on the way up. 'Do you really think you are going to understand what it is like to be poor by walking around a few streets and seeing a bit of dirt?' she had asked him.

'Well, it's a start isn't it?' he had replied, taken aback by her implicit criticism.

'You may think so,' she said with a shake of her head. 'But from what I see of being poor in Bethnal Green it will take a lifetime to really understand what it means to go without. I should introduce you to our neighbours there. Ten children crammed into two bedrooms with the parents sharing the settee downstairs, and the mother wondering every morning which half of the family she is going to be able to give any tea to that day. Mind you it's not all gloom. On the contrary. I think you would be surprised by how people keep up their spirits. On our plantation we had to lay off people when orders dwindled or the rains had failed to nourish the sugar cane. But they rarely complained. 'God will provide', they used to say. That's the mistake some people make, I think. They forget 'the poor' are not just some statistic to cause concern to well-off do-gooders, charities and the government.'

Julian had not answered. A memory of something his mother had told him years ago had returned to him with a thump of guilt. He had not forgotten a single detail of the story she had recounted more with amusement than pride. Before the war Mrs Richardson had travelled down south from her home in Yorkshire to visit a school friend whose wealthy parents lived in London. To fill in the long aimless periods between one evening party and the next the two young women had on a couple of occasions ventured in the family carriage into the East End. Two large wicker baskets containing thermoses of hearty carrot soup had been packed into the back of the carriage by the butler. For several hours the two friends had taken up their positions in a small room in the Bethnal Green Town Hall and distributed soup to the hungry and destitute of the area.

'I think the women appreciated us coming,' she said, 'though I certainly never considered slumming as my vocation. Nasty dirty work. Smelly too!'

'Slumming?'

'Yes, slumming. That's what we called it. Good description, don't you think?'

Appalled as Julian was by the memory of the smug superiority of his mother's tone of voice, a tiny suspicion that he might be about to embark

172

on a variation of the same sort of behaviour occurred to him. He dismissed the thought. The visit to Wigan was surely to be one of genuine information gathering, not the action of a self-satisfied hypocrite like his mother. He had Sir Philip to thank for making the trip possible.

'Excellent idea, my dear chap. I would like to hear your report. And what a good opportunity to give Rupert's car its inaugural outing,' Sir Philip had said with a smile at once regretful and grateful.

The pale-blue Talbot had been bought by Rupert's parents for his birthday nearly a year ago and was still sitting in the Cuckmere garage. Rupert had not yet got round to learning to drive it.

'I will ask Hooch to give the engine a once over and it will suit the two of you beautifully.'

Entrusting May with the new car was the Blunts' way of expressing how fond of her they had all become. Julian had seen the sympathy that the whole family felt for their young employee with the loss of her mother, and at a time when she and her brother were so far away from their remaining parent. Every one of them, even Bettina and Rupert, had been kindness itself to May. And Joan had put her own grief to one side and concentrated on looking after this motherless young woman.

Julian's response to May was becoming complicated. He had a tendency to vacillate over his friendships with women, enjoying the challenge of netting a woman and once netted, dropping her. And although this pattern of behaviour shamed

173

him, he had unquestionably been playing with the emotions of the young chauffeuse. May's huge eyes and unusual olive-toned skin intrigued him; but he was forever reminding himself that everything pointed against pursuing these thoughts further. Firstly there was a professional boundary to respect regarding her employment with the Blunts. Neither Sir Philip nor Lady Joan had actually said anything to caution him about becoming over-friendly with their driver, but Julian did not want to put them in a position where they felt they should comment. Secondly, while Julian had no pretensions to being socially superior to May, given his own parents' modest start in life, there was no denying his educational advantages. And finally there was the existence, even obstacle, of his steady girlfriend Charlotte. No. There was no question about it. May was hopelessly unsuitable as a romantic proposition. And yet. Despite her sweetness and willingness she sometimes demonstrated a steely confidence in her own opinions that made him like her all the more. She had certainly made him question his glib assumption that the visit to Wigan would deliver the experience and information he sought. Observing her capability at the wheel of Rupert's spanking motor, her forehead creased in concentration, it had struck him that 'deft' was the best possible word to describe her. But 'deft' as she may have been, he could not stop thinking how nice it would be to kiss her.

* * *

When Julian had planned the journey around the mining towns between Liverpool and Manchester he had not anticipated that the local mayoral entourage would be in town for a football match and staying in the only halfway decent hotel in Wigan. Mayoral influence was too big for its boots, he had spluttered to the receptionist when told that the two single rooms he had reserved were no longer available. It had been getting late and he was on the point of panic when May said she didn't mind, just for one night, where they ended up.

Relieved by her lack of fuss, Julian had taken May for a pint in the pub to work out what they should do next. They had fallen into a conversation with a man who was sitting at a table sticky with beer rings near the bar. With his short hair, small moustache and direct-gazing eyes, he appeared to be ten years or so older than Julian but looked quite different from any of the other careworn men in the pub. He introduced himself. His name was Peter Grimshaw. He was a professor of social history at London University and they soon discovered that he had read all the same books as Julian. The conversation went straight to politics. Peter told them he had come up to the North a couple of months earlier with a writer friend, Eric Blair, who was researching a book of his own about poverty in the North and had spent a despairing if illuminating (if that was the word) time down the mines. When Eric returned to London Peter had stayed on, gathering information for a paper he planned to deliver to his colleagues and students and eventually to write up and publish.

When Julian explained their predicament about where to stay the night, Peter offered to take them back to his own lodgings.

'Matter of fact, Eric and I both stayed there. They aren't up to much but the landlady seems to enjoy cramming as many people as possible into her house so maybe she can sort something out for you two, just for a night.'

★ ★ ★

After an uncomfortable night, Julian had woken up to feel Peter's toes nudging his shoulders beneath the filthy blanket. At least the warmth of another human body was some comfort in the freezing air and he hoped the combination of his shirt and the threadbare coverlet on the landlady's daughters' bed would provide something of the same for May. She had not baulked when the woman showed her the downstairs room that passed for accommodation. In better days the room must have served as a parlour because a piano was wedged up against a wall, its shape just visible beneath sheets of old newspaper. As luck would have it, the landlady explained, her daughters were away on a visit to some cousins in the countryside.

'Mind you,' the woman had cautioned. 'It's just for one night. You, young man, can go top to toe with Pete. If my girls pedal hard they will be back by tomorrow nightfall and I want you both gone by then.'

Julian had assured the landlady, Peter, and in

particular May, that they would both be gone first thing in the morning. He and May had planned to spend a few more days in Wigan and he wanted those precious days to unfold in lodgings more suitable for them both. Soon he would have to return to Oxford for his last summer term. He was not looking forward to the prospect of such finality. The weeks would be dominated by exams and by his own pressure on himself to excel. He felt unnerved by the uncertainties involved in leaving a town where he enjoyed an unprecedented sense of belonging. Although the undergraduate content changed so frequently, Oxford had bestowed on Julian and on almost every member of its shifting student body an easy and privileged connection to the place. He felt apprehensive at the thought of leaving the familiar little doors set within the large wooden entrace gates of the colleges, the innumerable grassy quadrangles, the layers of bicycles, leaning one against the other at the entrance to the courtyard of the Bodleian library, and the billowing black gowns, which when swollen by a sudden belch of wind gave the wearer his wizard-like silhouette.

Despite the stability of his surroundings, Julian's undergraduate mind was in a constant whirl. He was unable to work out exactly what he thought, what he felt, what he believed in, or even, latterly, whom he loved. First there was his degree. He had originally thought himself suited to the combined disciplines of philosophy, politics and economics. But latterly he had begun to question whether he was taking his studies seriously *enough*. He had an uneasy feeling that he was spreading himself thinly and not mastering the depth of any of them. That term T. S. Eliot had come to read some of his poems to the English Club. A little stunned to realise he had been sitting in the same room as a literary genius, Julian had later wondered whether he might find the greater truths of life in literature instead.

He was also troubled by the world's political polarity. Fascism was penetrating not only the furthest corners of Germany but was now flooding into the rest of Europe, enveloping countries as fast as a street becomes submerged beneath a burst water main. Maybe communism offered the only viable line of defence.

He could not understand the obduracy of the privileged classes with whom he mixed in refusing to acknowledge the reality of the German threat. The idea promoted especially by the Prime Minister and the Chancellor Neville Chamberlain of appeasing Hitler's Germany, a country still highly angered by the viciousness of the punishment it had received at the end of the Great War, seemed short-sighted and frankly unrealistic. And judging by that terrible exchange at the Bryanston Court dinner, the new King seemed as complicit in screening out the truth as the rest of them. Indeed, Julian had heard during the occasional private asides at Cuckmere with Evangeline that senior members of the Nazi party were sometimes invited to cocktails at Wallis's flat, when the King also happened to be present.

Evangeline had formed a breathy habit of

whispering nuggets of sensitive information in his ear while begging Julian to keep these confidences to himself. And while recoiling at the manner in which he acquired it, and annoyed that whenever he was alone in the library Evangeline would invariably appear, Julian remained fascinated by the information she passed on to him. Tucking herself close to him on the sofa, the not unpleasant smell of chocolate suddenly released into the air, she would lay her hand on his knee before hissing, 'Glad to find a moment when we can be alone. I have something to tell you.'

The detailed gossip that she delivered about life at Fort Belvedere, even down to the menus, interested him less than her inadvertent revelations about the hypocrisy of the King. The impression that he gave to the majority of the British people of minding more about their welfare than he did about his own was a falsehood that enraged Julian. The King appeared to care about one thing only, and she was not even British. Voltaire's two-hundred-year-old assessment of Louis XV that kings always deceive their peoples described Britain's new monarch perfectly, he thought.

Socialism was the dominant aphrodisiac in Julian's life, he concluded as he shifted his weight on the dirty Wigan mattress. Friendships with men, women, and even potential lovers, especially Lottie, took second place. At times he questioned whether he had ever properly loved anyone at all. Last week he had endured yet another uncomfortable lunch at his mother's

London flat. The reheated beef stew and a spoonful of tepid, lumpy mashed potatoes made him swear for the thousandth time that he would never repeat the experience. The absurd grandeur of Mrs Richardson's dining table with its white lace cloth, thick linen napkins and ebony blackamoors holding little saucers of salt aloft clashed with the standard of the food placed upon it. Yesterday, Julian had noted the absence of the usual jellied potted meat with relief. Going on past practice he had expected his mother to offer him a slice of what was almost certainly cat food, in her predictable attempts at economising for her son's visits.

'A little pâté, darling?' she would enquire as they sat down to the hideous meal, a lit cigarette in the holder that was as familiar to her mouth as cheddar to a mouse-trap.

The atmosphere in the sitting room was, if anything, worse than the dining room. The affectations of his mother's crocheted antimacassar on the back of the armchair, her Du Maurier in its little holder, which she puffed at distastefully, as if blowing into some sort of respiratory device, and her anti-Semitic, class-obsessing topics of conversation all coalesced to make Julian feel like screaming.

The phrase 'airs above her station' was one he had occasionally heard Cooky utter under her breath when Mrs Cage had left the room. The same phrase might have been invented for his mother, who had inherited her few fancy possessions from a distant cousin who had lived his life as an heirless bachelor.

The conversation between Julian and his mother rarely deviated from three topics: how she never saw enough of her only son; how difficult it was to make ends meet; and the Royal family. Extinguishing her cigarette before immediately lighting another, Mrs Richardson would mention the same long-dead cousin who had worked briefly as junior equerry for the last King, the connection apparently giving her licence to make judgements as if she were an intimate of the ruling family.

'I do think it is a pity that the King must wait so long for the actual Coronation. He must feel quite in limbo. I am convinced he is dying to walk around with that crown on his head!' she had observed last week.

'Don't be ridiculous, Mother,' Julian snapped but on she went, lighting another cigarette and positioning it securely in the dainty holder.

'You may think I am ridiculous but someone in my position has a good idea of how he must feel.'

And with that she got up to fetch an ashtray, a mist of Chanel No. 5 following her into the kitchen, the Duchess of York's favourite scent so her cousin had once divulged in the strictest of confidence. Julian remained at the table, trying not to react to his mother's habit of walking away whenever she heard something she did not like but knew to be true. Even if Philip had not asked him to keep the account of Mrs Simpson's dinner to himself, Julian would never have given his mother the satisfaction of hearing it. His mother's irritability was based partly on

181

her suspicion that Julian concealed from her the details of a life that she would have given her eye-teeth to hear about.

Julian never spoke to Mrs Richardson about his father either. When the irascible but heroic country doctor had married the prettiest and most spoiled girl in the North Yorkshire village where he had grown up, it had been a surprise to everyone who knew him. Dr Richardson's bride, one Margaret Cottesley, only wanted one thing in life, and that was 'position' (still her favourite word) and she was prepared to marry whoever came along, irrespective of age, looks, and character, in order to get it. For the one and only time in her life, Miss Cottesley had applied the powers of female seduction to her target and won. The truth was she had never loved her husband, although she kept that information to herself.

Julian knew all this past history from his old headmaster, Mr Bellington, his father's closest friend. Newly qualified after passing his medical exams with first class honours, Julian's father had decided not to go into practice as a GP but to follow an academic career instead. The two years he had spent teaching at Balliol College, in the convivial and stimulating company of Bellington and other clever men and boys, had been the happiest of his life. Even Dr Richardson's tiresome wife seemed content enough, basking in the invitations to cocktail parties that North Oxford enjoyed giving on most days of the week.

The outbreak of war in 1914 had meant that

Dr Richardson left his teaching post to become a medic in the trenches where, with instinctive calm and professionalism, he treated injuries so dreadful that no amount of training could have prepared him for. It was this spirit of getting things done in situations at which others had balked that had compelled him, just after Armistice Day, to take the lift down one of the local mine-shafts to help release a miner buried beneath a sudden coal fall. Inching his way out from beneath the sooty mass of fallen rocks, encouraged by reassuring words from the doctor, the trapped man finally emerged. As he leant across a small precipice, clinging to the doctor's hand below him, he made one final and successful leap to safety. But the agitation of the rock had dislodged another huge section of the coalface, which fell directly on top of the doctor, killing him instantly. The rich and philanthropic owner of the mine, on hearing of the accident, had put into trust a sum of money to cover the education of the doctor's three-year-old son, up to and including university fees, as well as a small allowance to permit Julian to concentrate on his studies without the distraction of financial worries. Julian's mother was prohibited from touching her son's settlement but would be taken care of by her widow's pension.

The widowed Mrs Richardson had never remarried, even though she had once made an undisguised play for her husband's old friend Mr Bellington, who had moved to Yorkshire after the War and become the headmaster of the local school. But Mrs Richardson's clumsy attempts at seduction backfired. The combination of an inappropriately low-cut blouse and a blatantly hollow bluff that she could use her 'position' to get a minor member of the royal family to 'grace', as she put it, the school sports day, had repulsed Dr Richardson's old Balliol friend. The headmaster's lingering contempt for Mrs Richardson surfaced during a lengthy farewell conversation in his study with Julian at the end of Julian's final term. Urging the young man to become a credit to his much missed and much-admired father, Mr Bellington had indicated that Julian's mother was a considerably less worthy parent. In that one conversation Julian's respect for his mother was given the final death sentence. He wished he had been lucky enough to have a mother like Joan Blunt, despite her fragility of mind. He had seen something reminiscent of her heart-breaking pain in the club in Pall Mall where he sometimes went for a drink with Rupert and Sir Philip. Hunched up in leather armchairs beside the fireplace, old soldiers lay lost in the reverie of their War, their minds filled with pictures of a destruction too dreadful to forget, and yet too awful to speak of.

Julian would escape from Mrs Richardson's cramped courtyard flat in Victoria as soon as he could and walk quickly towards the river. Sometimes he would jump on a passing bus and find that he had reached St Katherine's Docks way down the Thames in the East End. There he would see small groups of men standing together, leaning against a warehouse wall, not in a comradely way but more as if each one was waiting for something to happen, someone to arrive, and someone to offer them a job, and a bit of a life. Sometimes Julian went into a pub, ordered a glass of neat whisky ('That's right, lad, why ruin it with water?') and handed over tuppence for a packet of Woodbines before sitting down in a corner, his hat pulled down over his eyes. This vital place was a welcome contrast from the throttling atmosphere of Julian's mother's flat. In the pub, the chat was as real as the clashing smells of pipe smoke and sweat. Boxing was a popular topic. Success or failure on the horses was another. Bad practice at the pawnbroker was a familiar point of discussion. Cigarettes were inhaled deeply; royalty was acknowledged but not glorified. Mosley was condemned. War was feared.

Before arriving at Oxford, Julian had barely given *real* life a thought, freewheeling his way through a minor public school, courtesy of the charitable mine owner, wearing a nice flannel suit and playing a lot of cricket and a lot of football. Oxford had changed everything though. He had at last begun to ask questions. And Oxford challenged him to decide whether to devote himself to pleasure or to principle. Choosing to abdicate from a *duty* to do the right thing by society seemed increasingly to Julian to be the wrong option.

He had met Rupert Blunt on the first day of his first week of his first term at Oxford. Freshmen together, both undergraduates were in the university outfitters in Broad Street trying on their College gowns. The obsequious salesman

185

was trying to convince them both to buy a tailcoat.

'Delightful young men such as yourselves are *destined* to be invited to all the most important formal occasions in university life,' the salesman flattered transparently. Rupert rolled his eyes at Julian behind the man's back and they left the shop together without making any further purchases. Rupert, an old Etonian, already owned a tail coat from his schooldays and Julian could not have afforded to buy one even if he had wanted to, which he did not. But a friendship between the two men had been established there in Broad Street. Rupert was a generous-minded young man and enjoyed sharing his privileges with his clever new friend. Halfway through that first Michaelmas term he invited Julian to stay at Cuckmere for a weekend.

'My father is an MP and I know you and he would get on like the blazes, what with you being so obsessed with politics.'

Rupert had been right. Sir Philip Blunt had taken to Julian immediately, as had his wife, who was touched by the way Julian welcomed the maternal advice and encouragement that her own children rejected. Once a month, sometimes more, Julian had gone with Rupert to stay at the lovely grey flint house in Sussex. With his charming manners and eagerness to learn, as well as the respect and admiration he demonstrated for his friend's parents, Julian had been unofficially adopted by the Blunt family and the household that served it. Julian sometimes felt he had landed in clover. Rupert's parents fulfilled

186

for him all that Voltaire's 'best of all possible worlds' promised.

However, there were aspects of his friendship with Rupert that made Julian uneasy. A life formulated on self-indulgence was surely a wasted life, Julian argued with Rupert and his Bullingdon Club contemporaries, who uniformly believed that life was too short to devote to anyone but oneself and one's friends. The group of undergraduates who lived in spartan digs in a house at Beaumont Street near the Randolph Hotel represented a tempting intellectual stratosphere frustratingly far from Julian's reach. After poetry recitals and talks at the English Club, where Julian had shaken hands with members of this cerebrally rigorous crowd, he would return to the comfortable rooms he shared with Rupert feeling inadequate and angry, convinced he was squandering his Oxford years on inconsequences and misplaced values.

And then there were the girls. Julian's girlfriend Charlotte Bellowes was two years younger than Julian, lived in London and was in the middle of her coming-out year. She had confessed to him that she wasn't mad about books: 'take them or leave them', was her view. She and Julian had kissed of course, mainly at coming-out parties in deserted billiard rooms, in long galleries in which ancestral portraits hung beneath gilded ceilings or in the large darkened gardens of smart London houses that belonged to the parents of her fellow debutantes. Once they had found a derelict tennis court at the back of a huge Kensington mansion, and that night, after a great deal of pink champagne, Julian had been allowed to run his hand along the smooth stretch of thigh that emerged from the cuff of Charlotte's silk cami-knickers. It had been like plunging into a pool of melted chocolate.

Everyone agreed that Charlotte or Lottie, as her friends called her, was frightfully pretty. But there was something missing in the conversations Julian had with her. He had tried to discuss with her this ever-recurring feeling of guilt as they ate cucumber sandwiches in the Palm Court of the Ritz. But the subject invariably reverted to the next social engagement and to the people who might be invited to attend. To tell the truth, he was bored by her. Lottie didn't even like going to the movies, pronouncing cinemas to be a hot bed of germs, smelling of vinegar and chips. Chips were Julian's favourite food. One day he would find someone to love who also shared his passion for chips. And if she didn't, he would somehow make her.

He longed to actually go to bed with Lottie but the prospect was out of the question. Apart from the moment on the tennis court referred to half-jokingly by Lottie as 'Lottie's Lapse', she had once allowed Julian to bury his face in her neck although he had not enjoyed the experience very much. The bitter smell of her skin surprised him by reminding him of his mother. Lottie had anyhow made it clear that she drew a line at the point where her pretty emerald necklace settled in the hollow of her collarbone and Julian did not object. Once after another cocktail too many

Lottie had slumped against Julian on a pink velvet sofa in a Belgravia Square drawing room and admitted that her mother had told her that not only did 'it' hurt quite a lot but that the whole sticky rigmarole was frankly overrated.

If Julian had been older and married, the option of sleeping with another woman would never have arisen. Everyone did it. And even the older single man was able to pursue his options within the legions of bored, cooperative wives that glittered and littered the aristocratic drawing rooms of Britain. How had it come about that the older generation had it easy while Julian's own younger frustrated age group were compelled to wait?

Sometimes Julian wondered if he would ever acquire the expertise to become a good lover. The undergraduate women at Oxford, their never-quite-clean hair invariably pinned back to reveal proboscises developed for snouting out fact and never poetry, were universally unappealing. The idea of going to London and paying a tart for the experience did not attract him, although he did kick himself for not having answered the knock on his bedroom door at Cuckmere Park last weekend. Lady Bridgewater, the American wife of a senior member of the Cabinet, and at fifty-seven still lovely in a faded sort of way, had squeezed his knee most enticingly under the table at dinner. But Rupert had succumbed to a similar squeeze only recently, and even though Rupert had assured him the experience was a bit of a letdown, Julian did not feel like comparing first-time notes, good or bad, with Rupert.

Reflecting on his misplaced behaviour with Evangeline during that awful evening at Bryanston Court, he was annoyed that he had half-intentionally led her on. He could not think what had got into him. She was almost old enough to be his mother, although she seemed quite unbothered by the difference in their ages, her gauche behaviour suggesting she was quite innocent of any physical experience of love (or should he say lust) although God knows, by her age Evangeline must surely have had dozens of lovers. He kicked himself that on first sight of the overweight middle-aged woman in the unflattering and revealing dress he had tried to conceal his revulsion by making his usual mistake of going too far the other way and flirting with her. As soon as his fateful wink prompted that look of eager desperation Julian knew it would lead to trouble.

Rather to his relief, Lottie had been unable to come on the Easter expedition to the North of England. There was a stubbornness about her when she made up her mind. She had a dress fitting, she informed him, and two amusing-sounding tea parties already written into her engagement diary. And anyway, she had heard so often from Julian of his determination to see life in those northern towns and felt it might not be her cup of tea; she was bound to be a nuisance and get in the way. Far better that he borrowed May, the Blunts' driver, who would not interrupt, knew her place and would let Julian concentrate on everything he wanted to find out about up in the North, whatever it was. As the suggestion that May should drive him there had actually come from Lottie, who saw no threat in a servant joining her sweetheart on such a trip, Julian felt quite guiltless when he agreed with Lottie that it was an inspired solution.

12

The trip up North had begun with a minor catastrophe for May. In her anxiety to make sure the car was properly packed, she had left her overnight case behind. Julian could not guess what was so wrong, as his intriguing young companion fell silent. An uneven flush, an unruly series of blotches, was spreading upwards from May's collarbone. He had an awful feeling she was on the point of tears.

'Do you want to confess? Have you silently run over anything? Oh I am so sorry. Not funny. Sorry.'

May reddened even more.

'I have left my overnight bag behind.'

For a moment they were both silent.

And then Julian remembered he had two spare shirts. 'You can have one of them. We will buy a toothbrush and some soap. And after all, it is only for a few nights.'

What an idiot she was, she had told him. But she had accepted his old shirt and reported the next morning that she had slept better than she had for many days.

The three young people chose to have their breakfast in a nearby café rather than at the grubby linoleum kitchen table in the boarding house with its bottle of Worcester sauce, piles of ancient crumbs, and unidentifiable slops of liquid on its greasy oilcloth. Over a cup of tea and a slice of bread, Peter said he was intending to accompany his friend Eric to Spain before the year was out. Despite the short span of their acquaintance, Peter's passion for the cause made his invitation to Julian to join them sound persuasive. The Communist party could do with all the help it could get against the right-wingers, Peter told him eagerly. If Julian thought the mining industry was in trouble over here he should also take a first-hand look at the working conditions in Spain. A major conflict over there was not only inevitable but also imminent. Peter wanted to be there to record it and Julian assured him he would think seriously about his proposition.

As they left the stifling heat of the brightly lit café, thanking Peter and wishing him well with his research and the writing of his paper, they adjusted their eyes to the darkness outside. Both were in a jaunty mood as turning the corner, they were confronted with what looked like a giant orange gobstopper balanced on a tall black pole. Julian recognised the Belisha beacon at once. The Transport Minister, Mr Hore-Belisha, was a parliamentary friend of Sir Philip's and had stayed at Cuckmere the preceding summer just after the first beacon had gone up. He had joked to Julian that pedestrians had at last won their independence from the tyranny of cars.

'You are witnessing an historic landmark of the future,' Julian assured May in an exaggeratedly dramatic voice.

But May was looking bored.

'I thought you would be interested what with

you being a car buff,' he said in a tone of mock hurt.

'Interested in lamps on sticks? You must be mad. Anyway, I've seen them before. They're all over the place. You notice things like that when you drive a car, you know.'

She spoke in such a robust way that Julian burst out laughing at his pomposity. And then May laughed too. Together they walked through the streets, their carefree mood evaporating as they became conscious of the curiosity they invited in passers-by with their clean, neat clothes and their healthy, well-fed cheeks. At first the greyness and despair that Julian had anticipated seemed to be everywhere. Row upon row of identical buildings, built back to back, stretched out in front of them. Washing lines hung in the backyards, on which newly washed clothes were flapping, already grubby from air that tasted bitter with coal dust. Gutters were full of discarded crusts and tea-leaves. Miniature cemeteries crowded out flowerbeds that must once have brought some brightness to the front gardens.

May heard Julian's indrawn breath. A man was hunched against a wall for support, coughing the life out of his guts, gasping and heaving between each spasm. A sailor was crossing the road, carrying a parrot on his arm, the blue-and-green plumage of the ragged bird muffled as if it had been dipped in muddy water. A small boy flinched in the doorway of a shop, as a woman raised her fist, lowering it as soon as she noticed she was being watched, her anger temporarily thwarted from making contact with its target. Bunched up at the street corners, and standing outside the high iron-grilled factory gates, groups of men smoked, huddled together in twos and threes, their caps dragged well down over their eyes, their jacket collars pulled up firmly to their necks, the top button done up. Every moment or two one of them would suck in his cheeks, before landing a globule of foamy spit on the pavement.

'These men and two and a quarter million more cannot find work,' Julian said more to himself than May, shaking his head.

But May was not listening. She was looking at a man whose face was so ingrained with coal that it seemed that no amount of washing could ever remove the stains. May smiled at him, her gesture returned with an expression that lit up the young man's face, his smile revealing white teeth that dazzled in contrast to his sooty lips.

'For a moment that boy reminded me of my brother,' she said, smiling once again at the thought, as she and Julian walked on. 'Same sort of age, I think.'

And as they both looked more closely they began to see that among the scenes of hopelessness there was an intense vitality to these streets. Groups of shoeless children were playing near the steps of the houses, jumping, hula-hooping and chasing one another around the cold hard pavements with as much abandon as the children May had watched playing on the powdery sand of her island home. Women stood in animated conversation, sharing grudges and gossip, their arms tightly folded over their dingy aprons. Some knelt, their backs rounded over a pail of sudsy water, or squatted with a brush, demonstrating their pride in producing the most gleaming of thresholds. A couple of women were turning a skipping rope, their chatter uninterrupted by the children who hopped over the whirling arc between them. Two little girls were absorbed by something in the sky directly above them and, following their gaze, May and Julian made out a vapour trail emerging from the tail of a high-flying aeroplane, as it formed the word OXO in blurry white letters.

Julian closed his eyes as shame began to creep over him. What had he been expecting to gain by this cursory visit north? On the way up he had tried to defend the research-based purpose of the visit to May. His own words returned to him now and he regretted them. Over breakfast May had told Peter about some of the families who lived in her cousins' neighbourhood in East London. The children, many of whom had so little, played together and laughed together as if the riches of the world were theirs. Women who spent back-bending hours of the day cleaning and cooking and doing their best to manage viewed life with a cheerfulness that was instinctive, infectious. And men, even though unemployment meant they struggled to maintain their natural place in the hierarchy of society by providing for their families, were rarely beaten entirely. May's ability to look beneath the superficial was unmistakable. Her insight startled him.

That evening the mayor had moved on and two single rooms had become available in the hotel. Julian suggested they go out to a film and a plate of fish and chips afterwards. As Popeye, the spinach-eating sailor appeared on the cinema screen accompanied by his hoop-eyebrowed girlfriend, May was unable to suppress a shout.

'That's it! It's *her*! Different body but same face!'

'Who?' hissed Julian, taken aback by the little outburst.

'Tell you later,' she promised.

But later Julian had forgotten to ask her why she had laughed so much at the sight of Olive Oyl, although he did notice that May pushed the chips to one side of her plate, leaving them uneaten. By an unspoken agreement they did not dwell on the sights and experiences of the day they had just spent together. Both sensed a need to leave the subject alone for a while. Instead, May wanted to know about Julian's life in Oxford. She had glimpsed that beautiful city once from the window of a coach, she told him, and longed to visit it again properly. Julian told her how his father had taught at the University, how Matthew Arnold's dreaming spires, instead of sending him to sleep, had woken his mind, and how long hours in the Bodleian library raced by as he read everything he could lay his hands on. Locke and Berkeley and other writers May had never heard of seemed to be speaking directly to him, he said, although he couldn't get on with Kant. And for that matter he was having a hard time getting on with his flatmate.

'Rupert is a member of a club called the Bullingdon,' he told May. 'God alone knows what they all get up to except drink and eat and demolish as much precious property as possible. About ten years ago club members smashed up nearly five hundred windows in Peckwater Quad at Christ Church. They are a bunch of vacuous, spoiled, snobbish, stupid idiots,' he said, suddenly furious. 'And what's more, their current hero is Oswald Mosley, the fascist leader, one of the most wrong-headed men in Britain. God knows where it is all going to lead.'

'Why on earth do you share a flat with Rupert?' May wanted to know.

'I sort of fell into it,' Julian admitted. 'The truth is I am annoyed with myself for not having ended the arrangement. Too late now, though. But that's my trouble. I say I will do things and I mean it when I say it, but then the motivation slips away. But I do rate his parents. Especially her. Poor Joan. She worries so much about Rupert. She deplores all that right-wing talk.'

Julian changed the subject.

'Tell me about you,' he said to May. 'What sort of place did you grow up in? What do the West Indies look like? I know nothing about that part of the world.'

May needed no more prompting. She began to tell Julian of the monkeys who hung from their stringy arms in the trees around the plantation, waiting for the right moment to sneak a banana from the lunch table. She spoke of the rustling sound made by the wind that whispered its way up and down the green swaying sugar cane. She told of the brilliance of the new growth of the cane, the colour of crushed peas, and described the way she would peel the waxy skin from the stalks and suck out the sweet sticky juice. She spoke of the markets held in village squares, where the country people would come, balancing baskets on their heads packed high and tight with shiny avocadoes, olive- and coral-coloured mangoes, lemons still attached to their leafy branches, shiny green peppers and moon-crescent-shaped chillies. And without mentioning her mother, or the accident, May told him about the island's deserted beaches, which lay below cliffs lined with scrawny hawthorn trees, bent almost double by years of storms that had tried to dislodge them from their precarious footholds. Finally, when she began to describe the sea itself, in all its mesmeric, ceaseless, churning, dangerous, deep-blue beauty she fell silent, floored by the power of her memories.

When May came to the end, her eyes shining as bright as seawater, Julian gazed at her.

'Thank you,' he said, eventually. 'That was so lovely. *You* are lovely.'

★ ★ ★

Julian and May had stayed on in Wigan for two more days and when the time came to leave Julian had learned something, but not the lesson he had been expecting. Instead of the mixture of detached, analytical pity that he had anticipated as the legacy of his visit to the North, he was instead conscious of something more elusive,

199

more humbling and more valuable. He felt chastised by his self-importance.

During the long drive back Julian struggled to work out how he should respond to the preceding days. Something of his old confused thinking returned as he tight-roped between a sequence of intellectual and emotional choices. Maybe he could volunteer to teach at a local school once his exams were out of the way, to which May had ventured, 'Well now, that *is* an idea.'

'Education is everything,' he said, adding in a lighter voice, 'perhaps we should bring the King back with us on our next trip?' Between them, he suggested, they could dissuade the King from looking at Germany for answers, and force him to concentrate on the problems at home.

'He might hear us but do you think he would really be *listening*?' Julian asked her with a hard little laugh, not expecting a reply.

With May's prompting he talked about the Great War. He was studying its cause and effect as part of his degree. The economist Maynard Keynes predicted dreadful consequences to the harshly punitive treaty with Germany that had ended the four years of conflict. The trouble is, Julian explained, off on one of his rambles, that however hard you try to dissolve patriotism with the other ingredients of an emotional stew, it always floats to the top, just like grease finding its way to the surface of a meat broth. There were still so many older people alive who believed that it was a glorious thing to die for one's country. In Julian's view it was madness.

He looked at May. Her eyes were on the road ahead of her but the occasional affirmative nod confirmed that she was concentrating on what he was saying. He went on. An Oxford friend was being taught economics by a don who had once slept with Keynes and pronounced him ('only out of bed, mind you') to be the most terrifying of that group of artists and writers and thinkers who called themselves the Bloomsbury Group. The leader of the bunch was Virginia Woolf, writer of luminous, poetic prose and, with James Joyce, one of the most innovative novelists the century had so far seen.

'I have heard her speak on the wireless. She has a beautiful voice,' he said, clearly impressed by the woman. 'And come to think of it, she also has a beautiful face, judging by the photographs I have seen of her.'

Julian's offer to lend May his copy of Woolf's novel *Mrs Dalloway* was accepted at once although May did not mention she had met Virginia Woolf on several occasions. The well-known writer and feminist lived in the village of Rodmell near Cuckmere Park and May had driven Mrs Cage over there several times for lunch with her friend, Mrs Woolf's cook. Mrs Woolf was always most courteous to May on these visits. Usually she was busy putting on her hat and about to leave for the train to London but she never failed to ask May questions about herself.

'I have a terribly nosy habit of wanting to know every detail about everyone,' she had confided with a laugh, 'especially someone with an exotic life like yours.'

May thought Julian quite right to have remarked on Mrs Woolf's beauty. She had been struck by that long, elegant face and also by the movement of her large yet graceful hands as they adjusted the angle of her hat. Julian rattled off some more names associated with this illustrious bunch of writers and painters and thinkers but when he reached Morgan Forster, May stopped him. *A Passage to India* had been one of her mother's favourite books. And in this round-about way the conversation arrived at May's recent tragedy.

Although they were only separated by a year in age, there could have been no two young women more different than Charlotte Bellowes and May Thomas. Julian had been watching May as she emerged from those recent grief-sodden days and he had been amazed by the resilience with which she had handled her mother's terrible accident. He tried to imagine what he would feel if his own mother died and decided not to pursue the thought.

Shortly after Sam had arrived with the telegram at Cuckmere Park, the Blunts had insisted that May should take some time off in London with her brother and cousins but she had returned to Cuckmere the following Sunday at teatime, ready for the new week, assuring Sir Philip that she would prefer to be working than weeping. Joan had suggested that rather than stay behind alone in the house, May might like to come with them to evensong in the village church. Ever conscious of the healing power of a funeral, balm that she herself had once been denied, Joan thought that a service with some prayers might be of some help to May. For several generations, the Cuckmere custom had been for everyone at the house on Sunday evening, family, guests and staff, to go together to church. Mr Hooch had given May's arm a squeeze. This young woman, who no longer looked away when he spoke as so many others did, reminded him of someone he had once loved and lost.

'Don't mind me not coming with you tonight,' he said. 'I used to believe in all that Church and God rigmarole, although after this,' he gestured towards his face, 'I can't often think of much to be thankful for. But tonight, before I look out *Puck of Pook's Hill,* as I have promised young Florence I will, I am going to break a twenty-year rule and have a quiet word with Him up there about keeping an eye on you down here,' he said, tipping his battered chin skywards.

At what the poetically minded locals called 'the violet hour', the time of day when a rich purplish light would enfold the curves of the Downs, the geese set out on their evening journey, their abrasive cawing at odds with the grace of their synchronised wings. Sunday evening walkers, out with their dogs on the banks of the river, looked upwards as the birds flew towards the sea, horizontal ballet dancers, in perfect formation. Beneath the flight path the Cuckmere Sunday household walked the short distance to church in procession. Florence was at the back, kicking at the white flints that littered the mossy ground, and holding tightly onto May's hand. Inside the tiny church, not much more than a chapel, the Blunt family took their usual places in the front pew, bunching themselves up in order to make room for Evangeline. Mrs Cage and Cooky turned into the pew behind the family, with Florence and May beside them. The congregation settled itself, disengaging the needlepoint kneelers from the hooks, opening the hymn books at the right page, nodding across to the other side of the church to friends. The gentle sway of Bach's 'Jesu Joy' coming from the organ at the back of the church stilled the fidgeting. A late arrival, his honey-coloured hair hidden beneath a cap, hurried up the aisle and seeing there was no room in the front, squeezed in beside May. The service was short. The familiar words and tunes of 'Lead Kindly Light' and 'O God Our Help in Ages Past' sparked childhood memories in which May dared not indulge. Everyone had been so kind. Curiously enough, Miss Nettlefold had been the only person not to offer May more than a brief formal expression of 'her condolences'. Whenever May found herself alone with Miss Nettlefold, the subject of Mrs Thomas's death was never mentioned. May knew that Miss Nettlefold's mother had also died quite recently and assumed that the reluctance to talk of the accident in Barbados stemmed from her own as yet unsettled grief.

During the prayers, May was distracted first by Florence, who was dealing with her boredom by chewing the pew in front of her, and next by

Julian's insistent nudge at her elbow. Evangeline was struggling to raise herself from the tapestry hassock onto which her fleshy knees had sunk some ten minutes earlier. Julian, caught between horror and mirth, leant over to offer his help. But Evangeline made one more breathy effort and a huge bottom loomed up only a foot from Julian and May's noses before lowering itself onto the wooden bench. The pressure on May's elbow increased and for the first time in many days she felt like laughing.

However, as Julian sat in the passenger seat on the way down south from Wigan, he was nervous about opening up the pain of memory again. At first May sounded willing, even eager to talk. The ever-increasing remoteness of her mother's physical presence was one of the worst things about it all. As the gap between the present and the accident grew, May found herself working harder to remember what it was like doing ordinary things with her mother: walking, eating, talking, laughing. She was reminded how as a child she had longed to chase the setting sun, willing it not to disappear over the horizon.

'Please don't let it vanish forever,' she would beg her mother as the scarlet ball started to drop towards the smudgy line that distinguished sea from sky.

'Don't be so worried,' her mother would say. 'It will come back tomorrow before you are even awake.'

Appalled by the thought of infinite absence, May was abruptly resistant when Julian asked her about her father.

'I would rather not speak of him,' she looked up, her eyes angry.

'Of course, of course,' Julian replied, trying to calm her by resting his hand softly on hers. 'Would you believe me if I told you how much I envy you right now?' he asked. 'Do you know Tennyson's memorial poem to his friend Hallam? Sometimes the most hackneyed lines in poetry make the most sense. Everyone understands, I think, that it is better to have loved and lost than never to have had that experience. But there is another line that affects me more. Can I tell it to you?'

May nodded. Julian's hand remained resting on hers.

'Well, it's also from *In Memoriam* and is just this. 'An infant crying for the light'. My father died when I was three and although my mother is still alive she does not know how to love me. And so I have never known the light of parental love such as you have experienced. And,' he said simply, 'that is why I envy you.'

After May had dropped Julian off at Birmingham station to catch the train to Oxford he wondered if he had said too much. One of the two subjects that had not been discussed between them was one on which they were both sworn to secrecy. But if a disturbing love affair involving the head of state was taboo, then another matter, equally unspoken of, was forming between them. Even though he had removed his hand from hers soon after mentioning Tennyson and the nature of parental love, he had immediately wanted to put it back.

At the end of April Julian returned to Magdalen College for his final examination term and shortly afterwards, when the purple wisteria was trailing down the railings of Hamilton Terrace, May drove Sir Philip up to Oxford. After meeting with the Master of Balliol, who was also the vice chancellor of the university, an old friend from undergraduate days, Sir Philip was staying on at his old college for the night. May was about to make the long drive home but after a moment's thought she changed her mind. Somewhere within these ancient quadrangles and libraries, she knew she might find Julian.

She began her search at the café in the covered market where, according to Julian, they served the best homemade ginger beer known to man. For forty years Georges had sat undisturbed among the hallways of the market, the smell of exotic coffee lingering in the air above the fruit stalls, the fish market and the first-class butcher, an entire village of enclosed shops in the heart of the city. May took a corner table near the door which was pinned all over with notices advertising bicycle repairs, Mandarin lessons, spare rooms to let and all manner of activities including postings for amateur theatricals, film clubs, wine society tastings, a talk at Merton College by the Irish poet Louis MacNeice to the university literary society and the latest get together of the Oxford hamster club.

One flyer in particular caught her eye. There was to be an open-to-all meeting of Oswald

Mosley's New Party at three that very afternoon at the Carfax Meeting Rooms, just at the junction of the city's crossroads.

'Mosley here in Oxford in person!' the poster announced.

May looked at her watch. The meeting was to begin in half an hour. Asking directions from the waitress she made her way through the narrow streets, dodging cyclists in gowns and women with shopping until ten minutes later she reached the hall. Although the large room was almost full she found an empty metal-framed chair three rows from the front and sat down. Men were standing around the perimeter of the hall like sentinels, their arms folded across tightly fitting fencing shirts, their trousers tucked into the top of long boots and held up by belts with shiny buckles imprinted with an encircled jagged line. Despite the uniform, the men did not look particularly menacing and May could not help thinking that there was something rather attractive about their severe dress code. The woman beside May caught her admiring look.

'You wouldn't think much of them if you was married to a Cowley man,' she said with a sniff of disapproval. 'Can't get work for love or money, my Clive can't. We want to know what Mosley plans to do about the unemployment at the Morris works. It's all right for some, isn't it?'

May started at her accusing look, as the woman took in the smart chauffeur's uniform, relieved that she had parked the Rolls far out of sight of the hall. On the other side of the aisle just ahead of her, she spotted a familiar figure in

208

a tweed jacket with his back to her, deep in conversation with a youngish bespectacled man with wild-looking hair. But there was no time to go up to the pair as all at once a loud burst of marching music announced the arrival of the speaker. May recognised the tall figure of Oswald Mosley, leader of the British Union of Fascists, as he strode up the central aisle of the hall accompanied by two of his black-suited consorts. May shuddered inwardly, feeling yet again a disturbing physical excitement in this man's presence.

As Mosley reached the stage and saluted his audience, his elbow bent and his palm facing outwards as if directing the traffic, May took in every detail of the man. His hair was slicked back, not a strand out of place beneath its smooth, oiled pomade, just as it had been when he had passed by so close to her in the hall at Cuckmere several weeks before. Now that she had time to scrutinise him more closely, she saw that his small moustache looked as if it had been pencilled on and given the same greased-down treatment as his hair. His taut, athletic build reinforced his authority. May was near enough to see that instead of the thick, side-fastening cotton shirt favoured by his escorts, Mosley was wearing a far sleeker version made from silk. His eyes shone black. The audience was mesmerised, silenced and stilled by this dynamite combination of haughtiness and sexuality. A woman behind May whispered to her companion, 'My word, Glenda, what a virile animal!'

May knew exactly what she meant. She

wondered what would happen if one was quite alone in a room with Oswald Mosley. She might as well ask Mrs Cage, who would have discovered the answer when she took up the breakfast tray to the flowered spare room at Cuckmere and had returned so flustered.

Lifting his arms above him for silence, and taking a deep breath, Oswald Mosley's chest expanded like a swimmer about to take an Olympic dive. As he began to speak, several dozen people raised their newspapers and, pretending to read, produced a synchronised rustling that filled the room. The sentinels shifted on their feet. From behind a screen of *Daily Workers* came a barrage of offensive remarks as Mosley continued speaking to a wall of newsprint. After little more than half a minute of sustained interruption, Mosley paused in his attack on the Jewish financiers of the Labour party, warning that any disturbance in the hall would be firmly dealt with. The heckling continued from behind the anonymous protection of the newspapers.

'Red Front' came a cry from the back of the room followed by a burst of enthusiastic applause. Two or three black shirts moved into the central aisle.

'If anyone repeats those words they will be evicted from the room,' Mosley thundered, adding the single word 'Forthwith' to emphasise there would be no delay to his threat. His exaggerated vowels rang around the room.

'Stand fast!' he shouted.

The bespectacled man, his hair by now

sticking up in disarray, pushed his way into the centre of the hall to find himself trapped in a thicket of raised chairs and fists.

'Red Front!' came the cry once again from the back.

A steel chain held by one of the blackshirts was brought down in one stroke onto the spectacled man's face, while at the same time May saw a hefty knee rammed between his thighs. The spectacles tumbled to the ground. The noise in the room was fantastic. Another of Mosley's men had removed his belt, revealing the sharp, upright spikes that had up until then lain dormant behind the shiny buckle. Whirling the belt round his head the blackshirt brought it down with a whack on the buttocks of one of the Cowley men. And just as the confrontation began to escalate into something truly frightening, half a dozen policemen broke into the room.

'All women onto the platform at once!' May heard someone shout, but everyone, women included, was leaving the hall as quickly as possible by the main exit. May spotted Mosley vanishing through a side door escorted by two of his men, but there was no sign of the recently de-spectacled victim, nor of the familiar tweed jacket.

May was about to make her way back to the car when she turned round one more time to look at the empty platform. Something was moving beneath the piano, within three feet of where Mosley's black boots had been defiantly planted only minutes earlier. As she watched Julian emerge slowly from his hiding place, his legs stiff from the awkward position into which they had been folded for the past half hour, his usually firm-cheeked face buckled.

'Frank, have you seen Frank? Fucking Nazis! What have they done to Frank?' he shouted as he stumbled across the hall towards her. 'It was me that started the sign to attack!' Julian spluttered. 'It was me that cried 'Red Front'. If Frank's hurt it is all my fault.'

Tentatively, May put her arms around Julian as he buried his face in her shoulder. When Julian eventually pulled out of the embrace he looked up at May. His face was streaming with tears.

Summer

Expectation

13

May was looking forward to the summer. She had been missing the warmth that had been integral to her life until so recently. Her birthday month, for which she had been named, had delivered a welcome lift in temperature and she hoped June would bring more of the same.

The weekend after May's encounter with Mosley's henchmen there had been a small celebration at Oak Street. Another Fullers' cake, identical to the one that had been part of her and Sam's original welcome to the house, had appeared on the parlour table, except this time the soft icing had been punctured by twenty candles.

'Nothing like a moist bit of cake,' Rachel had remarked as May blew out the candles. 'Try saying 'pretty pussy' with a mouthful of dry sponge and you'll see what I mean,' she added, getting up to reach for a bottle of milk from the wall cupboard behind her.

Simon rolled his eyes at his wife's unmatchable way with words. But May was beyond care, existing in a state dictated by a slowly accumulating sense of anticipation at the way her friendship with Julian was developing, even though she kept the feeling hidden from everyone, especially Julian himself. He had forgotten to ask her to return the shirt he had lent her in Wigan and each night, in the secrecy of her bedroom, she slipped the shirt over her naked body, hugging her cotton-clad arms around herself. After returning from Oxford she had seen very little of Julian. He had remained there, working in the Bodleian library by day and in his college room at Magdalen by night, cramming for his final exams. But there had been one evening only two days after the drama of the Fascist meeting when she had bumped into him in the hallway at St John's Wood and he had asked her what she was up to.

'When?' she had asked him, willing her treacherous, flushing skin to remain dormant.

'Now. Right now,' he replied. 'I need to spend an evening when I am not thinking about dead philosophers or uniformed thugs or my nightmare of a mother. I must have covered hundreds of miles walking around Addison's Walk. The College cloisters help to concentrate the mind and give me a new perspective on the eternally fascinating question of why a table is still in a room when I am not in the room.' He paused, noticing the puzzled expression on May's face. 'Such are the preoccupations of a philosophy undergraduate about to sit his finals,' he explained apologetically. 'Anyway would you be a darling and save me from my thoughts by coming with me tonight to the Trocadero to see *Mr Deeds Goes to Town*? Gary Cooper's in it with Jean Arthur and she makes me laugh.'

And so they had gone to the Trocadero cinema and watched the film and then agreed that because they were both starving they would go for something to eat at the next door Lyons Corner House at Piccadilly. The place was even more packed than on May's earlier visit. But the maître d' had spoken conspiratorially to Julian and they were shown upstairs to a less crowded section. At the adjoining table two men were holding hands as one applied crimson-coloured lipstick to his friend's mouth. Julian had already sat down with his back to the couple and was studying the menu. He ordered fish and chips from the Nippy while May settled for a cheese omelette and decided, against her instinct, to say nothing about their neighbours. Half her concentration had been distracted by a decision that nothing was going to make her eat fish and chips out of choice, not even for the sake of someone who had sort of called her darling.

They talked of Wigan and of films and of mothers and of Oxford. Julian told her about his friend, the politics don Frank Pakenham, who was still suffering from the terrible bruises inflicted by Mosley's men. He told her how Frank's three-year-old daughter, adorable and curly headed, and innocent, had seen her invincible father groaning with pain in the darkened spare room. Julian had of course confessed to Frank at once that he had uttered the phrase 'Red Front', the two words that had triggered the violence.

'But Frank is one of the kindest men I have ever met,' Julian said. 'He told me he was even *glad* I had spoken those words and that he was *glad* of the chance to help break the fascists' power. And I too will do anything to help *him* in that effort.' There was a new determination in Julian's face as he spoke. 'You remember our friend Peter from Wigan?'

Of course she did. Those had been the days when she and Julian had been alone together for hours at a stretch. Peter was not yet in Spain but had sent Julian a card to say he was planning to be there by the end of the year. The Communist Party needed all the help it could attract.

'Are you going to join him?' May asked.

Julian was undecided. He admitted he was tempted. But he needed to get through his final exams first. And he had not discussed any of this with Charlotte.

'Not that she seems to be very interested whatever I do,' he muttered.

May changed the subject and began to talk about Cuckmere. Sir Philip had been busier than usual with more meetings, and urgent Parliamentary business than ever. He was worried about Lady Joan and her developing concern over Rupert's intended visit to Berlin later in the summer. She could not help fearing the influences he might fall under over there. The son of one of Lady Joan's friends had recently returned from Germany swearing loyalty to the Führer. But May kept all this information to herself. Instead she described her pleasure in seeing the drama of Vera's garden coming alive and how she and Florence had begun to explore the surrounding countryside together.

'There is a small river near the house that leads out to the sea and the cliffs there are enormous. Florence says she swims there in the summer and as soon as the weather warms up we have promised each other we will jump into the water.'

As May talked, Julian watched her intently and his encouraging smile emboldened her to a confidence, while making him swear on oath that he would not breathe a word of it to Rupert. The other day Miss Nettlefold had shown May her collection of wigs. There were looser ones for everyday wear, a cropped bob for the cocktail hour and an upswept chignon that was reserved for the occasional grand dinner, especially when Royalty was present.

'Wigs are part of my life,' she had told May. 'Mind you, I make sure no one ever sees me without one. I think I would *die* of shame if that happened!'

'She thinks we have a sort of friendship, you see,' May explained to Julian, after shifting her chair out of the line of sight of the two men beside them, one of whom had finished his chips and had now turned to the consumption of his friend's ear. 'She calls us 'soulmates' because we arrived in England on the same day. Of course, we can't be proper friends what with her being Lady Joan's god-daughter and me being the driver. But I feel sorry for her. I think she feels left alone on the outside of things.'

'Soulmates, you say?'

May wished she had not been so frank with him about the wigs.

'Yes,' she replied defensively. 'I do like her. She's different.'

'She's certainly different,' Julian agreed. 'But don't you think there's something not quite right about her? I mean apart from her size *and* her appetite? Not to mention those enormous teeth!

219

Like tombstones, they are! To be quite honest she gives me the creeps.'

May was irritated. She was damned if she was going to be lured into making unkind remarks about someone who had been so nice to her, despite the accident with Wiggle. They walked on in silence. *What a prig he is,* May thought to herself. Alarmed by how quickly she had found herself falling out with Julian she was relieved when they reached the underground. A sudden conviction that she was getting into something that perhaps she did not want to be part of engulfed her. She had intended to run down the stairs that led to the tunnel without looking back, but Julian caught her from behind, restraining her by both shoulders. Turning her to face him he kissed her hard on the lips, before releasing her.

She clattered down the stairs, her hard-soled lace-ups clicking on the hard surfaces like a castanet. Before she disappeared into the tunnel she turned to see him waving his cap to her. To her surprise and irritation his tobacco tasted as delicious as it smelt. *Funny that,* she thought. The power of taste. Uncooked cake and smoked tobacco. How strange that this most unlikely of the five senses could lead the way to new emotions. Afterwards she remained unaware whether he had removed his glasses to kiss her or had kept them on. All she did know was that they had managed the kiss without mishap and, despite her earlier misgivings, longed for a chance to do it again.

Rachel was still up when May let herself in to
Oak Street and with her usual unswerving
directness took one look at May and said, 'Don't
tell me you're not cracky on someone.'

Interrupting her scrutinising with a bone-
fracturing sneeze, Rachel blew her nose long and
hard into a large handkerchief before returning it
to the pocket of her floral apron. 'I can see it in
your eyes, my girl,' she continued looking hard at
May, before giving her a wink.

'I don't know what you're talking about,
Rachel,' she replied. May did not feel up to an
interrogation. She missed her mother. On most
days the awareness of Edith's death felt like a
muted hum. Sometimes the hum was so low
that it was almost inaudible, but then someone
would say something about mothers, or she would
come across a page in her book, or perhaps a line
of poetry, or a familiar tune on the wireless and
then the volume of the hum would be amplified.
Sometimes she would wake from a particularly
deep and satisfying sleep and for not much
more than a second or two, halfway between
semi-consciousness and wakefulness, she would
experience the treacherous relief of thinking she
had dreamt the whole thing. Her mother had not
drowned at all. Edith was still there in her little
book-lined room at the plantation, stretching out
her hands and waiting for her children to take
them. May would be overwhelmed with an
urgency to go to her mother. In fact, she must go
right now, today, this morning. But she had only

221

to lie there in her bed, sometimes in London, but more often in the quiet of Cuckmere, to realise that she was still dreaming. May dreaded these occasions of happy delusion. The cruelty of this sort of waking meant that early mornings could be worse than any other part of her day.

However, during the demanding schedule of the working week, May's mood remained buoyant. She was enjoying getting to know Sir Philip whose extra-curricular legal work had also increased twofold since the beginning of the year. He had been appointed to help advise the new King's legal team and May felt the privilege of trust when handling the related documents. She looked forward to the evenings when she joined the other chauffeurs who waited for their bosses to emerge from the House of Commons. Many of the drivers had been initially dismissive of a woman in their line of work but May's extensive knowledge of the machinery that formed the nuts and bolts of their profession soon silenced the sceptics among them. Even taxi drivers knew about Miss Thomas and occasionally wound down their windows at a traffic light and invited her into one of the green-painted cabman's shelters for a cup of tea. The elder drivers saw to it that no impropriety was ever ventured, although the level of flirtation was not insignificant. Between themselves all the drivers agreed that Miss Thomas was a bit of alright.

Most evenings May would stand by the passenger door of the Rolls-Royce, her cap in hand, waiting for Sir Philip who would rush out from the Commons main door, the *Evening Standard* under his arm, and almost fall onto the leather seat of the Rolls. When he was on his own he chose to sit up at the front beside May, who sometimes caught a look of surprise on the faces of passers-by. At times he would be consumed by a story in the newspaper, and at others he would look directly ahead in silence. May had come to interpret his moods. He could give the impression of aloofness, even arrogance. But there was nothing in him of the smug, self-satisfied ways of his children. He often asked how May was getting on. She had told him of her pride at how Sam had been selected as part of the naval volunteer team at the imminent maiden voyage of the *Queen Mary*. He was to join the crew of a naval launch bringing an Admiral from Portsmouth to Southampton in preparation for the Admiral's transatlantic voyage on the new liner.

Sir Philip was delighted to hear the news of Sam's advancement. The launching of the *Queen Mary* promised to be the last word in magnificence. Sir Philip had been discussing the ship with Duncan Grant at a recent party in Sussex. Grant was a most engaging man who lived near Cuckmere at Charleston, a farmhouse cocooned by the embracing sweep of the surrounding South Downs. He shared the house with the artist Vanessa Bell, and the Cunard directors had commissioned paintings from them both to decorate the vast amounts of wall space that lined every floor of the ship. As part of her contribution, Vanessa had painted a scene set near a fountain in London's Kensington Gardens, inspired by a memory of that park near where she and her two brothers and sister Virginia had grown up. The quintessentially English painting with two children and their nanny playing on a summer's day at the foot of a fountain was to be hung in a private dining room on board the ship's first-class accommodation. Mr Grant, on the other hand, had fallen out badly with the Cunard authorities after they rejected his nude murals as 'inappropriate for the elegant taste of the new vessel', and at the party Sir Philip had been left in no doubt at the painter's outrage at such censorship.

★ ★ ★

On the day of *Queen Mary*'s maiden voyage May drove the Rolls-Royce down to the Southampton docks. Lady Joan had been invited as one of several MPs' wives who were making up a party of distinguished guests. She had invited Evangeline to join her, knowing that the occasion promised to be the sort of British outing that Miss Nettlefold enjoyed so much.

Mrs Simpson regretted she would not be joining them in Southampton.

'She is remaining in London to help the King put the finishing touches to an important dinner planned for tonight at York House,' Miss Nettlefold explained to Lady Joan in the car on the way to Harrods to collect their new hats for the ceremony. 'Of course, I quite understand why at the last minute Wallis feels there is no room for me at the dinner. The King already has his full complement of guests what with the Duff Coopers, the Mountbattens, Lady Cunard and the Prime Minister himself. But Wallis has told me that the King intends to introduce Mr Baldwin to 'his future wife'!'

May listened to Miss Nettlefold's newly animated chatter through the not-quite-closed glass partition. The American woman had been noticeably subdued over the past few weeks, her buoyant mood dipping at the same rate as the number of visits to the Fort had dwindled. She confided to May that she had looked into the price of a ticket to sail back to New York on the new ship but the price was beyond her reach, and anyway there wasn't really anything to return to America *for*. Her brother wrote her the occasional postcard, but the cards never convinced her that her family were missing her very much. Looking on the bright side, however, Mrs Simpson had mentioned something about spending a few weeks in the Mediterranean later on in the summer and Miss Nettlefold was hoping the invitation would soon be confirmed.

'I always say it is the things that you don't do in life that you regret, May,' she had said with a girlish little jump before climbing into the back seat of the car beside Joan.

They had reached the outskirts of Southampton in good time. May had eased the car onto the narrow wooden deck of the Woolston floating bridge and to the sound of clanking chains and the hiss of steam, the Blunt party had remained in the car as they floated across the River Itchen

225

to the Port on the opposite bank. The *Queen Mary* was scheduled to depart at 4.30, allowing time for lunch beneath the Tudor beams of the old Court Room in the Red Lion Inn. A table had been reserved in the very room where, five hundred years earlier, traitors plotting against the life of Henry V had been found guilty and sentenced to death.

'How quaint this is!' Miss Nettlefold had exclaimed. 'Don't you applaud a grim death for those who deserve it, May?' she continued, as Lady Joan teased her for looking in the corners for signs of dried blood.

'Shall we have a good talk about everything when we get home, Evangeline, darling?' May heard Lady Joan ask. 'You seem worried about something, and I want to help if I can.'

May saw Miss Nettlefold nod, and rest her hand gently on Lady Joan's arm.

'I would like that very much,' Miss Nettlefold replied quickly. 'The sooner the better. I do feel a bit uncertain about things.'

After leaving the women to their lunch, sisterly pride fluttered through May as she watched her brother march smartly along the dock towards her, smoothing down the front of his blue naval trousers. The cut was difficult to get used to but he had found that the uniform with its white, sharp-edged collar and side fastening buttons had an instant effect on girls. Sam had been given half an hour of free time to meet up with his sister before rejoining his colleagues for the moment of the sailing. An hour earlier he had stood to attention at the bottom of the gangplank with the rest of the small naval party, as the Admiral had boarded the ship. Sam had been permitted to take the suitcases to the Admiral's first-class stateroom and his glimpse of the grandeur and comfort inside the ship was, he told his sister, something he had never seen before.

'Bit of a change from what we sailors are used to. Not a bunk in sight!'

Now the brother and sister stood side by side on the quayside staring up at the two thousand inaugural passengers who were already leaning elbow to elbow along the upper rails. Even at a distance their faces demonstrated the novelty of being celebrities for one afternoon.

At a thousand feet long, the word was that if one of the three funnels was placed on its side six locomotive engines would be able to pass through abreast. May wondered what their father would think of the vessel people were calling 'not so much a ship as a gesture'. The newspapers had been full of extravagant statistics for days and May, whose interest in machines did not stop at cars, had been gobbling up every detail she came across. Nat had been given a hand-me-on copy of the *Illustrated London News* by his butler friend and last week's full-colour commemorative issue had been devoted to the anticipation of the maiden voyage. Not only did the ship weigh more than that of the combined fleet of the Spanish Armada but the throb of the engines was so powerful that reporters feared that a well-shaken martini would spill over the edge of its glass with the vibrations. There were decks as long as entire village streets and as well as including hundreds of photographs of the interior, the magazine had commissioned drawings of the lay-out of the different classes of accommodation. A side view section of the ship indicated not only the whereabouts of the sleeping cabins, the libraries, and the drawing rooms but also the position of the two acres of sports and recreation decks, the garage with its capacity for three dozen cars, the two swimming pools, the hospital, the printers' shop (for the daily newspaper, the menus and entertainment programmes), the cinema and the hairdresser. The ship's gardener was to make sure that the hundreds of pot plants were well watered while the pets' own promenade deck came complete with a convenient lamp post, although curiously the kennels were to be overseen by the ship's butcher. The memory of Wiggle momentarily interrupted May's concentration. But turning to the next page of the magazine she came to the diverting charts that showed the huge quantities of linen on board, including 21,000 table cloths and 31,000 pillow cases, and a larder containing vats of caviar.

The clever illustrator had shown how, with its funnels stretching up to two hundred feet from the ship's keel, *the Queen Mary* would have reached a height of more than thirty feet above Lord Nelson's tricorn on top of his plinth in Trafalgar Square. An ingenious sketch of the ship's dining room demonstrated that the Pilgrim Fathers' *Mayflower* would have fitted into just a corner of the new saloon.

On the quayside the Portsmouth division of the Royal Marines were standing to attention. Decked out in white helmets that shimmered like full moons above the red blue and gold uniform, some of the smaller band members looked as if they might be toppled not only with the weight of the huge drums hung around their necks but with the self-importance that the day's role had thrust upon them. Many of the buildings that ranged around the dock seemed taller that day, extended vertically by thousands of spectators who had crowded onto every square foot of roof available in order to get a better view. It was already 4 p.m. and May hugged Sam goodbye before hurrying back to her seat in the cordoned-off area for chauffeurs near the packed VIP box. Below them Sam's svelte figure had taken up its place among the small group of naval officers who stood to attention, wishing the Admiral Godspeed. May managed to catch Miss Nettlefold's eye who beamed back at her after spotting May proudly identifying her brother.

Soon a huge cheer went up from what the wireless had estimated would be a quarter-of-a-million-strong crowd, accompanied by 'Rule Britannia' oom-paahing out from the band on the quayside. Flags were flicking in the air, hats were waved and handkerchiefs contributed to the breeze-borne flutterings. Everyone hoped the rain would hold off. Seaplanes skimmed the surface of the water and touch-landed with the agility of dragonflies before lifting off again. Small aeroplanes equipped with cine cameras buzzed in low circles through the threateningly grey sky. Pathé News had guaranteed that the resulting haul of footage would appear on the cinema screens within three days.

Almost imperceptibly the gap between the ship and the quayside increased. Smoke started to appear from the huge funnels. Bunting-draped vessels varying in size from large yachts to the most diminutive of rowing boats sounded their horns to wish the *Queen Mary* well on her way. A small cry coming from the VIP box distracted May's attention from the colour and drama of the scene. Leaning forward as far as she could she was just in time to see Lady Joan fall sideways into Miss Nettlefold's arms. Quickly May clambered over the partition wall to reach the still figure of Lady Joan.

'I had a fearful feeling that something like this might happen,' puffed Miss Nettlefold, who was scarlet in the face with the effort of lifting her limp godmother to a chair. 'She has been feeling rather off-colour these past few days. I had a word with Cooky about tempting her with some special dishes but for the life of me I could not get Joan to touch anything. Philip has been beside himself with worry. You should have seen the chocolate tart that came up from the kitchen yesterday but all Joan would do was shake her head at it.'

One look at the colour of Lady Joan's face and her badly distorted mouth had alerted a steward to go and fetch help. With the lower part of her face fixed in a twisted grimace and two buttons of her silk blouse missing after it had been

230

urgently loosened, Lady Joan was laid at an awkward angle on top of a stretcher, carried down the stairs and out of the back entrance. Once Lady Joan was settled gently in the back of the car and Miss Nettlefold had taken the passenger seat, May set off slowly for the journey back to London.

14

Word of his wife's sudden illness had reached Sir Philip in London and he was already waiting with the family doctor and another gentleman on the doorstep as May pulled up the car outside Hamilton Terrace. Lady Joan had not stirred throughout the journey, and even Miss Nettlefold, shifting constantly in the cramped conditions of the front seat, had spent much of the time in silence. Every so often she had looked backwards through the open dividing screen just in case Lady Joan had recovered consciousness.

An hour later Sir Philip came to find May in the kitchen. He looked exhausted.

'My dear, I am most grateful to you. Miss Nettlefold has told me how efficiently you have dealt with things this afternoon. I am afraid Lady Joan has suffered a stroke. Mr Hunt, the consultant, thinks her recent anxiety about Rupert and his politics might have contributed to this. Her nerves have been terribly weak for years I am afraid.' Sir Philip sounded unlike his usual reserved self. He seemed to want to tell May every detail of his wife's condition as if to reassure himself that everything was being done to help her.

'I know Hunt through the old boys' network at Balliol. He's already a distinguished man of medicine, even though he must still only be in his early thirties. He is just about to move to the

Neurological Clinic at St Bartholomew's and we have had several talks over the years about Joan. You know, the way she is about her younger sister's death?'

May nodded.

'Well, John understands that Joan is still unable to recover from the tragedy. He is one of those few people really interested in that sort of psychological condition. It *is* such a relief he could come at such short notice and see her. Oh, forgive me May, I am going on a bit aren't I?' He buried his head in his hands. 'As if the loss of her sister has not brought her enough suffering already. And now this,' he half-whispered to himself.

* * *

The following day a still unconscious Lady Joan, accompanied by a uniformed nurse, was driven down to Cuckmere Park in an ambulance. If she was to stand any chance of recovery, Hunt considered absolute inactivity and peace to be an essential ingredient for healing. The nurse was to take up permanent residence and would attend to all Lady Joan's basic medical needs, Sir Philip explained, unless his wife's condition showed no sign of improvement, in which case she would have to be admitted to hospital for closer monitoring.

During the next few days the rest of the staff at Cuckmere vacillated between subdued discussion about people they knew who had been struck down with something similar, and the good news at least that the date for the Coronation had been confirmed for next May, less than a year away. In the kitchen Mr Hooch held his cup of elevenses coffee in hands ingrained with engine oil and grease and shook his head slowly from side to side. His pessimism at the prognosis for the much-loved mistress of the house was all too evident in his face. Cooky advised everyone to try and look on the bright side. She was certain that her Ladyship would be fully recovered in time for the big Coronation celebrations in St John's Wood next summer. Cooky would probably be asked to help London Cook with the preparations.

'I will agree for her Ladyship's sake but only if London Cook can manage to keep her temper under control for two whole days,' she said pursing her lips in and out in quick little movements. 'I remember my mother telling me about the red and blue jellies she made for the old King's Coronation street party in Battersea in 1911. God bless his soul.'

And Cooky picked up the corner of her apron and wiped a tear from her eye, a gesture which May considered a trifle theatrical given that it was now six months since George V's death and May had heard the story at least half a dozen times before.

Getting up from the kitchen table, she excused herself and went outside into the garden. At last a pattern of sunshine had established itself, bringing with each successive morning long stretches of warmth that allowed sweaters to remain in drawers unmissed for days on end. At the far end of the lawn, near the large fig tree, Vera was busy tying up the trailing ends of a purple clematis that were tumbling over a wicker archway. She raised a hand to May in greeting. Severely dressed in her habitual dungarees and fearsome beneath her distinctive earth-smeared cheekbones, Vera's magic fingers brought the chalky flowerbeds of Cuckmere to life.

Sir Philip's reading glasses and the newspaper lay in a deck chair that had been placed against the shady curve of the long flint wall. The green-and-white-patterned chair, with its own fringed canopy, had been Sir Philip's gift to his pregnant wife during the summer their son was born and the sag of the fabric on the seat showed the evidence of much use. The garden looked like the juxtaposed brushstrokes of an impressionist's canvas with the flowers packed so closely together in the earth that it was impossible to distinguish where one bloom ended and the other began. Roses flung themselves over flint walls and the pink and red hollyhocks had beaten all their previous records in height, their delicate pink flowers scaling the top wire of the tennis court. At the other end of the lawn, Vera put the ball of string and secateurs into her pocket and sat down on a bench beneath the fig tree. It was too early for the tree to produce any fruit but the large leaves provided the dappling shade that was welcome on such a hot day.

Whenever May had some time to herself she would sit by the door of the ancient dovecot and listen to the velvety crooning that came from inside. The inner walls of the squat stone building were slatted with hundreds of deep square shelves, a stone-built library filled not with books but with doves, each one snug in the individual slots in which they and their antecedents had nested for several centuries. May looked around this lovely place, absorbing the beauty of it. In April, the thick yew hedges had been clipped back to the cleanest and smoothest of profiles but the new growth was already beginning to blur the crisp lines. Petals borne on the occasional breath of a breeze drifted across the lawn from the rose garden and floated into May's lap. The air was so still that she could only tell the direction of the wind by training her gaze on a landmark, a chimney, or a tree, and watching a cloud make its snail-slow progress across the sky towards that fixed point. That day the sun was so bright that May found it impossible to read her book even when she scrunched up her eyes to see the words on the page. She went inside the house.

As usual Lady Joan was on her own, apart from the nurse who sat saying nothing in a corner of the room. Miss Nettlefold had admitted to May that the sight of her godmother, so indisposed and helpless, had upset her dreadfully and, concerned she might make a scene at the bedside, Evangeline thought it wiser to stay away.

The two Blunt children rarely came upstairs to their mother's once-pretty bedroom that was now filled with medical equipment. In fact, Rupert and Bettina rarely came at all to

Cuckmere during those summer months. Bettina explained to her father that she was in the middle of her busy London Season and Rupert, having recently finished his exams, was giving himself an extended and well-earned period of celebration with his friends. Despite the intense demands of his work in London, Sir Philip tried to be near his wife as often as possible and May found herself driving him up and down to the city four or five times a week.

On the day Lady Joan had returned home in the ambulance, May offered to take her turn sitting with Lady Joan. Sir Philip had agreed at once.

'My wife is very fond of you, my dear,' Sir Philip said, 'and when she wakes I know she will be grateful to find you nearby.'

Taking up her position at the head of the bed, May would try to ignore the smells of stale decay, medicinal chemical, and the uneven sounds that came from beneath the oxygen mask. There was no knowing if Lady Joan would ever wake. There had been talk of her having an operation involving an electric current being passed through her brain but Sir Philip could not bring himself to subject his wife to such a frightful invasion. The only confirmation of life came from the intermittent misting up of Lady Joan's oxygen mask and the flickering butterfly hover that stirred beneath Lady Joan's cream nightdress. May had once leant over to interrupt the path of a ladybird that was in danger of becoming trapped under the mask as it tracked its way across the invalid's pale cheek. Feeling her gaze becoming intrusive May had stood up. Such contemplation should be reserved exclusively for the absorption either of a daughter, or a lover.

* * *

May had heard nothing from Julian since they had parted at the underground station nearly a month ago. She missed their conversations. Julian was so easy to talk to. He made her think and he made her laugh. What's more, he listened to her, one of the most important points on her mother's list of qualities to look for in a man. Above all, she could not stop thinking about the taste of his kiss. And those thoughts had led to others that had never before entered her head. Part of her felt she should put a stop to anything further developing between them. She was aware of the professional barriers, even though Sir Philip had not cautioned her in any way. And there was something else that deterred her. While she did not like the idea of either of them deceiving Miss Bellowes, she was conscious of her own new physical longing. The truth was she did not trust herself.

Over the past few months she had seen and envied and admired the love and the physical affection between Nat and Sarah, whose baby was due in October. Memories of her revulsion at Duncan's touch had slowly begun to fade and alone in her bed at night she had begun to experiment with new feelings that were emerging with a not unpleasant regularity. Running her fingers up the long line from her ankle to her waist, she would linger for as long as her instinctive modesty would allow her at the dark hair-sown softness between her legs. She tried to imagine what that sort of caress might feel like if it came from the hand of another. Sometimes she succeeded in giving her body up to the deep-sourced pulse that began as a faraway tremor, and then enveloped her entire body, clearing her mind of everything except an unprecedented and sublimely delicious sensation.

Julian did not find out about Joan's stroke until well after it had happened and was furious with Rupert for not telling him. He travelled down straight away to Cuckmere, arriving one scorching hot day from London by train. His visit had coincided with one of Miss Nettlefold's rare appearances but she had already exhausted her tolerance for a distressing bedside vigil and had gone to take some air before returning to London.

Julian went straight to Joan's bedroom, while in the kitchen his arrival dominated lunchtime conversation. The staff were delighted. The notion that over the past few years Lady Joan had become more attached to her son's undergraduate friend than she was to her own son had not gone unnoticed; nor was it possible to ignore the closeness that seemed to be developing between him and May, although each member of staff had their own reasons for keeping that particular observation to themselves. Cooky believed that it was bad luck to encourage a romance before it had even begun. Mr Hooch did not want to see any harm coming to the young woman for whom his protective affection was beginning to feel paternalistic. And Mrs Cage did not want to find herself in a position where she had to remind May that she was an employee in the house. Best to leave any suspicions well alone and they might simply disappear.

An hour after his arrival Julian left the sickroom and went into the study. Sir Philip was in London and May was sitting at her desk alone.

'I hoped you would be in here,' Julian said, slowly scrunching up the pale blue cap in his hand into a ball. He looked nervous and flushed.

May stood up so quickly at the sound of his voice that she dropped her pen and stumbled over the wastepaper basket at her feet.

'Oh look at me, all fingers and thumbs. I didn't know you were here. Have you come to see Joan?'

'Yes. That bastard Rupert hadn't even told me about her illness. I was horrified by the news.'

'I knew you would be, which is why I didn't tell you myself. I didn't want to upset you in the middle of your exams.'

'Oh May, it isn't you I blame,' Julian said, coming closer.

'Oh well, that *is* a relief.' She stood awkwardly next to her desk, not sure whether to sit down again or to remain facing Julian, inhaling his distinctive smoky smell.

'I hope you aren't going back to London

straight away? Must you? Please stay on a bit?' It was now May's turn to look flustered.

'I should probably leave,' he replied slowly. 'I promised my mother I would go and see her this afternoon. But I want to see you. I have missed you.'

May tried to keep her voice from betraying her excitement. *Did he really say what I think he said?* she wondered to herself, suddenly alarmed that if she didn't keep him there now, she had no idea when she would next see him.

'Actually, I was just going for a swim,' she said as calmly and nonchalantly as possible. 'Would you like to come with me? You could take my bike. I can borrow Florence's. She's still at school.'

'Yes, yes, I think I would love that,' Julian replied.

* * *

Together they pedalled out of the drive, down the lane, through the village and into the open country, taking the path that led towards the river's meanders. Whole families of rabbits lifted their heads from their steady consumption of clumps of clover and ran for refuge in the tunnels that honeycombed the surrounding fields. A herd of brown and white cows were chewing rhythmically on the grass verges and walking towards them was the unmistakable bulk of Miss Evangeline Nettlefold. A huge smile broke out on her face as she recognised the figure in the cap.

'I have been trying to telephone you,' she

241

began, holding up her hand in an attempt to get him to slow down. 'I have got some tickets for the ballet at Covent Garden next week. Just for the two of us to celebrate the end of your exams.'

'Can't stop now, I'm afraid,' Julian shouted out as they sped past her. 'We're off to swim.'

And Miss Nettlefold found herself forced to step so quickly to the side of the path in order to avoid being run over that she did not have time to notice the fresh-smelling cowpat into which her new walking shoe plunged with slippery ease.

Following the curves of the sharp bank where the small water lilies sucked up the marshy water and produced their sharp butter-yellow flowers, the smell of wild peppermint in the air, May and Julian made their way to the mouth of the river. Lying the bikes on their side they skipped over a thick black cable that emerged from beneath the seabed and slithered reptile-like across the pebbles before disappearing through the wall of a hut set twenty-five yards above the sea line.

'Philip told me about this place,' Julian said. 'Even so, I find it hard to believe that a telephone line runs all the way under the sea from Dieppe to us over here at Cuckmere. Such a small piece of kit for all those voluble French! Shall we leave our towels here by the hut?'

That morning, in anticipation of what she had thought would be a solitary swim, May had put on her old faded bathing suit beneath her summer dress. Julian was less prepared, but several terms of plunging naked into the Isis near Magdalen College had dissipated his inhibitions.

And then he remembered the unusual item of clothing he was wearing beneath his shorts. A few weeks after that appalling dinner party at Bryanston Court during one of the snatched moments when Evangeline attempted to advance her futile suit, she had slipped a parcel out of her bag and placed it gently in Julian's lap.

'I hope you won't mind such a, well, shall I say 'personal' gift, but my brother found his life transformed by this garment so I asked him to go to our local department store and buy one for you.'

'What a surprise,' was all Julian could think of to say, as he removed the wrapping paper to reveal a pair of elasticated swimming trunks with a horizontal vent and a sort of pocket that resembled a kangaroo pouch at the front.

'No time for preparing for summer fun like the 'present', excuse the pun!' said Evangeline, moving her cheek near Julian's mouth, undeterred by the delay she was forced to endure before receiving a perfunctory kiss of thanks.

Evangeline's present had lain untouched, shoved at the back of a drawer, but that morning, searching for a clean item of underwear, Julian had come across the unwelcome gift. He hoped May was not looking too closely as he steadied himself, preparing to make a deep dive into the final stretch of the Cuckmere river before it merged with the sea half a mile further on. A few hundred yards from where they stood a sequence of white chalk cliffs undulated above the coast in a pattern of seven graceful rises, before culminating at Beachy Head. There, at the highest point, where the drop down to the thunderous crashing of the water against the rocks was over five hundred feet, the sea appeared at its most beautiful and its most threatening.

Standing above the swift flowing river, Julian and May were alone except for a tall, elegant woman sitting on the grass on the opposite bank and looking out to sea, an open book in her lap. She was wearing a long, pale-blue, linen jacket, her hands thrust deep within its pockets. Suddenly she looked up and across at May and Julian. May waved to Mrs Woolf in greeting who immediately waved back.

Julian stared, first in recognition at the woman and then back at May. Allowing himself to take in the long legs and brown body in its pretty, flower-patterned suit beside him, he felt suddenly and intensely exhilarated.

'You are one of the most surprising people I have ever come across,' he declared. 'Ready?' he asked, taking off his glasses and putting them carefully on the grassy bank. 'Let's jump *now*!'

A moment later the water enveloped them. The current was travelling at speed and they found themselves spinning round in circles as the rush of water pulled them towards the river mouth. In less than a minute they reached the open sea, whooping and shouting to one another at the top of their voices above the noise of the waves.

After several minutes, Julian who, unlike May, had been deprived of a childhood in which swimming was as much part of the daily routine as the brushing of teeth, suggested they turn back to the shore.

Afterwards May was not quite sure how it had all happened. Julian had returned to the bank to get his glasses before they climbed together up the pebbly shore towards the little telephone exchange to retrieve their towels. Shivering from the temperature of the water as well as the intoxicating swim, May pushed at the door of the hut and to her surprise it gave way. A broken down armchair, so large that it was almost the size of a sofa, was wedged in a corner. Julian's teeth were chattering.

'Shall we go in and get warm?' May said. 'I'm sure no one will mind.'

Inside the hut, sitting on the chair big enough for two, May began to rub her hair dry with the towel.

'Let me help you,' Julian said quietly, sitting down and taking the towel from her. Several minutes elapsed during which he kissed every part of her face, even her eyelids, before he slid the straps of her costume off her shoulders. Gradually he eased the flowery suit down the length of her body, until she was completely naked. For May this long-anticipated moment had become one of imagined resistance. And yet the dreadful memories of Duncan's sustained abuse now vanished in the presence of the warm, patient, loving touch of a man whose uninhibited desire for her was suddenly impossible to resist. The lightness of Julian's fingertips, stroking her back and running at first all the way to the base of her spine, and then, cautiously, slowly, round to the curve of her breast, made her want the feelings he was awakening in her to last forever.

245

As he gathered May towards him she felt his arms gently circle her waist. Leaning into the cool smoothness of his bare skin she allowed herself to sink deep, deep into a previously unimaginable state where nothing at all mattered, nor would ever matter again. For what seemed like a lifetime, May remained inside that small wooden hut on the pebble beach wrapped in Julian's arms. As he kissed her at first with such tenderness, and then with a reciprocated passion as powerful as the motion of the sea itself, she thought she might dissolve with happiness.

★ ★ ★

Later that evening Mr Hooch arrived back at the garage after leaving Mr Julian at the station. The trip had been his second to Polegate that day. He had already taken an unusually taciturn Miss Nettlefold to the train, remarking to himself that not only here was a woman decidedly out of sorts but also one who, judging by the pungency that still lurked in the back of the Talbot, had taken to economising on baths.

May was inside the Rolls-Royce, oiling the partition window that divided the driver from her passengers when Mr Hooch walked in.

'Mr Julian's visit has certainly put a big smile on your face, young lady,' Mr Hooch remarked as he shut the door of the Talbot. 'He seems to think he will be back here soon. To see her Ladyship, I expect,' he added, a smile detectable in his own voice.

Mr Hooch found himself unexpectedly moved by the sight of this beautiful young woman who was unable to stop herself from grinning. And yet at the same time he feared for her.

'Mind you, I imagine he will have to tear himself away from the charms of Miss Bellowes if he is to have time to come down here on any sort of regular basis.' There was a note of caution in his voice that May was in no mood to be troubled by.

'I am sure Mr Julian will manage somehow,' she said gaily. 'And now I must be off to London to see my brother. Would you mind dropping me at the station, Mr Hooch?'

Mr Hooch and May stood together on the platform as they had done on the day they had first met. He shook her hand, his glove leaving a small oily mark on her palm although no blemish could dampen May's elated mood.

'Here we are then, and cheer-oh, as we soldiers used to say in the old days. Stay safe, my dear. I don't mind telling you I am already looking forward to your return on Monday.'

As the train rumbled towards London May briefly considered her feelings of relief that Duncan had always just stopped himself from advancing his foul interest in his daughter to its horrible conclusion. Whatever he had done to her, he had left her essential purity intact for another to discover. Mr Hooch's mention of Lottie had made no impact on her that afternoon and it was not long before she drifted back to the memory of Julian's parting kiss and his promise that he would be back with her at Cuckmere soon.

Oak Street felt musty when May let herself in the front door. Despite the spic and span order of the house, the Castors and the Greenfelds rarely opened a window, even in the summer, and the small downstairs rooms could become clogged with smells of cooking and Simon's pipe smoke. She was pleased to find Sam home on a day's leave, making a cup of tea.

'Let's go outside to the park before dinner,' she urged, pulling him away from the teapot and handing him his overcoat. 'I haven't seen you for ages and I've got loads to talk to you about.'

15

There had been times recently when Evangeline had felt lonelier than at any moment since her arrival in England. With the absence of Wiggle and the incapacity of her godmother, the diversions that had previously filled her London days were becoming fewer. Walks in the park, visits to the dressmaker, outings to the cinema, and even treats to the outstanding patisserie department at Fortnum and Mason lost their appeal when there was no one to enjoy them with.

The London house had developed a sense of abandonment. Philip often spent the night at the house but left for work immediately after an early breakfast, returning only to change into his evening clothes before going out again until after dinner. Even Julian never dropped by any more, although Evangeline knew from May how often he visited Cuckmere. She had no longer felt quite as well disposed towards May since noticing her inappropriate and frankly ridiculous need to follow Julian all over the place: up to the North, down to the South, over the fields and yonder. Poor Julian. That flat-chested young woman must be driving him mad. And May was certainly close to overstepping the limitations of professional relationships. Evangeline had even considered mentioning the matter to Philip but was not confident she would get the response she was seeking.

Rupert and Bettina came and went as they wished but were as tedious as ever, obsessed by their own social engagements, arriving at all hours of the night with their loud-mouthed friends. An invitation to Evangeline to accompany Bettina and her friend Charlotte in loco parentis to their formal presentation to the King at the Buckingham Palace garden party had resulted in a wash out. In truth, Evangeline had felt sorrier on that occasion for the girls than for herself. The presentation was to have been the high point of their debut year. Fittings for white silk dresses and discussions about the feathered headdresses had even begun to bore Evangeline. But the garden party had been rained off.

Well over a hundred girls had been waiting for their big moment, running over the Presentation Curtsey in their heads, trying to ignore their mothers' fussing while fluttering their fans, and doing their best to keep their feathers dry. Suddenly it was announced that not only would there be no more presentations that day but that the King had decided that the curtsies of those debutantes who had been foiled by the rainstorm were to 'be taken as made'. No alternative arrangements were to be scheduled, rendering entire outfits and the rest of the grand hullabaloo redundant.

'I know Daddy hobnobs with HM day and night, but I call it *extremement* rude to treat us that way.' Bettina was close to tears. 'And I have a good mind to say so to his face.'

Even the invitations to dine with Wallis had dried up or become subject to last-minute cancellations. Evangeline tried to forgive Wallis's erratic behaviour by reasoning that her increasing involvement with the King left little time to spare for old friends. Although Wallis's presence at the Fort had been established since well before Evangeline's arrival in England, Wallis was now running many other parts of the King's life, including his London engagements. Evangeline was amazed that nothing about the romance had ever appeared in the British Press. Wallis's name had been published a couple of times next to Ernest's in *The Times* Court Circular but that was the extent of it. What a difference between the newspapers here and those back home! Her brother had sent over a clipping from Ed Sullivan's column in the *New York Daily News*, together with a couple of others from popular magazines. Headlines had included 'Yankee at King Edward's Court' and 'Baltimore girl who won friendship of King'.

Mostly the stories were anodyne and even friendly, except for a cartoon showing an olde worlde English pub in which the regulars, bucolic strings of straw hanging from their mouths, were enjoying a game of darts. The caption read, 'We don't want no Yanks upsetting things over here, do we?' The dart-board was covered with a picture of Wallis's face. No one in Britain outside a charmed circle would have had any idea what the cartoon meant or recognised the face that had become the players' target. Nevertheless, the published existence of anti-Wallis sentiment across the Atlantic was worrying. That nice Lord Rothermere who

251

Evangeline had met briefly at a Sunday lunch at Cuckmere Park was certainly most cooperative about the way he did not indulge in gossip in his pages. But how long could a good story be suppressed? Evangeline wondered. Did his newspaper, the *Daily Mail,* not honour the people's democratic right to know what went on in their country? Perhaps Lord Rothermere was unaware of the full truth behind this woman who wielded such influence over the King?

If that was the case, he was certainly in the minority among the powerful and influential members of society who came in and out of Hamilton Terrace. The subject was rarely off the agenda. Evangeline had often heard Philip discussing the problem with Joan before she became ill. Members of the Cabinet were becoming agitated about the deepening relationship between the King and a married (and divorced!) woman, while Winston Churchill reassured Philip that Mr Simpson was still on the scene and was always included in the King's invitations. There was still a hope within both the upper and lower House, Philip had said, that this current infatuation would 'blow over', just like the King's other romances with married women, notably Mrs Dudley-Ward and Lady Furness. Certainly no one felt able to speak directly to the King about the matter. Queen Mary was thought to be '*hors de combat*', and still fragile at the loss of her husband. And Mr Baldwin had pointedly refused to interfere in the King's private life. Many members of the Cabinet felt that as long as the constitution remained intact, and the plans for next year's Coronation went ahead unchallenged, the matter of the royal love life should be left well alone.

Neglect had a bad effect on Evangeline but Wallis would always come up with something at the last moment. Recently there had been the offer of several nearly new hats, which Evangeline had accepted with alacrity, especially as she was missing her expeditions to the millinery department at Hochschild Kohn. The choice, as well as the price range in the equivalent department in Harrods, was far too rarefied for Evangeline's taste and purse except for very special occasions. There had also been some cast-off handbags and gifts of redundant dresses, although even the most resourceful seamstress had been defeated by the challenge of adapting any of Wallis's diminutive frocks to fit Evangeline.

One evening, knowing that Evangeline shared her love of music, especially jazz, Wallis had proposed dinner at Quaglinos on a night when she could be sure the debonair singer, Leslie Hutchinson, known to everyone as Hutch, would be playing a medley of romantic tunes.

The candle-lit nightclub, just off St James's, had been hazy with cigarette smoke. The King's table was in the centre of the room, while the less exclusive clientele would be shown to tables placed at the outer edges, several yards from the intimacy of the dance floor itself, and fairly close to the gents and ladies 'facilities'. The waiters never made this segregated positioning explicit but relegation to the second division was evident to those selected for such discrimination. The air around the outer tables was perfumed with Elizabeth Arden's cloying Blue Grass, while the oxygen around the King's table reeked of something headier and more expensive. Women with money to burn on smelling good would anoint the pearl-hung cleavage of an otherwise naked back with the pricey scent of Guerlain's distillation of orange blossom, jasmine and sandalwood.

When Evangeline accepted an offer to step onto the dance floor (in truth her only such invitation of the night) she was swept into the centre of the room in the arms of the King himself. His manners were so exquisite that he had danced in turn with each of the four ladies in the party, although Evangeline hoped that he had not asked her out of pity but more in genuine friendship. She liked him, this charmfull man who had taken such a shine to her old school friend. She was still not certain of his intentions towards Wallis but the fascination between the two of them was noticeably weighted on his side. At the Fort only the other day Wallis had snagged her fingernail. Although she had dismissed the break as mattering 'not a jot' the King had nonetheless dashed across the marble-floored hallway, returning a moment later with an emery board from his own dressing room.

When Evangeline rose to dance with the King, finding her way through the cramped tables to the dance floor, she was determined to glide round the floor with the grace she had attempted to learn at school. Unfortunately her dress was a little long and as the pair lurched past the piano Evangeline felt a little squeeze of her red satin bottom. Letting out a squeal of surprise, every eye in the restaurant turned on her.

'Oh, don't mind Hutch,' the King hushed her, as Evangeline twisted round to find out where exactly the unwelcome pinch had come from. 'Hutch is such a naughty man, but we forgive him everything for that voice, don't we?'

A little later a man at a neighbouring table was asked to leave when a waiter spotted a badly concealed camera beneath a bowler hat. The following day the *Star* newspaper carried the pictures of Wallis on the dance floor, although no accompanying text identified her as the woman in the arms of the King, and Evangeline was relieved that the shot had missed the earlier moment of the bottom pinch.

Evangeline's summer plans took an upturn when Wallis telephoned to confirm an invitation to join the King's annual summer cruise round the Mediterranean in August. And when a blue envelope arrived in the post at Hamilton Terrace the following day, Evangeline knew the invitation was securely in the bag. The assurances that Wallis proffered when 'on the horn' often came to nothing, but if a telephone call was unreliable, the written word counted. Wallis had added a PS that it would be helpful if Evangeline could accompany her on the way home from the holiday on a shopping expedition to Paris. Mrs Simpson had evidently now become a woman who required a lady in waiting and Evangeline was happy to accept the position, even if she was tactful enough not to acknowledge that this was the service being required of her. The prospect of such a glamorous holiday on the yacht would require more than a little weight loss, Evangeline pledged to herself. She felt distinctly apprehensive at the thought of undressing in front of people with the physique not only of Wallis but also of the alarming Lady Diana Cooper, whose name was also on the cruise guest list.

One Friday lunchtime in the middle of July Evangeline was discussing the holiday wardrobe with Wallis over a rare lunch in the King's new apartments at Buckingham Palace. The King had never liked the grey building at the top of the Mall, associating it with the stuffy years of his childhood, and as a result he spent as much time as possible at the Fort. But official duties such as Trooping the Colour and the presentation of medals involved short overnight stays in the London residence, and Wallis often accompanied him there.

That day her expansive hand gestures showed off the ruby-and-diamond bracelet that encased her wrist, while pinned to her navy-blue jacket was a huge diamond brooch that Evangeline could not remember seeing before.

'Fortieth birthday presents, perhaps,' Evangeline wondered, twisting the signet ring on the little finger of her own left hand, a confirmation gift from her godmother Joan all those years ago. The finger beside it seemed more naked than ever. As Evangeline contemplated her absence of jewels Wallis shifted nearer her on the sofa and was now sitting slim thigh alongside thick.

'So, Vangey, perhaps we should think of getting you a new canine friend? I expect you are still missing Wiggle and we have had some happy news. Slipper is about to become a father. Let me make you a little happier, with a new puppy, Vangey. You always look so anxious.'

And suddenly Evangeline's unadorned fingers found themselves clasped within those encircled by precious stones, the physical contact returning Evangeline in a moment to the distressing events of two decades ago. Confessing to a sudden rush of heat Evangeline got up and moved over towards the open window.

Below her in the Mall all appeared orderly. The Union flags were flying and a small crowd was waiting for a glimpse of the King, who was expected to ride past at any moment. Earlier that afternoon, the wide-open spaces of Hyde Park had provided a perfect stage for Edward VIII's presentation of the King's Colours to three Guards regiments. Horses huffed and stamped and pawed at the grass. Helmets gleamed in the sunshine. London was July-blowsy with the weight of full-grown leaves on the trees. A military band wound its way through the Wellington Arch at Hyde Park Corner, the drums and trumpets alerting those royalists waiting at Constitution Hill that the King was on his way.

As the small figure on horseback wearing his ceremonial scarlet uniform and bearskin emerged through the Arch, he passed a man in a brown suit with a snappy moustache holding a newspaper. Suddenly the newspaper fell from the man's hand revealing a revolver pointed directly at Edward VIII. With impressive speed, the King's personal detective knocked the gun from the

257

man's hand to the ground as a policeman moved forward quickly to arrest the would-be assassin.

Throughout the day worried officials were shown in and out of the King's private apartments, trying to unravel the security lapse that had made such an incident possible. Given that two further rounds of ammunition had been found in McMahon's bag, the fragility of the King's physical safety as he went out and about doing his 'Kinging' job had been exposed. Special Constable Anthony Dick, who had been detailed to look after the King that morning, arrived to explain what the police had discovered. An Irish journalist, George Andrew McMahon, had pulled a loaded gun on the King, and the quick thinking of the detective had saved the King's life. Constable Dick confirmed that the assassin was mentally unbalanced. The words 'May I love you?' had been found written on his discarded newspaper. The full implications of the gunman's intentions were received by the King with impressive calm.

An equerry knocked at the door. He was holding a telegram. 'Please forgive the interruption, Sir, but this is a message of some importance, Sir.'

The few words pasted in tickertape onto the cream paper conveyed the Chancellor of Germany Adolf Hitler's anxiety at 'the news of the abominable attempt on the life of Your Majesty' and included his heartiest congratulations on the King's lucky escape.

'Interesting how fast news travels these days,' observed the King. 'Who would have thought Hitler had heard of the incident already? He must have his spies everywhere.'

Wallis and Evangeline had been sitting quietly in a corner of the room for the past hour. Wallis had been unnaturally subdued. However, on hearing about the telegram Wallis jumped up.

'That will be down to Ribbentrop, David. He is already taking his ambassadorial duties most seriously, you know, even though he hasn't yet arrived in London for the appointment. I hear he is due in a month or so, which is rather nice. Even so, he never misses a trick! We must remember to give him a welcome dinner as soon as he arrives.'

Evangeline and the King caught Constable Dick's concerned expression.

'What is it, Constable?' the King asked, a note of defensiveness in his voice.

'Excuse me, Sir, but I have neglected to point out one further detail we have discovered about McMahon. He was seen only a few days ago selling the *Blackshirt*, Sir, the fascist party newspaper, Sir.'

'Yes, well, that is most interesting, Constable. And we are most grateful for everything you have done.'

Realising he had been dismissed, Constable Dick made a neat little bow, and then, as an afterthought, a formal nod of his head in the direction of Wallis before leaving the room.

Wallis was more shaken after the assassination attempt than Evangeline had ever seen her. Despite being kept on the periphery of her friend's social life, Evangeline remained eager to be useful. The complications of Wallis's relationship with the King were becoming greater with

259

each passing day and friends should stand by one another no matter what. Although Wallis spent most of her time in the company of the King, her affection for Ernest had never been in doubt. Evangeline wondered how far the tolerance of a husband could be pushed. And she had not been certain where Wallis's genuine romantic centre lay. Was it with the King or with Ernest? But things were changing. Recently Ernest and Mary Raffray had been spending a great deal of time together and Wallis had begun to mind. Just two days after Wallis's fortieth birthday on 19 June, a waiter had carried the breakfast tray up to the room occupied by Mr Ernest Simpson in the notorious Hôtel de Paris in the village of Bray. Not more than half a dozen miles from where Mrs Simpson was in discussion with the fashionable interior decorator Lady Mendl about altering some of the furnishings at Fort Belvedere, the Bray waiter noticed that a woman in a yellow floral hat who gave her name as Buttercup Kennedy had joined Mr Simpson under the covers. Whipping out a camera from beneath a white napkin, the waiter took a picture of the couple in bed. That same day, when presented with the photograph, Wallis wrote immediately to Ernest to inform him he would be hearing from her solicitor. Not long afterwards, Wallis made arrangements to move out of her marital home, Bryanston Court, and into a flat of her own in Cumberland Terrace in Regent's Park.

16

One day in late July Evangeline was invited by Wallis to join a 'family-only' weekend party at the Fort. Wallis's splendid aunt, Mrs Bessie Merryman, had arrived for a short visit from New York and soon the three Americans were catching up on news from back home. The *Queen Mary* had sailed into New York Harbour for the first time to a huge welcome. A heat wave in North Dakota had reached over 120 degrees Fahrenheit, resulting in a series of terrible fires that had killed many people; Mrs Merryman was reading *Gone With the Wind,* a marvellous new novel about life on a plantation in the Deep South. She recommended it.

As if in mind of high temperatures, the King announced he was going to have a steam bath and disappeared into the basement, re-emerging some time later dressed in his evening clothes, scarlet in the face, and beaming as he gleamed. The steam bath, along with the bathrooms 'en-suite' and the central heating system, were all additions to the Fort that the King had made himself under the influence of the luxuries of the New World, which he had visited several times when Prince of Wales. Not even Chatsworth could boast such modern comforts, he told his guests with pride.

After dining on oysters brought up from the Duchy's own oyster beds in Cornwall, accompanied by several glasses of pink champagne, the

King had impressed Wallis's aunt by playing a song from the Scottish highlands on his bag-pipes. Gratified by her applause, the King told her that there were some who failed to share his passion for the pipes. The conductor Thomas Beecham had once been bold enough to remark to the King himself that he preferred the sound when safely seated the other side of a mountain.

The next morning, after standing on the highest point of the garden and showing 'Aunt Bess', as the King affectionately called her, the dome of St Paul's Cathedral through his eyeglass, the King had insisted on a Saturday afternoon expedition to have tea with his brother Bertie.

'David just loves his new car,' Wallis explained to her aunt indulgently. 'It's an American station wagon, would you believe? Yes! And he far prefers it to the stuffy old Rolls.'

'And where are we going in this lovely new car, Wallis darling?' her aunt asked, amused by her niece's sudden enthusiasm for machinery.

'Oh, we're going to take a short hop over to see the Duke of York at Windsor,' Wallis replied as she went to her room to put on her driving hat.

As the party from the Fort arrived, whirling with a dramatic flourish twice around the circular driveway at Royal Lodge, the Duke and Duchess of York were waiting for them at the front door.

'Don't you think it's a bbbbb, a bbb a bbb-it rrracey for the lanes of BBBerkshire, David?' Bertie began.

'Oh goodness, Bertie, you *are* an old stick in the mud,' retorted his brother, grinding out his cigarette in the gravel. 'This car is all the rage, don't you know? Have you seen the way it moves? Wallis arranged it for me! Isn't she the most clever girl?'

Elizabeth stood at her husband's side, her brilliant blue eyes radiating scepticism. Evangeline knew of Wallis's suspicions that 'Bertie's little wife' disapproved of her and assumed this disapproval to be founded on jealousy. Wallis was convinced that the Duchess of York secretly regretted settling for the second son in the family. Bertie was without doubt the less exciting brother and Wallis was keen to cushion these tense family meetings with other people, preferably outsiders. However, on that particular afternoon the atmosphere over at the Lodge was lightened by the arrival of the King's young niece Elizabeth.

'*You* like my new car don't you, Lilibet? More fun than others, isn't it? It's like settling for a bowler instead of a stuffy old topper, isn't it?'

Elizabeth and the King got along famously with one another. They had a running joke that involved Lilibet curtseying to her uncle every time she saw him. At her every appearance, whether emerging from the shadow of a tree, peering round a door or popping up from behind the car, the sight of this charming child always prompted the same question from her uncle. 'Have you forgotten your manners, Lilibet?'

In response the curly blonde ten-year-old would stretch the pockets of her jodhpurs outwards with her hands as if she was wearing a full ballgown and drop down to the ground in one respectful sweep. And every time uncle and niece would roar with laughter.

Inside the lodge tea was served, with orange juice for Lilibet and her six-year-old sister, Margaret Rose. Evangeline was enchanted by the girls. Lilibet reminded her of Florence down at Cuckmere Park. Both girls were exactly the same age, but Evangeline was conscious of the difference between them. One had all the freedom in the world, while the other was restricted by the weighty protocol that came with being the niece of the King.

*   *   *

The next morning, back at Fort Belvedere, Wallis was busy attending to matters of the household, instructing the servants to anticipate her guests' every whim. Wallis's preference for blonde-haired staff was evident beneath the white lacy caps of the housemaids. The King was pruning his ubiquitous rhododendrons as he did at every spare opportunity, as well as weeding the herbaceous borders. Mrs Merryman was catching up on her sleep in the blue bedroom upstairs, just across the corridor from her niece. Evangeline seized her moment. Struggling into her stretchy black swimming costume with its clever front fastening and thigh-concealing over-skirt, it occurred to her that it was not unlike a ballet dress that might be worn by Tchaikovsky's black swan. Fleetingly she wondered if Julian was enjoying those cunning elasticated swimming trunks she had given him before adding her raincoat over the top of her costume as an extra layer of concealment and hurrying out of the front door.

Passing the old battlements, with some two-dozen ancient cannons ranged along their front, Evangeline half-slithered down the slope that led to the high walls surrounding the swimming pool. Climbing roses tumbled over the stone, and a few petals had fallen in the wind, making a confetti puddle on the grass below. Several years ago, the King had transformed the area around an old lily pond into something resembling an outdoor sitting room with comfortable upholstered chaises to stretch out on and little trolleys filled with everything necessary to fulfil the urge to drink and smoke.

At the centre of this beautifully arranged scene, the pool glittered in the morning light. The pool was the hub of summer life at the Fort. On tables in front of the curved wall into which a long low stone bench was set, the drinks trays were already in place. A choice of wines, spirits, and jugs of freshly squeezed orange juice faced the thirsty guest. Any Sunday morning weariness might be relieved by a champagne cocktail or the restorative elixir of a Bloody Mary, a concoction that had arrived two years earlier on the menu at the St Regis Hotel in New York when Wallis was visiting friends in the city. Wallis liked to be up with the very latest in fashion so Evangeline was not surprised to see this spicy tomato juice and vodka make its way to the Fort luncheon table.

Buffet lunch would follow a few hours later, a meal unrecognisable from an average British al fresco menu. Evangeline had been to several lunch parties in Philip's constituency half an hour's drive from Cuckmere, where under-cooked slices of chicken accompanied by slices of overcooked egg and congealed swirls of mayonnaise meant that she returned home ravenous.

Lunch at the Fort was eaten on guests' knees while seated in the cushioned cane chairs by the side of the pool. The spread changed in composition daily and was always supervised by Wallis. The Fort staff would lay monogrammed white cloths over the trestle tables, spread out the buffet, cover the dishes with little bead-scattered cloches made of fine-meshed wire to keep the flies and wasps away, and retire to the kitchen, leaving the guests to help themselves. There was a deliberate code of informality. The King insisted it should be that way. Guests could choose to eat as much or as little as they wished and although people may have remarked on the extreme slenderness of Mrs Simpson's frame, everyone agreed there was no faulting her when it came to providing mouth-watering menus.

Those fortunate enough to be staying for the weekend would find thick ham roasted in honey, piled high onto blue willow-patterned plates. There would be a whole salmon, cold with a herb dressing, and biscuity pastry cases filled with mushrooms settled within a rich cheese and parsley sauce, still warm from the oven. Silver lids concealed mounds of waxy new potatoes with knobs of butter melting and seeping deep into the dish. Bowls of home-grown baby broad beans, as small and irregular as green-coloured sea pearls, sat beside plates of tender stemmed asparagus tied in bundles with black cotton bows. Nutty avocados, sent down each day to the Fort in a green Harrods van, were added to lettuces picked from the kitchen garden only moments earlier. And 'club sandwiches' of cold turkey, tomato, and pickle were piled between layers of toast and pinioned to avoid collapse by a wooden sausage stick. The Fort staff were sceptical about this American innovation but there was no deterring Mrs Simpson about something when she had made her mind up. For pudding there were bowls of sweet strawberries and raspberries and blueberries gathered from the Fort fruit cages and trays of meringues sandwiched together with whipped, sugared cream from the Windsor Home farm. There had been one much talked of error when Wallis had served a local dish from her own southern states back home. A diamond-backed terrapin had been sent over in a refrigerated container from Baltimore. Wallis explained that her mother had often prepared the dish and that it had become a family favourite. Apart from the single portion that Wallis placed on her own plate, complete with a wedge of lemon, the rejected reptile was returned to the kitchen intact.

That Sunday morning, several hours before lunch, Evangeline removed her coat and laid it on one of the chairs. She stood alone at the top of the pool steps and put out a tentative toe.

'Not too unbearably cold,' she thought to herself. 'I can do this. I can. I must. I will dazzle them all with my confidence on board the *Nahlin* in August. People will be amazed at my prowess as a swimmer.'

Moss grew in velvety clumps around the edge of the pool, and the sounds of wildlife coming from the nearby undergrowth were a little too close for Evangeline's liking. But willing away her life-long fear of water she began to walk down the steps. She could hear the bells of St George's chapel at Windsor Castle, some six miles in the distance, ringing out for the early Sunday service and the birds were calling gaily to one another in the nearby trees.

Evangeline braced herself to take two more steps. The water was lapping at her waist now and the overskirt was floating out around her as if her body was the jam in the middle of a doughnut. Only one more step to go, and she would be afloat. But as she put out her hand to steady herself on the edge of the pool before making the final plunge, her fingers encountered something slippery, and living. Evangeline let out a scream, shoving the startled frog away from her but at the same time losing her balance as she fell with force into the water. Managing to recover her footing she was relieved to discover that the water level had come no further up her body than her rib cage and she began to wade back to the steps. But the violence of her fall had disconnected several of the hooks at the front of her bathing dress, leaving Evangeline's bosom exposed to the air. Before she had succeeded in getting any of the hooks to close a man came running from the surrounding woods and down the path towards her.

'Help is here,' he shouted, as with a small splash the King of England dived neatly into the pool.

17

Evangeline had been spending a lot more time down at Cuckmere now that circumstances had changed. John Hunt had advised Philip that perhaps Joan would be better off in the nearby excellent cottage hospital where a full complement of nursing staff could assess and note even the tiniest of changes in her condition and Philip, wearied by the length of time it was taking for his wife to recover, had reluctantly agreed. With Joan no longer resident in the house, Evangeline was relieved to think she could stay at Cuckmere without the guilt of avoiding the invalid.

Evangeline's mother had always said that August was a wicked month and Evangeline was hoping that the monthly characteristic would hold true this year. She felt she could do with a bit of wickedness. Checking the contents of the silver dishes on the sideboard, she placed two sausages, a spoonful of kedgeree, three rashers of bacon and a grilled tomato onto a plate and settled herself down at the head of the Cuckmere dining-room table. An envelope addressed to Joan in green ink was sitting next to a basket of scones. Evangeline was surprised to see scones at that time of day and had quietly blessed Cooky for anticipating how they would be just as welcome at the beginning of the day as they always were at teatime.

270

Evangeline and Cooky were on excellent terms, unlike Evangeline's shaky relationship with Cooky's opposite number in the Hamilton Terrace kitchen. That particular liaison had never really recovered from the suggestion that London Cook's marinade of onion and wine-soaked kidneys might be responsible indirectly for poor Wiggle's 'unfortunate demise', as the Blunt staff referred to it. London Cook remained adamant that any finger of suspicion pointed against her was quite unjustified and Evangeline had been unable to diffuse London Cook's claims of false accusation. Evangeline had stressed on numerous occasions that Wiggle had long suffered from a congenital heart complaint and that the 'demise' was neither the fault of May nor anything to do with a saucer-full of offal. But London Cook remained affronted and a frost between the two women had continued to hang in the air well into the balmy summer months.

However, it was all sunshine and sugar between Evangeline and Cooky, an important relationship that Evangeline took trouble to preserve. Cooky, a solid monarchist, had been impressed by Miss Nettlefold's friendships in high places and as a result showed the American visitor an extra degree of respect. And Cooky had another reason for fostering this happy rapport. It made London Cook jealous. Cooky would flatter Evangeline by referring to Wiggle in altogether human terms, asking about the small dog's 'lineage' and assuming a doleful expression whenever there was cause to mention 'The Passing-On'.

'Mark my words, Miss Nettlefold, Wiggle will be given in heaven the soul he was denied on earth,' Cooky assured Evangeline mysteriously but somehow comfortingly.

This reverence for Evangeline's feelings complemented Cooky's genius in the pastry department and cemented their mutual regard. All in all, Evangeline was beginning to prefer life in Sussex to that in London. Philip had begun to ask her for a little help with the running of the household. He had sought her opinion on flowers for the weekends, consulted her on menus, even discussed the composition of guests at one of the recent house parties that he felt professionally compelled to give, despite Joan's incapacity. Evangeline soon forgot last week's regrettable occurrence when the daily had walked into her bedroom just when she was hiding the shards of an eighteenth-century French vase beneath the chocolate wrappers in her waste paper basket. That day Wallis had cancelled an invitation to a formal dinner at Bryanston Court and Evangeline had demonstrated her disappointment by throwing the pretty object at the fireplace.

Now at last she had the chance to host dinner parties of her own. Last Saturday Evangeline had taken Joan's place at one end of the dining-room table as proxy hostess for her godmother, and afterwards Philip had gone so far as to say that he did not know quite how he would manage without Evangeline's help.

'Thank you, Philip,' she said, risking a small kiss of gratitude on Philip's cheek. 'That means a great deal to me.'

As a result of her unexpected promotion, Evangeline was enjoying a new social confidence. She felt needed. When arranging the dinner-party placement by pinning miniature handwritten name flags onto a leather-covered cork board imprinted with the outline of a table, she positioned herself between the guest of honour, the Director-General of the BBC, Sir John Reith, and the Mayor of Eastbourne.

Ever since Evangeline's arrival in England, she had found dinner parties something of an ordeal. The British adhered fiercely to the etiquette of having equal numbers of each gender around a dining table although the rule was treated with laxity by the Blunts. Even so, women guests entering the dining room either at Hamilton Terrace or Cuckmere Park would raise an eyebrow when they saw that their name card had been put next to that of Evangeline; her single status invariably threw the numbers out of kilter. In London the search for a spare, single man was less of a challenge. Several distinguished individuals, mostly confirmed bachelors, were happy to fill the role. The choice in the country was more limited and had become an even greater problem for the Blunts since the Cuckmere vicar's announcement that he would no longer be available for that purpose. His wife was so fed up at being left at home that she had threatened to stop doing the church flowers.

The day before the dinner Sir John's secretary had telephoned to say he would be coming alone, and even though Bettina had already been persuaded to come down to Cuckmere on one of her rare visits, Evangeline and Philip found themselves a woman short. At the last minute the headmistress of the village school had been asked to occupy the spare chair between Rupert and the senior librarian from the London Library who was in residence cataloguing Sir Philip's books.

'Do you think Miss Dobbs will have the right clothes?' Philip asked Evangeline at teatime. He was uncharacteristically nervous, his uncertainties about such matters no longer eased by his wife's reassurances. 'I hope she wears something other than those moth-eaten trousers, and remembers to brush that chewed hair. Honestly, sometimes she looks more like a Mr than a Miss.'

Evangeline was too preoccupied with thoughts about her own gown to be much interested in Miss Dobbs's dress sense.

'Between us,' Philip continued, 'I have instructed Mrs Cage that Miss Dobbs is not to be given too much wine. You never know when tongues unaccustomed to alcohol may run away with themselves, do you?'

Evangeline finally gave Philip her attention.

'I think you have nothing to worry about, my dear. I am certain the evening will go with a swing. And Miss Dobbs may surprise us as a marvellous addition to the table. Don't they say teachers and librarians go together like . . . ' Evangeline sought for a comparison, ' . . . like a spoon and fork, or toast and marmalade? And now, if you will excuse me?'

And after giving him what was threatening to

become a habitual peck on the cheek, Evangeline headed upstairs to begin the preparations for her evening toilette. Philip made sure she was out of sight before looking in the mirror and touching the spot where Evangeline's lipstick had left an imprint the colour of a holly berry. As he wiped his cheek with his handkerchief he resolved to treat her with more kindness.

★ ★ ★

By the time the quails' eggs had been cleared away, Evangeline was doing her best to fulfil her duties as a hostess. She had succeeded in feigning a rapt interest in the Mayor of Eastbourne's plans for new town housing. It had not been easy. Every time he lifted a forkful of egg to his mouth, the gold mayoral chain would swing forward and hit his plate with a clang. As soon as the plate of shellfish and asparagus was placed in front of her Evangeline turned her attention to her right in relief. Sir John Reith had barely touched his first course and, as he watched Evangeline helping herself to a generous dollop of hollandaise, he explained that he suffered from 'the terrors of a poor Scottish digestion'.

Sir John's physical indisposition prompted a discussion between them of a case featured in the past few days in the newspapers. Recently a back-bench MP representing a Leicestershire constituency had died in puzzling circumstances. Although the MP had been a married man it emerged that he had been having a secret affair with his much younger constituency secretary. For several years he had complained to his cook of breathlessness and had eventually died in some agony. A post-mortem revealed that the cumulative effect of small quantities of mercury in his stomach had caused his death. The cook had reported her suspicions to the police and the MP's wife was arrested on suspicion of poisoning her husband.

'I would conclude several things from the case,' Sir John said, rubbing his stomach. 'First of all, infidelity is not a good idea. Secondly, murder is hard to get away with. And thirdly: make sure all poisons are hidden from would-be assassins.'

His lack of interest in food freed up Sir John's attention, allowing him to concentrate on his companion as she surprised him with a thorough knowledge of the differing strengths and weaknesses of various poisons.

'We had a swell teacher at my school back home in Baltimore,' Evangeline told him. 'Professor Meredith had a long beard and my favourite lessons were the ones with him in the chemistry lab. Once his beard caught fire in my friend Wallis's Bunsen burner, although I managed to put it out with water from the goldfish bowl. After that Professor M kind of took a shine to me. When the other girls were taking extra tennis classes I would go to the lab and help him experiment on the rats with poison.'

'This is fascinating. Do go on,' Sir John said encouragingly.

276

'Well, sometimes we used a dab of the Brazilian wandering spider venom and that was very effective: loss of muscle control, paralysis and then death. Then there was cyanide, speediest of all, and strychnine — that took a little longer. My favourite was sarin, a kind of gas that we once tried on a rabbit, the size of a puppy. I'll never forget it.' Evangeline's voice had become trance-like at the memory. 'The rabbit lay down on its back at the first whiff. The Professor never let us test mercury as the process takes too long to take effect. Mind you, strychnine and cyanide can both be concealed in drinks, which makes it dangerous stuff as we all have to drink, don't we, Sir John?'

Evangeline drew a breath, followed by a swig from her wine glass and allowed herself a moment to assess her solo audience. Sir John was a handsome man about the same age as herself, Evangeline guessed, perhaps a year older, but what a position of power he had reached in the same time span!

Evangeline was enjoying herself. Not since her first few weeks in England had anyone been quite as interested in what she had to say, let alone someone who was *such* a someone. Julian, for example, never seemed to listen to her. Of course, at his age Julian did not have the sophisticated maturity of Sir John. That long-ago encouraging wink before Wallis's dinner party had proved his interest in her, of course, and it had been her own clumsy behaviour that night that had discouraged him from pursuing those feelings. She was pretty certain that he was not committed to his silly girlfriend Charlotte with her unnecessarily suggestive behaviour. No. Evangeline had no one to blame but herself that no matter how hard she tried to command Julian's attention he appeared distracted. Come to think of it, he was always wanting to go somewhere in the car, whether it be to see Joan in the hospital or be taken to the station. Not for the first time did she consider how dreary it must be spending so much time travelling about in the car on his own with only the foolishly besotted May for company.

However, in her place at the head of the Cuckmere table, Evangeline was able to put Julian from her mind. She also forgot her frustration of earlier in the evening when the flat-chested androgynous look, currently so in vogue, had persisted in evading her despite all her efforts with a stretchy crêpe bandage. Sir John's eyes were directed not at the substantial cleft of her chest but on her mouth and the words that were tumbling from it. He was clearly much more than a pinch-and-tickle man.

'Good gracious,' he said, 'you have the makings of a most effective detective! I wouldn't wonder if you are a fan of Agatha Christie stories or should I say Dashiell Hammett from your side of the ocean? Marvellous book that, *The Thin Man*, didn't you think?'

Evangeline would have been happy to pursue the discussion about crime fiction but Sir John seemed keen to return to her account of life at school in Baltimore.

'You must have been one of the most popular

girls there,' he observed confidently as he offered her the use of the silver pepper grinder that lay between them.

Evangeline blushed and smiled as prettily as she could. Perhaps it was the new French style of chignon into which Wallis's hairdresser Antoine had cleverly arranged her lighter coloured wig that was contributing to the beneficial effect.

'I understand from Philip that you have been acquainted with Mrs Simpson since your school days,' Sir John was saying, 'although you do not appear to have left those days behind very long ago!'

Evangeline found herself a little more forthcoming than she had intended, realising that she had already drained a third — or was it a fourth? — glass of Chablis. She looked across the table to Miss Dobbs, who was performing admirably in her seat between Rupert and the librarian. Rupert was being at his most Etonian-charming, despite Miss Dobbs's green tie. Evangeline turned back to her own dinner companion.

'We all wonder a little about exactly what *is* going on there down in the woods at Fort Belvedere,' he was saying, 'although it is far for me to pry. What I really want to ask is did anyone ever tell you what a most unusual voice you have? Forgive me my professional interest, but I cannot help but notice a voice. And yours is pure velvet in texture.' Sir John was aligning his unused fish knife and fork in exact parallel with the pudding spoon and fruit knife as he spoke. He was evidently a precise sort of man.

Evangeline was glowing both without and within.

'And if you will not mind a further professional observation?' Sir John continued. 'Yours is a voice that asks, one might even say *demands* to be heard on the wireless.'

'I am not sure I follow you exactly, Sir John,' Evangeline replied eagerly.

'Oh, please let me explain. We British are most interested to hear how you do things on the other side of the Atlantic. And what the audience wants is the truth about a place and its people. Truth. That's what's missing from life. The wireless can help fill some of the gaps that the newspapers are unable or even reluctant to address. Even George V was a little sceptical when I first suggested he make a Christmas broadcast to the nation, and it took me nearly ten years to persuade him to sit in front of a microphone to give a seasonal message to the people. Eventually he took to it like a duck to water and for the final four years of his life he didn't miss one of them. You should consider coming into the broadcasting studios and recording a little about your wonderful country and all the excitements going on over there.'

Evangeline blinked at him, for a moment quite speechless.

'Well I never, Sir John,' she said at last. 'No one has ever paid me such a compliment.'

'I promise you I am perfectly sincere about this,' Sir John replied. 'Do think about it. Any mistakes or hesitations can be easily changed before the recording goes out on the airwaves.

And I warn you, I am an impatient man and I will be looking forward to hearing from you very soon.'

Such talk, Evangeline assured herself, was mere professional flattery, but nonetheless flattery was a most agreeable courtesy.

'You certainly managed to animate Sir John last night,' Philip remarked the next day. 'Never seen him so jolly. He can be rather a fusspot. Has to have things just right, nothing out of order. In fact, he is often a curmudgeonly old so and so. I do congratulate you, my dear, on taming the beast. You certainly had more success than I did with the trappist Lady Mayoress. Couldn't get a word out of her. And as for the librarian's wife! Give me Miss Dobbs any day. Life and soul she was; except for yourself, my dear, of course.'

* * *

The scones were still giving off the heat of the oven and the smell was irresistible. No one else had yet come downstairs and Evangeline helped herself, adding a dollop of butter that was absorbed into the doughy surface. Her mouth was still full when Philip walked in and caught her eyeing the envelope.

'Is that for me?' Philip asked trying to conceal his irritation at knowing Evangeline received little from the postman other than a forwarded copy of the American *Good Housekeeping* magazine.

'Oh I *am* sorry. It's for Joan, actually, but of course it is for you to open. I was just struck by

281

the unusual colour of the ink,' Evangeline began as a couple of half-chewed sultanas tumbled out of her mouth onto the tablecloth.

'Not *green* ink is it?' Philip asked as he turned to pour himself a cup of coffee from the pot sitting on the electric hotplate.

'More like emerald, I think you might say,' Evangeline replied examining the envelope more closely.

Philip came over to the table, raised a puzzled eyebrow at the sight of the scones swaddled in their snowy napkin, and took the envelope from Evangeline. The grandfather clock in the corner of the room struck nine times. Philip opened the envelope and read the contents. Only after he had swallowed a mouthful of coffee did he speak.

'Myrtle, damn it. I might have wondered when we would hear from her. And just when things were settling down, what with you here to cheer me up,' this last phrase inserted just in case he had upset his wife's god-daughter by any earlier brusqueness. God knows Evangeline meant well, even if she got in the way some times. The other evening he had run into John Reith in their club. John wanted Philip's view on a confidential matter. At a recent lunch in Claridge's a mutual friend, Lady Reading, had suggested John would make a good Ambassador to Washington.

'Excellent plan, my dear fellow,' Philip had exclaimed. 'Although I sometimes wonder if there are any Americans left over there. They seem to have descended on this country in droves.'

They had both laughed a little at the eccentric

ways of Joan's American god-daughter.

'Expert in poison of all things, so it seems!' John had remarked, adding however that the beauty of her voice was an asset none could deny. Philip had been grateful to share a word with someone else about his houseguest's strange and often infuriating ways. Worryingly, Evangeline had not spoken of any plans to return home to America and out of loyalty to his poor wife, who was so fond of this large bewigged woman, Philip felt reluctant to raise the subject.

'You know all about Myrtle, Joan's elder sister, don't you?' he said to Evangeline at the breakfast table. 'Need I expand on the reasons why we always fear the arrival of a communication written in green ink?'

Philip was half smiling but Evangeline could see he was rattled. And from her conversations with Lady Cynthia Asquith she knew why. No one else on this earth was capable of unnerving Joan or Philip to the degree that Myrtle was. Unlike Joan's younger sister Grace, whose death and its consequences had at times blighted the spirits of the entire Blunt household, Myrtle had rarely been part of their family life either in general conversation or in bodily presence. Throughout her adulthood Myrtle had demonstrated her supercilious manners. She hated anything that smacked of 'modern ways' especially those adopted by people who should know their place. For example she could not abide 'hatches' that linked a kitchen with a dining room.

'What's the difficulty in carrying the plates

through a door, I ask? Oh no. Nowadays people knock a hole in a wall instead and save themselves the effort. Typical new-fangled laziness is what I call it.'

The foul-tempered Lady Myrtle Bradley had lived on her own in a tiny village in Yorkshire since her own tragedy of the war years had condemned her to spinsterhood. There had been a fiancé but his position at the controls of one of the new tanks had not protected him from the jagged fragment of shrapnel that had sliced into him from ground level. Joan had never felt her sister to be sufficiently distressed by the loss of Jack. In fact, Joan had always wondered if her sister was capable of feeling anything at all for another human being. An exchange of Christmas cards now formed the extent of the two sisters' contact with one another. Goodness knows what Myrtle did with herself all day up there in Yorkshire. There had been talk that she was involved with a group of keep fit fanatics, a current rage in parts of the country. Myrtle had always been an outdoorsy type. In her late twenties, before meeting Jack, she had been one of the first to adopt the bifurcated skirt in order to sit more comfortably astride her bicycle as she pedalled the lanes around their childhood home in Hampshire with a couple of like-minded young women. Her chief reading material consisted of *Time and Tide* magazine and printed lists of garden bulbs. Joan knew this because Myrtle had once asked Joan to save her any catalogues she no longer had use for at Cuckmere.

'Too tight to take out a subscription herself, you see,' Joan had explained to Vera when she asked her to make sure that any out-of-date gardening publications were sent on up to Lady Myrtle in Yorkshire.

'Certainly, my Lady,' Vera had replied, before embarking on quite a correspondence with Lady Myrtle, comparing the fertility levels of the peaty soil in Yorkshire with the chalky earth down on the south coast. Last year this unlikely connection had encouraged Vera to take a few days of her holiday up in Yorkshire. She planned to visit the Minster and perhaps call in on Lady Myrtle and make her acquaintance in person.

'Lady Myrtle was most accommodating and we spent a very enjoyable time together in her garden,' Vera reported on her return, her dry upper lip twitching as she spoke.

After Joan suffered her stroke, Philip had written to his sister-in-law. The letter was as friendly as he could make it, but he explained that medical advice cautioned against any new visitors until Joan regained consciousness. Even though Joan had recently been moved to the cottage hospital, a meeting between the sisters at this time would not benefit either Joan or Myrtle. Joan would be oblivious to Myrtle's presence and the sight of her unresponsive sister would inevitably distress Myrtle.

It was therefore with surprise, alarm and displeasure that the letter in the distinctive green ink indicated that Myrtle would be coming down to Sussex this week. Myrtle fancied a spell near the south coast. She had been feeling a little anaemic of late and thought the sea air might invigorate her. Philip looked up from the letter, lowering his glasses onto the tip of his nose.

'She has no telephone. An unnecessary expense, she thinks. And of course she's too mean to pay for a telegram. She is breaking her journey by staying in her club at Hyde Park Corner, an all-female establishment if my information serves me correctly. And then she will take the train from Victoria arriving at Polegate station on Friday afternoon. And that's tomorrow.'

Philip put the letter down, took off his glasses and rubbed his eyes.

'She really is the giddy limit, Evangeline. A visit will not be *at all* convenient or indeed welcome at this time. The children are away in Berlin. I am spending several nights at Chequers in discussion with the PM and am not planning to return until after the weekend.'

Evangeline could feel his anger getting the better of him. She offered him a scone but he waved the basket away.

'Mrs Cage and Florence leave for Bognor Regis tomorrow,' he continued, his voice rising, 'and Hooch is already off for his annual break with his brother up in Holkham. Cooky is going to visit that strange vicar friend of hers in Winchester. Thank God London Cook is on duty. I suppose I could spare her to come down here for a day or two while I am away but that only leaves the two daily cleaning ladies to hold the fort at home and May to take Myrtle to and from the hospital.'

'Why not let me stand in?' Evangeline interrupted. 'Explain to Myrtle that you are busy this weekend. It's the truth, after all.'

Putting his glasses back on, Philip looked doubtfully at Evangeline.

'Trust me, Philip. I assure you May and I can manage Myrtle together. Don't bother London Cook. May is perfectly capable of preparing the odd dish or two; she learned how on that sugary island of hers. Something that involves beans and rice I believe, and I daresay I could try and lend her a hand. What do you say?'

Philip looked at her, his cheeks doing that curious nervous thing of puffing in and out that she had seen him do when he was about to interview Rupert about some misdemeanour or was preparing for a difficult talk with a senior politician. The cheek puffing was Joan's habit, too. Strange how husbands and wives picked up each other's little tics.

'Well I don't know. I mean I suppose it *is* an idea. Could you really manage? I mean Myrtle may well be more than even you can chew, if you get my meaning,' he added, feeling an explanation for the phrase might be called for.

Evangeline was insistent. 'I have heard she can be a handful but I have handled more than one difficult woman in my time, believe me.'

'Well, you are certainly confident, I will say that for you,' said Philip, his acquiescence to the plan implicit in his air of relieved gratitude.

Evangeline took a bite from a tepid scone, filtering her words through flour-smeared lips. 'After all that you and Joan have done for me, it is a pleasure to be able to help.' And in a gesture that demonstrated her new sense of purpose Evangeline picked up the small brass hand bell that lay at Philip's place and rang it.

A moment later Cooky put her head round the door.

'Could you be so kind as to find Miss May please and ask her to come in for a moment?'

Philip excused himself to get ready for Chequers and the smile on Evangeline's face remained long after he had left the room. If she could not be appreciated by either Wallis or Julian then at least the kindly husband of her poor godmother understood her worth.

★ ★ ★

On the afternoon of Myrtle's arrival things had not quite gone to plan. A taxi had been waiting at the front door when May returned from taking Sir Philip to Chequers, packed tight with Mrs Cage and Florence's holiday luggage including the red bucket and spade that May had bought Florence from the little stand in the Cuckmere post office a few days earlier.

Evangeline had gone with May to post a card to her brother in Baltimore and meeting Mrs Jenkins for the first time had been taken aback by the postmistress's remark about May having a touch of the tar brush about her. May had ignored Mrs Jenkins and bustled Evangeline out of the post office but not quickly enough to prevent her from hearing a comment about large sunhats failing to disguise overweight women.

288

Florence had been in a foul mood for a week, despite being allowed to wear shorts for the first time that summer. Shorts were her favourite article of clothing, their appearance from the drawer proving that the school term had finally come to an end. But Florence announced she hated making sandcastles so what was the point of the bucket? Sandcastles were for boys or sissies. And anyway there was almost no sand at all on Pagham beach. It was covered in nasty pebbles. She had hated the pebbles last year and was certainly going to hate them again this time.

Everyone had noticed how Florence had recently been hanging around the kitchen, watching Cooky make junket. Florence had always made her hatred of junket clear, the slimy consistency reminding her that the only time she was forced to eat it was when she was ill. A freshly made bowl of the slippery pudding had become a familiar sight in the Cuckmere kitchen since Lady Joan's illness and despite Lady Joan's recent absence in hospital, Cooky had continued to make quantities of the stuff just in case her ladyship returned at short notice. On the day before her departure on holiday Florence had been helping herself from Cooky's mixing bowl. It was as if she wished to behave in a manner as contrary to her true self as possible.

Mrs Cage had already issued her daughter with a warning that if she did not pull herself together she would remove Florence's swimsuit from the suitcase and there would be no swimming at Pagham. There were girls who would give their ruddy eye-teeth to be taken on holiday, Mrs Cage told her sharply. Florence didn't know what a lucky girl she was. This reprimand resulted in a sullen look and a sharp kick of the green baize-covered door. Florence's sulky restlessness continued right up until the moment of departure when May stood by the taxi to see them off.

'Have a lovely time, darling,' she said, bending down to kiss Florence whose curly hair was for once free of restraining elastic bands and ribbons. 'Enjoy the swimming, won't you?'

Florence looked down at the driveway, refusing to catch May's eye. Threaded through the loops of Florence's shorts was a belt with an unusual but somehow familiar buckle, marked with a circle and a line like a pictorial flash of lightning inscribed through the centre of it.

'What a lovely belt!' May said. 'Is it your special holiday belt?'

But Florence said nothing, and with a low-slung wave of her hand got into the car beside her mother looking miserable.

May went to her room to change into her chauffeur's uniform. On her pillow was an envelope containing a photograph. The note that accompanied it was short.

'This is where I have got to go, *again*.'

May picked up the photograph. Florence, looking a little younger than she had a few moments ago, was standing on a pebbled beach surrounded by a group of smiling women dressed in black. Florence was wearing her shorts and the unusual belt was looped through the waistband of her shorts. May turned the picture over. 'Pagham. 1935' was written in pencil on the back. She looked back at the picture, studying it closely. All at once she recognised the symbol on Florence's belt. She had seen the same one on the Blackshirt belts at Mosley's meeting in Oxford. May put the picture in her trouser pocket and went down to the garage to fetch the car. For a moment she considered showing the photograph to Mr Hooch. And then she remembered his response to Sir Oswald Mosley's visit to Cuckmere and decided against the idea.

May and Evangeline arrived on the platform at Polegate just in time to see the train from London draw into the station. It had been Evangeline's suggestion that they face Myrtle together from beginning to end of her visit, although it did not seem quite right to May. The proper thing would have been for May to meet Lady Myrtle in her capacity as chauffeur and for Miss Nettlefold to stay behind to greet Lady Myrtle as the acting Lady of the house. However, Miss Nettlefold had insisted on coming to the station.

'It's the sort of things friends do together,' she had said firmly.

The tall woman who came towards them with the same lengthy strides as Lady Joan was unmistakably a Bradley. But the similarity in carriage between the two sisters was not replicated in their choice of dress. Instead of the elegant silk and wool femininity of the woman who lay in a coma in a nearby hospital, here was a figure dressed for an afternoon on horseback or for a spot of weeding, in her tweed jacket, knee breeches and sturdy brown lace-up boots. With a copy of *Time and Tide* magazine tucked under her arm, in one hand Lady Myrtle held a thick walking stick, and a metal birdcage in the other.

'Nice suit,' was her opening remark to May as her eyes travelled the length of May's willowy body. 'Glad to see you take your professional duties seriously. And who on earth are you?'

Myrtle's deep voice was directed at Evangeline and had a strong hint of the northern accent that May had heard used by the sailors on the sugar consignment ship to Liverpool.

'I am Evangeline Nettlefold, your sister's god-daughter from America,' Evangeline began.

'Oh yes. The overweight charity case.' Myrtle spoke in short truncated sentences as if she was economising within a telegram. 'Well, make yourselves useful. The reading material. Remove it please. Now,' she said, indicating to May that she expected her to retrieve the magazine from beneath her armpit. 'Rum business with my sister. Mind you, hardly ever see her. What a chatterbox she is. Relief to know she has shut up for a while.' And then sensing disapproval, she rather surprisingly corrected herself. 'Mustn't speak ill of the ill, I suppose.'

In no time they reached the long driveway up to the house.

'Not a bad place. Typical of Philip not to be here to show me round. Hasn't turned up to see me for years. And no sign of that stuck-up nephew of mine or his idiotic sister? Some things to be grateful for I suppose. Hand me Dorothea,' Lady Myrtle said, indicating the birdcage on the back seat. 'Don't want her gnawing at the bars,' she added as she strode through the front door.

The canary was tossed from one side of the cage to the other, and May feared for its well-being within its hurdy-gurdy transport. Inside the hall Evangeline disappeared for a moment, only to reappear breathing heavily and pushing a trolley across the uneven flagstones. When Mrs Cage was at home, the trolley was only used in the passages behind the kitchen baize door. But in the housekeeper's absence Evangeline had laid it with cups and saucers on the upper level, and a large cake on the bottom shelf, and brought it upstairs.

'Good gracious,' cried the visitor. 'A hostess trolley? Whatever next? Permission to dunk pieces of cake in the tea, I suppose.'

However, she declared herself satisfied with the chocolate cake that Cooky had baked before her departure, and ate two slices before asking to be shown the way to the garden.

'Would you like May to take you over to the hospital to see Joan?' Evangeline asked. 'It's only a mile down the road.'

'No thank you very much. That particular engagement can wait a while,' Myrtle replied. 'It's not as if my sister's going anywhere, is it? No, I am going out to the garden. It's no good waiting around inside a stuffy house all day. I will see you later.'

Lady Myrtle walked onto the terrace leaving Evangeline and May staring after her. She seemed to know her way through the garden as if she had studied a plan of it. Ducking under the rose arch, and turning left at the red-tiled dovecot, she strode off in the direction of the pond and disappeared from sight. Inside the house, Dorothea began to weep in her stuffy cage. May longed to open the cage door and release her. She could not imagine why Lady Myrtle kept such a bird, unless it was to derive pleasure from its beautiful singing voice, and May doubted whether Dorothea had sung freely for a long time.

Later that evening Evangeline and May waited with minimal enthusiasm for Myrtle's reappearance. May was grateful she had often watched Rachel prepare her thick tomato soup and roast chicken for the Sabbath meal and now both dishes were sitting warming on the kitchen stove. Evangeline had mixed herself a strong and very dry cocktail in the manner in which she had often observed Wallis employ, coating the inner rim of the glass with vermouth before adding the ice-cold gin, and finishing the glass with a slither of lemon and an olive. Half an hour later, Evangeline was halfway through her second drink, and there was still no sign of Lady Myrtle. A glance into the dining room laid for two, followed by a check in Myrtle's bedroom, revealed that she was definitely not in the house. May had run to the end of the garden to see if there was any sign of her but had returned alone. As May passed through the stone hall she saw an envelope sitting on the table marked in green ink. The single sheet of paper was addressed to

Evangeline. The message was brief.

'I will be otherwise engaged for dinner this evening. I will see you in the morning.'

Evangeline and May had been puzzled but not concerned. Myrtle seemed like a woman capable of taking care of herself. It was getting late. Evangeline went upstairs to her own bedroom, while May set off along the little lane that led to Mrs Cage's house. On her way she passed the small cottage that was home to Vera Borchby. Vera's lace-up muddy gardening boots were sitting on the porch. The lights were still on; the sound of music and what sounded like two very low male voices drifted through the open bedroom window. May hurried home to bed.

18

Wallis's excitement about the forthcoming cruise on the *Nahlin* was proving infectious and for once Evangeline did not feel quite so left out.

'Of course, we have had to remove all the books from the ship's library, in order to make enough space for everyone to have their privacy. But I don't think anyone will mind sleeping in a slightly musty room and no one will miss those old books when there is so much else to do, don't you agree, Vangey!'

Wallis had laughed, waving her hands in the air, drawing Evangeline's attention to a charm bracelet from which dangled several different coloured crosses. Noticing the direction of Evangeline's gaze, Wallis explained.

'David inscribes the date on one of these crosses when something important happens that he wants me to remember. Look at this last one! Can you see that it says 'God Save the King for Wallis 16.vii.36' in his own handwriting? That's to remember the day he avoided being shot at in the Mall! Isn't he a hoot?'

Evangeline hoped without much conviction that the extra room on board the *Nahlin* had not been created to accommodate her. She loathed must. The yacht sounded wonderful though. She belonged to Lady Annie Henrietta Yule, the widow of a man who had made a colossal sum of money in India out of tea, jute and paper. Lady

Yule had asked John Brown, the famous Clydebank shipyard, to build her the first privately owned steamship.

There was no limit to the extravagance to which the King intended to go, in order that he and his guests should enjoy their summer holiday. The crew, the food, the drink, the opportunities for lazing, dancing, sleeping and loving were all to be of the highest standard.

'David has even ordered a huge supply of golf balls to be packed on the ship so that it doesn't matter how many he drives into the ocean!' Wallis chuckled.

However, security rather than luxury was the uppermost consideration in the minds of the King's advisors. The *Nahlin* was to be guarded by two destroyers, the *Glow Worm* and the *Grafton*, and by chance, May's brother had been billeted to join Royal Navy officers on board. Sam had been impressing his superiors since the day he joined the RNVS and the responsibility for guarding this precious cargo, and for making sure that certain papers of state were delivered to the *Nahlin* on a daily basis, was only entrusted to the most promising and reliable of young recruits.

Among the crew were several lads who had grown up on Scotland's Western Isles, the connection with his maternal homeland making Sam happier than he had been since the day before hearing the news of his mother's death. The crew was informed that the *Nahlin* had been rented for the month of August by the reclusive Duke of Lancaster, who no one knew anything about and no one could remember having actually met. But whoever he was the joint crews of the destroyers would ensure there would be no security mishaps for the mysterious Duke.

Evangeline had packed her black bathing suit with some misgivings. She had been troubled by her ignorance of cruise wardrobes especially after Wallis's advice on what to pack had not been any help at all even though she was in no doubt that Wallis had planned her own shipboard trousseau with her usual meticulous flair and precision.

'Oh, just bring any old thing, Vangey!' Wallis had said airily. 'I will be dressed most informally myself and David's valet has only included one proper suit for the obligatory emergency royal funeral rig. Otherwise David plans to be as casual as he is at the Fort, and you know what that means?'

Evangeline knew only too well. The well-worn shorts that had done double duty as bathing trunks during the unfortunate rescue mission at the Fort swimming pool had made many subsequent appearances. Evangeline herself had not ventured into the water since the mishap. No unkind remarks had been made to her face but she suspected that her little accident had been discussed extensively behind her back.

Evangeline had intermittently wondered if it might have been wiser to remain at Cuckmere for August, even though Philip had assured her he would just about manage the hosting of any country dinner parties on his own. Most of the time, however, he would remain in London but never too far from a telephone, just in case Joan woke up. His optimism was impressive. Joan had remained in hospital and had barely moved a muscle of her face since Myrtle's abortive visit and she remained fearfully thin. The truth was Philip was so distressed by his wife's unchanging condition that his visits had become increasingly infrequent.

* * *

The Royal party arrived in Yugoslavia on 10 August 1936 for the final leg of their outward journey to the coast, having exchanged the Orient Express for the Yugoslav Royal train. While the party made a brief, diplomatic stop to take tea with Prince Paul, a couple of well-informed photographers were waiting at the railway station, hoping to bag a shot that would confirm the shared holiday plans of the King and Mrs Simpson. They had been rewarded with a single frame that they intended to sell for a tidy sum to as many European newspapers as possible.

The *Nahlin* was moored in the harbour at Sibenik on the Dalmatian Coast, a three-hundred-foot vessel with the pleasing simplicity of her outlines reflected in the clear mirror of the Adriatic waters. The ship that was to be home to the royal party for the next four weeks gleamed white against a backdrop of tree-covered mountains, and the first sight of her took away the collective breath of her distinguished passengers.

'Oh my!' Evangeline exclaimed, overcome by a rare move to literary eloquence. 'What happiness it will be to bask in the sunshine of eternal bliss!'

She had a feeling this might have been a quote from William Shakespeare, because it sure sounded like one. She wished Julian could be there to hear her say it instead of indulging himself in the hedonistic playgrounds of Berlin. She comforted herself by thinking how tired he would become of the empty-headed Lottie, and at the same time how relieved he would be to escape May's persistent proposals for bicycle rides.

Finding themselves torn between the beauty of the ship and the unexpected sight of crowds of strangers gathered on the opposite side of the port, the King's guests could not disguise their anxiety at what they had let themselves in for. The captain of the *Nahlin* estimated twenty thousand Yugoslavs, splendid in their national costume and alerted by the latest newspaper stories, complete with photographs, had come out to look. It was immediately evident that the Sibenik crowds were interested less in the figure of the King than in his female companion.

After a few days spent in absolute privacy cruising the sparkling waters the holidaymakers docked at a small harbour off one of the Greek Islands where it was confirmed that the pseud-onymous cover of the Duke of Lancaster (in truth, one of the King's own subsidiary titles) had been rumbled. With a look of doom mingled with disapproval, the King's equerry, Sir John Aird, informed his employer that an ever-increasing number of publications in America and Europe were covering the royal cruise and that interest in the King's personal relationship with Mrs Simpson was mounting by the day. As well as revealing the basic itinerary the newspapers had announced the names of 'Britain's King's guests' including 'a divorced woman from Baltimore'.

The couple around whom so much speculation fizzed was sharing one end of the yacht, while the guests were marshalled in the state rooms at the other. Evangeline comforted herself that although the former library was indeed rather musty, she supposed she should count her lucky stars that she was on board at all. All her early hopes that the romantic focus of the cruise might be expanded were soon dashed. The guest list comprised the King's various equerries as well as several safely married couples, including the formidable Lady Diana Cooper and her parliamentary husband Duff. Sadly Mrs Merryman had decided to stay put for the summer on the other side of the Atlantic, as her presence would have made the ignominy of being an unmatched woman more bearable. There were of course several singletons among the crew, but even Evangeline had to concede that there wasn't much chance of a middle-aged dame from Baltimore finding a non-English-speaking deckhand from Greece to be a suitable beau, in order to teach Julian a lesson in what he might be missing.

The guests settled into a routine of want-for-nothing indulgence. With staff ready to satisfy every whim, much of the time was spent doing nothing much at all. Lazing in the luxurious state rooms, stretching out on soft-cushioned and deep-mattressed chaise longues, eating fish that had been swimming in the warm waters beneath the boat only an hour earlier, puzzling over jigsaws, playing cards, reading, dozing, flirting and chatting of inconsequences all amounted to justifiable activity of a holiday nature. The King was certainly in a holiday mood. He had acquired a shrimping net that he would dangle in the water, while floating around the *Nahlin* in a small dingy. His cooperative subjects would lean over the side of the ship encouraging him.

'There's a big one, Sir,' they would say, pointing helpfully, while the King whooped like a schoolboy each time he trapped so much as a jelly fish. Around his neck two crosses on a silver chain glinted in the Mediterranean sun, matching the answering glint of those on the bracelet around Wallis's wrist.

Whenever the guests wished to go on shore to explore the islands or to have dinner in a local restaurant, a pack of photographers waited to greet them and whenever the King disembarked for a morning of sightseeing, a jaunty holiday pipe in his mouth instead of the familiar cigarette, there would be loud shouts of 'cheerio' in an exaggerated British accent. In Dubrovnik romantics reminded the romantic couple how important it was to 'Long Live Love' by shouting *'Zivila Ljubav'* in their own language. One day the *Nahlin* slipped along the four-mile-long waterway that sliced through the isthmus joining the Peloponnesian peninsula to the Greek

302

mainland. The towering sides of the Corinth Canal resembled the entrance to an Egyptian tomb, opening out not onto a long-abandoned burial place but instead onto the golden light of the Ionian Sea. The King remained on the bridge of the ship throughout the passage, mesmerised by the delicacy of the exercise, as the Captain guided the *Nahlin* through the narrow cut. A pair of binoculars swung from his neck, and he was so engrossed in the manoeuvre that he appeared oblivious to the attention his half-naked state was attracting, delighting cheering onlookers with such informality. Evangeline noticed Lady Diana Cooper's moue of disapproval as she watched the scene from the ship's rail.

When the other guests left the yacht to go on land, Evangeline took to staying behind in the shade of the yacht. During the first week she had been determined to keep up and join in. But she had found herself quite out of breath and also vertiginously queasy on the precariously narrow paths. These walkways had been created over centuries by hundreds of indigenous black-and-white goats which continued to criss-cross the rocky islands without a stumble. But each step of a canvas-shoe would send hundreds of little pebbles cascading down the cliff face, each mini-avalanche eroding the breadth of the path still further. Most of the *Nahlin* guests learned to navigate their way with confidence but such physical agility was denied Evangeline and the beauty of the view, high above a light-dancing sea, was compromised by her fear of falling hundreds of feet below into the water.

Evangeline's habit of dawdling, whether to recover her breath or re-tie her laces, meant that she often ended up a good fifty yards behind the person in front of her. From time to time the King would stop to tie his own lace and everyone would wait for him to complete the task. If there was a knot in the lace he would pause for longer, and during these interludes Evangeline would catch up with her companions, each one trying hard not to stare at the King's bottom which was stuck up in the air, quite unselfconsciously, as he bent over his shoe. Despite the benefits afforded by the King's recalcitrant laces, after a couple of hours of wheezing and clutching in terror at tuffets of wild thyme to steady herself, Evangeline was always relieved to arrive at a crumbling temple, a lunchtime shelter from the heat and the glare. But these ancient buildings were hard-won goals and she soon decided that the quietness on the empty yacht offered an appealing alternative.

Sometimes she pleaded seasickness. This excuse was a beauty as it succeeded in absolving her from joining a terror-laden swimming party. On other occasions she would announce a previously undeclared passion for jigsaw puzzles, sentencing herself to a frustrating morning staring at hundreds of bits of odd-shaped pale-blue-and-white fragments of wood and the impossible challenge of reproducing an impressionist's cloud-spattered sky.

Evangeline had a further reason for wanting to be alone. She had begun to notice the

304

increasingly tense atmosphere that existed between Wallis and the King. Wallis was often impatient and critical of her besotted suitor, who hovered anxiously and ever closer to her as if the earth beneath her feet would crumble at the faintest upset. He would go to every length to accommodate Wallis, agree with her or fetch things for her, giving an impression that the role of King and subject had been reversed. Evangeline tried to make sense of it. Wallis of course was not exactly a 'subject', and maybe that was the nub of it: respect. It was neither asked for nor given.

Everyone who spent time with the King, even those whom he claimed as his closest friends, treated him with a deference they showed to no other living person — everyone except Wallis. The oddest thing about her critical manner was not the King's unquestioning acceptance of such behaviour but the enjoyment he apparently derived from it. The more of a bully she became, the more he seemed to like it. There was something school-mistressy about the way she spoke to him that reminded Evangeline of the way a mother treats a wayward child. Could it be that Queen Mary had never devoted the time to discipline her eldest son? Or perhaps the explanation lay with his father, George V, who had been by all accounts an excessive disciplinarian and had squeezed out the gentler motherly instincts of his shy and slightly frightened wife. Either way, their eldest son, now in his forties, appeared to have at last found a variation of the maternal bond he had craved for so long.

Whatever the explanation for the strangeness of the relationship, Wallis seemed tenser by the day. Evangeline even wondered if some sort of breaking point was imminent. If so, the build-up was not enjoyable to witness. She wished for the dozenth time that Julian or even May were there to talk to. Lady Diana seemed aware that something was up but Evangeline did not dare introduce the subject and Lady Diana did not invite chattiness. Besides Lady Diana had recently been struck down with a bout of tonsillitis and was confined to her cabin.

Turning these thoughts over in her mind while the others were safely on land and out of sight, Evangeline would sometimes take off her summer dress and lie down on the shady deck in her patched-up bathing suit, with no threat of being watched. Occasionally she would remove her sweltering wig, and pop it on the stool beside her, while at the same time ensuring her exposed and sensitive scalp remained well out of the sun's glare.

One member of the crew became endearingly attentive to Evangeline. Georgio spoke nothing but Greek but he would always spot Evangeline sitting on her own, bent over a half-completed jigsaw of a wooden Renoir seascape. Her concentration was instantly and willingly side-tracked whenever the muscular young Greek appeared beside her, indicating with loud smacking noises of his fingers to his lips, that he would be happy to bring Evangeline something refreshing to drink, or maybe one of chef's pastry and honey cakes.

One afternoon when the rest of the party had gone ashore to look at a temple that predated the birth of Christ by five hundred years, Evangeline had chosen a favourite chair in the shade, near where the retractable sea ladder was stowed. As Georgio came up the ladder from the sea, she was about to call out in greeting when she saw he was not alone. Georgio did not notice Evangeline in the afternoon shadow because all his attention was focused on the figure that was following him up the steps from the water. A young woman appeared at the top of the ladder wearing a matching two-piece garment of pink gingham that had never featured in any of Evangeline's fashion magazines. A brassiere encasing a pair of enviably firm breasts was separated from its matching pants by a flat, milk-chocolate torso. Georgio helped her onto the deck, his wet, green trunks clinging to every contour of his formidable physique.

Motioning with a finger to his lips for the girl to stay silent, Georgio was doing all he could to contain his laughter. As the dripping couple stood together on the firm surface of the boat the semi-naked woman gripped the salty wet material of her swimming pants and licking her lips with the tip of a raspberry pink tongue, she squeezed. A fine horizontal jet of water shot into the air before falling in shimmering droplets onto the deck. The party trick was answered by an appreciative kiss blown through the air from Georgio's moistened lips.

Evangeline was unable to look away. Hand in hand the couple disappeared below deck, as

307

Evangeline stared after them. Suddenly there was a movement in the shadows opposite. Muffled in a blanket, a bowl of yoghurt and a thermometer on the table beside her, Lady Diana Cooper was looking over at Evangeline and smiling very broadly indeed. Evangeline, flattered by the invitation to conspiracy, smiled back.

A sailor was polishing the handrail near the ladder up which Georgio and his friend had recently climbed. Evangeline thought she recognised May's brother from the day when May had pointed him out at the maiden voyage of the *Queen Mary*.

'Sam?' she said enquiringly.

'Oh, Miss Nettlefold, what a nice surprise it is to see you!' Sam knew how fond his sister was of this large American lady and how kind she had been to May after the accident with the dog.

'Sam, what in the world are you doing here?' she asked.

He explained that he was one of several sailors who had been brought aboard from the *Glow Worm* and the *Grafton* to help out with the evening's dinner party.

'Oh you have come from what Lady Diana calls the 'Nanny boats'?' Evangeline asked, looking over to Lady Diana with a smile, emboldened by her recent overture of friendliness.

But Sam was beginning to look uncomfortable. The family blush seeped up from his neck.

'Oh right. That's good. And it's very bald to be here. I mean nice.' Sam was mumbling. 'Sorry,

Miss Nettlefold. I hope you will excuse me. I must get on.'

As Evangeline went to her room in the former library to change for dinner and to contemplate the art of erotic arousal, she tried to work out exactly what Sam had said. Only when looking in the mirror for any horrible sign of sunburn did his words become clear. Appalled by her reflection, she opened the door to an urgent knock. Georgio was grinning as he held up what looked like a small, limp, black rodent.

'Lady Diana. She find it,' he explained, handing over the wig.

*　*　*

The King of Greece and his own house party were to arrive for dinner on the *Nahlin* from a nearby island, escorted across the water in a square scarlet gondola rowed by two oarsmen from the Nanny boats. Edward VIII's own piper stood on deck playing 'Over the Sea to Skye', one of the few tunes in his limited repertoire.

The King of England was the last member of the party to appear on deck. He was wearing a natty pair of white flannel trousers, blazer and a yachting cap and looked terrific. Wallis appeared equally glamorous, in an ankle-length white pleated skirt and a cream silk short-sleeved shirt with a square nautical collar edged in brilliant blue ribbon. Evangeline had not seen Wallis in the same outfit twice throughout the cruise except at lunchtimes when a sunhat of white broderie anglaise, resembling a baby's bonnet, would make its appearance as protection against the full glare of the sun. Beneath the rick-rack trimming Wallis's adult face looked frankly absurd. One morning the bonnet was in its customary place at breakfast, and as Lady Diana Cooper's glance travelled swiftly across the table from the bonnet to Evangeline the two women's eyes were, for a second, locked in a conspiratorial mirth born out of mutual contempt. Evangeline had felt a brief surge of hope that this beautiful, intimidating, clever, funny woman might wish to deepen her acquaintance with Evangeline into something bordering on friendship.

Wallis had been so caught up with the King throughout the cruise that Evangeline continued to question what she was doing on board the *Nahlin* at all. During long, airless nights in the old library she considered whether the invitation to join the yacht had been born out of nothing more than Wallis's guilt. The idea that Evangeline was some sort of pitiable figure, the charity child that Lady Myrtle had so cruelly identified, did little for her confidence. Rather than enjoying herself on the cruise, her perceived ostracism only exacerbated her resentment of her old school friend. Evangeline was determined to make further affable overtures to Lady Diana.

As the piper continued with his wailing tune, Sam stood to attention with the other sailors, his skin once again restored to its usual pale and unblemished state. The King of Greece's party had almost reached the *Nahlin* and Wallis tried to stand up, ready with her greeting. But the hem of her skirt had become caught on a leg of

310

her chair and she fell suddenly and awkwardly backwards. Sam moved forwards to the deck to release the trapped material but was beaten to it. As the King of England scrabbled on the deck, crumpling the knees of his perfectly laundered trousers, Wallis hissed at him loudly enough for everyone on deck to hear her.

'David! What *are* you doing? This is the most extraordinary performance I have ever seen! Are you mad?' Catching hold of his hand, she gripped it fiercely.

The King rose from the floor, his crestfallen expression bearing the mark of Wallis's rebuke as he picked up one of Mrs Simpson's fingers, and bringing it up to his open mouth kissed it.

Guests and crew alike had watched the humiliating episode, wondering with some foreboding where all this kingly subservience was leading. The attention of the foreign press on the King and Mrs Simpson could perhaps be contained from the British public for a while, but small, public indiscretions such as witnessed on the deck of the *Nahlin* only contributed to an ever-widening circle of gossip.

★ ★ ★

Eventually, after one long, sunny and largely indolent month the cruise came to an end and the guests dispersed in different directions. For Evangeline the magnificence of the Parthenon remained with her as the best moment of her holiday, a day when even she had managed the long climb up the Acropolis to the summit. In

311

the sweltering heat of the last day of August she had reached the walls of the astonishing temple, so settled in its ancient place. Wandering into the vast open space of the Parthenon, built by an ancient civilisation for the virgin goddess Athena, she noticed Lady Diana and eager for the chance to put the wig incident behind them, walked quickly towards the elegant straw-hatted figure. But she was not fast enough. Lady Diana's husband had beaten her to it. Together the pair stood, their backs to Evangeline, presenting a unity that was unmistakably intimate. Evangeline moved away from them and looked out at the sea. The colour of the water reminded her of the glitter of the sapphire brooch that Wallis often wore, fashioned from her favourite gemstone.

'It matches the colour of my eyes so well, don't you think, Vangey?' Wallis had asked with a coy little smirk.

Dragging her thoughts away from the woman who had puzzled and influenced her since her schooldays, Evangeline wondered if she would be able to find the right words to evoke the visual power of Greece, or to convey something of the extraordinary beauty of Athens. She knew who it was she so desperately wished to impress with her observations. But the prospect of warm baths and steady land beneath her feet convinced Evangeline that the end of the holiday had arrived not a moment too soon. It was already September by the time they disembarked from the *Nahlin* for the last time. Evangeline and Wallis continued their journey to Paris while the

312

King returned to London alone. He intended to spend the last two weeks of the month up at Balmoral and hoped his decision would please Queen Mary, a stickler for all traditions, especially the Royal Family's annual Scottish break. His relationship with his mother had deteriorated over the past few months as Queen Mary made her disapproval of Wallis increasingly obvious. Her son hoped he might be able to repair the damage although he was not looking forward to returning to 'real life'.

'Striped trousers and coats again. Back to school,' he grimaced to Wallis and Evangeline, as he said his goodbyes.

As soon as Wallis and Evangeline arrived at the Meurice, a hotel familiar to Wallis from a couple of visits to the Parisian dressmaker earlier in the year, Wallis succumbed to an extreme tiredness. She had planned to visit the Avenue Georges V salon of her favourite couturier Mainbocher but she announced apologetically that a day or two to rest and recover her health was in order. The holiday seemed to have exhausted rather than energised her. The elasticity of her wide grin had sagged and she was even thinner than usual. Her quick wit and high spiritedness had noticeably ebbed over the past two weeks and been replaced with frequent outbursts of irritability, largely directed at the King himself.

'I am in such a gale, Vangey darling. I have a mountain of correspondence to deal with, and a difficult letter to write, so will you forgive me if I leave you to your own devices for the evening? If anyone asks, tell them I have a cold. Matter of fact, I am feeling pretty ropey. Overdone things a little, I guess.'

Several large envelopes addressed to Wallis in her aunt Bessie's handwriting were awaiting her arrival at the hotel. Evangeline's brother had also sent over a small packet of cuttings from the Baltimore and New York papers, among them a photograph of a scene on board the *Nahlin* of Wallis's manicured hand resting gently on the King's naked forearm. Goodness knows where the photograph had originated but the intimacy between the pair was undeniable. An accompanying note from Evangeline's brother informed her that a New York publishing company already had a biography of Wallis in the works, titled *From Baltimore to Balmoral*.

For the whole of the next day Wallis refused to see anyone. She remained in her room, ordering room service to bring her plates of cold trout and salad and ears of American corn that were then left half-eaten on trays outside her bedroom door for every passerby to see until the waiter came to remove them. The following morning Evangeline knocked on Wallis's door and, not hearing an answer, turned the handle. Wallis was still in bed, her usually immaculate centre parting marking an untidy line across her scalp. She was wearing a pale, peach-coloured bed-jacket made of a silky material and edged in swans' down. The washed-out colour emphasised the sallowness of her complexion. Wallis had long suffered from terrible skin problems and Evangeline knew that the celebrated smoothness of her face was courtesy of Mrs

314

Gladys Furlonger, a queen in her own right, not of a kingdom but of the art of facial massage. In Mrs Furlonger's hands lay the secret to eternal youth, until the effect of her pricey ministrations wore off. Denied Mrs Furlonger's healing magic and exposed to undue amounts of Mediterranean sun, despite the baby bonnet, Wallis looked worn out, unattractive, and beaten. For a moment Evangeline felt a combined surge of pity and affection.

'Vangey, come and sit here,' Wallis said softly, patting a coverlet almost invisible beneath the mass of newspaper clippings scattered across it. 'Thank the Lord you are here. You are my oldest and dearest friend, especially now that rat Mary has betrayed me.'

Evangeline folded her arms across her chest, determined not to allow her hands to be caught in that claustrophobic knuckly grip. Wallis had begun to sniff and soon tears were running with abandon down her cheeks, making little rivulets through a thick coating of Elizabeth Arden foundation.

'What is it, Wallis darling?' Sensing an imminent confession, Evangeline's lovely voice was full of compassion.

'I just can't do it, Evangeline. Do you hear me? I cannot and I will not.'

There was a pause followed by an extended indrawn sigh. Evangeline waited.

'The date for my divorce hearing has already been fixed for late next month. Ernest has agreed to some sort of arrangement suggested by the King and both men assure me all is amicable between them. Ernest is too sweet to make any fuss, though I confess I sometimes wish he would. But Vangey, I don't think I can go through with it. Ernest and I belong together. Mary means nothing to him, I know that much. And I also know some people consider Ernest a bit dull, but for me he is a safe pair of hands. We get along together just fine.' Wallis continued, her voice now emphasising the inflexibility of her resolve. 'That's it. Ernest gives me security. That is definitely what he gives me. So I must escape from David as soon as possible. I never *ever* meant it to go as far as this. Never.'

'Surely you cannot mean this?' Evangeline interrupted, her own voice now trembling a little, but Wallis waved her silent, struggling to steady herself as she continued with her extended confession.

'He keeps quoting the Bible at me, Vangey. He says there is a time to weep, a time to smile, a time to rend, a time to sew . . . and — '

And breaking off for a surprisingly fierce laugh, Wallis continued.

'And he does not mean those damn tapestries that he is always stitching away at. Anyway, he says there is a time for everything and that now is *his* time to *marry*. God help me, Vangey, but what kind of a mess have I gotten myself into here? I feel I am going to go mad! In fact, I think I am getting ill again. Not just this damned cold but all those stomach troubles that I had earlier in the year have returned.'

Wallis fell back against the pillows as if defeated by life. Both women were shocked into silence by the implications of what Wallis was saying.

'Pass me my sable wrap from over there, Vangey, will you, there's a dear.' Wallis instructed eventually, indicating a chair with a feeble wave of the hand.

The knuckly fingers were naked of their usual cluster of rings but as Wallis pulled the fur around her bony shoulders she seemed to gather a new strength.

'I want to add one more thing, Evangeline, in case you are in any doubt about my intentions. I want you to know that I am convinced of one unshakeable truth. David and I as a married pair would create disaster together!'

She reached over to the small table beside the bed and picked up a sealed blue airmail envelope. Her voice was much calmer now.

'I am going to tell you a secret, Vangey. I want you to know that I have broken the whole thing off. Matter of fact, I have written to David to tell him that this is the end of it.' Wallis waved the blue envelope at Evangeline. 'I have told him that we would never make each other happy. The money and the jewels, well, most of the jewels, perhaps not the sapphires, will be sent back to him. And when I get back to England I am going to return to Ernest and then we will all go back to America and you will come with me and we will find you another Wiggle as a reward for being the most stalwart of all friends. Perhaps the King would still let you have Slipper's puppy. What do you say, darling Vangey?'

The tears had dried and the old familiar

confidence had returned as unexpectedly as the appearance of stars on a cloudy night. Evangeline was so taken aback by this dramatic turn of events that she could only stare at Wallis open-mouthed. Of course she had not been the only cruise member to notice the signs that all was not right between Wallis and the King, but this momentous decision was a volte-face that even Evangeline had not anticipated. The idea of giving up the unconditional adoration of a man was inconceivable to Evangeline, in any circumstances. But to give up the love of a King was something that only a lunatic would consider.

And yet Evangeline found herself moved by Wallis's confession and by the trust Wallis had placed in her by making it. The two of them would be proper friends again. They could make plans together. Their lives would be set in some kind of direction. Rapidly Evangeline thought through some of the consequences of Wallis's decision. Evangeline was certain that the King would put up a pretty fierce fight to keep Wallis. She had seen too often the way he looked at her. Despite (or was it *because* of?) the firm way in which Wallis treated him there was no question that he was deeply in love with Wallis. Nevertheless, Wallis was stubborn. Whatever obstacles the King might put in her way, Wallis would triumph. Of that Evangeline was certain.

Evangeline felt an unfamiliar rush of relief. It had been a difficult year but one which she would look back on with much affection especially for the time spent with the Blunts before Joan's terrible illness. She wondered how she could have doubted the loyalty of her old school friend. In an unprecedented gesture, Evangeline found herself stretching out her own plump hand and giving Wallis's naked knuckles a reassuring squeeze. It felt like gripping a leftover Sunday joint after poor Wiggle had chewed all remaining flesh from it.

'I admire you, Wallis,' she said, overcoming the impulse to withdraw her hand. 'Most women would not have the courage that you have just demonstrated. And I want you to know you can count on my friendship. Your trust in confiding in me will never be forgotten.'

★   ★   ★

After returning to England, Evangeline heard nothing from Wallis for more than two weeks. She was not concerned. She knew that patching up things with Ernest and the unravelling of all the legal procedures previously set in motion for the divorce would take a while. And then there would be the business of moving back into number 5 Bryanston Court from the house in Regent's Park that Wallis had taken after the temporary rupture with her husband. She expected that Wallis had already booked the passage for the three of them to New York. Wallis had promised they would all sail on the new *Queen Mary* as a treat.

One evening Evangeline was dining alone in St John's Wood with Philip. She had stopped reading all the newspapers, even the clippings sent by her brother from America. She was tired of all the false rumours that swirled through the European and American press and the British papers were so self-censorious about what they could and could not print that she saw no point in reading them either. The wireless had become her favourite means of staying in touch.

With a smug sense of knowing better, she listened to Philip mentioning stories that Wallis had been in Scotland with the King, the Mountbattens and those old friends of hers, the Hunters. The rumours had been confirmed in yesterday's *Times* Court Circular he said. There had been some critical muttering in the House that the King had begged off an official 'Kinging' engagement while up in Scotland, only to be seen by a press photographer driving himself to Aberdeen railway station to meet 'a special guest'. Philip had also heard that the tartan halls of Balmoral, still decorated with the original plaids chosen by Queen Victoria, had witnessed quite unprecedented levels of gaiety over the past two weeks. With a knowing smile, Evangeline assured Philip that the rumours were definitely unfounded. *The Times* Court Circular must have included Wallis's name by mistake. Tapping the side of her nose Evangeline apologised that she could not fill him in any further on Wallis's plans as she was sworn to secrecy.

When the telephone eventually rang a week later on Joan's long-unused desk in St John's Wood, Evangeline picked up the receiver and on hearing Wallis's steady voice at the other end was pleased to know that her recovery from the momentous Paris decision had been speedy.

Wallis was certainly a woman of considerable resilience.

'Vangey, darling. How are you?'

'Never better, Wallis my dear, and looking forward to seeing you.'

'Ah yes, well there is a slight difficulty about making any plans for the week or so I'm afraid,' Wallis replied, sounding apologetic. 'I expect you have seen from the Court Circular that I have been away up in Scotland? Well, without going into matters that I feel are best left unspoken now,' and at this point Wallis's voice assumed a conspiratorial tone, 'I am going to lie low for a while. I have been staying in Claridge's but as a matter of fact I am just off to spend a few days in a little house in Felixstowe in Suffolk. Kitty and George Hunter are coming with me so I won't be on my own, just in case you were worrying. That legal matter, you understand, for which I want only my closest married friends near me. But there is nothing to worry about. Sorry that I can't stop to talk just now. There are so many people making demands on my time. On my return from Suffolk I think we have dinner engagements every night for three weeks! But I will be back on the horn just as soon as I can.'

And then, just before hanging up she added something.

'Oh, and Vangey, be a dear and agree to walk Slipper's puppy while I am away? I have asked Osborne to have him brought up from the Fort and delivered to Hamilton Terrace. We have taken up your suggestion and called him Loafer, just to keep the shoe theme going, and to remind

321

him he belongs to an American! I know you will be pleased to take care of the precious animal for me.'

The voice was extinguished with a click so sudden that Evangeline had no time to respond. Clearly the conversation in Paris had meant nothing. Talk about basking in the sunny company of kings! Surely Wallis must realise her mistake in prolonging her relationship with the King instead of returning at once to Ernest? Was she entirely lacking in common decency by not ending her dalliance now? What was in her head by going through with the divorce from her husband? Had Wallis not learned her lesson with her first marriage that decent men like Ernest were hard to come by? The business with Mary Raffray had surely only come about because Wallis had inadvertently pushed Ernest into it. After all, if one's wife were conducting a steamy relationship with a king, most men would run for the arms of another woman. Fickle, that's what Wallis was, Evangeline concluded, the sort of female who is seduced by position, sycophancy, power and gemstones. As well as the betrayal she had made to the hapless Ernest, Wallis's behaviour amounted just as much to a betrayal of Evangeline herself. And the assumption of the woman, lumbering Evangeline with the dog without so much as an 'if you please' was the final straw.

Evangeline remained sitting at Joan's desk considering the nature of treachery. She was angry and tried to calm herself down by analysing the reasons for her anger, even forcing

322

herself to admit that she had drawn pleasure from the gradual collapse of Wallis's relationship with the King. The concept of 'WE', the combined initials of the two names of the lovers, Wallis and Edward, their own private cipher, had nauseated her while at the same time brought up the memory of her and Wallis's own schoolgirl code. Gel-lis. Suddenly Evangeline was overwhelmingly and dangerously jealous, the oath of friendship she had made so recently in the hotel in Paris wholly invalidated.

Evangeline opened Joan's telephone book, and turned to the entry marked Sir John Reith. As soon as the call was answered she came straight to the point.

'Oh, Sir John. This is Evangeline Nettlefold speaking. You remember? Well, yes, I do recall you saying something to me about the velvet voice! Most kind! I have been thinking over our delightful conversation at Philip's dinner at Cuckmere back in the summer, and I have decided I would be more than happy to take up your suggestion that I introduce a flavour of my country to your listeners. I have just one proviso. Could we keep the plan to ourselves for now? I would like it to be a surprise for Wallis.'

And having arranged to meet at a discreet rendezvous to discuss the idea further, Evangeline put the receiver gently back in its cradle feeling that she perhaps was gaining the upper hand at last.

Autumn

Loyalty

19

May and Sarah were sitting in the Queen's Arms, even though it was only eleven in the morning. The once negligible swelling of Sarah's waist had billowed into a size that made it difficult for her to get in and out of the armchairs at home with ease and she had recently discovered the high stools in the pub to be more comfortable. Danny the publican brought the two women cups of tea and a plate of his wife's ginger biscuits, reminding May of the Jewish way of associating food with welcome. Apart from the ever-present plateful of sugar cookies in Bertha's plantation kitchen, there had been no such custom while May was growing up when meals were an ordeal to be endured rather than enjoyed.

May was glad to be back in London. She had wanted to see her brother, of course, and hear about his adventures in the Mediterranean, but it was Sarah to whom she felt the most pressing need to speak. May had made few friends in Barbados, largely because she told herself she was always so busy with her work. But even at school there had been no particular girl to whom she had felt close. In fact, there had been times when the teasing about the unusual colour of her skin, neither white nor dark, had made her feel quite alienated from the tiny community that lived and worked near Speightstown. She suspected that she was viewed as an oddity, and longed to be part of a group. Now, with Sarah she had at last found the non-judgemental, mutual affection of a woman and the feeling was uplifting. Sarah had been the first person, other than the oblique references made by her own mother, to have spoken to her about what it felt like to fall in love. Now it was May's turn to share her own response to that experience, with all the consequent joy and agony that seemed to be integral to it. She very much wanted Sarah's advice about Julian but was curiously shy about how to ask for it.

Cuckmere had been a gloomy place during the past few weeks. Most of the staff were away on their holidays and Sir Philip continued to spend most of his time up in London, working on the confidential legal matters that consumed his professional attention. Both the birdlike Lady Emerald Cunard and the tall, diaphonous Lady Sybil Colefax had been heard saying how grateful they were for the appearance of another decent single man on the dinner party scene. Lady Joan remained unconscious in the hospital and Sir Philip had not been able to bring himself to agree to the course of electric-shock treatment some shell-shocked war veterans in his club had spoken of as effective in such situations. The physical intrusion into the brain sounded too dreadful to contemplate. John Hunt understood Philip's reservations but remained baffled by Joan's case. He had been meticulous about visiting Lady Joan in hospital at least once a week, but was unable to give her husband much reason for hope. The photographs of Lady Joan had disappeared from Sir Philip's desk and May knew the reason. The photograph of her own mother, brought with her from Barbados, was still secured facedown by an elastic band in the back of her diary. The visual reality of her mother's gentle smile was still too painful to look at.

As well as Lady Joan's unchanging condition and the effect it was having on her tense and over-worked husband, several other things had seemed out of kilter to May during those few hot summer weeks. Florence's puzzling behaviour and the photograph of the beach at Pagham continued to trouble her. Julian had confirmed for her that the sign on the belt was indeed the symbol of the British fascists but although Mrs Cage's secret sympathies were now clear, both May and Julian agreed that for Florence's sake it would be unwise to say anything to Sir Philip. However much they might condemn Mrs Cage's allegiance to Mosley's party, no harm seemed to have been done, beyond Florence's evident discomfort about her holiday. For the moment Mrs Cage's secret was safe.

But Florence's absence meant there had been no one to accompany May on bike rides and Sam was away in the Mediterranean guarding, so Sam believed, the Duke of Lancaster. Miss Nettlefold had divulged to May the Duke's real identity but May did not expect Sam to have any direct contact with the *Nahlin* passengers. The special nature of the cruise had not remained entirely confidential. A new titivating weekly publication had been left in Oak Street by one of Sarah's clients and Rachel had been agog at photographs of the King walking down the narrow streets of a town somewhere in the Mediterranean. He was accompanied by a smartly dressed but un-named lady and they were both laughing.

'I am glad to see the King enjoying himself,' Rachel remarked approvingly, flicking through the pages of the magazine. 'Why don't those other papers that Nat brings home show such nice pictures, I wonder?'

During those summer weeks May missed Julian more than anyone. But she was also furious with him. They had parted in unfortunate circumstances. After she had shown him the photograph of Florence at Pagham he had admitted that he was still planning to spend August in Berlin. He argued that he had no choice. Arrangements had been made. Somehow May had convinced herself that the conversations, the bicycle rides and above all the magical, heady, daring, surprising, addictive hours they had spent secretly in the seaside hut together on probably half a dozen occasions meant that Julian's relationship with Lottie must be at an end, even though they had never specifically discussed it. Whenever May felt brave enough to ask the question Julian had changed the subject. And yet an inadvertent remark made by Bettina had smashed her optimism. Perhaps men of that class and that upbringing just do things differently, she tried to reason, while all the time nearly broken with disappointment. But every time she vowed to think no more about him, the memory of his laugh and of the touch of his fingertips returned all the stronger.

On the morning before Rupert, Julian and Bettina's departure by car for Berlin, Bettina had woken to find her stomach covered in red spots. By the time she had scratched them, covered them in thick calamine lotion to pretend they weren't there and eaten her breakfast, the rash had spread to her arms. She could already feel her forehead and her back beginning to itch. In the practical absence of her mother, she went to find Mrs Cage.

'Yes, my dear, those blasted chicken pox are the cause of the trouble, without any doubt. I heard from Mrs Jenkins in the post office that there was an outbreak in the village. Shame you escaped it in childhood when Mr Rupert came down with it. Grown-ups with chicken pox feel much sicker than children do. So I am afraid it is up to bed with you, my dear,' she instructed in her best no-nonsense tone as if Bettina was still the same age as her daughter.

Bettina was beginning to feel so sick that the thought of cool white sheets, a darkened room and the privacy and freedom in which to scratch seemed at that moment infinitely more enticing than a long journey in Rupert's Talbot, accompanied by rations of dark beer and fatty German sausage.

'I didn't want to play goosebugs to Lottie and Julian anyway,' she muttered on her way up to bed as May sat at the kitchen table, listening to every word. 'Tongue sandwiches in the back seat? *Non, merci.* I will leave that role to Julian *avec grande plaisir!*'

Rupert made it clear that he was damned if he was going to allow his roommate to learn to drive before Rupert himself had mastered the skill. After all, the car belonged to Rupert and it had been galling enough to discover back in March that his father had lent Julian the Talbot even if it had been a woman driver in charge of the wheel. Rupert's pride in his recently acquired expertise had been dented by the news of his sister's illness and the subsequent unwelcome role of chaperone. Rupert found Lottie rather attractive and did not understand what she saw in his decent but terribly serious friend. But the small blue car had left Cuckmere in the final week of July, as Bettina remained behind in bed wreathed in the antiseptic aroma of calamine lotion. With Rupert at the wheel and Lottie and Julian in the back seat, the car had made its way to the nearby Channel ferry at Newhaven. The launch of the Games was to take place on 1 August, and May, hurt, angry and confused at what she had heard, had tried her best not to dwell on what might be happening over there.

★   ★   ★

May had been catching up on Sarah's news for over an hour without Rachel's inhibiting running commentary. For the moment, May kept her own hopes and worries to herself as she deferred to Sarah's infectious excitement about the baby which was due in about six weeks' time. Gladys was the first choice of name for a girl. Indeed, it was May's own middle name, chosen by her mother in memory of Edith's sister.

'But if you have a boy?' May had asked.

'We think Joshua,' Sarah replied and for a moment the two young women were silent as the long-awaited arrival of the baby suddenly seemed very near.

And then Sarah made May laugh describing how Rachel and Simon had reluctantly given the parents-to-be some time alone together before the birth. Somewhat to their mutual surprise Sarah's pregnant state had intensified Nat and Sarah's physical desire for one another and the only drawback was finding time to be alone in the house to take full-voiced, uninhibited advantage of it. Rachel's eyes and ears seemed to fill every corner of the house even when she wasn't in it.

At first Rachel had been indignant when Nat had suggested his in-laws take a holiday on the south coast.

'I've heard about that Billy Butlin up in Skegness with his scheme for making everyone join in on games as if we were all part of a performing circus. I ask you? Whatever next?' Rachel asked him.

Holidays were unprecedented for the Greenfeld parents.

'Who is going to make sure the kitchen floor is swept, Nat? Sarah can't see her feet any more let alone bend over a broom. She even makes some of her clients stand all the way through their hair appointments. She says she can get at them more easily that way. And what is Simon going to do down there in the heat? Not much to eat at the coast either, I wouldn't wonder. Simon says it's a place for ships not chips. And how is number fifty-four going to manage without my leftovers? Did I say I was indispensable, Nat? Did you ever hear me say I was? But mark my words, Nat, this place would come to a standstill without me.'

Nat was undeterred and eventually found a bed and breakfast in Eastbourne with a view of the sea and round the corner from the gaiety of the pier. Even so, it had been Simon in the end who finally persuaded Rachel to go. One day he came back from Schein's Gentleman's Hairdressing Saloon in Bethnal Green Road having discovered that Mr Schein had been to Eastbourne himself quite recently.

'I went with a 'special' friend, if you get my meaning, Mr Greenfeld? Eastbourne's a good place for what I like to call 'discretionary assignations'.'

Simon assured Mr Schein that all indiscretions were safe with him, and as Mr Schein doused Simon's thinning locks with Levy's Patent Hair Restorer, he described for Simon a concoction of ice cream, whipped cream, syrup and nuts known as a 'knickerbocker glory' that was sold in a café on the famous pier.

'Nothing like a bit of whipped cream to get the heart fluttering is what I say, Mr Greenfeld.'

There was also an excellent pub and a most accommodating betting shop with generous tick that Mr Schein had discovered tucked far down the maze of Eastbourne's genteel side streets. Simon walked out of Schein's, with his newly razored cheeks and a shining pate, feeling quite converted to the idea of himself and Rachel spending a few days at the coast.

The holiday was such a success that on their return Rachel urged her neighbours to take a few days of sea air down on the south coast where you could get ice cream in a container that resembled a small vase and the added bonus of all the fish and chips you could eat just on the doorstep. There was no mention of the betting shop. Simon had kept that information to himself.

During their absence Sarah and Nat had been left alone for the first time in their marriage and she and Nat had fallen in love all over again. However, a tragedy had occurred next door at number 54 that had blighted those happy days. Mrs Smith, the mother of ten, had recently discovered herself to be pregnant. One evening after their tea, Mr Smith had taken two of the youngest children 'out for some river air'. Neighbours had noticed how anxious he had been looking in recent days after the discovery that yet another mouth to feed was on the way. Times were already hard enough, with paid work still so scarce. Mr Smith was at his wits' end with worry. He must have concluded that the only solution to reducing the weekly food bill was by eliminating the need to fill hungry mouths. His actions had shocked the entire Oak Street neighbourhood.

According to a witness, the three members of

the Smith family had been holding hands when they jumped from Blackfriars Bridge. In seeking to reassure Mrs Smith the policemen said the little ones would probably have thought they were playing a game. They would have hit the water with such a smack, said the report in the *Hackney Gazette*, that death would have come very quickly. A black ribbon hung from the door knocker at number 54, indicating that visitors were not encouraged. Knots of shaken neighbours had stood outside talking in low voices about how anyone could reach such a level of despair as Mr Smith must have done. The cloud of grief billowed out from behind their closed front door.

As Sarah told May this terrible story, her hand stroked her distended belly. *What a lot of luck you need to be born into happiness*, May thought. She wondered, not for the first time, whether she had already met someone who could sustain her as Nat did Sarah. She was still hesitant to confide to Sarah about what was happening between her and Julian and her persistent fear that his relationship with Lottie had been reignited in Berlin. So instead she talked about Florence. Sarah listened carefully as May described how much she had come to care for the child and how Florence had recently appeared so unsettled. The unusual belt Florence had reluctantly been wearing on the day she left for the beach gave the biggest clue to the nature of Florence's strange mood.

'There was a mark on the belt that I discovered to be the symbol for Oswald Mosley's

Blackshirt party and I think her mother might be a Mosley follower,' May explained.

She was about to describe Mrs Cage's badly disguised excitement at the Blackshirt leader's visit to Cuckmere but stopped herself. She was sworn to secrecy, of course, but she also knew that Sarah would have been horrified. The Greenfelds would not begin to understand the reason for Mosley's visit to Cuckmere. Sir Philip would not have tolerated such a guest under his own roof were it not to discuss a matter of national importance: the King's relationship with a married woman. May wondered what Sarah, a Jewish woman, would make of Mosley and felt dreadfully ashamed of the physical attraction she had felt for a man whose actions threatened the very London family with whom she spent her time. Racial and religious prejudice was not something of which May was ignorant. In Barbados, and outside their own plantation, there had been some notorious racists among the white community and the experience in Oxford's town hall was still vivid in her mind. She remembered the angry wife of the Cowley motorcar worker, she remembered the noise of the clashing steel chairs, and she remembered the blood that had oozed from the cuts on the face of Julian's friend. And then she thought again of the tall dark figure that had crossed the stone floor at Cuckmere and vanished upstairs with Lady Joan. And she remembered the sight of Mrs Cage carrying the tray with its vase of delicate flowers. The current of anti-Semitism was running fast even through May's small world. May said nothing.

But as if she was reading May's mind Sarah brought the very subject up herself. 'I don't expect you have come across the rumours while you have been down in Sussex,' she began, 'but Nat has been reading reports in the newspaper and talking to several tailors he works with and the word is that Mosley is planning a march through the East End any day now.'

Sarah returned her hand to rest on the swell of her stomach.

'If he comes I would like to be here with you,' May said.

'Oh good. Mum will be pleased. She says she is not worried but I know she is.' And with that Sarah and May moved back to the subject of motherhood and on to Lady Joan.

'She looks so old now,' May said. 'Her hair is completely white and her skin is almost transparent.'

May and Sarah both struggled to imagine what it felt like to have more of one's life behind one than in front, reaching a level of such closeness between them that May at last felt ready to talk to Sarah about her confused feelings for Julian.

At that moment Sam came flying in through the pub door. 'I came straight home as soon as the ship docked.' His were eyes shining and he was so out of breath that he was close to unintelligible. 'I've been looking for you two everywhere.'

'Oh, Sam, I am so happy you are here. When did you get back from the ship? Come and tell us everything.'

'I wanted to see you right away, of course. I had a wonderful time. There were some lads from Mum's part of Scotland. They are really looking forward to meeting you, May. And we swam every day, and olives are my new favourite food. Oh and the King is cracky on someone! An American. She's a friend of Miss Nettlefold.'

May looked at Sam, suddenly appalled.

'Shush, Sam. Keep your voice down. Have you already been to Oak Street?' she asked him quickly.

'Oh yes! Of course! I was looking for you.'

'And did you speak to Rachel at all?'

'Well, I sort of mentioned it, but only briefly,' Sam half-apologised, sensing his sister's caution. 'She was *really* surprised! Actually a lot more surprised I might say than *you* seem to be,' he added a little reproachfully.

'Oh, Sam! What have you done? I must go and talk to Rachel at once,' May said, pausing to kiss a rather confused Sarah before dashing out of the pub without even stopping to put on her jacket. If Rachel knew the secret of the King's love life, then the whole street would be buzzing with the news within the hour.

May was still talking to Rachel and Sarah, who had followed her home from the pub, when Nat returned unexpectedly at lunchtime. She was still doing her best to convince them that Sam was confused about the identity of the woman who had caught the King's eye on board the *Nahlin*. May had it on impeccable authority from Miss Nettlefold, she assured them, that the King had been flirting with a member of the

Greek royal family. Sam's imagination must have been running away with itself. What would the King be doing with a married American lady? May did all she could to make the idea sound absurd. No. The King must have been giving the glad eye to a Greek princess. All those Royals ended up marrying each other, didn't they?

Rachel had humphed a bit and went to put the kettle on. 'Strange things happen in love and war, May, I'm telling you,' was all she said, filling the kettle, scepticism evident in every line of her face.

Nat too had some urgent news. The voice at the end of the workshop telephone that morning had been posher than any of those belonging to Nat's regulars.

'So sorry to disturb you, Mr Castor,' the man had said. 'That *is* Mr Castor, isn't it? Oh good, good. Glad to reach you. Would you very kindly pass on a message to May?'

The man, Mr Richardson, Julian Richardson, was in London for the day visiting his mother and wondered if he might call round to see May later that afternoon? Nat, who, together with his wife and mother-in-law, had an inkling of May's romantic notions from the blush that crept over her whenever she mentioned Mr Rupert's university friend, had just avoided sewing his thumb to a buttonhole before throwing the jacket he was stitching aside and racing home to find May.

★ ★ ★

Three hours later, back in the pub for the second time that day, May was sitting enthralled at Julian's tales of Berlin. Lottie's name had not been mentioned. What was quite apparent was Julian's ambivalence about the appeal of the German people. On the plus side, the country was so well organised, Julian enthused. There was so little unemployment. Everything in Germany worked. There had been some extraordinary parties.

'Despite not being much of a party person myself, even I confess to having enjoyed some of those Berlin balls,' he told her, lighting a cigarette.

The grandeur and opulence of Berlin had been astonishing. Comparisons had been made with events staged by Nero and Louis XIV. There had been music, and dancing and fabulous ballets performed under the light of the moon. There had been caviar and oysters, oceans of champagne and evanescent galaxies of fireworks. Footmen dressed in pink uniforms copied from those worn in the eighteenth century and bearing miniature torches had greeted guests at a banquet at the opera house to which Julian had been invited at the last minute through the exemplary connections of Chips Channon. Julian felt horribly out of place at a table decorated with water lilies, watching obscure members of European royalty mingle with German officers of state as Chips pointed out remote foreign cousins of the British Royal family, all descended from old Queen Victoria.

May barely touched her drink as she listened

to Julian's story, inhaling the smell of his cigarette, happier as well as more anxious than she had been at any time since he had left to go to Berlin. She did not know what had happened between him and Lottie in Germany. But she was prepared to wait. At that moment sitting alone with Julian in the pub was all she wanted to think about.

Julian described how the power-aspirant British had been anxious for their moment with Herr Ribbentrop, the German foreign minister about to take up residence in London's German Embassy.

'Chips thinks that Ribbentrop's elegant and charming manner is something of a façade and that there is steel under all that suavity,' Julian told May with the air of a privileged insider. He described how one afternoon, with a little time to kill, he had explored parts of the city on his own. Something prevented Julian from mentioning how Lottie had been more than willing to stay behind in the hotel with Rupert and how she had announced they were both keen to try the hotel's special German beer. Lottie had been ill-tempered throughout the holiday, and on one occasion had suggested that Julian might be happier driving around the lanes of Sussex. Her tone had been unequivocally sarcastic. Instead, Julian continued by describing for May how many of the shop fronts had been boarded up and doors had been covered in graffiti. The paint-daubed phrases were often beyond Julian's knowledge of German, but sometimes a door bore the one word 'Jud' meaning 'Jew' or just two letters, an image that recurred again and again throughout the Jewish back streets.

'I was told that PJ stands for 'Perish the Jews',' he explained to May, shaking his head in disbelief.

'How truly dreadful,' May said, with an involuntary shiver, 'that so much prejudice could be conveyed in just two letters.'

Eventually Julian had become lost in a maze of streets and after asking for directions in hesitant German, had found himself standing among a small crowd of curious onlookers gathered directly opposite Hitler's house in the Wilhelmstrasse. The house was surrounded by several men in the ubiquitous uniform of black breeches. They all stood to attention as the sound of hooting horns preceded four black cars that drew up simultaneously outside the house. The small figure who emerged from the middle car disappeared inside the house quickly but not before Julian had managed to get a good look at him.

The Olympic Games themselves had been an event Julian would never forget. The opening ceremony had taken place in front of a capacity crowd of 100,000 spectators, assembled under heavy-clouded skies. A new spectacle that year, in the form of a flaming torch brought in relay all the way from Mount Olympus in Greece, had been carried into the stadium in the hand of a tall German athlete. The flame had burned continuously throughout its twelve-day journey. Thirty thousand members of the Hitler Youth and the German Girls were crammed into the stadium. The scene resembled the biggest military tattoo the world had ever seen. At the moment

Hitler took his place in the stand, thousands of spectators cheered their ear-splitting acknowledgement of his presence. Right hands were raised in salute towards the diminutive figure in brown uniform as they shouted in unison two words: 'Heil Hitler.' Julian had felt as if he was witnessing the second coming of the saviour of the world.

However, a man not only of a different nationality but a different colour had stolen the Olympic show and confirmed Julian's horror at the intensity of Nazi Germany's racism. With his superhuman performance Jesse Owens, or 'Ovens' as the Germans pronounced his name, was a black American from Alabama, whose limbs covered the ground at lightning speed. The grandson of a slave, his skin clashing with the Aryan paleness of the German competitors, Owens won a sensational four gold medals in the sprint and long jump. The word was that Hitler had hidden his fury at the result by rationalising Owens's triumph. Athletes with monkey-like features owed the strength of their limbs to their tree-leaping antecedents, Hitler had declared to the press.

Julian stubbed the cigarette out with a vehemence that made May jump. 'You have no idea how happy I am to be home again,' he said reaching for her hand.

'And you have no idea how happy I am that you have come back,' May replied cautiously as she allowed him to stroke each of her fingers in turn.

For a moment they looked at each other, both unsure where the conversation was going next.

'Will you tell me all your news, then? What's been happening at Cuckmere?' he asked, gently releasing her hand and reaching again for his packet of cigarettes. 'Any news of Joan? And how is Florence?'

'I haven't seen as much of Lady Joan now that she is staying in the hospital for tests. But whenever Mrs Cage and Cooky and Mr Hooch and I visit her we still try everything we can think of that might wake her,' May said. 'We have played music to her, shown her photographs, read to her, sang to her, whispered to her, even, in occasional moments of exasperation, shouted at her.'

'Does anyone think she will recover?' Julian asked looking truly saddened.

'The doctor thinks she may spend years in a coma. I hope she doesn't know enough to feel lonely. Her sister came down to Cuckmere but left without even going to the hospital to see her.'

'Her sister?' Julian asked, surprised. 'You mean Myrtle? The avid reader of *Time and Tide*, otherwise known as the *Sapphic Graphic?*'

May could not help laughing. 'Yes, how do you know?'

'Joan told me all about her. I once met the magazine's editor, Lady Rhonda. She had ditched her living arrangements with a perfectly good husband for a strapping young woman.'

'Well, maybe Lady Myrtle was inspired by Lady Rhonda,' May said, still laughing. 'I would say that Vera is certainly on the strapping side.'

'Vera? Where does she come into it? And tell me about Florence? Did you manage to ask her about the belt?' Julian asked.

He wanted to hear everything, as May had hoped he would. So she told him how the day after Lady Myrtle's disappearance she had suggested they celebrate Florence's return from Pagham by baking a cake with raspberries from the Cuckmere fruit cages. To begin with, Florence had been subdued, still stuck in that strange mood in which she had left for her holiday, but with the promise of a bike ride and a swim in the river she had gradually recovered her good humour. The belt had been nowhere to be seen. They had not been able to find Vera anywhere in the garden to ask if they could go into the locked cages. In fact, no one had seen the gardener for days but she was a free spirit and the Cuckmere community were used to her disappearing at the drop of a hat. A knock on the open front door of her cottage remained unanswered.

'I wasn't that keen to go in,' May explained to Julian, 'but Florence said we must if we were to be given the key.'

'I think you enjoy being wrapped round little fingers,' Julian said. He had pushed his white-blond hair right off his face, taken off his glasses and was grinning at her.

May hesitated, feeling the beginnings of a blush just beneath the collar of her shirt. 'Oh well, you know, I'd do anything for some people. Well certainly for Florence.'

Vera Borchby must have left her door open by mistake. She had certainly not been expecting visitors and did not notice May and Florence standing in her sitting room. Her uninvited callers could tell that one of the two figures on the sofa was definitely Vera by the laced-up gardening boots that were sticking up in the air. The jaunty chords of an Irving Berlin song floated from the wireless in a corner of the room but they failed to drown out the grunting noises coming directly from the sofa. May had grabbed Florence's hand and pulled her outside.

There had been loud protests followed by hundreds of questions. And finally after buying an ice cream from the man who travelled round villages with an icy box attached to the front of his bicycle, Florence promised she would not say a word about Lady Myrtle hugging Miss Borchby upside down and about the two women being what May described rather desperately as 'convivial'. As Florence had assured May so many times before, Florence was good at keeping secrets.

'And what happened to Myrtle afterwards?' Julian asked eager to hear the conclusion.

'She left the next day. None of us saw her again, except Mr Hooch who took her to the station. But I am afraid we could not help discussing it. Cooky was impressively knowledgeable about 'them that swing the other way'. She told us about a woman called Hall-something, I think, who wrote a book about it not long ago.'

'Quite a disappointing book in that way,' Cooky had remarked with rare knowledge of the printed word. 'A friend of mine even asked the bookshop for her money back. I expect there are dozens of women at it behind closed doors,' she surmised with a pronounced pout of her lips and a quick whip round their over-dry surfaces with her tongue.

Mr Hooch had been less outraged although equally captivated by speculation over the goings on in the gardener's cottage.

'Whoever would have guessed it?' he said to May, with the jolly twinkle he reserved exclusively for her. 'Nothing more than a couple of girl pansies, aren't they? Right in the middle of our village! I say! But no harm done, eh?' he chuckled. 'It's the after-effects of that bloody war again, excuse my language. Not enough of us decent men left to go round are there? Does funny things to women, war does.'

May was coming to the end of her story. 'When Sir Philip came back from Chequers he gathered us all (except Vera, of course) in the drawing room and asked us to keep the incident to ourselves, and to realise what a blessing it was that Lady Joan knew nothing about it. He asked me privately to mark 'return to sender' on all the envelopes that came addressed to him in green ink and give them back to the postman. He had a word with Vera too. The beauty of the garden is what persuaded him not to sack her, although he was very keen to stress to all of us that she had not done anything wrong. She even offered to find a good home for that poor canary. And Mr Hooch is more pleased than anyone that Vera is staying because he says she grows the best lettuces in Sussex.'

May was reluctant to finish her account of the recent weeks at Cuckmere. As long as she kept talking, she told herself, there would be no chance for Julian to tell her how happy he had been with Lottie in Berlin. She watched his tweedy back as he waited at the bar for Danny to refill their beer glasses.

'I've got some good news to tell you,' he said at last, putting his glass down on the table with a flourish. 'I have decided to train for the law and become a barrister. An excellent crammer has offered me a place to study for the Bar exams starting in September. And, even better, I have been accepted as a student at the Middle Temple. And the best thing of all is that now that I have escaped from the manicured clutches of Lottie I will have all the time in the world to concentrate on the Bar exams.'

'I am sorry. What did you just say?' May asked him.

'Lottie. Charlotte. You know? Well, when I left Berlin she decided to stay on for a bit and Rupert was decent enough to say he would drive her home so at the moment I am fancy-free. And I desperately need someone to come with me to the movies. You wouldn't consider being that someone would you?' He was smiling as he asked May the question.

May nodded back at him.

'Oh good, good, good,' he said. 'Because the truth is that not a single day has passed over the last month without me thinking about you.'

May did not trust herself to reply.

20

Julian wanted to know whether May would be staying down at Cuckmere during the coming weekend. He was intending to visit Joan. At least, that was the reason he gave. But May was thinking of returning to Oak Street as Sarah's baby was due so soon. Sir Philip confirmed the decision for her as soon as he sat down at his desk. His frequent absences from Cuckmere during the past few months meant that the old cigar smell was less evident than it had once been. Nearly a year had passed since May had first sat in this room, her hair falling all over her face, and anxious to give a good first impression at her interview. But today it was Sir Philip who looked anxious.

'Lady Joan?' May asked quietly.

'No, my dear, another matter I am afraid. And it concerns you.' He put the tips of his fingers together, his hands forming an airy cage, and leant forward on both elbows. 'Your cousins are Jewish, are they not?'

May nodded.

'I think you should know that there is a real possibility that the Blackshirt march planned for next Sunday might make its way to Cable Street and through the streets of Bethnal Green. And against the advice of the police, the government has refused to ban the march. I would far rather you stayed here in the safety of the countryside.'

Sir Philip could see an objection forming on May's face before she even began to speak.

'Thank you so much, Sir, but I would feel very worried if I wasn't at home looking after my family in Oak Street. And my cousin is about to have her baby so I think they need me there.'

'Of course. I am not at all surprised by your response,' Sir Philip said, looking at May with affection. 'They will value your calming presence, May. But whatever happens I urge you to stay inside throughout the weekend. It is hard to over-estimate the lengths to which anti-Semitic feeling will go. I will tell you in confidence that six thousand policemen as well as the entire mounted force are going to be out on the East End streets on Sunday. I think that shows you that people are frightened and that things could get nasty.'

* * *

When May reached Oak Street the atmosphere was more one of determination than fear. The threat to the neighbourhood had diverted Rachel from her interest in May's romantic hopes as well as her persistent suspicion that May and Sam were trying to keep from her some enthralling piece of information about the King's love life. Here instead was the prospect of a real-life drama on Rachel's own doorstep.

As a precaution, Nat had positioned his truncheon directly inside the front door. Some of the locals had armed themselves with catapults and knuckledusters and one of the fatherless children next door had shown Nat an evil-looking homemade instrument fashioned from a torn-off piece of iron grating. The weapon was nothing in viciousness, however, compared with the ingenuity of the Cyprus Street barber who had tied a piece of string to a potato embedded with several of his brand-new razor blades.

At breakfast that morning Simon had read aloud from the *Jewish Chronicle*. 'Jews are urgently warned to keep away from the route of the Blackshirt march.'

However, the generally accepted information, gathered from the anti-march organisers, the information in the *Daily Worker*, Nat's second-hand copy of *The Times* and pamphlets that had been pushed through letterboxes, as good as confirmed there would be no trouble anywhere near Oak Street itself. It was rumoured that the demonstrators condemning the actions of the Blackshirts would include 100,000 anti-fascists, Spanish Civil War activists and a good number of people who were joining in for 'the hell of it'. The plan was to congregate at Aldgate, a couple of miles from the Greenfelds' home. All over the East End the same notice written in chalk had appeared on pavements and walls.

'Everybody to Aldgate on 4 October 1 p.m.'

Early on Sunday morning Sarah announced to her mother that she was feeling cooped up. There was little likelihood of the baby appearing for several days yet, and Sarah always went out on a Sunday. This Sunday was no different. She was going for a stroll.

At first Rachel had been adamant that Sarah

was going nowhere. 'Over my dead body, you are going out in your condition, my girl,' she had said through a mouthful of one of next door's eggs. But Sarah had inherited her mother's obstinacy and was hearing none of these objections.

'If you must know I am going to Gardiner's to buy Nat a tie for when he becomes a father,' she replied. 'You can come with me or stay put, it's up to you, Mum.'

Gardiner's department store was known by everyone in the East End as 'The Harrods of the East', and no other shop would be good enough for Nat's paternal tie.

'Whatever will Nat say if anything happens to you, Sarah? Tell me that?' Rachel asked, pouring herself a cup of tea from the pot.

'Nat and Dad do not need to know where I am going. There is a sale on at Gardiner's and a special Sunday opening for two hours this morning. I can be up there by ten and be back home by after eleven.'

Rachel sipped her tea. She could not allow her daughter to go out on her own but realised there was no dissuading her from abandoning the expedition. Rachel was a woman generally possessed of profound common sense but had never been able to refuse her daughter anything. She tried to convince herself that on a day when the perils of being Jewish, female and pregnant were at their most heightened, her presence would be protection enough.

Standing up Rachel reached for her coat. 'Right, my girl. We better get going then if we are to be back before any trouble starts.'

Sarah stood up and hugged her mother.

As far as Simon and Nat were concerned the two women were going round the corner to Victoria Park. What with the days drawing in and the October winds about to sharpen their bite, mother and daughter planned to take advantage of an unusually balmy autumn day. Even so, Nat did his best to forbid them both from going. 'You tell them, Simon, there is madness in the air.' But neither woman paid him any attention.

'My advice is to give up on them, Nat,' Simon said. 'Ill-advised is a man who challenges the will of a determined wife,' he said, returning to the betting pages of the newspaper. But Nat was not yet ready for defeat, warning Rachel and Sarah that he was prepared to restrain them physically from leaving the house.

'Look here,' Rachel said pulling on her gloves, 'I'm telling you straight, Nat, you must not worry about us getting caught up in this march. It's not going to come within miles of us, and anyway nothing is supposed to start till this afternoon, two o'clock at the earliest. Let the poor girl have a break, for pity's sake. Your wife is about to spend the rest of her days tethered to a pram. God in heaven, Nat, do you honestly think that I, Rachel, her mother, a future *grandmother*, no less, am going to let Sarah come to any harm?'

'Well, make sure you are back by noon, that's all I am asking,' Nat said with a sigh, smiling at the familiar obstinacy of his mother-in-law as, putting on a convincing show of being affronted, Rachel ushered her swollen daughter out into the street.

While the women were out Simon sat in the parlour, listening to the news bulletins on the wireless, the sound turned up at deafening volume, the *Jewish Chronicle* lying open across his large stomach. Nat had finished catching up with yesterday's *Times*, collected first thing from his butler friend, even though it had been a Sunday, and made himself and his father-in-law a hefty chicken sandwich which they ate on their laps, before falling into a Sunday afternoon doze.

'Things don't sound too good up at Aldgate,' Simon said a while later, gesturing towards the wireless. 'Shouldn't Rachel and Sarah be back by now?'

Both men looked at each other all of a sudden concerned. But just then there was a double rap at the front door and a young man in glasses with white-blond hair stood there, a summery linen cap in his hand and a striped college scarf round his neck.

'I am so sorry to call without any warning. My name is Julian Richardson. I am a friend of May Thomas. I do hope I have got the right number?'

For a moment Nat quite forgot about Rachel and Sarah as he put out his hand to Julian in greeting. 'Delighted to meet you,' he said. 'Really delighted. Do come in. May is upstairs. I'll fetch her at once.'

'I wondered if she might want to come up and join me at the march,' Julian explained.

Nat hesitated on his way up the stairs. 'The march? Are you planning on going up to Aldgate?'

'Yes I am. And I thought May might want to come with me.'

On hearing voices, May had already begun to make her way downstairs, her surprise at seeing Julian lighting up her face.

'I thought it would be Sarah and Rachel back from the park. You are always turning up when I least expect you,' she said, beaming at him. 'Nat, this is Julian. Nat's my cousin. You know.'

But Nat was looking worried. 'My wife and her mother are somewhere out in the streets. I was expecting them home an hour ago.'

May turned to him. Her earlier smile had vanished.

'Gardiner's. They've gone to Gardiner's. Up at Aldgate. You're right, Nat. They should have been back quite a while ago. We must go and find them at once. We can take the bikes. Julian, will you come with me? Nat, you wait here in case they turn up.'

Without a moment's hesitation, Julian followed May out to the back where she was heaving two bicycles out of the shed.

'I know the way,' May shouted to Julian over her shoulder as she began to pedal. 'Follow me.'

★　★　★

Gardiner's was about half an hour's walk from Oak Street, or ten minutes on a bicycle, perhaps less. May pedalled fast, passing the boarded-up shop fronts at speed and hoping that Julian was close behind.

A thunderous commotion was coming from the direction of Aldgate and as they approached the junction of Commercial Street and Whitechapel

High Street, they found their way blocked by an overturned lorry, weighted down with bricks. Whole chunks of concrete had been dug up from the pavement, the square patches of bare earth turning the pavements into giant, uneven chessboards. By now they could hear the cries and shouts of a huge crowd ahead. Dismounting from their bikes and squeezing through a gap beside the lorry, May and Julian turned the corner, where the full force of the protest hit them.

Hundreds of police, many on horseback, were struggling with a threateningly volatile crowd as bricks and stones and lemonade bottles flew through the air. Although there was no sign of Mosley himself, all of humanity seemed to be there as Jews and fascists and communists and police jostled with the angry, the curious, the young and the old, the fearless and the fearful. The hefty slabs of pavement had been smashed up to provide weapons that were now in the hands of the protestors who pushed and shoved their way through the crowds. All along the pavement, people were sitting with their heads in their hands, blood streaming from wounds to their faces as doctors and ambulance workers did their best to attend to the dozens of injuries. Red flags were flying from the lamp posts. A couple of parked tramcars had been emptied and were lying on their sides outside Aldgate underground station. Placards held up high announced marchers variously affiliated with the Stepney Jewish People's Council against Fascism and Anti-Semitism, the Labour Party and the Communist Party. The words 'Bar the Road to

Fascism' had been written in huge chalk letters on several walls. Some people were shouting the Spanish Civil War slogan 'Non Pasare' — 'They Shall Not Pass'.

A familiar tune reached May above the incredible noise, although the words given to the old American socialist solidarity song, 'Solidarity Forever', a song popular with the plantation workers back home, were new.

'We'll hang Oswald Mosley on a sour apple tree, when the red revolution comes,' the marchers sang in the streets of London's East End, before an ominous chant drowned out their words.

'The Yids, the Yids. We must get rid of the Yids.'

Fear flushed through May's face as she and Julian paused to catch their breath. Julian put an arm round May's shoulders. A lad of perhaps eight years old was standing on the pavement in front of them. Reaching into his pocket he scattered a fistful of glass balls across the street. A mounted policeman opposite cursed at the boy.

'What do you think you're doing? *Bloody* marbles. Should be *bloody* banned.'

But the policeman was unable to prevent his horse's feet from beginning to slide uncontrollably as if the street had turned suddenly to ice and the horse began to slip and slither across the road its reins became tangled, rendering its rider powerless. Somehow the animal managed to remain upright, stumbling to a halt within inches of where May and Julian stood.

'Go back to Palestine,' came a cry from Gardiner's Corner, followed by two words, chilling in the brevity of their message. 'Perish Judah.'

'They must be in there,' May said to Julian, pointing to the shattered doors of the main entrance of Gardiner's.

Tying their bikes with Julian's scarf to a lamp post, Julian put his arm tightly round May's waist as together they made for the shop. The display windows at the front had been smashed in and a couple of women were climbing out through the jagged edges of the plate glass, bolts of Harris tweed and flowered poplin tucked beneath their arms. Sarah was crouching on the floor next to an almost empty display of ties, her back humped over her knees. She was moaning softly in the way that May had heard the women in the plantation moan when the time for their confinement had arrived. Rachel was bending over her, for once unable to speak. Relief at the sight of May filled the older woman's eyes.

'Don't worry, Rachel. We are here to bring you both home,' May said to her as she ran back out to the street with Julian.

An ambulance was making its way slowly down Cable Street heading away from Gardiner's, its bell clanging. Looking around in desperation May spotted the mounted policeman from earlier, once again in control of his horse.

'We need help,' she yelled at him. 'My friend. She's having a baby! *Now!*'

'Right away, Miss,' he said. 'I'll find you a driver right away.'

* * *

Simon had been looking for the doctor for more than an hour. Judging by the reports of violence that was breaking out up at Cable Street, he had an intuition that Rachel's nerves might get the better of her. He was also terrified that the drama of the demonstrations might bring on his daughter's labour pains and was uneasy at the thought that he and Nat might have to deliver a baby themselves. No one had seen the doctor all day and although Simon had hammered several times on the door of his house in nearby Cyprus Street, there had been no response. On Simon's final attempt the door was opened by the doctor's wife. She was wearing a dressing gown.

'For goodness' sake Mr Greenfeld, what a lot of noise,' she had snapped, furious at the disturbance. 'He's not here. He's gone up to help up at Aldgate.'

As she closed the door in Simon's face, a window opened above her and the red face of Mr Schein the barber appeared.

'Not in Eastbourne now, I see,' Simon could not resist saying before hearing the window slam shut and going to wait at the corner of Cyprus Street until the doctor eventually returned from treating the injured.

When the taxi appeared in Oak Street, Nat and Simon were waiting on the doorstep of number 52. May and Julian got out of the cab first, followed by an unusually silent Rachel. The pins securing her ever-elegant bun had fallen out and her hair was hanging unconstrained round her shoulders. Simon took his shocked wife's hand and led her inside while Nat reached across to the seat and lifted Sarah out of the taxi. He carried her across the threshold of number 52 as if they were newlyweds, kissing her forehead and stroking her hair as he took her upstairs to their bedroom where the doctor was waiting.

Inside the house, May fetched all the towels she could find and a large enamel bowl filled with hot water. For the time being, the doctor and Sarah were to be left alone. Meanwhile Simon insisted that Rachel should lie down on her own bed until the baby arrived. The wait would not be long, the doctor had assured them, and for once Rachel deferred to her husband's instructions.

May went to put on the kettle. Julian and Nat were in the parlour. Now that the danger of the streets was behind them she felt elated to have Julian here in Oak Street for the first time. She could tell that he and Nat were going to like one another. Already Julian was trying to divert Nat's anxiety from what was happening in the bedroom above by describing the earlier scenes around Aldgate and discussing how and when it might be safe to go and retrieve the bicycles and Julian's scarf.

Outside in the street May heard the sound of a group of children arguing with one another. Julian and Nat were too deep in conversation to notice her opening the front door. She was just in time to see a dozen boys and girls huddled conspiratorially by the War Memorial, holding paintbrushes and pots of paint. Their attention was centred on a girl with long, reddish, flyaway plaits who stood in the middle of the group giving instructions. May's heart lurched. She was about to shout out at them but catching sight of her, the children began to run. May ran after them, turning right at the War Memorial, but once she was round the corner the entire group had vanished.

Reluctantly May walked home. As she approached the door of number 52, she could see at once that the two clearly delineated, painted letters were still wet. She put her hand up to touch them, as if to be sure they were not a work of her imagination. She pulled back her fingertips as if she had touched a burning coal. The threat to Jews that Julian had seen in Berlin had reached the streets of the East End.

Inside the house a long steady cry more like an announcement was coming from upstairs and she could hear Nat's voice carrying the news across the backyard walls and along the terrace of house.

'It's a boy. Sarah and I have a boy. A son!'

Would that those letters could stand instead for Peace for Joshua, May whispered to herself, before going inside to ask Julian for his help. She wanted the paint removed before it had time to dry and strengthen its vile message.

21

Julian had got himself into a muddle. He had been sitting on a bench in Hyde Park for a good half hour wondering how to make some order of his life. It was late on a Friday morning and he was grateful that there were so few people about. Nearby a small number of bowler-hatted men were reading newspapers and preparing to eat their lunch, their grease-proofed sandwiches lying unwrapped in little packages on their laps, as the pages of the *Financial Times* flapped in the wind. A few yards away on another bench a large woman in a fur coat sat with her back to him, deep in conversation with a distinguished-looking man. Every now and then the woman would stop talking and reprimand the restless terrier at her feet with a fierce little jerk of the lead.

Julian turned away from the pair in an effort to concentrate on his own thoughts as he vacillated between deciding on one course of action and then another. His tendency towards consistent inconsistency both infuriated and exhausted him.

Julian had only seen Lottie once since her return from Berlin and Rupert not at all. Julian was sharing a flat near the law courts with a gregarious fellow graduate and had diffidently resumed something of his old social round of dances and dinners and weekend parties. After long bibulous evenings in the Mirabelle and the Café Royal he had come home disgusted with himself for his continued association with the vacuous Bullingdon crowd. He had intended to be definitive about ending his relationship with Lottie but although he had intimated to May that it was over, the truth was he hadn't actually got round to telling Lottie. At a recent Mayfair ball finding himself, as usual, bored by the same old people, the same old music and same old chat, he had even kissed her. He had been drunk, he told himself, by way of excuse, and on leaving her discovered that any lingering feelings of physical desire had entirely evaporated. In fact, after giving way to Lottie's strange vinegary-smelling skin and her scarlet-painted lips he felt as if he had swallowed a mouthful of stale beer. He was glad she had decided to go and stay with her grandmother for a few days in Cornwall. He could do with a bit of time to think.

He had not planned to fall in love with May. She was the most unsuitable person for a girlfriend. And up until the moment they had plunged together into the river at Cuckmere Haven and had floated out to sea he had been determined to live a less anarchic, more exacting, and impressively responsible existence. But in the presence of the slender body in the water beside him, and the dark hair swept back from that lovely face with her wide grey eyes looking at him from the swell of the waves, he was confronted with the clarity he had so long sought. As he had walked up the beach with her towards the hut all his apprehension about what was about to happen had magically disappeared. If there was a skill involved in the act of love, he had been eager that they discover it for the first time together. And during that first afternoon, by the sea, in the small hut at Cuckmere Julian had barely been aware of time or place, certain only of one thing: that life was, in that moment, perfect.

And yet, away from the hut, and from May's embrace the reality of day-to-day life nudged its way into his conscience. Reverberating memories of the violence at Cable Street reinforced his conviction that he was living in a country at odds with itself, riddled with selfishness, hypocrisy, prejudice, double standards and secrets. Last week he had received another card from Peter Grimshaw, the professor he and May had met in Wigan, urging Julian to join him and his friend Eric in fighting the cause in Spain. Julian was tempted to go. And yet. And there he went again! Dithering, procrastinating. For one thing his law term began in a matter of weeks, he argued with himself, and for another he found himself increasingly loath to travel to a country, fanciful as it sounded, in which he would not be breathing the same air as May.

The strengthening wind was beginning to deter Hyde Park's lunchtime visitors from delaying any longer, and newspapers were folded with the finality that preceded a return to the office. Julian adjusted his striped scarf, pulling it up high around his neck and tucking the ends tightly beneath the collar of his coat. The large woman and her gentleman companion continued to sit absorbed in animated conversation on the bench a little way along the path. The small dog was lying obediently at their feet. Julian's thoughts turned to his mother. She was unwell. The doctors had initially told him it might be tuberculosis but until they could be certain they had advised Julian not to say anything to worry her. He had spent a difficult evening in her flat a week earlier when Mrs Richardson had taken advantage of his presence to observe what a selfish young man he had become.

'Instead of looking after your old mother when she needs you, you tell me you are still thinking of taking off for Spain. You don't even know this boy, Paul did you say his name was? And what about that other one? Eric something? Flair? Blurr? What sort of families do they both come from? Not ones I have ever heard of, I'm sure.'

As a consequence of that dinner and a sign of tentative guilt, Julian had consulted an expensive chest specialist from Guy's Hospital whose son had been his contemporary at Magdalen. Julian had always been careful with his money and was glad he had saved a sufficient sum from his benefactor's allowance to pay for this medical advice.

'I understand your mother is widowed,' the specialist had said sympathetically to Julian on the telephone after examining Mrs Richardson in his Harley Street rooms, an encounter for which she had worn her best hat and diamond pin.

'I am told on excellent authority that it is *very* like one in the possession of the Duchess of

York,' she told Julian afterwards while appearing vague about the diagnosis of her illness.

'We only have our parents for such a short precious time, don't we?' the specialist had said to Julian. 'But do we make the most of it while they are here, that is what I ask myself sometimes? However, that is exactly what I would advise you to do, Mr Richardson. Your mother is not at all well, I am afraid. She has cancer of the lung, which I assess to be inoperable.'

Julian remained ambivalent about this news. He was not certain if it was his duty to care for a woman he did not love even if she was responsible for giving him life. He could, at least for the short-term, pay for her medical needs. And the recent conversation with her, or more accurately her latest lecture, had left him feeling unusually defenceless. Perhaps his mother had a point. Apart from the temptations of London, here he was, enjoying the benefits of his Oxford education, the luxuries of Cuckmere, and ever-deeper feelings for May, while responding with a half-promise to Peter that he might come out to join the communists in Spain. Was he simply trying to impress his left-wing Beaumont Street heroes with those plans? Should he stay near May and look after his mother, or should he reassess his life by leaving the country? Or was there a halfway measure in all this? He did not know. At times he despaired of himself.

He had brought a copy of *Jude the Obscure* to the park but the wind was whipping round him and it felt too cold to settle down and read.

Pulling his afghan collar even more tightly round his neck he stood up to leave. He planned to call in at Heywood Hill, the new bookshop in Mayfair that one of the Beaumont Street crowd had recommended for the most interesting and up-to-the-minute political titles. He would have to hurry there if he was to arrive in time for the birthday luncheon of an old university acquaintance, a Bullingdon Club member who had been born with half the silver of Mayfair wedged in his mouth.

Just then he heard a 'whooee', and tilting and swaying towards him came the unwieldy hulk of Miss Evangeline Nettlefold, being pulled from one side of the path to the other by a small dog of deceptive strength. Plumping herself down on the bench, Evangeline patted the seat beside her and still swaying a little, clamped a hand firmly on Julian's knee for balance. He tried not to flinch as he felt her kiss dampen his cheek.

'My, am I surprised to see you on such a blowy day! This is Loafer, Slipper's puppy. You know? Wallis's dog. Wallis had to go to Suffolk. On business. They were so busy at the Fort so I said I would take care of Loafer while she was away. I chose the name. You know? Like the new shoe everyone is talking about?' Ignoring Julian's bemused expression, she rattled on. 'Wallis was amused to think that a slipper would give birth to a loafer! But to tell you the truth, I think Loafer is a little unhinged and he is driving me a little crazy.'

And as Julian looked more closely at Evangeline she did indeed look a little crazed. Her hair

(Oh yes, a wig, he suddenly remembered) was in a state of unusual disarray, a little hat with a veil was propped precariously on the top of her head, her cheeks were aflame, and her brow simmered with perspiration.

'You look very hot in that coat,' Julian said.

'Oh well, I wasn't expecting to run into anyone,' she explained.

'But didn't I notice you sitting over there with a gentleman just a few moments ago?' Julian asked her.

The cheeks flamed anew. 'Oh yes, well, that was just an acquaintance of mine. I hardly know him.'

She is not telling the truth, Julian thought to himself. She was certainly more than just 'acquainted' with the man with whom she had been in such deep conversation and who looked decidedly familiar from the newspapers, even though Julian could not quite pinpoint his identity. But out loud Julian said, 'How strange that you should 'run into' two people you barely know in one morning!'

Evangeline looked startled and stood up quickly. 'Yes, well, I must be getting on and leave you to your book.'

And without another word she set off on her uneven path, a tall, hunched-over figure led on by the little dog. Julian watched her as she rolled away into the distance. Every so often she would give the animal's lead a vicious little tug, that had it been any stronger might have broken the poor animal's neck.

*   *   *

There had been a sudden burst of rain, and as Julian reached the elegant Georgian house that faced onto Piccadilly, he was aware of water seeping through the collar of his coat and onto his neck. He rang the bell twice. He had rushed from the park, regretting that the conversation with Evangeline had delayed him and prevented him from making the detour to the bookshop. As the butler opened the door he caught Julian checking his watch.

'Not the last to arrive, by any means, Sir,' he assured him. 'Must be the weather, Sir,' he continued in the deferential manner that all the best servants adopted to ensure the upper classes never felt themselves to be in the wrong.

The dining room was on the first floor, facing the street. Julian helped himself to a glass of champagne from a tray, and went over to join the other members of the lunch party who were standing at the open window.

He was surprised to see Lottie, swinging her elegant legs, sitting on the high window seat next to Rupert. Why wasn't she in the country?

'Hallo, Julian, you didn't think I would miss a good party did you?' Her carefree tone was at odds with the apprehensive expression on her face.

Julian managed a smile.

'Hallo, old chap,' Rupert said. 'Good of you to prise yourself away from all those lectures to join us! And how is the world of the legal wizard?'

'The law term hasn't begun yet,' Julian replied

370

quickly. 'But you made it safely back from Berlin in the Talbot then I see?'

'Ran like the wind, it did,' Rupert replied confidently, but looking strangely sheepish.

'So sorry your mother isn't getting any better,' Julian said.

'Thanks. I must remind Bettina that we should go down and see Mama soon. Awfully difficult to know what to say to someone who doesn't even know us. And that sister of mine is so busy playing games with a new German soldier friend she had met at a party for the new German Ambassador. She says he's going to take her to Berlin to show her the sights! Anyway, have you been down to Cuckmere recently?'

Julian murmured that he had, not wanting to admit that he went to see Joan (and everyone else at Cuckmere) every week, and more recently every couple of days. He kept to himself the disapproval felt by the Cuckmere staff who had not seen either of Lady Joan's children for a good couple of months.

Julian turned his attention to the noise coming from the direction of Piccadilly Circus. As the sound of chanting grew louder, the first of several hundred brown flat caps appeared in the street below the window, looking like a field of flattened molehills, their blue and white banners plainly visible, rising above the caps. Two of the men were carrying a coffin-sized container beneath the protection of several battered umbrellas. Another was holding the lead of a Labrador. The dog was moving as slowly as the men.

'It must be the shipbuilders from the North with their petition for Downing Street,' a member of the lunch party called out from inside the chandelier-hung room.

'Yes, that's right,' confirmed another leaning precariously far out of the window to get a better view of the street. 'I can see that red-headed MP Ellen Wilkinson,' he added. 'Apparently she has marched with them all for miles. She cannot be more than five foot tall.'

Julian was silent. The sight of the slow steps of the Jarrow marchers who had been on their feet for over three weeks was one of a desperateness that he had not encountered since his visit to Wigan over six months ago. He had read about the march in the newspapers of course and barely a day had gone by since last April without him thinking of the men standing on those street corners, looking forward to nightfall when another day without work or pay would be over. Further north eight men in ten were said to be unemployed, and since business at Palmers' shipyard on the Tyne had dried up, the figure was sometimes even higher. But these men who had arrived in the heart of London, just a few feet from where Julian held a brimming glass of champagne, were passing through one of the richest, most privileged areas in the country. Oh yes, he thought, cynicism washing over him. Most onlookers agreed they were witnessing dignity, pride and courage. But the point was what was anyone, what was *he* doing about it?

Slamming his glass down hard on the table beside him he heard it crack. He turned away

372

from the window, tripping over a well-known member of the peerage, who was lying at full stretch in an armchair, blowing smoke rings from a cigar and managing to yawn at the same time.

Lottie looked up from her position on Rupert's knee.

'You off then?' she had obviously drunk a good deal of champagne and did not bother to disguise the truth of her relationship with Julian's erstwhile university roommate. 'Off to find the back seat of a Rolls-Royce, I expect,' she added, with unmistakable bitterness. Julian did not answer her. Coatless, he dashed out into the street, banging the front door behind him before the surprised butler could reach it. An hour later, after he had signed up at the Holborn Headquarters to become a card-carrying member of the Labour Party, he made his way back down Piccadilly feeling disturbed. Skirting the back wall of the gardens of Buckingham Palace he headed for Victoria Railway station. Barely pausing to think what he was doing, he bought a ticket to Polegate and an hour later walked through the gates of Cuckmere Park just as the light was fading. Mr Hooch was putting the Talbot away in the garage and waved in greeting.

'Good afternoon, Sir. Nice to see you. Come to pay a surprise visit to her Ladyship, have you, Sir?'

The Cuckmere kitchen staff's united approval of Mr Julian had not abated both for his loyalty to Lady Joan, and for his still unspoken but obvious attachment to young May.

'Yes, that's right, Hooch. I came to find a bit of peace and sanity if you really want to know!' Julian told him, suddenly overcome by a need to tell the truth to the older man. 'Is anyone about?' Julian asked.

Mr Hooch was not innocent of what lay behind the question. 'Sir Philip has gone to his study and I am just this moment back from collecting Miss May from the station. You must have walked along the back lane or we would have passed you on the road. You'll find her in the kitchen, I expect. I'll tell Sir Philip you are here.'

The kitchen door was empty but Julian knew where May lived. He found Mrs Cage's front door unlocked. May was crouching in the hallway beside a cupboard sniffing a paintbrush. She started when she saw Julian.

'You! Sorry! You gave me such a shock! A lovely shock, though,' she whispered. And laying the brush on top of the paint pot, she closed the cupboard and put her finger up to touch his lips.

'Can we go inside the cupboard?' he whispered back, grinning at her with a mixture of delight and puzzlement and catching her finger and kissing it. 'And you can tell me why you are suddenly so interested in paint.'

'Oak Street, you silly,' she said quietly.

'Oh yes, of course,' he replied. May had not been the only one to see the letters on the Greenfeld door in Bethnal Green on the evening of Joshua's birth. Both Nat and Simon had been safely upstairs with the new baby when May had beckoned to Julian to join her outside and with

374

the help of a wet cloth and some turpentine the two of them had managed to remove the evidence before any of the inhabitants at number 52 had seen it.

Without another word, May motioned Julian to follow her up to her room, taking his hand as they climbed the stairs. A small and silent figure was lying face-down on May's bed. Florence was shaking all over, rigid to May's gentle touch. On the floor beside her was a small picture frame. May picked it up. Together she and Julian looked at the full-length photograph. A young, unsmiling man of about twenty years old, Julian's age, looked back at them. His hair was greased and smoothed away from his face. Julian recognised the uniform at once. The knee-length socks, lederhosen and beige-brown shirt with epaulettes identified him at once as a member of the Hitler Youth.

'Florence. Speak to me,' May said as she sat down on the bed beside the child. Her red-gold plaits hung down the back of her checked shirt. But as May tried to turn her over, Florence stood up without looking at her and ran from the room. Julian and May looked at one another. Julian came over to the other side of the bed. Putting both arms round May's waist he kissed her so hard that she had to lean right into him to still her sudden dizziness.

'That felt like a goodbye rather than a hallo kiss,' she said eventually. 'It felt like a final and never-to-be forgotten kiss. Will you do it again? Just so I can be certain it isn't the last one?'

'I would like to kiss you all day, darling May. A

thousand times a day,' Julian said, sounding a little wistful. 'But Philip knows I am here so I better go and say hallo.'

Julian found Philip in the drawing room. The older man was pleased to see Julian and was half surprised that he was alone. He was aware of the attraction between these two young people and if Joan had been there they would have discussed the implications, good and not so good, of a potential romance between a member of his staff and a friend of their son. On the face of it the situation was most unorthodox. And yet Philip could not help thinking that Joan would approve. Her regard for Julian, his loyalty, his intelligence, his efforts to do the right thing, and all this despite his complicated and in some ways tragic background, had developed in her a real affection for the young man. On his part, Philip found May, despite her inexperience of life, and her very young age, to be a woman of admirable, even remarkable substance.

Philip had not been in a good frame of mind. He had been irritated to learn on his arrival at Cuckmere that Mrs Cage had taken to her bed. According to Cooky she had 'come over all queer' when she had returned from London about three weeks ago and the rest of the staff had barely seen her since. Meals had been taken over to her house in the village and housekeeping instructions had been delivered from her bedroom. Apparently Florence had been rather down in the dumps as well and according to Hooch had been most withdrawn on journeys to and from school. Hooch had read her any number of Kipling stories whenever he had a free moment, but the words had been lost on her and even the suggestion of ice cream in October had failed to do the trick.

Joan would certainly have taken the trouble to discover why the child was suffering. But at the moment Philip could not afford the time to look after the personal problems between Mrs Cage and her daughter when there was so much else to preoccupy him.

The romance between the King and Mrs Simpson was no longer simply a matter for speculation in the smart dining rooms of Belgravia and the Home Counties. Things had moved far beyond the boundaries of Society and the situation was changing by the day. The day after the Decree Nisi had been awarded in the Ipswich court in October, America's most prestigious broadsheet the *New York Times* had begun its leader with the words, 'From Mayfair's most exclusive drawing rooms to Whitechapel's most plebeian pubs one question was on everybody's lips.' Several paragraphs had been devoted to speculating on 'the question', stopping just short of stating what was becoming increasingly obvious.

Philip gestured for Julian to sit down. 'How good to see you, Julian. Help yourself to a drink,' he said, gesturing towards the whisky decanter. 'How did you find Joan today?' Philip asked.

'Forgive me, Sir, but I arrived too late to get to the hospital. I have had rather a strange day. The hunger march from Jarrow reached London and the sight of it has turned me upside down a bit.'

'I know what you mean,' Philip replied with a sigh. 'The whole world seems upside down to me at the moment too.'

'Are you able to tell me about your side of things at all?' Julian asked tentatively, anxious not to pry too deeply.

'Yes. Matter of fact, I trust you enough to tell you, on the proviso that all I say is kept within the confines of these walls.'

Philip knew he was taking a risk in speaking, but sooner or later the whole story was going to be out in the open. He had wondered on several occasions how much speculation there had been among his own staff after the unfortunate visit from Sir Oswald. The Prime Minister himself had originally suggested that it might be a good idea to invite him for a private talk, as Mosley seemed genuinely concerned about the catastrophe into which the besotted King was heading. Philip had agreed with the utmost reluctance to welcoming such a man to his house for a discussion about the best way forward and it had taken all his powers of persuasion to make Joan relent.

But after that meeting, and many subsequent meetings of a similar nature in various private rooms around London, neither Philip nor Mosley, nor innumerable other powerful men, had been able to convince the King to change his mind. And now the King's intransigence over his intention to marry Mrs Simpson had reached a crisis point. Indeed, Philip himself had an air of resignation about him.

'I will try and put you in the picture. Perhaps I

378

should begin by saying that there are some things the British public will never accept and Queen Wallis, a twice divorced American (with two former husbands *still living!*), is one of them. I fear it is already too late to make the King see reason, even if there had once been a time for that, which I doubt. He is obsessed with the woman and I suspect his mind was made up to marry her as much as a year ago. I doubt even Mrs Simpson herself was aware of his decision at that stage. People think it is all her fault but I feel the opposite. In fact, she has not only told the King's legal friend, and latterly my colleague, Walter Monckton, but also the Prime Minister, that she has been trying to call the whole thing off for several weeks. However, the King is as stubborn about listening even to her as he is weak in what the American papers are calling 'matters of the heart'. And I am afraid Alex Hardinge's plain speaking has cost him the King's confidence. By advising the King that the newspapers will not hold their silence for much longer, a devoted Private Secretary has been sent into some sort of purdah.'

Philip paused. He wondered if he was saying too much.

'Some people can see the funny side of it all,' Philip continued in a lighter voice. 'For example, the Duchess of Devonshire suggested at dinner the other night that a new post of 'Master of the Mistress' might be created for Mr Simpson. More worryingly, Lady Colefax says she has it on first-hand authority that the King has threatened to slit his throat if Mrs Simpson leaves him.

Anyway, we have reached a stage where there are four options. Firstly the King gives Mrs Simpson up, which does not look at all likely. Secondly, the King marries Mrs Simpson and she becomes Queen, an option ruled out by the Church on account of her two divorces. Then there is the suggestion that the Church and Parliament, and not forgetting the Dominions, might accept Mrs Simpson as the Sovereign's wife, but not as his crowned Queen, as has been tried at various times throughout our history. Baldwin and the majority of the House, barring the old maverick Churchill of course, and Oswald Mosley and the King's holiday companion, Duff Cooper, have already indicated they would not give their support to such a plan, although I fear the King continues to think this may indeed be a solution. And of course the final and most drastic choice would be for the King to renounce the throne.'

'Abdicate?' Julian asked, the word zipping into the air like a firework.

'Yes. It is true. There is the option of an Abdication. But that would be a last resort,' Philip added hastily. 'I don't think it will come to that. There are so many arguments against it and the King is not unaware of them. For a start he knows the country loves him and would never forgive him if he abandoned them. And for another thing, it is uncertain where he would go. The King is not a man who would take easily to permanent exile.'

Philip was suddenly furious at the King's wilful selfishness. 'The whole thing is the most hell of a mess,' he snapped. 'The man is behaving as if no one in the world matters except him.' Clearly exasperated, Philip went over to the whisky decanter and refilled his glass.

'Do me a favour and dine with me tonight?' he asked Julian. 'I can find my own company both exhausting and lonely.'

★ ★ ★

May had remained in her bedroom, writing in her blue notebook. After half an hour Florence returned looking pale, and very serious.

'Do you want to talk to me about the photograph?' May asked her.

Florence nodded.

'And do you want to talk to me about the paint?'

A second nod. As Florence sat down on the bed beside May a few feathers escaped from the silky quilt and floated up into the air.

'It's a secret though,' Florence began, sounding anxious and looking at May in the face for the first time that day.

'Of course,' May replied, 'I promise.'

'You really promise not to say anything?'

May nodded.

'Well,' Florence began, her eyes now looking down onto the bed. 'That person. The one in the picture?'

'Yes.'

'Well, he isn't my brother. Not properly anyway, just half properly.' And gathering confidence, she continued. 'Actually, I've never even met him. He's called Carl and Mum says he belongs to her other life when she was married to a German. She says that was a long time ago and I don't need to know about it. It was when she was living in Germany. And that husband died ages before I was born. Carl's uncle and aunt agreed that Carl could live with them when Mum came back to England.'

For a moment Florence's voice shook. A storm of tears that had evaporated earlier had left behind an intermittent shudder. Florence moved further up the bed and May could smell the sweetness of her breath, like a meadow in early summer.

'Is your father in Germany too?' May asked gently.

'No, he met Mum when she came back to England. My dad was in the army and Mum was an army wife, she says, but Dad died of pneumonia when I was only one. And after Dad died Mum came to work here.'

'So both your mum's husbands have died? That is so sad for her.'

Florence looked up at May, grateful for her sympathy. 'Yes. Sometimes Mum is very sad but she always says at least she has me with her, even if the others aren't here any more. That's why I try and do the things she wants, like the painting.'

A small hand crept across the eiderdown and put itself quietly into May's own hand. For a few moments they sat there silently, side by side, hands joined, as Florence wavered between loyalty to her mother and a wish to confide long-held secrets.

'Promise you won't say anything when I tell you that Carl told Mum how to do the letter painting?'

Once more May gave her word.

'Well, he said I should do it too. He said Mum should teach me about the Jews taking over everything and ruining people's businesses. And he wrote her a letter about doing the painting. They do that over there in Germany.'

'Is that why you didn't want to go on holiday to Pagham?' May asked.

'Yes. We had to go last year and afterwards all of us children said we didn't want to paint on the doors any more. I don't think Mum would have made me do it on my own but Carl and the other women in the camp at Pagham encouraged her. They said it was easier for children to do it as they could run away more quickly than the grown ups. I told Mum I didn't want to but she said it was for England, not for Germany, and that I was English, wasn't I?'

A second shudder rippled through Florence and May felt the effect of it through their joined hands.

'I didn't mean to do it to Nat and Sarah and you. I didn't even know I was in your street till you came out and found us. We were only in that part of London because lots of Jewish people live there. I was trying to tell all the others that we should stop doing it, I knew it was wrong.' Florence spoke calmly now, as if what she was saying was an unarguable fact.

May drew Florence closer. An image of Sarah with Joshua in her arms flashed into May's mind.

'Florence, what you did was very, very wrong. If I ask you, and you agree never to paint on doors again, will your mother be angry with you?'

'I expect so, but I don't care. I am going to tell Mum that I don't want to do it again. If she makes me I will tell her that I will never speak to her again. Ever.'

And Florence got up from the bed and just as she had on their first ever meeting, kissed May on the cheek.

'I never told Mum about Vera and Lady Myrtle, you know.'

May smiled at her. 'I knew you wouldn't.'

'Will you keep Mum's secret?' Florence asked. 'For me?'

'Yes. I promise,' May said as she watched Florence skip out of the room.

★ ★ ★

The following morning Mr Hooch came to find May having breakfast in the kitchen and handed her an envelope.

'Mr Julian must have left this in the garage before the taxi came to get him.'

Inside the envelope was one sheet of Cuckmere Park headed writing paper.

Saturday 31 October 1936
Darling May,

I am sorry to leave without saying goodbye but if I had delayed my departure this morning by speaking to you, I might have changed my mind and not gone at all.

I am catching the boat to France today and then taking the train to Paris to meet Peter. From there we will probably travel on to Spain and meet up with his friend Eric. I am going to Spain because I think, well, I hope, it is the right thing to do.

I don't know how long I will be away, perhaps a good while, but I will get a message to you to tell you I have arrived safely.

Look after Joan, won't you? You know I think of her as a mother. And give Florence a kiss from me.

I am going to miss you more than you know.

With love from
Julian

May read the letter twice and the final two sentences three times. After a moment she realised Mr Hooch was still standing in the corner of the kitchen.

'I am going back to Polegate now to collect Miss Nettlefold from the ten o'clock from Victoria. Would you like to come with me? I would welcome the company,' he said.

Mr Hooch did not have to explain an invitation that May knew was kindness of the best sort. But she declined the offer and went to her desk intending to immerse herself in her work, the certainties of life unravelling around her. She remembered how as a child at home in Barbados she would sometimes wake in a panic in the middle of the night, fearful that she had built her sandcastle too close to the shoreline, and that in the morning she would find it had melted clean away in the waves. Just as the foundation stones of the pavements around Oak Street had been forcibly uprooted in the East End only a month ago, so the way of life and the friendships that she had begun to trust in over the last ten months no longer seemed so secure.

Sir Philip was waiting for her in the study.

'I have got to go to London tomorrow for a meeting at Downing Street with the Prime Minister, Sunday or no Sunday. Things are truly coming to a head. Can you get Lord Beaverbrook on the telephone for me right away?'

Half an hour later the sound of the dogs barking in the big hall confirmed that Miss Nettlefold had arrived but May did not actually see her until she spotted the fur-clad figure, outside on the lawn with Loafer. May watched the pair of them through the window. Loafer was limping along behind his temporary mistress with the gait of an animal dragging itself through life. May turned back to her desk where the telephone was ringing for what seemed like the dozenth time in as many minutes.

At teatime Miss Nettelfold came looking for May. The small study felt dreadfully cramped as the large woman eased her abundant form past the desk and sat down, her over-tight skirt revealing fleshy knees that merged together as one.

'Have you left Loafer outside?' May asked. 'Because I know Sir Philip wouldn't mind if she

386

came in here for a moment.'

But Loafer was having a snooze on the bed upstairs, Miss Nettlefold explained, and did not wish to be disturbed. In fact, Miss Nettlefold had been asked to return the dog to the Fort in a couple of days' time and May was to drive them both there. And she and May were to spend the day together tomorrow as well, Miss Nettlefold announced with a theatrical clap of her hands. The day of the wireless recording with Sir John Reith, about which Miss Nettlefold had confided to May some weeks ago, had almost arrived. Miss Nettlefold had some appointments in the morning in Mayfair and was expected at the recording studio in Crystal Palace in the south of London by noon. May nodded, trying not to think about Julian's letter, and to share in Miss Nettlefold's excitement. Miss Nettlefold was certainly in a very ebullient mood.

'Things have been going well for me, May, I am delighted to report. Some people choose to reject one in life, but I have found that another door always opens, especially when you are least expecting it!' And off she went, praising the British and especially the Scottish, whom she had recently discovered to be among the most loyal of friends. 'Loyalty, May, that's the quality I put at the top of the tree. That's why I like you, May.' And with a generous smile she wanted to hear how May was doing. 'How is that nice young brother of yours? Going to go far that Sam, I know it. Trust me. Oh, and by the way Hooch tells me Julian Richardson has gone off to Spain.'

'Yes,' May replied. 'He left rather suddenly this morning.'

'Well. Forgive me May if I use an English phrase when I say 'a jolly good riddance' to him. Now, don't think I hadn't noticed you developing a certain, shall we say 'interest' in him although personally I can't think what anyone could ever see in glasses and albino hair. And there's more to life than swimming, believe me. Interested in everything and nothing he is. Never could make his mind up, dithering about all over the place, in politics and in friends. Poor Lottie. No wonder she decided she would be better off with Rupert. Anyway, perhaps the sights in Spain will knock some sense into young Mr Richardson.' She pronounced the word 'young' with contempt.

May turned back to her typewriter. Tears blurred the typed words in front of her but she managed to mumble what sounded like an agreement before Miss Nettlefold went to see if tea had yet arrived in the drawing room.

22

Shortly after leaving London, Evangeline heard May flick the double switch on the walnut dashboard, illuminating first the sidelights followed by the headlamps. Evangeline was surprised that darkness had already fallen even though it was barely teatime. She was staring up at the roof of the car, stretched out across the back seat, her elegant lace-up boots protruding from the edge of the tartan rug that covered her. She felt incapable of rousing herself to look out of the window. There was nothing to see in the dark anyway. Loafer was equally comatose, slumped across his proxy mistress's stomach, rising and falling with Evangeline's breaths as if he was sleeping on top of a live anthill. Evangeline was aware of the slothful impression she must be making on May, especially compared with her upbeat mood of the beginning of the day before. But Evangeline was beyond caring. In fact she had barely spoken a word to May for the entire journey.

The humiliation that she had experienced yesterday at Crystal Palace in the secret wireless recording studio was worse even than anything she had suffered at the hand of her mother. With hindsight she kicked herself for her stupidity at thinking such an apparently simple plan would work, and for allowing her contempt for and disappointment in Wallis to get the better of her.

Of course she had convinced herself that the motivation for what she was doing lay in a desire to tell the truth, just as Sir John himself had advocated at dinner. But the real truth was that Evangeline's plan was born out of jealousy and hurt at Wallis's rejection of her.

Everything had begun so well. She had told no one but May of the honour of being chosen for Sir John Reith's experimental broadcast. She wanted the whole thing to be a surprise. A coolness had developed between herself and May during these past few weeks as Evangeline found it impossible to ignore Julian's obvious affection for the young chauffeur. Now he was safely out of the way Evangeline wanted to mend any differences between herself and May. Evangeline had explained how, by the miraculous medium of the wireless, a handful of individuals of different nationalities were to bring insights from their own countries right into the heart of British homes. Sir John had decided America would be the best place to begin, given that country's close links with Britain. Evangeline, with what Sir John Reith had called her 'beautiful velvety voice', was to be the first of his foreign broadcasters. The only detail of the plan that she withheld from May was the existence of two handwritten pages that she had been working on in secret for several days.

★ ★ ★

The build up to the recording had been thrilling. Evangeline had spent the morning in Mayfair, first with the manicurist at Elizabeth Arden and then in Antoine's hairdressing salon having her wig adjusted in a private room. She had taken particular trouble with her clothes. Although Evangeline had not a drop of Scottish blood in her, she was glad she had indulged herself in a new tartan suit with deep pockets, especially when Sir John commented on how well the dark-blue-and-green checks became her. She was gratified that Sir John had appreciated her little gesture to his own country.

From the moment May dropped Evangeline off at the side entrance to the Crystal Palace, Sir John had treated her as if she was nothing less than royalty, agreeing to Evangeline's request that her broadcast be kept as a surprise for her compatriot friend, Wallis Simpson. He had personally ushered Evangeline through the corridors and down in the lift to the basement. Everyone they passed had doffed their cap and made a little bow not only to him but to Evangeline too. They were used to seeing what the technicians referred to as 'eminent personages' visiting the television studios, particularly as the broadcasting of the first television pictures to a few affluent private homes had only begun a month earlier. But a visit from the head of the BBC Wireless service to the discreet studios reserved for broadcasts that for one reason or another had to be conducted in secret was a particularly great honour.

Once they reached the studio Sir John introduced Evangeline to George Barnes, the BBC's senior producer for 'special talks'. Mr

Barnes, a friendly-looking man with a wide-open face, short haircut and most reassuring manner, ran through the practical details with Evangeline. He reminded her of how she should speak slowly and clearly, pausing if she encountered a problem; the recording technician would be only too pleased to begin again if she made a mistake. As the programme was not going to be broadcast live, there would be every opportunity to correct any small hesitancies, he assured her with a warm smile.

Mr Barnes made sure Evangeline was comfortable in the capacious schoolroom chair, sending off for a cushion from one of the television prop rooms to soften the wooden seat. The technician settled a pair of headphones over her newly lacquered wig. The typed script, already approved in every detail by herself and Sir John, was placed on the table in front of her and they were ready to start.

As instructed, Evangeline began reading as soon as the green light on the fist-sized microphone began to shine red. Looking up briefly, she could see Sir John's tall figure on the other side of the glass screen nodding at her encouragingly, with Mr Barnes, full of reassurance, beside him.

The first minute was taken up by Evangeline expressing the pleasure she felt at speaking to a British audience about the land of her birth. None of the three men on the other side of the glass noticed as Evangeline discreetly slipped the two pages of handwritten notes out of her pocket. After completing a vivid description of how the skyscrapers in New York were now dominated by the six-year-old Chrysler building and the even newer and taller Empire State, Evangeline cleared her throat, and placed her handwritten pages on the table.

'But tonight as an American who loves your country, I feel it is my duty to let you in on 'the world's worst kept secret',' she began.

Sir John was frowning on the other side of the glass, looking across at George Barnes for clarification.

'And by that,' Evangeline continued, 'I mean the object of your own King's affections. The British Press may be an exemplary institution but during this past year they have been operating a censorship programme that has left their foreign counterparts astonished.' She took the next part extra slowly. 'I believe that the British have a right to know that Edward VIII is in love with a twice divorced American woman.'

Evangeline looked up. The expressions on the three faces in front of her reflected their mutual shock. Evangeline went on with her surprise.

'You should also know that the King intends to give the British people a new Queen. This woman with whom he is currently conducting a romantic relationship is named Wallis Simpson, and when Wallis Simpson marries Edward VIII, Queen Wallis will join him on the throne.'

When Sir John burst through the door of the studio a moment later the microphone light had once again turned green. Evangeline could see the technician frantically pushing buttons on the control panel as Mr Barnes mouthed urgently at him.

'How *dare* you abuse my time?' Sir John said, lifting Evangeline's headphones off her head with some roughness. 'You stupid, stupid woman. Sir Philip warned me that you were unpredictable. No wonder! I kick myself for not listening to him.'

'I was only telling the truth, like you said to,' Evangeline replied angrily and full of reproach, conscious that in the hasty removal of the headphones her wig had slipped sideways. 'If you don't want to listen to the truth, then I give up on this goddamn hypocritical country.'

But as she tried to stand up to leave, she realised that she was stuck. A couple of blobs of not-quite-dry glue on the extra cushion had attached themselves to the seat of the chair and to the fabric of Evangeline's skirt. With a little straining she managed to release herself, and pushed the chair out of her way but not before the engineer, Sir John and Mr Barnes had all heard the sound of ripping cloth.

'No one ever tells the truth, that's your whole problem,' Evangeline said, flinging herself through the door with as much dignity as she could muster.

Walking quickly towards the lift, the tear in her skirt flapped open behind her, as the furious voice of Sir John followed her down the corridor. 'This treacherous incident will not go unnoticed. I can assure you of that, Miss Nettlefold.'

On the drive back to Hamilton Terrace May had asked politely if the recording had gone well.

'I am a little tired, May, if you don't mind, and would rather not speak.'

May had been apologetic. Even so she ventured further, hoping that Evangeline had not had words with Sir Philip? Evangeline was not in the mood for imparting confidences and responded with a shake of the head. She knew why May had asked the question. These days, with the tensions in the House escalating by the day and monopolising Philip's time, he was quite capable of being tetchy to anyone.

May had enquired after Loafer as well. She had remarked on how the dog had appeared unusually lethargic for these past couple of days. In fact, May could not remember when she had last seen the dog conscious. But Evangeline offered no insight into the dog's recent behaviour and the rest of the journey had passed in silence.

★　★　★

The following afternoon the car made its way up the graceful loops of the Fort drive, and soon the floodlit walls appeared, silhouetted against a sky in which rain clouds obliterated the stars. The King's stationwagon was parked in the semi-circular driveway but for once no one was waiting at the front door. A full minute elapsed before Osborne the butler appeared, as immaculate as ever in his black suit and tie. Greeting Miss Nettlefold with a handshake, and all but ignoring May, he retrieved the suitcase from the boot of the car. Evangeline, with a sleeping Loafer in her arms, followed him into the house, with May carrying her own overnight bag walking close behind her.

It had been Evangeline's idea for May to stay the night at the Fort. After agreeing to return Loafer to Wallis, she had become nervous of the likely consequences of yesterday's scene at the Crystal Palace. Secretly she planned to feel so unwell that it would become necessary for her to return to London early the next morning. She had telephoned Wallis before she set off for the Fort from London.

'Wouldn't it be fun if May stayed and took us both for a drive tomorrow? I have never been to Eton School and the Blunts are always telling me there is a dear little village nearby with an excellent tea shop.'

Osborne led the way into the octagonal drawing room where the velvet curtains were closed against the night sky. The tea things had not been cleared away and a plate of egg and cress sandwiches lay untouched on the large stool in front of the fire. Two men, one dark the other blond, were standing near the fireplace holding flower-patterned cups. They were so absorbed in their conversation that neither noticed Evangeline come into the room.

'Mrs Simpson remains rather taken with Rothermere's suggestion,' the King was saying. 'We would go ahead with the Coronation next May as planned but as the decree absolute becomes law in April, that gives us an opportunity to fix a wedding date before then. And then, do you see, Wallis will be at my side when I am crowned but she will not take the usual royal rank due to a King's wife.

396

Morganatic is the term, I believe? I think this plan may solve all our problems, Walter, don't you?'

'Of course, the plan is certainly worth a shot, Sir,' the dark-haired man replied, 'but I am bound to say that I can't see Baldwin or the rest of them liking the idea very much. Mind you, Winston and Mosley might be supportive, for what that is worth. Leave it with me for now, Sir.'

Just then the King caught sight of Evangeline. She had learned how to make him the briefest of curtsies so as not to draw attention to a process she still found both tricky and embarrassing.

'My dear Evangeline, what have we here? A sleeping Loafer! You must have been running him ragged in the Sussex fields! Osborne, take the poor dog to the kitchen and see if he might like something to eat.'

Evangeline deduced from the King's friendly tone that he had heard nothing of yesterday's aborted recording.

'Come and meet my guest.' The King beckoned Evangeline over to the fireplace. 'I believe you may already have been introduced to Walter Monckton, my lawyer? Wallis will be with us shortly. Cigarette?'

Evangeline declined the offer as she had so often before, irritated that the King never remembered that she did not smoke. She felt jumpy. She had not seen Wallis since her return from Suffolk three weeks ago nor had she heard a word from Sir John during the past twenty-four hours and did not know if, or how, he would implement his parting threat. Perhaps he had forgiven her. Evangeline hoped that for once she would be given the benefit of the doubt. Behind her back she crossed her fingers for luck.

Mr Monckton, a friendly-looking man with prominent spectacles and a central hair parting that reminded Evangeline of Wallis's own style, shook her hand firmly. 'Pleased to meet you again, Miss Nettlefold. I trust you had a safe journey from London?'

'Oh, Evangeline knows her way to the Fort with the instinct of a treasure seeker, Walter! She has been one of our most frequent visitors this year, although we have not seen enough of you recently. And how is the splendid Miss May Thomas?' the King enquired.

Despite his ever-present politeness of manner, his smile momentarily fell away revealing a face that appeared to have aged a decade in a month. Turning to the lawyer he explained that Evangeline's driver worked for Sir Philip Blunt, the man whose legal advice over these past few days had been invaluable.

'Grew up in the plantation fields of Barbados, May did. And I tell you, even though she's not yet twenty-one, there is nothing she doesn't know about the inside workings of a car.'

Mr Monckton looked interested. 'Funny thing that. My daughter Valerie is not much younger and she too is crazy about motors. She drove me here today and is having a cup of tea in the kitchen. I hope Miss Thomas is there too. They should meet.'

At that moment Wallis came into the room.

The yellow of her collared cardigan matched the yellow of the King's tie. A new diamond pin in the shape of a bow sparkled from her lapel.

'Vangey, darling, how lovely to see you. It has been too long. Now have you brought Loafer back to me? Oh yes, don't tell me, he's resting after all those walks in the park?'

Evangeline submitted herself to her old schoolfriend's embrace, feeling the boniness of Wallis's shoulders protruding through the wool of her cardigan. To Evangeline's relief she could detect nothing but warmth in her old school-friend's greeting even though Wallis looked exhausted.

'Shall we leave the gentlemen to their talk and go to my room to catch up?' Wallis asked her, taking Evangeline's hand and leading her upstairs. 'Aunt Bessie is on her way here from across the ocean, thank goodness, but I am so pleased to have you here with me now, Vangey. I could do with one of my own at the moment in this crazy country.'

As soon as they reached the first-floor bedroom Wallis sat on the bed and patted the cover for Evangeline to sit down next to her. 'I expect you have heard on the grapevine that the Suffolk judge gave us the nisi?'

'Yes. I had heard.'

'Oh good. I thought you would have. I must say that is a relief for all of us. I cannot tell you how unenjoyable it was in that cold little house in Felixstowe, even though Kitty and George did their very best to keep up all our spirits.'

Evangeline, along with everyone else who was

following the unfolding drama, was well aware that the decree nisi had been granted in Ipswich more than three weeks ago. The first stage of Wallis's legal separation from Ernest had been reported in the British Press on 27 October but with the minimum of embellishment. However, Evangeline had been fully briefed by the American papers sent over by her brother. The journalists had gone to town. The *New York American* had been unequivocal when it stated that a wedding date between 'Wally' and the King of England was already scheduled for next year. The decree absolute would finalise the divorce at the end of April and speculation hovered over whether the marriage would precede the Coronation, confirmed for 12 May 1937, or whether the union between Wallis and Edward would follow shortly afterwards. What seemed to be in no doubt, however, was the inevitability of the marriage itself.

'So now we have all that business, including the Coronation, hanging over us and who knows where it will all end.'

Wallis was looking at Evangeline, her dark little eyes suddenly hardening. 'Now look here, Vangey,' she said, drawing Evangeline's hand once again in amongst her bejewelled knuckles. 'I know you think I have forgotten all about what I said to you back in September in the *Meurice*. The truth is that even though I have still not convinced David how much better off he will be without me, I am still trying my best. He must have it his way at the moment, you see?'

Evangeline was listening.

'But I am pretty sure that when he speaks to Mr Baldwin this coming Monday he will see sense,' Wallis went on. 'I know that the British people, who love David, will never accept me. I'm divorced twice over, well, almost, and I am a Yank with far too much pep. But David won't take it from me. He is full of crazy talk at the moment about giving up the throne. In fact, Walter thinks I should leave the country for a while to let things calm down, and maybe out of sight will mean out of mind. To be frank, life has been pretty good hell for some of these past few weeks and I miss my freedom.' Wallis paused, smoothing down her hair with her hand. 'I couldn't even get out of my flat in Cumberland Terrace to go to Antoine so my hair is a complete mess! Even this place, where I have been so happy, now *seems* like a Fortress and I feel like a caged bird. If I can manage to get away,' she went on, 'you will have to look after Loafer and maybe Slipper too for a while longer.'

Evangeline murmured her agreement trying at the same time to pull her hand free. She suspected Wallis was dissembling. Only half an hour earlier in the drawing room downstairs Evangeline had heard the King discussing Wallis's interest in a morganatic marriage.

'The thing is, Vangey,' Wallis was saying, 'I give you my word now that David and I will never be married. You know me, Vangey. I love life too much, and I am talking about the old secure way of life that I had with Ernest, to even consider becoming Queen of England!'

Even now Evangeline could not work out

whether Wallis Simpson was in love with the King or not. She no longer believed a word Wallis said. In fact she was only relieved to conclude that Sir John Reith had decided not to mention yesterday's little disagreement in the recording room. Perhaps some men *were* actually decent. She was about to go and change for dinner when there was a knock at the door.

'I am sorry to disturb you, Madam,' Osborne said, 'but there is an urgent telephone call for you. I explained to Sir John Reith that you were speaking with Miss Nettlefold but he insisted I interrupt.'

'I will take the call here, Osborne. Just put it through to the bedroom extension.'

Evangeline made a move to leave but Wallis put her hand on her arm. 'Don't go, Vangey. Reith may have something interesting to say.'

* * *

Ten minutes later as Evangeline was making her way down the staircase, the King emerged from the door to the cellar steam room. 'Are you all right, Evangeline?' he asked, 'You look upset.'

'Yes, Sir. I am upset,' Evangeline almost snapped back at him. 'I think you should know that Wallis is not all she seems. She is treacherous and dangerous. She says one thing and does another. She cares only to benefit herself. She is not worthy of you, Sir. Don't let her betray you, Sir, in the way she has me.'

At that moment Wallis appeared at the foot of the staircase in the octagonal hallway.

'Wallis,' the King said, 'tell me what is going on.'

Without looking at Evangeline, Wallis took the King's arm and turned him to face her. 'One's schoolfriends should be loyal,' she began. 'Even fat, spinster, hairless ones whom one has spent a lifetime feeling sorry for and being kind to out of pity. Above all, one's countrymen should be loyal. But if I have learned one thing in life, it is that one will always have enemies and that, however you choose to spell the word, it is *jealousy* that will eventually destroy everything that matters.'

Together the King and Mrs Simpson went arm in arm into the yellow curtained drawing room followed by Osborne who shut the door firmly behind him.

23

Early on Sunday morning, with the late November sunshine struggling to make any impact on the cold temperatures, May set out once again on the road from London to Fort Belvedere. Sir Philip was sitting in the front seat as he so often liked to do. He had been helping Mr Monckton with legal advice for many weeks now and was planning to stay the night at the Fort. He had been given the small bedroom at the back of the house that was usually reserved for the use of a visiting valet and May had been given the rest of the day off.

'I fear these comings and goings from London might last a good few days yet, my dear, so try and conserve your strength while you can.'

May was pleased to get home to Oak Street and had been enjoying looking out of her attic window watching the scene below. Mrs Cohen was scrubbing her front-door step opposite. She was as lean as her husband had been fleshy. Next door Mrs Smith was also hard at work on her own doorstep, her pride ensuring standards were kept up, even though her high spirits had been extinguished by widowhood. Mr Smith's desperate leap into the river, his two children holding trustingly to his hands, had not been forgotten by anyone in the street. It was common knowledge that the unwanted pregnancy, the catalyst for the tragedy, had been seen to by a kindly woman who lived above the butcher's.

'Gave me a good price, she did, seeing we are all part of the same neighbourhood,' Mrs Smith had informed Rachel with a touching acceptance of her lot.

At lunchtime the following day the children were at school while their parents were at work or busy inside their homes. The street was unusually still. No one was at home at number 52 Oak Street except May. On hearing a double knock on the door May took the rungs of her attic ladder at well-practised speed and skipped down the flight of stairs. There was always the unlikely hope that Julian would tire of Spain and turn up at Oak Street out of the blue as he had done once before.

Sam was waiting on the doorstep.

'Are you all right?' she asked him as he followed her into the house. 'You look so pale.'

'Actually, would you mind if we went out?' he asked her. 'I want to be with you. But not here. Somewhere where it's just us? I was coming to see if you fancied a trip to Sydenham to see the Crystal Palace? If we hurry we could take the train to Forest Hill and still get there in the light.'

May quickly recovered from her disappointment that Sam was not Julian, and went to get her coat. She had seen so little of her brother recently. He had not been home on leave since before the birth of Joshua and had missed the whole drama of Mosley's march.

They reached the park and sat down on a bench within sight of Paxton's spectacular glass structure. The building had been designed as the showcase for Queen Victoria's Great Exhibition and for eighty years it had been a source of pride for Londoners. Brother and sister stared in admiration at the biggest and most beautiful greenhouse they had ever seen before Sam reached deep into the pocket of his navy greatcoat and drew out a white envelope covered with muddy fingerprints.

In handwriting familiar to May and Sam ever since it had appeared on the flyleaf of their first schoolbooks, the name May Gladys Thomas was inscribed on the front and beneath it Sam Benjamin Thomas. May looked at Sam, puzzled and alarmed.

'A friend, well actually you know him. William? From the consignment ship? Well, he brought this over with him last week and posted it from Liverpool. It arrived at my digs in Portsmouth yesterday.' Sam explained. 'Bertha got in touch with him. After Mamma died she sorted through all her things and came across this letter. Apparently it was in a box containing a huge stash of correspondence with postmarks from India. Knowing William was a friend of mine, Bertha asked him to bring the letter with him to England when he next sailed.'

For the past few months, May's grief had subsided like an exhausted butterfly beating its wings against a closed window. The sight of her mother's writing threatened to revive the receding pain.

'You open it,' Sam said encouragingly. 'Your name is on the top. Girls first.'

The seal on the envelope gave way easily and

cleanly. The date at the top of the page was the date of their sailing to England, in December 1935. Sam moved closer to May on the bench and she began to read aloud.

My beloved children,

I have no idea in what circumstances you will read this letter, if indeed you ever will. What I would like best is to come over to England, and hold both your hands as we always do when there is something important to speak of, and then I would read this to you myself. The purpose in writing the letter is as much for myself as for both of you. Sometimes (as I know I have said so many times that it makes you groan) I feel that the very act of writing things down makes truths true and whole.

I want to begin by saying that the only consistent source of emotional happiness in my life has been my love for you, my children. And now, on the day in which you have both sailed away from me, perhaps to a new life that I will never know, I feel it is the right time to tell you the truths that, as my children, you have the right to know. So here is the story of my life as simply as I can set it down.

I was not in love on the day of my wedding. I married on an impulse, probably for security, possibly as an adventure, but whatever the reasons were, I soon realised I had made a terrible mistake. Duncan (as I will call him here) devoted more care to his work than to anything or anyone else. I was lonely. I missed

Scotland. I missed my sister. I missed my parents. And I felt I had missed out on life's opportunity to love and to be loved.

At the beginning of the Great War, Duncan left Barbados and joined the Navy, expecting to be gone for just a few months and I stayed behind to care for our son Sam, who was by then two years old. I longed for companionship and while Duncan was away I fell in love.

Gabriel Nischal Ramsay was half-Indian and his middle name, that suited him so well, meant calm. I used to call him Nishy. His British father, Mr Ramsay, had worked for the Maharaja of Jaipur looking after the regal elephants, just as his grandfather had before him. Time and science moved forward and with the arrival of the motorcar, working elephants were no longer used for transport at the royal court. One of Mr Ramsay's chief responsibilities was to oversee the upkeep of the Maharaja's cars, a job in which he took pride and from which he derived much pleasure. Although Nishy's parents were happy enough together, his mother, an English teacher to the Royal children and a woman of great beauty, had a brief affair early in her marriage with the Maharaja's younger brother and conceived a child. Nishy's phial of royal blood was well known to those at court, accepted although never discussed.

Looking for adventure, Nishy left the court at Rajasthan in 1912 and travelled to the West Indies where he got a job at Duncan's plantation. He worked hard and was well liked, particularly

408

by Duncan. Soon Nishy was promoted to the role of deputy manager while in his spare time he made sure all was well with our car.

Duncan was given leave for one wartime visit to the plantation in the early autumn of 1915, (and here I apologise to Sam for revealing something that no child should hear from his mother) I could not bear to be intimate with him.

Duncan took the rejection badly and a few weeks after he returned to the Navy, angry, and humiliated, I discovered I was pregnant with Nishy's child. Nishy and I told no one except Bertha, a woman whose unconditional loyalty has sustained me throughout all these years. When our olive-skinned daughter, one-quarter Indian and blessed by royal blood, was born in the early summer of 1916 Nishy and I called her May after the month of her birth and a time of year when all the world seems full of hope and promise.

Duncan returned to Barbados in the summer of 1917, took one look at the year-old baby, saw the touch of darkness on her skin and realised what must have happened. There was a violent and dreadful row and Nishy, fearing for his life, returned at once to Rajasthan. He wanted me to follow him but Duncan's threats of recrimination eroded my resolve. I prayed daily for the courage to scoop my children into my arms and escape to Nishy in India or to my parents in Scotland or to my sister and her family in London. I will never cease to regret that fear prevented me from doing so. I remained on the island, sustained by motherhood alone.

I have not seen Nishy since the day we were parted but we have written to each other every single week. For eighteen years I have brought my letter to the plantation office where Bertha's husband, Tom, conceals it within the outgoing pile of mail. Nishy's letter to me waits for collection from the Speightstown post office in an envelope addressed to Bertha. She continues to run the risk of being questioned about receiving letters from her cousin in India. When you, May, my daughter, began taking the post to Speightstown a few years ago, you were unaware that the documents you carried in your hands were letters of love between your parents. I have saved all Nishy's letters and I hope that one day they will be given to you so you can both understand and forgive.

Duncan's one condition in allowing you, May, to live in the family house was that neither you nor Sam should ever be told the truth of May's parentage. I agreed to keep the secret. No one challenged the assumption that the beautiful child with her dark skin was Duncan's daughter. Duncan's own war injuries had resulted in a cruel infertility and with my infidelity, the loss of his manhood and the death of an adored elder brother, he began to drink. In the navy, rum had been a fifth element, like air or water. The alcohol exacerbated his anger and his moods were and are often terrifying.

At first he could not bring himself to look at the new baby, aware perhaps that no child of such beauty could have been conceived out of anything other than love. But after a few years his behaviour towards you began to evolve into one of stifling affection. He told me that if he could not love you as a father he would love you 'better than a father'. I did not object. I reasoned that it was better that he loved you too much than not at all.

Throughout the years Duncan's regard, even love for you, Sam, remained intact. He was proud of you and it was only because of that pride and the hope that you gave him amidst his own failure, that he agreed you should both go to England. My own fears for your safety were softened by knowing you would be in the care of Nathanial, who I trust with you both on my sister's life.

I count the days I have already spent without you and wonder how long I can continue with an existence that feels so empty. Duncan is angrier than ever. He blames himself for letting you go just as he blamed himself for leaving me during the war.

But if he had not left me then I would never have known the love of Nishy, nor spent three years with my beloved son all to myself or had the joy of becoming the mother to my precious daughter.

Whatever happens to me, never forget that I have always been

Your adoring

Mamma

May put the letter back in the envelope feeling dazed. The tragedy on the beach no longer seemed accidental. She put her arm round her brother's shoulders.

'I hated Duncan too,' Sam said quietly, his use of the first name for his father unmistakably cold. Sam had been five years old when Duncan returned home from the War, old enough to remember the day in which he had witnessed his mother's terror, a day when his father and Nishy, gentle and soft-spoken, with his dark skin and the pointed beard, had a huge argument. Sam also remembered how his mother had continued to weep long after Nishy had inexplicably disappeared. Sam stood up from the bench, put his hands into his pockets, and kicked at the few remaining autumn leaves that were skipping across the wide, deserted avenues of the park. A fireball of a sun was already setting ahead of them.

'I saw what Duncan did to Mum. When he was away at the War I came to love Nishy too. After he left I saw Mum's unhappiness and I saw how strangely Duncan behaved towards you. He sort of loved you and yet at the same time he could speak so unkindly to you. It was almost as if he possessed you. But he was my father and I was not sure what to do. Now I am not sure I will ever forgive myself for doing nothing.'

May looked at Sam through her tears before glancing down at her hands. For the first time in her life their colour seemed beautiful. She pushed one of them deep into the pocket of her brother's coat, hoping her touch would confirm

412

that she blamed him for nothing. But she did not want Sam's opinion of his father to be damaged further. She knew then that she would never tell him the full truth of Duncan's abuse. Her mother had never known of Duncan's secret bedtime nips and his subsequent mistreatment of the girl who was not his daughter and May was glad. Her mother had suffered enough and Sam should not be made to inherit that suffering.

Their hands remained linked as they made their way out of the park and towards the underground. They continued to talk. They promised each other that they would write to Nishy, the man who had made their mother so happy. And they would write to Bertha and to Tom to thank them for their courageous selflessness. And they pledged to one another that if they ever saw Duncan again they would confront him together, fearlessly.

★ ★ ★

They returned home early that evening from the Crystal Palace exhausted. A few hours later the famous building was almost completely destroyed by fire. The colossal blaze stained the whole sky red and was rumoured to have started with a smouldering cigarette thrown carelessly into a dusty grating. *The Times* reported how it had been possible to read newsprint at several hundred yards distance so bright were the flames. Soot-blackened goldfish had been seen swimming in a fountain filled with the fallen debris of stone effigies of British Kings. Days later, smoke had continued to swirl around the two central water towers that had miraculously escaped intact. Rachel swore that she had actually heard the roof of the Egyptian Hall fall in.

'The man on the wireless said the noise of the crash had travelled five miles. And Mrs Cohen said her Benjamin saw the glow from down at the coast. Are you listening to me, Simon?'

But Simon was listening to the news on the wireless.

'I don't know about buildings,' he replied, 'but it looks like something else is about to go up in flames.'

★ ★ ★

May said nothing to the Greenfelds or the Castors about the revelations contained within her mother's letter. The news of her mother's love affair made her long more than anything to talk to Julian but she did not know when her chance would come. He had sent her a postcard to say he had arrived safely in Paris and that he would write again when he reached Spain. Since then she had heard nothing more. She was grateful that her work for Sir Philip had become even more demanding. There were more letters and reports to type and more telephone calls to make, to receive and to field than she could remember. And the secretarial work had somehow to be squeezed in between driving to and from the relentless number of meetings, lunches and dinners that packed Sir Philip's every waking hour. At least May had no time yet to dwell either on the momentous discovery about her parentage, or on Julian's silence.

Sometimes she dropped Sir Philip off at Number 10, sometimes she waited late into the night outside the Houses of Parliament until he emerged looking ever more anxious. The story of 'the King's matter' finally reached the daily newspapers on Thursday 3 December, triggered by a public remark from a voluble cleric.

The Bishop of Bradford had put a question to the Diocesan Conference about whether the King had a comprehensive understanding of the full spiritual significance of the upcoming Coronation. The British press, silent for so long over the King's relationship with Mrs Simpson, allowed themselves to interpret the Bishop's doubts as their long-awaited licence to reveal the whole story.

Each morning for a week Sir Philip had sat in the front seat of the car either on the way to the House of Commons or to Fort Belvedere, reading *The Times* aloud as May drove him through the streets of London and the lanes of Berkshire and Surrey. Under a headline entitled 'King and Monarchy', *The Times* revealed how parts of the foreign press were 'predicting a marriage incompatible with the throne'. The Prime Minister had not yet commented publicly although the surprisingly modest prime ministerial car was often parked in the Fort driveway during those few frenetic days. On Friday 4 December, under another headline, 'A King's

Marriage', *The Times* reported that Mr Baldwin had assured the House that 'No constitutional difficulty exists at present' and a couple of days later two lines at last gave some information concerning the woman at the centre of the whole drama.

'Mrs Simpson left England on Thursday night. It is believed her destination is Cannes.'

On Sunday May was again given the day off and went to the pictures with Rachel. Both women joined the cinema audience as they jumped to their feet and sang the national anthem louder than ever followed by a rousing round of 'For he's a jolly good fellow'.

Mrs Simpson had released a personal statement to the press.

'Mrs Simpson is willing to withdraw forthwith from a situation that has been rendered both unhappy and untenable,' it read.

'Well I never. The cheek of it!' Rachel fumed. 'She might have thought of that before, Simon, don't you think? What must his mother be feeling now? It's Queen Mary who I feel sorry for. Queen or no queen, she's a mother, and must be as worried as any of us would be.'

On each successive day of the following week Members of Parliament packed the chamber in anticipation of a statement from Stanley Baldwin. Each day they returned home no wiser about the King's final decision. Sir Philip and Mr Monckton were only two of the advisors who hurried through the doors of the Fort, Buckingham Palace, the Houses of Parliament and 10 Downing Street. Chauffeurs in the employ of the Archbishop of Canterbury; the Prime Minister; Mr Joseph Chamberlain, the Chancellor; Mr Anthony Eden, the Foreign Secretary, and Mr John Simon, the Home Secretary, gathered in servants' halls and in car parks and in the street with the drivers working for Mr Winston Churchill, Mr Duff Cooper and Sir Oswald Mosley.

May was well known to most of these drivers. During the preceding eleven months she had spent long hours in their company, waiting for Sir Philip and their employers to conclude meetings on which major national decisions depended. If at first these hard-talking, tobacco-inhaling chauffeurs had shown surprise at a woman's inclusion among their number, they, like the taxi drivers, had quickly come to respect her for her professionalism, and to secretly admire her for her comeliness. Indeed, there was more curiosity in Sir Oswald's driver than in May. Over packets of Woodbines and cups of tea the man who had driven the leader of the British Fascists to the march at Cable Street and once to Cuckmere Park was asked to justify his presence within this distinguished group.

'From what I hear on my side of the glass screen,' he explained, 'Mr Baldwin thinks Sir Oswald could help in making the King see sense about his fancy woman. And he's not all bad, Sir Oswald, you know. He has ideas that some people find appealing. Take my missus for example. She says Mosley wants to give women a good deal, what with offering them the same party member rights as a man. Her women friends agree with her that Sir Oswald talks

417

sense. Can't see it myself,' he added. 'But a job's a job isn't it?'

The other drivers muttered their support for Mosley's inclusion in the King's team of advisors. All the chauffeurs were united in their fear that the monarchy was on the verge of collapse and when they were joined late in the proceedings by the driver employed by the Duke of York they all speculated on the role *his* boss might be playing in a few days' time.

★ ★ ★

On Thursday 10 December Sir Philip climbed wearily into the front seat of the blue Rolls-Royce. As May pulled away from the kerb Sir Philip took off his hat and buried his head in his hands. The car crossed over Westminster Bridge, the murky grey water beneath running at speed with the turning tide and Sir Philip tugged his fingers through his long uncombed hair. Eventually he spoke.

'Thank God it is all over. Edward VIII has signed the documents and Mr Baldwin read us the statement this afternoon. By tomorrow Britain will have a new King, and you and I will deserve a rest.'

24

Sam was on his way home after a pint with Nat in the Queen's Arms. He was glad it was a Friday and was looking forward to spending the weekend with his sister and their cousins, especially Nat. Sam had come to regard Nat with the affection and trust worthy of a brother.

The pub had been packed with regulars, and Danny, Bethnal Green's most royalist publican, had greeted the cousins with his usual friendly welcome.

'I would be glad of a bit of advice from you two,' he announced as he filled two glasses to the brim with his home-brewed beer. 'I've got a problem,' he said, gesturing behind him. 'I want to know which one of them I should put in pride of place?'

The same three photographs still leant against a collection of dusty bottles of liquor at the back of the bar as they had done since the beginning of the year, Queen Mary in her pearls sat next to George V on his Coronation day and they both looked out from their carriage on last year's triumphant Jubilee tour of London. Danny's wife Ruth had put her Jubilee embroidery kit beside the picture of George V. Two lines:

Prince of Sportsmen, brilliant shot,
But happiest aboard his yacht.

had been stitched onto the outside of the tapestry case. A fourth photograph had been added to the collection since Nat last looked, showing a grinning Edward VIII, a much-reproduced image taken when the King was the Prince of Wales, a cigarette stuck jauntily in one side of his mouth.

'Now, do I dare put up the new one, is what I am wondering?' By now Danny was laughing. 'I mean, you never know who is coming next. George and Mary to start with, then Edward, here for a moment and then gone in a blink of an eye, and now Albert. What a merry-go-round it has all been, hasn't it, Nat?'

Nat and Sam drank their first pint at the bar, and discussed with Danny the shocking news of the abdication and it was only when they ordered the second pint that Sam suggested they go to a quieter table in the corner. He wanted to talk to Nat alone. Privy as he already was to the knowledge of May's parentage, Nat did not show any surprise when Sam outlined the contents of the letter sent by Bertha. With considerable relief Nat now confessed how, on his last visit to his mother in Holloway Prison, Gladys had sworn him to secrecy about an exotic Indian who had once loved her sister. Although Gladys was horribly weak from her prolonged lack of food, she was determined that the family secret should not die with her. Despite his young age, Nat had understood the depth of love his mother held for her sister. When he turned fourteen, he had begun to develop a curiosity in the workings of the adult world and had written to his aunt Edith in Barbados, asking her to tell him something of those circumstances which his mother had hinted at during her final days. Edith's reply, possibly written out of relief of finally sharing her secret, contained the entire story of her love affair with Nishy. By return of post, Nat promised that if ever she and her children needed help, he would do all he could to supply it, for his mother's sake.

'There are two things I want to say,' Sam began with a new confidence that was not lost on Nat. 'The first is that I know you're going to be a wonderful dad to Joshua and I envy him. And secondly,' and here Sam's voice wavered for a moment, 'you are the best cousin May and I could ever have had.'

As they left the pub both men walked for a while in silence, the younger, slighter, blond figure contrasting with the elder, robustly built and dark-haired. As they turned the corner to Oak Street Sam stopped in front of the War Memorial.

'I remember how you said these men had done their duty,' he said, almost shyly. 'I think we could all learn a lesson from them, don't you?'

Nat linked his arm through Sam's and together they walked the short distance to number 52.

'Come in, come in, Shalom Shabbat,' Rachel said, bustling them into the kitchen. The table was laid for the Sabbath feast. 'We are having our meal punctually, Nat, as we all want to hear the King, that's the latest old King, if you see what I mean. He is going to be making a speech on the wireless at ten o'clock tonight.'

Rachel had noticed the newspaper in Nat's hand. 'What have you got there? More terrible news, I suppose?' she asked.

'I made an exception and bought myself today's edition,' Nat told her. 'Couldn't wait for tomorrow. Take a look.'

Rachel, Simon, Sam and May crowded round the paper.

'Well, I never,' Rachel said, sighing loudly. 'I mean seeing it written down there like that. He really is going. Makes you think, doesn't it? I mean who can we trust, Nat, I'm asking you?'

'I agree with you,' Nat said. 'It's hard to believe that a man who seemed to care so much about this country, our country, I should say, has gone and abandoned us. Love is one thing, I know, but perhaps it should sometimes take second place for kings.'

'Mind you, May knew something was up, didn't you, May?' Rachel was smiling at her approvingly. 'I like a girl who keeps a secret when she's asked to and you've done well to respect the monarchy. I am sure Sir Philip respects you for keeping secrets, my girl, and Sir Philip's judgement is good enough for me.' Rachel was not the sort to hold a grudge, and had quite forgiven May for pretending the King was enamoured of a member of the Greek royal entourage. She could even have a laugh that things would have been different if he had been. Later that evening, after the Sabbath meal, the whole family gathered round the wireless. As soon as they heard Sir John Reith introduce the

422

former King as 'Prince Edward', Rachel insisted they all stand out of respect.

'You must believe me when I tell you,' the former King began, speaking very slowly in his curious accent, that mixture of truncated vowels and transatlantic roll that was so familiar to May, 'that I have found it impossible to carry the heavy burden of responsibility, and to discharge my duty as King as *I* would wish to do, without the help and support of the woman I love.'

In a voice sounding steady and as clear as if he was speaking to them from the leather settee, the man who had once been King lingered over the personal pronoun, emphasising, lest anyone be in any doubt, that his decision had been taken by him alone. The Oak Street family, along with a captivated nation, heard his entreaty for understanding, a message intended for anyone, even cynics like Nat, who had ever known what it is to be in love. When the broadcast came to an end Rachel was the first to speak.

'And just to think he could have had his pick of those foreign princesses. Princess Wallis, if that's who she is to be, is no more royal than Mrs Cohen or me. Still it takes all sorts to make a world. Put the kettle on, will you, Sarah? I think we all deserve a nice cup of tea.'

★ ★ ★

May came downstairs the next morning to find the coal fire in the front room already lit. What with the rustling of newspapers, the voices coming from what felt like the ever-intrusive wireless, and the cries of hunger that engulfed Joshua at regular hourly intervals, May needed some air. She went to find Sarah who agreed at once to go up to Gardiner's with May to buy Nat his long-overdue tie. A generous bottle of milk before leaving ensured that Joshua slept the whole way in his pram and while Sarah was choosing the tie, May noticed some pretty photograph frames edged in delicate blue flowers sitting on a nearby counter.

'Forget-me-nots, they are,' the sales lady told her. The frame was the perfect size for the picture that had been strapped face downwards for so long at the back of her diary. The time had come to turn it over. May bought a matching pair. She would write to Bertha and ask her to look for a photograph of Nishy in the old trunk of letters so that she could keep the image of both her parents near her. On their return to Oak Street May went to her room running through in her mind the muddle that the whole world and specifically her own world seemed to have stumbled into. Taking her blue diary from the drawer beside her bed, she slipped the photograph of her mother out from beneath the elastic band. The picture fitted the frame perfectly and with Edith watching over her, May filled several pages of the diary with the confusing sequence of the past days' events, as if by setting them down on paper they would become real.

★　★　★

During the long hours before the King made his final and lonely decision, May and Valerie Monckton had sat together in the Fort Belvedere kitchen waiting for their instructions. They discovered much common ground between them, indulging their mutual fascination for car engines, an interest they did not often get the chance to air with many others. Sitting in the servants' sitting room they had both inadvertently learned of the extent of Mrs Simpson's unpopularity among the Fort servants. Loyalty was not a quality to be found here, and a maid with a particularly loquacious tongue spilled the beans about how Mrs Simpson would come into the empty kitchen at all hours of the night and cook herself bacon and eggs, leaving behind an unholy mess. For months, the Fort staff had despised her insistence on strange American concoctions such as club sandwiches. In fact, Mrs Simpson's demands on the staff bordered on the unacceptably high-handed. There was even a story that she regularly snapped off the lead tips of pencils before asking for them to be re-sharpened into severer points. Suggestions of her imminent departure had been welcomed whole-heartedly.

Two weeks before the final crisis, May had been with Valerie in the Fort kitchen comparing the petrol consumption of the Rolls-Royce with that of the Monckton's Daimler when Osborne announced there had been a change of plan. Miss Nettlefold was leaving immediately for Portsmouth. A ship for New York was sailing the following day and Miss Nettlefold had arranged for an overnight stay in a hotel near the port. There had been no sign of Mrs Simpson or the King when May had fetched the car from the garage and driven up to the front door of the Fort. Miss Nettlefold was standing alone in the hallway, her small overnight suitcase at her feet.

'I don't really want to explain my reasons for leaving, if you don't mind, May,' Miss Nettlefold announced as soon as she was settled in the back seat of the car. Her voice was so weak that May had to concentrate hard to hear her through the open partition behind her. 'But I should like to explain to you, a woman who has so often been a friend to me, that I have suffered a disappointment of a personal nature and have concluded that I am no longer needed here. It is time for me to return to my own country.' Miss Nettlefold sounded defeated even by the effort of speech. 'None of this would have happened if Joan had been able to take care of me,' she said, almost inaudibly, 'the mother I had never had.'

The snap of a bag's clasp being opened was followed by the muffled but unmistakable sound of weeping during which May remained silent. Eventually Miss Nettlefold spoke again, her voice less audible than ever.

'I want to thank you for being a friend to me, May, and to apologise if there have been times when I have behaved a little curtly towards you. I have only ever wished to protect you from your own innocence. I hope you will learn soon that people, especially men, cannot always be trusted and that friends, however close you may think

426

them to be, can abandon you at their whim.'

May was uncertain to what the older woman referred. Miss Nettlefold had, it was true, made some unkind remarks about Julian but May could barely remember what they were. When Miss Nettlefold asked her to send her clothes to Baltimore, May confirmed that of course she would. On arrival at the Portsmouth hotel May considered whether it would be in order to attempt the intimacy of a farewell embrace. But Miss Nettlefold had folded her arms across her chest and was looking out to sea as the hotel porter retrieved the small bag from the boot. Both women stood by the car and for a moment looked steadily at each other. And then May Thomas watched Miss Nettlefold walk alone into the small quayside hotel, her broad shoulders hunched beneath the flapping fur coat. May had rarely seen anyone look so lonely.

★ ★ ★

Shortly after Miss Nettlefold's voluntary exile, Mrs Simpson also fled the country under cover of darkness and no one, let alone Mrs Simpson herself, knew when she might be reunited with the man who was no longer king. In a way, May felt sorry for Mrs Simpson. May knew what it was to be separated from someone who you longed to be with every moment of the day. As if the distressing circumstances of the departure had not been enough, Mr Monckton's daughter Valerie had told May of the sad news of the death of Loafer, Mrs Simpson's puppy. When

Osborne the butler found Loafer in a cupboard at the top of the stairs, he initially thought Loafer had gone into hiding to escape the raised voices and unsettling hurly burly of the house, but the body had obviously been stone cold for a while. The local vet made some tests on the dead animal and was puzzled to discover that Loafer's blood had been contaminated by an inexplicable and lethal dose of rat poison.

★ ★ ★

During the car journey down to Cuckmere at the end of a week in which a king had chosen the love of a woman over duty to his country, the subject of Miss Nettlefold had arisen between May and Sir Philip for the first time since Miss Nettlefold's unexpected departure. Something had happened the day she spent with Sir John at Crystal Palace to prompt Miss Nettlefold's unexplained flight and yet May doubted whether she, Sir Philip or anyone would ever be able to guess the truth. A good lunch with Sir John Reith in the club might shine some light on the mysterious affair, Philip thought to himself.

'I wonder whether she would have allowed herself to become so unhappy if Joan had been here to help,' Sir Philip said aloud after May had described how she had driven Miss Nettlefold to the hotel near the Portsmouth docks. 'She always seemed like a lost soul to me. The world is an indiscriminate place,' he said. 'There are those who succeed despite themselves, and there are others who cannot escape the weapons of sabotage that they wield on themselves. It is as if an instinct for self-preservation sometimes fails us.'

As Sir Philip brought out his handkerchief and blew his nose, he brushed both of his eyes lightly with the palm of his hand before picking up his pipe and packing the bowl with tobacco. A little embarrassed by his emotion May looked away but not before noticing that Sir Philip's favourite photograph of Joan was once more sitting in its old place in front of him on his desk.

*　★　*

Mrs Cage finally left the seclusion of her bedroom, her usual energy restored together with an air of purpose as she set about the complex business of decorating the house for Christmas. The Blunt children would both be joining their father for the holidays and were each bringing a friend to stay for the festivities. Mrs Cage asked Mr Hooch to select a suitable spruce from the estate and to position it in the echoey stone hallway. Florence was looking forward to helping with the decorations. Cooky had begun drawing up mouthwatering menus and gradually a sense of gaiety and optimism returned to the servants' hall. Florence had secretly persuaded her mother to buy May some skates for Christmas and was planning to show off her skill at balancing on ice as soon as the water in the lake froze over. And Mrs Cage had promised Florence a special holiday early in the New Year. She was waiting for the right moment to divulge to her daughter that they were going to spend a few days with her friends in Bavaria.

On the morning after the King signed the papers renouncing the throne, May joined Mrs Cage in the smaller spare bedroom at Cuckmere. Together they began to sort through Miss Nettlefold's possessions, packing them into one of Rupert's old school trunks. Miss Nettlefold's sad, final request had touched May and she was determined to protect the woman from any further indignity. But the box containing Miss Nettlefold's wigs was already full, each wig wrapped in the tissue paper Mrs Cage usually reserved for Lady Joan's own clothes. Not a word had passed between May and Mrs Cage of Florence's confession about Mrs Cage's son. May had decided that she could only stick to her promise to Florence by steering clear of the whole subject. It was Mrs Cage who broke the silence.

'Poor Miss Nettlefold. I wish her well. And I think all we can both do is to agree that there are some things in life and some ways of behaving that are best left unexplained, don't you agree?' Mrs Cage stretched her hand out to May who was putting the wig box carefully in the trunk next to a small silver letter opener, and touched her gently on the arm.

'Yes, Mrs Cage, I could not agree with you more.' May replied abruptly, and excusing herself went next door into the adjoining bathroom. The room smelled of antiseptic and the shelf above the basin was quite empty except for a couple of unused crêpe bandages and two brown bottles

430

half full of liquid. She recognised the labels at once, surprised to find the poison Mr Hooch used on the rabbits and rats in Miss Nettlefold's bathroom cupboard. It was not long, however, before she remembered how Mr Hooch had mentioned only a few weeks ago that he must order a new supply of poison.

'Either I have miscounted my supply or this year I have got through the stuff at a faster rate than ever before.'

An image of Loafer lying in the back of the car unconscious on the rise and fall of Miss Nettlefold's ample stomach was in May's mind as she emptied the remaining liquid into the basin, put the bottles in her pocket and, thanking Mrs Cage for her help, went to find Mr Hooch to take her to the station. On the way to the garage she passed the garden dustbin, opened the lid and buried the two empty bottles among a wheelbarrow load of dead plants. Miss Nettlefold would at least be saved from one final betrayal.

25

Julian could hardly believe he had only left England six weeks ago. Since his departure, constitutional Britain had undergone an astonishing transformation, as described at titillating length in the French newspapers. What was equally surprising to Julian was the change in his own outlook on life which had been stimulated, pummelled, extended, inflated and reordered in ways he had never dared hope for.

He had left his letter for May on Mr Hooch's workbench in the garage knowing Mr Hooch would make sure May got it as soon as he saw her. The taxi had picked him up before anyone else was awake on that late October Sunday morning and he had been driven in the dawn light to the port at Newhaven. He had sat on the ferry to Dieppe even then trying to convince himself that he had made the right decision. Despite the earliness of the hour, he soon emptied the demi-carafe of Beaujolais the waiter had brought over to his table and had immediately ordered another. Wine had never tasted so good, especially after the mild headache he attributed to the previous late night's talks with Philip.

Julian soon cheered up as the wine worked its magic and he began to concentrate on the prospect of a few weeks in Paris. He had often dreamt of spending time in the city that had at times been lost to Voltaire and Gide, Proust and Hemingway, culture and intellect, wine and beauty. And after six weeks he was able to conclude that the experience had not disappointed. Peter had proved to be the most knowledgeable of guides and stimulating of companions. He had introduced Julian not only to his earnest friend the writer Eric Blair, but to the outspoken Spanish surrealist painter Joán Miró who had a habit of staring at ceilings before jotting sketches in his notebook. Henry Miller, an American novelist, and his lover, a writer Anäis Nin, were Julian's favourite couple although the sexual connection around them both sometimes so strong that it felt indecent to remain in the same room.

For six weeks Julian found himself absorbed into the company of this group of individuals all of whom held the Spanish Civil War at the forefront of their creative and political lives. For six weeks he had argued and listened, learned and laughed, raged and marvelled about politics, books, paintings, poetry, love, sex and death until the sun came up over the Seine.

'Ici, en ce moment, on peut trouver le sens de la vie et le but de vivre,' Miró had pronounced one evening.

And yet, Julian's own reasons for living were incomplete. And when after six weeks his companions came to a decision that it was time to leave Paris for Spain, Julian hesitated. If he joined them he would be closing down that part of his life that he was now certain mattered more than any other. He felt only a little guilty at

433

having abandoned his mother to suffer her illness alone. He did not regret that he had missed a whole term of his law course. There would be time to catch up. But he had left Cuckmere without telling May what he felt about her and he did not want to wait any longer. He said goodbye to Peter and Eric at the Gare du Nord and boarded the Thursday morning train for Dieppe. If he was lucky he would arrive in London by the following afternoon in time for the weekend.

★ ★ ★

May finished writing in her diary and decided to walk over to Smart's Picture House and see if the Friday afternoon newsreels were yet carrying the official news of the Abdication. In the packed cinema May took the only available aisle seat in the back row. The sound of crunching peanuts was unusually subdued that evening, although the familiar mix of praise and abuse was still being hurled unabated at the screen.

A woman in the seat beside her was in a terrible state, wringing her hands and shaking. 'How will we manage without him?' she said turning to May. She did not seem to expect an answer. Although the lights had already dimmed and the film had already begun to roll, she pushed past May and headed for the door.

May watched the black-and-white pictures moving in front of her, reaching instinctively up her woollen sleeve to check the silver bracelet was safely in its place and running her finger along the slightly worn line of forget-me-nots. In front of her the scenes of snowfall in Argyllshire with the caption promising the 'proverbial snowy Christmas' were followed first by news of the Varsity match, and pictures of the victorious muddy faces of the Cambridge team and then by coverage of a dreadful air accident. A Dutch plane had crashed into a row of terrace houses in Purley shortly after leaving Croydon Airport in fog and fourteen people had been killed. There was no mention at all of the Abdication, no film of the hasty departure abroad of Mrs Simpson a week earlier, no footage of the man who had been King up until the day before, as he went between the Fort and the Royal Palaces working out the details of the biggest decision of his life.

Just as May was beginning to wonder if she had invented the whole Royal spectacle as a distraction from the uncertainty of her future with Julian, a photograph of the Duke and Duchess of York appeared, captioned 'Our New King and Queen Elizabeth'. The film footage continued to roll amid collective gasps and cries of 'God Bless them' as the narrator's voice with its cut-glass accent recounted how in 1923 the Duke of York had chosen 'a charming Scottish bride' from Glamis Castle.

A castellated building, at least ten times the size of the Fort, filled the screen at the same time as a tall man in a cap appeared at the end of May's row and indicated she should make room by budging along to the empty seat beside her. Barely glancing up, May sighed slightly with irritation as she moved across, while keeping her eyes firmly ahead on scenes of a curly-haired girl, wearing a white coat and holding the hand of her pearl-laden grandmother. 'Princess Elizabeth Alexandra Mary is now in the direct line of accession to the throne,' the plummy voice announced as the newcomer beside her unwrapped a roll of newspaper, releasing the familiar vinegary smell into the air. May suddenly felt hungry. She had eaten very little these past few days despite Rachel's protests that these were times for everyone to keep up their strength.

'Would you like a chip? They're still quite hot,' the man whispered, taking off his cap and untying his stripey scarf. Still May did not look round but the voice was as familiar to her as if it had been the voice of her own mother. It was the same voice that whispered to her in her dreams and was the first sound that she tried to summon to her mind in the morning.

'In the hands of King Albert we may rest assured that the dignity of the Crown, so well established by his beloved father King George V, is in safe keeping,' the commentator was saying. 'To King Albert and Queen Elizabeth we wish long life, happiness and courage in the years to come,' the voice concluded. May forced herself to eat the chip, surprised to discover that it tasted delicious.

'Thank you, darling,' she murmured as Julian reached across the seat for her hand. Interlacing her fingers with his own, he took off his glasses and bent to kiss her, lighting up the cinema with his head of white-blond hair.

436

Acknowledgements

I am most grateful for the information provided by Anne Sander at the Archives at Balliol College Oxford, Luke McKernan at the British Library Newsreel, Mike Lamden at National Express Coaches and the ever-helpful staff at the London Library. I have consulted dozens of biographies, histories, essays, novels, newspapers, magazines, diaries, personal letters both published and private, as well as masses of photographs and several movies during the research for this book. Among the publications I found especially valuable were the Duke of Windsor's own memoirs, *A King's Story*; Wallis Simpson's autobiography *The Heart has its Reasons and Wallis and Edward, The Intimate Correspondence 1931–37 of the Duke and Duchess of Windsor* edited by Michael Bloch; *Queen Mary* by James Pope-Hennessy; *Edward VIII* by Philip Zeigler; *Blackshirts-on-Sea* by J. A. Booker; *Journey through a Small Planet* by Emanuel Litvinoff; *The Age of Illusion* by Ronald Blythe; *The Long Weekend* by Robert Graves and Alan Hodge; and *Chicken Soup with Barley* by Arnold Wesker. I would like to single out one other book that I cannot recommend highly enough for its illumination of the decade, Juliet Gardiner's *The Thirties: An Intimate History*.

First novels are intimidating undertakings at every stage of the process and from conception to birth I have been guided and encouraged by a number of amazing people. I would particularly like to thank Patricia Anker, Kitty and Michael Ann, Frankie Baldwin, William Boyd, Kevin Brownlow, Paul Calkin, Debo Devonshire, Sophie Ford, Antonia Fraser, Arthur Fyne, Hugh Harris, Dr Jonathan Hunt, Diana Kelly, The Hon Mrs Charles Kitchener, Katie Law, Pam Leigh, Dr Kate Murphy, Adam Nicolson, Molly Nicolson, Rebecca Nicolson, Rosie Nicolson, Vanessa Nicolson, Cate Olson, David O'Rorke, Tim O'Rorke, Shirley Punnett, Sarah Raven, Nash Robbins, Julia Samuel, Julian Smith, Tom Stoppard, Joanna Trollope, Hugo Vickers, Henry Wyndham and Rachel Wyndham. I am indebted to Hilary and Galen Weston for their invitation to Fort Belvedere and for the invaluable sense of place the visit gave me. My research has been backed up by the unflagging energy, imagination and intelligence of Clementine Macmillan-Scott.

Ed Victor has radiated confidence and encouragement in the book from the beginning. He is the best. And I am as grateful as ever to his colleagues Charlie Campbell, Maggie Phillips, Morag O'Brien and Linda Vann. My forensically intuitive editor Michael Fishwick has taken unprecedented trouble over the book and I am also blessed at Bloomsbury with the enthusiasm, professionalism and flair of Katie Bond, Oliver Holden-Rea, David Mann, Alexandra Pringle, Anna Simpson and Alexa von Hirschberg.

My agent in America, William Clark has worked harder on my behalf than I deserve. At Atria Books I would like to thank Sarah Branham for her unflagging passion and perceptiveness and Judith Curr for her belief in me as a writer.

I could not have imagined life in the Britain of 1936 without the memories of Jeremy Hutchinson who was a young man on the cusp of adulthood during the extraordinary events of that year. His arrival in my life has been one of the huge joys of writing this book.

My biggest thank yous are for the unwavering insight and love of my girls, Clemmie, and Flora, and for my saint of a loyal and loving husband, Charlie. The book is for them with all my love, and more.

Juliet Nicolson
April 2012

We do hope that you have enjoyed reading this large print book.

Did you know that all of our titles are available for purchase?

We publish a wide range of high quality large print books including:
Romances, Mysteries, Classics
General Fiction
Non Fiction and Westerns

Special interest titles available in large print are:
The Little Oxford Dictionary
Music Book
Song Book
Hymn Book
Service Book

Also available from us courtesy of Oxford University Press:
Young Readers' Dictionary
(large print edition)
Young Readers' Thesaurus
(large print edition)

For further information or a free brochure, please contact us at:
Ulverscroft Large Print Books Ltd.,
The Green, Bradgate Road, Anstey,
Leicester, LE7 7FU, England.
Tel: (00 44) 0116 236 4325
Fax: (00 44) 0116 234 0205